DETECTIVE FIRST GRADE

DETECTIVE FIRST GRADE

Dan Mahoney

St. Martin's Press
New York

Editor: George Witte
Copyedited by Karen Pilibosian Thompson
Design by Karin Batten

ISBN: 0-312-09288-1

First Edition: May 1993

10 9 8 7 6 5 4 3 2 1

Books are available in quantity for promotional or premium use. Write to Director of Special Sales, St. Martin's Press, 175 Fifth Avenue, New York, NY 10010, for information on discounts and terms, or call toll-free (800) 221–7945. In New York, call (212) 674–5151 (ext. 645).

For Detective Louie Miller (1925–1987)
My "Tommy Pacella"

and

Detective Bobby Gallagher
The "Gun-collar Man"

DETECTIVE FIRST GRADE

1

July 9   3:30 p.m.

Yogi was no dope, Detective Brian McKenna thought as he drove along Empire Boulevard. This is déjà vu all over again.

McKenna looked at his partner, Richie White. Stuck in deepest, darkest Brooklyn again and working with another hoople. No more bright lights for me for a while, no fine restaurants, no high-fashion good-looking women. How many times have I been sent down? Four? Five? How many times have I been caught breaking their rules?

McKenna was bored and began feeling sorry for himself again. Seven-one Detective Squad. Certainly not very glamorous, the main mission being to keep the Hasidic Jews and the Blacks from killing each other or burning each other out. Angelita disgusted with both me and the police department and threatening to leave. Not much to smile about. And nobody to blame except myself for this current state of affairs. Myself, and those jerks in the FBI. They don't appreciate anybody doing the "right thing" when it conflicts with their plans.

But the worst thing about banishment to Brooklyn is the boredom: there isn't enough worth doing. Nothing important anyway. After all, it's only Brooklyn. Who cares what happens here? Nobody I know.

McKenna drove what the New York City Police Department called an unmarked car. The car fooled no one in this neighborhood. Everyone knew that two white guys wearing ties in a four-door Plymouth were the "DTs," the detectives, "the Man." They might as well have been in full police uniform driving an ice cream truck.

It was a hot and muggy July afternoon and the streets were packed with the darker and poorer shades of humanity. McKenna and White were stuck in one of those Brooklyn traffic jams that occur for no good reason and only end by Divine Intervention. McKenna observed the difference between this particular jam and typical midtown Manhattan gridlock. Nobody was blowing their horn here, probably realizing that a show of annoyance could upset the crowded and delicate balance and could lead to a serious confrontation with fellow motorists. Confrontation was more dangerous here than in the Bright Lights. This was a notoriously well-armed neighborhood.

But the healthy fear evaporated as soon as anyone noticed that the police were around. The middle-aged, well-built black man in the car on McKenna's left started blowing his horn and gesturing in an attempt to get McKenna's attention.

McKenna smiled and stole a quick glance at his fellow motorist. Everything about the man was big and solid, including the chunky Buick he was driving. Their eyes met while the big man simultaneously leaned on his horn and shouted in McKenna's direction. McKenna couldn't understand because the big man's windows were closed.

Perfect! McKenna thought. A way to break the boredom. He faced forward and made a pretense of studiously ignoring the big man. This implied insult enraged the man and he continued blowing his horn and shouting at McKenna through his closed window. McKenna continued to ignore him. Finally the man leaned over, rolled down his passenger window, and yelled, "Hey, Officer, why don't you get out of your car and do something about this traffic?"

Rising to the occasion, McKenna answered in his best LAPD–Adam 12 voice, "Excuse me, sir, but I just happened to notice that you aren't wearing your seat belt. Do you realize that, in the event of an accident, you could be seriously injured if you were ejected from your auto? Not to mention the fact that you are currently risking being cited for a fifty-dollar fine and two points on your license, if any. I remind you that a conviction for this violation would automatically entail an increase in the amount of automobile insurance that I am sure you know you are required to pay by Section six-eleven of the New York State Vehicle and Traffic Law."

"Say what?"

"If, by your present conduct, you are going to force me to start doing my sworn duty of enforcing the law, I feel that I must start on the first violation I encounter, which is the violation that I have just finished discussing with you, sir."

"Huuhh?" Confusion was engraved all over the big man's face.

McKenna watched as this confusion was slowly replaced by resentment.

McKenna smiled, leaned out of his window, and said in a stage whisper, "I sure hope this bullshit works on you, pal, because, just between us, I don't have any summonses and I think I forgot how to write one anyway. So, please let me slide on this one so this knucklehead sitting next to me doesn't call me a pussy and break my balls for the rest of the day. How about it?"

Finally he got it. The big man smiled and said, "Ain't this a bitch, Officer!"

"Thanks, pal. By the way, would you mind saying that once more, but a little louder so the knucklehead can hear you?"

The big man leaned forward in his seat, looked at Richie White, and agreed with McKenna's assessment of his partner.

"Sure, Officer. AIN'T THIS A BITCH!"

"Thank you, sir, and happy motoring."

"One second, Officer! I just got to know your name."

"Brian McKenna, expert detective at your service, sir," answered McKenna with a salute and a smile.

"Pleasure to meet you, Detective McKenna. I've got to catch you at a party sometime," the big man said as he returned the salute and rolled up his window.

"I just love that seat-belt law," McKenna said to White.

White didn't look the slightest bit disturbed about McKenna's disparaging characterization of him. "Let's keep this straight, McKenna. You have to play by the rules and be consistent. Call me either a knucklehead or an asshole in your stories to these guys. One or the other. Otherwise, the bet's off."

"OK, knucklehead. Let's add it up. Correct me if I'm wrong, but so far today I've got three *Ain't that a bitch*'s, eight *Say what*'s, and three *Damn*'s. Subtracting that 'Officer, you ain't nothing but a no-good motherfucker,' I figure you owe me thirteen dollars."

"Settle for five bucks?"

"For you, anything," McKenna replied. Sucker, he thought. This guy belongs in Brooklyn. He even likes it here. He's just like the Eskimos. They think they've got a great place, too. Richie White and the Eskimos just don't know any better.

McKenna's eyes were drawn to the pulled, frayed thread hanging from the elbow of White's jacket. He couldn't help himself.

He doesn't even know it's there, McKenna thought. A 100 percent no-wrinkle, no-iron polyester sports jacket. What a buy! Looks like one-size-fits-all. I can't even tell what color it is. How can we possibly get any respect for this police department when it looks like our detectives get dressed in the dark? These Brooklyn detectives don't know that this job is 50 percent appearance. If you look good, people want to talk to you. If people want to talk to you, the rest of the job is easy. Now, who would want to talk to this guy? It's not that he's a bad guy. It's just that he hasn't learned the tricks to make it easy.

White caught McKenna staring at the jacket and said, "Like it? My wife got it for me for my birthday. She's a great shopper. Most comfortable jacket I've ever had. And it never wrinkles. I took it right out of the dryer before work today."

"Yeah, it's nice. I'd like to get something like that for myself. It looks like it goes with anything. You can wear it anywhere," McKenna said.

"The great thing about it is that I can wear any tie I want with it."

"That's great," answered McKenna. Any tie but that one, he thought.

"I'll bring you in the catalog tomorrow, if you like. Then I can have my wife put you on the mailing list."

"Great, thanks," McKenna said. If my mailman sees that catalog, I'll have to move.

The auto air-conditioner was going full blast. McKenna looked at White, who was rolling up his window to keep the July heat out. He disapproved, but didn't say anything.

"McKenna," asked White, "How about rolling up your window before we roast in here?"

"Sorry pal, but I prefer to hear all the good things that our citizens are saying about us. I never miss an opportunity to make sure that we're still winning their hearts and minds."

They were headed eastbound in the stop-and-go traffic, slowly approaching the intersection of Bedford Avenue.

McKenna had never been able to suppress the warm feeling of nostalgia that swelled inside him every time he had to pass this place, now the site of the Ebbets Field Houses. He thought back to his childhood, when the city had been different. Many times his father had brought him here to watch Duke Snyder, Pee Wee Reese, Roy Campanella, and those other Boys of Summer. "Dem Bums," he remembered his father saying. Won the National League Pennant in '52 and '53 and did it again in '55 and '56. They even finally beat the Yankees and won the World Series in '55, and suddenly Brooklyn wasn't good enough for them. They started looking around and after the 1957 season they took the money, packed up, and went off to the sunshine. They were the first to leave the neighborhood.

McKenna took another look at his surroundings. Of course, he thought, anyone with sense and enough money took the hint and soon followed them out.

Look what they did to this place, McKenna thought. The site of the famous ballpark, once the home of the Brooklyn Dodgers, was now occupied by six separate twenty-three-story buildings that comprised the Ebbets Field Houses, a low-to-moderate-income New York City housing complex famous only to the cops who spent a lot of time trying to catch the assortment of robbers, drug dealers, rapists, and murderers who lived in these high-rises among their victims and customers.

Four cars in front of the detectives a man exited the rear seat of a taxi. He walked to the sidewalk, looked around, and started strolling in their direction. McKenna's instincts startled him out of his daydreams. He sized up the man instantly. Male, probably Hispanic, about forty years old, five feet nine inches tall, medium build, one hundred and sixty pounds, mustache and goatee, swarthy complexion, well dressed, wearing green snakeskin shoes, green pants, a white shirt, and an open green nylon Windbreaker.

It was the shoes and the Windbreaker that caught McKenna's attention. The shoes were out of place in this neighborhood. Too expensive. And it was too hot to be wearing a Windbreaker. As the man approached, McKenna saw that as he walked his left shoulder was slightly lower than his right shoulder and that he also swung his left arm slightly away from his body.

Without moving his lips, McKenna said to his partner, "Don't look now, but get ready! This guy's got a gun in a shoulder holster." The man was now about ten feet from the front of their car.

Naturally, White turned his head and looked right at the man as he approached. Why do I bother talking to this guy? McKenna wondered.

So McKenna also turned and his eyes locked with the man's as he passed their car. He was right; the guy was definitely one of the piranhas. In that instant McKenna saw recognition, fear, and apprehension in the man's eyes. Although McKenna and this man had never seen each other before, they recognized each other. The hunter was about to become the hunted. They both knew their roles and began formulating their plans. The game had begun.

The man turned his head forward and continued walking. McKenna saw that his gait had picked up almost imperceptibly as he continued down Empire Boulevard.

"Are you sure?" White asked. "I didn't see it."

McKenna ignored the question. "Let's get him," he said as he slipped his 9-mm Glock semiautomatic from the holster on his belt, turned off the car, removed the keys from the ignition, and handed them to White. He was relieved to see that White had finally caught on and was removing his own pistol from its holster.

5

"Don't forget the radio," McKenna said, meaning the police walkie-talkie. They both took a deep breath and opened their doors.

Their quarry was sharp. He was thirty feet behind the detectives when they got out of the car. As soon as he heard the sound of the doors opening, he took off. He was fast and he wasn't looking back. Leaving their car right in the middle of traffic, the detectives gave chase. The race was on.

The piranha ran across Empire Boulevard through the lanes of stopped cars and headed toward the Ebbets Field Houses.

McKenna was delighted. Now there would be no need to tell any little lies in court about this upcoming arrest. Flight of a suspect was one of the mitigating circumstances that, in the eyes of the courts, justify an officer's action when he stops and frisks a person before he arrests him for unlawful possession of a firearm.

It never even crossed McKenna's mind that this man might get away. For the past ten years he had run in three marathons a year. He was fond of saying, "They might be faster for the first block, but to get away from me they have to run twenty-six miles in under three hours fifteen minutes." They never could.

The detectives were fifty feet behind the man by the time he reached the first building in the housing complex. He hadn't slowed down a bit. McKenna judged the man's pace and started to pull a little ahead of White.

"Should I put it over?" White yelled, meaning, Should he transmit this foot pursuit over the police radio he was carrying?

McKenna looked over his shoulder at White and saw that he was red. Looks like I'm going to be on my own in this one in a little while, he thought.

"Not yet," McKenna answered. He figured that he might want to have a little private chat with their man when they caught him, and he wouldn't want to have any other officers present during this "interview" who could be called to testify against him later.

The chase continued through the sidewalks of the complex of buildings. McKenna slowly narrowed the gap while White fell farther and farther behind. The suspect made a series of right or left turns at the corner of each building, so that by the time McKenna was twenty feet behind him, they were at about the same point as when they'd first entered the housing complex.

By now, this foot pursuit had attracted quite a bit of attention in the crowded neighborhood. McKenna felt as though they were running across the infield of Ebbets Field on opening day. People were everywhere and they all stopped whatever they were doing to watch the game. Both officers knew that the police weren't considered the home team here.

The man now heard McKenna's footsteps behind him and he pulled a large, ugly-looking automatic pistol from his shoulder holster. McKenna saw the weapon and slowed down a bit.

Not just yet, McKenna thought. He didn't want to risk a gunfight on these crowded streets.

The suspect ran toward a group of tough-looking Spanish punks wearing gang colors and yelled to them, *"¡Ayúdenme, hermanos!"* imploring them for help.

The group gave the man a cheer as he passed through them. McKenna followed and one of the aspiring gangsters stuck his foot out as McKenna was passing, catching the instep of McKenna's left foot while he was in midstride. The result was spectacular. McKenna sprawled face forward on the concrete and slid into second base.

McKenna got up as quickly as he could and turned in time to see White grab the owner of the offending foot. The rest of the pack was giving a demonstration of the Big Bang Theory, scattering to all corners of the universe at close to the speed of light.

McKenna shouted to his partner, "Let him go and put it over!" The suspect was now about one hundred feet in front of him.

He heard White shout into the police radio the New York City Police Department code call for "Officer needs assistance." "Ten-thirteen. Ebbets Field Houses. Officers in civilian clothes chasing male Hispanic armed with a gun."

In the nine radio cars then on patrol in the 71st Precinct, eighteen hearts skipped a beat and the adrenaline started flowing. In one instant, nine hands reached for the dashboard and turned on roof lights and sirens. All assignments were put on hold. Nothing else mattered. A fellow officer was in trouble and requesting assistance. Within five seconds the front of every police car on patrol in the 71st Precinct was pointed toward the Ebbets Field Houses.

McKenna heard the wail of the sirens and wondered, How many collisions did I just cause?

He poured on the speed and as he ran he heard the sound of White's footsteps behind him. He felt pain in his right knee, looked down, and saw that he had torn the pants knee of his Botany 500 suit. For the first time McKenna felt anger. Man, do I want to talk to this guy!

The gap was quickly beginning to narrow. He's finally getting tired, McKenna thought. Thank God!

The man made a left when McKenna was once again fifty feet behind him and, gun in hand, ran into the lobby of 277 McKeever Place in the heart of the housing complex. In the lobby were three middle-aged black women from the building Tenants' Safety Committee, sitting behind a desk placed near the front of the inner lobby door. Their mission was to screen all nonresidents entering the building, an attempt to keep criminals from using their building as a place of business. The gunman rushed past them and tried the inner glass door of the lobby. It was locked. He was cornered.

In unison, the three ladies resigned their position of trust, got up from their chairs, and headed for the front door.

The gunman turned. "Stop!" he yelled, and the three ladies froze in the doorway. They were between McKenna and the gunman. The gunman raised his weapon and placed the short barrel on top of the shoulder of the closest woman. McKenna dove behind one of the thick, old, pollution-scarred sycamore trees that dotted every New York City housing complex in the city.

The gunman fired a four- or five-round burst. McKenna heard the outer glass doors shatter as the rounds slammed into his tree. The volley of rounds hit the tree with repetitive thumps.

Christ, full automatic! McKenna thought. Thank you, God, for this tree.

McKenna peered around the tree and saw that the three ladies in the lobby were frozen in terror. He couldn't shoot.

"Get down!" McKenna yelled. Everyone in the lobby, including the gunman, instantly dropped to the ground. From the prone position he fired another burst at McKenna's lucky tree. Each round hit the tree, but this time the rounds struck closer to the ground, very near where McKenna had just shown his face.

McKenna looked behind and saw that White had also dropped to the ground about one hundred feet behind him. He was yelling excitedly into his radio.

The sound of approaching sirens promised that help was very close.

McKenna heard another burst of fire from the lobby and dug himself deeper into the pavement. This time the bullets weren't meant for him. He peered around the tree and saw that the gunman had fired into the heavy inner glass door, shattering it. He was gone.

McKenna ran in a crouch into the lobby of the building. The three ladies still lay frozen on the ground.

"Which way?" he asked, and three index fingers pointed up.

McKenna stepped through the blasted door and ran toward the two elevators in the inner lobby. The floor-indicator lights showed one elevator on the tenth floor and the other on the seventeenth.

No way he's in the elevators, thought McKenna. These elevators were notoriously slow, when they worked at all. He couldn't have gotten so high so fast in these elevators.

McKenna ran to the stairwell, opened the door, and heard the sounds of his man running up about three floors above him. The stairs were made of steel, and in the enclosed stairwell the footsteps rang like coins dropping into a tin cup.

McKenna started up and noted with alarm that he was making as much noise as the gunman. He counted twenty-four stairs between each floor. There was a small landing after every twelfth step where the stairs performed a U-turn on their way up to the next floor. He took the steps three at a time. When he got to the fifth floor the gunman's footsteps sounded louder, maybe just two floors above.

This guy's good, McKenna thought, but he's getting tired now. I've got him.

Suddenly the footsteps above him stopped. McKenna heard the sound of metal hitting metal and it echoed down the stairwell. He recognized the sound. The gunman was reloading. He had just dropped his used magazine from his weapon and was inserting a loaded clip of ammunition. McKenna heard the distinctive sound of the bolt snapping closed on a fresh cartridge.

He kept climbing until he estimated that he was one story below the gunman, who, he knew, was waiting for him. The sounds of many footsteps from the floors far below him meant his reinforcements were arriving.

Let me try this one, McKenna thought. He yelled up the stairwell, "Give it up, *hombre,* so we can both walk out of here."

The gunman's answer was swift and unexpected. McKenna heard the sound of rapid gunfire, saw the sparks of ricochets striking the steel and concrete of the stairwell, and staggered from the force of one of these rounds hitting his bulletproof vest.

McKenna cried out, more from surprise than from pain.

The gunman yelled down the stairwell, "How do you like that, *maricon?* Did I get you?"

McKenna resented the gunman's Spanish insult, which implied that McKenna's sexual orientation was a little off. He could also hear in the man's voice that he was tired and breathing heavily. Making his voice sound like he was in pain, McKenna shouted up, "Just a scratch, partner!" using his best patent-pending John Wayne imitation. Regretfully, he ripped open his white-on-white custom-made shirt, popping all the buttons, and with his left hand felt his chest under his vest. No blood. Much of the force of the bullet had been spent during its course of flight when it had ricocheted off the stairs and walls of the confined stairwell.

Thank you, John and Yoko, he thought. McKenna had received one of the one hundred vests that John Lennon and Yoko Ono had donated to the Patrolmen's Benevolent Association in 1977, in the time before the Police Department gave free vests to its officers.

McKenna realized that he was up against the best he had ever seen. Skip shooting was something one learned only during intensive military training in house-to-house combat.

The way this guy banked his bullets in the stairwell, I'm glad that I'm not playing billiards against him, McKenna said to himself.

For the first time the thought crossed his mind that he might not win this one.

At the sound of the gunshots the footsteps below him had stopped. McKenna breathed a sigh of relief when he heard their noise resume. At the same time he heard the sounds of the gunman's footsteps as he continued his climb.

McKenna took off his shoes and placed them on the stairs. I should have done this before, he thought. He noticed with some satisfaction that the sound of his footsteps was now indistinguishable from the racket that his fellow officers were making about three floors below him.

McKenna kept himself two floors below the gunman as he continued his now silent pursuit. When he reached the tenth floor he heard the squeal of the stairwell door opening on the twelfth. He could tell by the sound that the gunman's footsteps made on the concrete of the building hallway that he had finally left the steel stairwell.

McKenna climbed until he reached the access door on twelve. He could hear the gunman banging on one of the apartment doors and yelling, "Open up, Paco. It's Rico."

The stairwell door was half open. McKenna hesitated a second and then slipped quickly and silently into the hall.

The gunman was twenty feet away. His back was toward McKenna. He pounded on the door of the end apartment in the hallway with the butt of his gun.

McKenna raised his pistol and lined up his sights on the middle of the gunman's back. He savored the moment of victory and said, "Surprise, partner!" As the gunman started to turn with his gun hand raised, McKenna fired three quick shots. The force slammed the gunman flat against the apartment door. He dropped his gun and his feet slipped from under him as he slid slowly to the floor. He moved slightly as McKenna cautiously approached him. When McKenna was standing over him, the dying man tried to push himself up off the floor. He managed to turn his head and face McKenna.

McKenna looked into the man's eyes for the second time and saw that he was right. It was a surprise. He died just as the first uniformed officers, led by Detective White, reached the twelfth-floor stairway door.

"Police officer!" McKenna yelled to them. "It's all over!"

It was then that he saw the hole in the apartment door that one of his bullets had made after it had passed through the body of the dead man. And it was then that he heard the moaning coming from the other side of the door. McKenna knew he was wrong. It wasn't all over.

Detective Second Grade Brian McKenna had just fired his weapon in the line of duty for the second time in his twenty-three-year police career, a career during which he had effected more than eighteen hundred arrests.

McKenna took quick stock of his situation as he was surrounded by a sea of his fellow police officers. He smiled slightly as it dawned on him that he was barefoot and without a glove in left field of the Ebbets Field Houses.

2

July 9   3:45 p.m.

Detective Richie White pounded on the apartment door and rang the bell. No answer.

Images of doom flashed through McKenna's mind. His doom. Every second the hallway grew noisier and more crowded with uniformed police officers, breathing heavily. They sounded like a porno movie. The twelve-flight journey up was grabbing everybody's lungs, including McKenna's. The constant crackle of voices from each cop's radio made it worse: "We need the sergeant. We need Emergency Service. We need an ambulance." Everyone was needed at 277 McKeever Place, twelfth-floor hallway, and everyone was coming. The circus had begun and the spotlight was fixed on McKenna, center ring. The other officers were asking him questions and he couldn't focus. All he could see was the small hole in the door and all he could concentrate on was the moaning on the other side.

How could this be? McKenna knew that he had hit the gunman with every shot. How could a bullet go through his body, go through a steel door, and hit somebody on the other side of the door? And who was the injured person, moaning with the pain caused by his bullet and unable to answer the door? He imagined the worst. A grandmother on her way to church. A small girl on her way to buy ice cream. The police commissioner sneaking out of his girlfriend's apartment. He concentrated on that one and started to feel better.

Then things actually got better. White stood over the gunman's body with his ear to the door. "I hear lots of movement inside," he said. "Somebody's running around in there." Good. Next came a radio transmission from a cop outside the building. "There's a male Hispanic throwing guns from the window of the twelfth floor at 277 McKeever Place. We've got two automatics and a revolver so far. We need more units outside for crowd control." Better. Whoever was in apartment 12G was with the bad guys.

White stood up and called McKenna over to the door. "This guy really stinks," he said, pointing down at the dead gunman.

McKenna smelled it then. The gunman had defecated in his pants as he died. But White also had some good news.

"Look at this, Brian. There's just a trace of sheet metal welded to the door where your bullet went through. It's painted over, the same color as the door. Knock on it." McKenna tapped the door around the edges. Solid steel. Then he knocked in the center where his bullet had gone through. Just a thin sheet of metal.

"All right!" McKenna exclaimed. "Drug dealers." Everyone in these housing projects knew the setup. Drug dealers cut illegal mail slots into their doors. You want drugs, you knock. Put your money in the mail slot and the drugs come out the same way. Very clean arrangement. No face-to-face deals. No chance of the dealer getting robbed during the transaction. Except the building management doesn't permit mail slots for that very reason. The mailboxes for each apartment are located in the building lobby. After a while, the other people who live on the drug dealer's floor start to complain, anonymously of course, about the steady stream of visitors to their neighbor's apartment. So every once in a while the building maintenance crews pull out the mail slots, weld on a piece of sheet metal to close the opening, and paint the door. But the drug dealers are still there, inside.

Lucky shot, McKenna thought. I managed to send a dealer a Special Delivery through his old mailbox.

The elevator doors opened and the 71st Precinct patrol sergeant, an Emergency Service sergeant, and two Emergency Service police officers came out.

Short and young, the patrol sergeant looked annoyed by the scene that greeted him. His name tag said Rocco Diluvio. That grabbed McKenna's attention. Nobody but a pompous ass would put his first name on his name tag, McKenna thought. Especially if it was Rocco.

The Emergency Service sergeant was the exact opposite. He was big, gray, with a heavy flak vest, and he looked delighted to be there doing the job he was trained to do. Everyone knew Sergeant Leo Smart. He was a legendary character. This job was going to get done right.

The two Emergency Service cops with him wore the same vests

13

and helmets and were loaded with equipment. One carried a large machine that looked like a combination portable generator and vacuum cleaner. The other dragged what looked like a do-it-yourself swimming-pool kit, boxes of heavy rubber lining and steel braces. Both of them had shotguns slung on their shoulders.

Emergency Service went right to work. They tied a taut rope from the doorknob of apartment 12G to the doorknob of apartment 12H, the adjacent apartment, so that neither door could be opened. Then the two cops began setting up the mysterious apparatus.

Rocco Diluvio watched them for a moment, then turned to the gunman's body. "Who's the shooter?" he asked.

"I am," said McKenna.

"Then I don't want to talk to you yet." He turned to White and asked, "You his partner?"

"The honor is mine for today, Sarge."

"Did you fire any shots?"

"No."

"Good. You I can talk to. Tell me what you've got inside and why we're all here."

White very briefly described the chase. When he was finished, Sergeant Diluvio said, "Tell me where there might be any evidence."

"Spent shells in building hallway. Spent shells and empty magazine on seventh-floor stairwell landing. Oh yeah, McKenna's shoes down on sixth-floor landing. And over here..." White took him over to the twelfth-floor stairwell entrance and pointed out McKenna's three expended shells.

The young patrol sergeant looked McKenna over. He took in the torn pants, the ripped shirt, and then he focused on McKenna's left hand. McKenna looked at his hand and saw that it was bleeding from a scrape across his knuckles. He didn't feel any pain and figured that he got the injury when he was tripped outside.

"You want to go to the hospital, Detective McKenna?" Rocco Diluvio asked. "You look like you could use some kind of treatment."

"Maybe later, Sarge. I don't feel a thing yet."

There were now about fifteen uniformed cops in the hallway. As their patrol sergeant took careful note of them, they started slowly drifting toward the freedom offered by the stairwell door.

Rocco Diluvio stopped the drift with the magic words: "Everybody's on overtime." He sent two cops to the sixth- and seventh-floor stairwell landings to establish a crime scene. Three cops went to the lobby and another one to the tree outside the building where McKenna had taken cover from the gunman's bullets.

"Nobody touches anything," he told them. "And nobody up or down the stairs through the crime scene."

14

Diluvio posted a cop at the stairwell and another at the elevator, with orders to permit no civilians or any more cops on the floor unless they were accompanied by a boss or acting on higher orders. "And no press," he said.

He turned to McKenna. "Where's your car?"

"We left it in the middle of Empire Boulevard," White interjected. "Want me to move it?"

"Not you," the sergeant said. "Give me the keys." He tossed them to one of the uniformed cops. "You take care of this."

He took the radio off his belt and gave a rapid series of requests to the dispatcher. "Seven-one Sergeant to Central, K. I need the Crime Scene Unit, the Hostage Negotiating Team, the Brooklyn Homicide Squad, the Medical Examiner, and a supervisor from the Seven-one Detective Squad to respond to the twelfth-floor hallway of 277 McKeever Place. And the Duty Captain."

The dispatcher confirmed that everybody was already on the way. Then Rocco Diluvio turned to McKenna and asked, "Anything else?"

With a smile that hid his growing respect for the young sergeant, McKenna pointed to his feet and Diluvio sent a cop down to the sixth-floor landing to get McKenna's shoes.

He next directed his attention to Sergeant Smart. "Can I do anything for you, Leo?"

"Yeah, kid. This skell's body's in my way, and he's smelling up the hallway. I also need a layout of this apartment," he said, pointing to the doorway of 12G.

Diluvio thought this over for a moment. Then he had two uniformed cops pick up the dead man and carry him down the hall to just beyond the stairwell. "Nobody touches that body," he ordered.

A cop went off to the building management office for a diagram of 12G. Diluvio stepped to the doorway of the apartment and picked up the dead man's weapon, a TEC-9 automatic pistol. It resembled a rectangular box, with a two-inch barrel protruding from one end and a pistol grip and trigger attached to the bottom.

"Looks nasty," Rocco Diluvio said. He gave the pistol to White. "Your partner's going to be spending a lot of time talking to the chiefs and the DA, so it looks like these are going to be your collars, right?"

"Sounds OK to me, as long as my boss agrees."

White took a pad from his pocket, handed it to McKenna, then crouched in the hallway and unloaded the weapon.

"One live round in the chamber, a magazine loaded with fourteen rounds of live nine-millimeter ammunition. Weapon defaced, serial number filed off." McKenna wrote as White was talking. White smelled the muzzle and chamber of the weapon. "Evidence of recent discharge present," he said as he stood up.

White gave the weapon back to the sergeant, who handed it to a nearby officer.

"Welcome to the case, Rogers," Diluvio said. "You're now the official property officer. Keep track of everything recovered and write it all down."

There were still a few happy uniformed cops without assignments left in the hallway. Diluvio took care of that, telling them, "Go downstairs to help the units outside with crowd control."

Sergeant Rocco Diluvio, Mister Personality himself, had made everybody less happy but more productive in the shortest time possible.

An Emergency Medical Service ambulance crew arrived on the floor to officially pronounce the gunman dead. The attendant leaned over the body and felt for a heartbeat, then stood up and said, "Yup, he's dead." He looked at his watch. "Officially pronounced dead at four-o-six P.M."

McKenna took the attendant's name and wrote it down on his pad. Diluvio told the ambulance crew to stand by until they had cleared out apartment 12G.

Meanwhile the Emergency Service crew had been busy working on the door. They took the rubber lining and placed it all around the doorframe of apartment 12G. The steel braces held the rubber lining in place. It looked like they were building another rubber door in front of the apartment door. Two more Emergency Service cops came up with shotguns and additional tools. Leo Smart took a crowbar and hammer and used them to widen the bullet hole in the door by ripping away the sheet metal that covered the former mail slot.

Smart bent over and peeked through the opening. "There's a male Hispanic lying right in front of the door. He's breathing, but it looks like he took the bullet in the chest. There's another male Hispanic at the far end of the apartment. He appears to be unarmed right now. He's looking at me and giving me the finger." The Emergency Service cops finished their work at the door.

While McKenna tied his recently returned shoes, he stared at the contraption. "Nice job. How does it work?"

He got a quick lesson on the Rabbit Tool from one of the Emergency Service cops. "Start the generator and a pump fills the rubber bladder that's forced into the doorframe with air. Eventually, the pressure becomes too much for the door. It starts to bend a little and pulls the hinges and the lock from the doorframe. Door goes down. It's the only thing short of dynamite that works on these steel-frame doors."

Rocco Diluvio knocked a few times next door on 12F. After a few moments it opened just a crack. All McKenna could see of the occupant was a black hand holding the edge of the door slightly open.

Diluvio said, "Sorry to bother you, but we're going to blast your neighbors out in a couple of minutes. You got a phone?"

"Uh-huh."

"We'd like to use your apartment as a temporary headquarters. I hope you don't mind. As a matter of fact, you might want to go to the store or something, because there might be some more shooting around here."

Enough said. The circus continued. McKenna was reminded of the clown car when eight chidren and five adults left the apartment and headed for the elevator. Then came a large black woman pushing an old man in a wheelchair. "It's all yours, Officer," she said, and joined the rest of the displaced occupants.

The elevator door opened. Out stepped Deputy Inspector Jerimiah O'Shaughnessy, the recently promoted commanding officer of the 71st Precinct. Not the duty captain, as everyone expected, but something worse.

O'Shaughnessy was known far and wide as Deputy Dog Dick. Rumor had it that he had gotten that name while working as a desk officer in a Harlem precinct. One day he had been busy berating a prisoner who had a sense of humor, something O'Shaughnessy lacked. What he did have was bright red hair and a tendency to blush violently whenever he was angry, embarrassed, or under pressure. The more O'Shaughnessy yelled at the prisoner, the redder he'd gotten, and the more the prisoner had convulsed with laughter. Finally, while the entire four-to-twelve platoon of that Harlem precinct stood in front of the Desk waiting to be inspected before they went on patrol, the prisoner had said to O'Shaughnessy, "You know, Lieutenant, you're red in the head like a dick on a dog."

That was it. From then on he had been Lieutenant Dog Dick, until it was Captain Dog Dick; now it was Deputy Dog Dick, which the cops in the Seven-one Precinct agreed had a nice ring to it. They were all looking forward to the day when he would get promoted to full inspector and finally be transferred. Then he would be the Dog Dick Inspector. And he had the perfect personality to eventually become the Chief Dog Dick. O'Shaughnessy's arrival was good news for no one. He was the perfect act to follow Sergeant Rocco Diluvio.

Diluvio saluted O'Shaughnessy and brought him into the new temporary headquarters to fill him in. The assembled officers felt it was a good idea to wait in the hall. After five minutes Diluvio came to the door and told McKenna that the inspector wanted to see him. McKenna found O'Shaughnessy standing in the living room of the small apartment. He was on the phone, and by his deferential manner, McKenna guessed that he was talking to the borough commander, who probably wanted to know what the hell was going on. McKenna saluted and O'Shaughnessy asked, "How long have you been in Brooklyn this time, McKenna?"

"Two weeks, Inspector."

"Why you here?"

"A little incident in Manhattan with a diplomat. I haven't gone to Department Trial yet." McKenna mentioned the Department Trial for a reason. Under the rules of the game, O'Shaughnessy couldn't ask McKenna specifics about the incident until the trial was over.

"So we're stuck again. Two weeks and you've already managed to get bullets spread all over the borough, shoot somebody in the back, and maybe get some innocent people shot. Not to mention you caused a radio-car accident when one of my cars was rushing here to help you out. You're lucky no one was hurt. But I'm still short a car now, thanks to you. Tell me, McKenna, did this whole mess have anything to do with your assignment today?"

"No, sir. Just a crime in progress that we observed on our way back to the station house."

"And what was that crime in progress, McKenna?"

"Illegal Possession of a Loaded Firearm, sir."

There it was, a little red, starting at the neck. "Care to tell me more, McKenna?"

"I'd rather wait until I speak to my delegate, Inspector. You understand. Just in case there are any criminal charges against me later. I would hate to have you testifying against me for something I might tell you now."

The red had reached his cheeks and was still climbing. "I'm talking man to man, McKenna. Just so I have something to tell the chief when he asks me. I've got a large, disorderly crowd outside and there's going to be a lot of press. You've got to give me more."

"No offense, Inspector. But I think I'd rather talk to my delegate first. Then he can talk to the union lawyer, and our lawyer can whisper to the chief and tell him what he needs to know."

O'Shaughnessy was red right to the top of his head, Ready for Blast-off.

Just then Diluvio came in and said, "Inspector, they've got a lot of drugs in the apartment and they're flushing them down the toilet. The Emergency Service sergeant wants permission to blow the door and go in before they flush it all."

Countdown delayed. O'Shaughnessy snarled, "I'll talk to you later about this, Detective McKenna. All I can say is that you'd better have your story straight."

The men went back into the hall to see what was going on and to await the inspector's decision.

18

Smart was still looking through the hole in the door. Out of the corner of his eye he saw O'Shaughnessy, stood up, and saluted. "They just started flushing drugs down the toilet, Inspector."

"How do you know, Sergeant?"

"A minute ago I saw one of the guys inside bring about ten one-kilo bags of dope into the bathroom. Then I heard the toilet flush. What do you think, Inspector?"

The toilet in Apartment 12G was flushed again and the sound was clearly heard by everyone standing in the hallway.

"Don't worry about it too much, Inspector," Smart said. "I called our dispatcher and ordered a couple of Emergency men who were on their way up to cut the water off into the building. That'll stop our pal inside from flushing his dope, but it's gonna take a few minutes."

O'Shaughnessy didn't look happy. He was thinking the situation over when the toilet flushed again. Smart decided that it was time to have some fun with O'Shaughnessy. Fun for Smart consisted of forcing the big Bosses to make a decision. They hated that.

"It flushes every couple of minutes, as soon as the tank fills up," said the old sergeant. "We're losing a lot of evidence. I've got another two men coming up with a bulletproof shield. We're ready to blow the door and go in now. It only takes about a minute to get this generator going. As soon as you give the word, Inspector."

Without answering, O'Shaughnessy went back into the temporary headquarters apartment and turned on the water faucet in the kitchen.

Smart winked at McKenna and McKenna replied with a smile.

After two minutes and a few more flushes the water stopped. O'Shaughnessy came back out and told Smart that the water was off.

"I already knew that, Inspector," replied the sergeant. "The guy inside just asked me what happened to the water."

"The people inside may still be armed and just waiting for us," O'Shaughnessy said. "There might be ten people in there. We'll wait for the Hostage Negotiating Team to try and talk them out."

Smart took these instructions in stride. He didn't look surprised. O'Shaughnessy had just given him the Official Department Line.

Two more Emergency Service cops came up carrying a large Plexiglas bulletproof shield. With them was the cop who had been sent to the building management office for the apartment plans, which he gave to Smart. Four rooms: two bedrooms, a living room, and a kitchen. With O'Shaughnessy listening, Smart and Rocco Diluvio made their own plan to deal with the people inside 12G.

O'Shaughnessy added his two cents before he approved the plan.

"If and when the time comes, only Emergency Service men with flak jackets and helmets go in."

Rocco Diluvio and Smart looked at each other. This was standard procedure and news to nobody.

"When the apartment's secure, White as the arresting officer, and his partner, McKenna, will be the search team," O'Shaughnessy added.

Then Lieutenant Schnieder arrived. He was McKenna and White's boss, the commanding officer of the Seven-one Detective Squad.

"Glad you're here, Lieutenant," O'Shaughnessy said with genuine sincerity. "Do you need to be filled in?"

"No, sir. I think I've got the picture. The chief called me in my office."

"Good You can supervise the search team."

"That's what I'm here for."

O'Shaughnessy was happy to be off the hook. He had managed to place responsibility for the search with the Detective Bureau. If anything went wrong, it wasn't his fault.

It started suddenly and ended quickly. Smart, who was looking through the hole in the door, suddenly shouted, "Something's up!"

He had everybody's attention. "The skell's bringing the dope to the living-room window. He's got a knife. Shit! He's ripping the bags open and pouring the dope out the window."

At that moment the radio crackled with a message from a unit outside. "He's throwing cocaine out the window. There's coke all over the grass. We need more units for crowd control. They're going crazy."

That did it. This made for bad headlines. O'Shaughnessy gave the order. "Take the door."

Leo Smart backed away, reached down and started the generator. Its racket was deafening. The rubber bladder inflated and the Emergency Service men deployed behind their Plexiglas shield. The door burst off its hinges and fell into the apartment, landing on top of the wounded man in the apartment's hall. The cops ran over the door and the man under it. The last one in pulled the door off the shot man and handcuffed him. While they searched the apartment, McKenna stood outside. Two minutes later they came out with a second handcuffed prisoner. It was over.

"Ready for the search team," Smart said on his way out.

Rocco Diluvio lifted his radio and canceled the call for the Hostage Negotiating Team. McKenna breathed a sigh of relief. We would've been here till tomorrow night if the Hostage Negotiating Team had gotten here before Emergency Service knocked the door down, he thought.

Lieutenant Schnieder, McKenna, White, and Rogers, the uniformed officer who had been designated as the property officer, went into the apartment together. They were to confiscate all evidence and contraband that were in plain view. They worked room by room, starting with the bathroom. Two unopened one-kilo clear plastic bags filled with compressed cocaine sat next to the toilet bowl. There were also five ripped clear plastic bags with some cocaine powder left in them scattered around the bathroom. McKenna saw a lot of cocaine powder floating in the toilet bowl, so he went into the kitchen and found a ladle and a large pitcher with a cover. He scooped the powder from the bowl and put it in the pitcher. He gave everything to Rogers, and then they started on the living room.

On the windowsill were seven kilo bags of cocaine and a knife. A long table along the wall held two digital scales, stacks of unused clear plastic bags, a compressing machine, and a bag-sealing machine.

McKenna looked out the window. Directly below, twelve stories down, the grass was covered with white powder. It had a real shine to it. There were also a lot of large white rocks of coke on the grass. The scene below was one of barely controlled pandemonium. About fifty feet from the building a line of twenty cops struggled to maintain formation against a crowd of what looked like two hundred people. McKenna heard the wail of sirens; more cops were still arriving. A television news van and the reporters were just beginning to set up, raising the antenna of the van and running wires to a spot near the line of police from which they would broadcast.

McKenna yelled to the cops downstairs and a few of them looked up. He threw a stack of unused clear plastic bags and the ladle out the window. A sergeant directed two cops to the stuff on the ground and they started scooping up the rocks of coke.

"Rogers!" Lieutenant Schnieder said, "Bring whatever we've got so far into the temporary headquarters."

Schnieder, McKenna, and White went to the first bedroom. It was a real mess. The bed was unmade and clothes were thrown all around the room. A blue canvas travel bag lay on the bed and McKenna opened it. Money, and lots of it. The bag was stuffed with wrapped stacks of bills: twenties, fifties, and hundreds.

McKenna turned to Lieutenant Schnieder. "Plain view?"

Schnieder smiled and answered, "It was open when I got in here."

Good enough, McKenna thought. He gave the open bag to the lieutenant and they went to the second bedroom. It had been used as an office of some kind. A small desk along the wall was stacked with notebooks. McKenna opened one; it was a record of drug transactions. He scooped up the pile and asked Schnieder, "We got enough yet?"

"More than enough for us. We're not Narcotics. As it is, we're going to be counting this stuff all night."

They went back to the living room and helped Rogers carry the rest of the evidence to the temporary headquarters next door. Lieutenant Schnieder logged down the time in the Temporary Headquarters Log that had been set up. It was now 4:19. Under five minutes in there, McKenna thought. That should sound good in court.

McKenna and White left Lieutenant Schnieder, who had to tell O'Shaughnessy what they had found in apartment 12G. In the hallway were the prisoners, Rocco Diluvio, Sergeant Smart, and about ten uniformed cops. Smart was busy supervising his men while they packed up their equipment. The shot prisoner still groaned on a stretcher while being worked on by the ambulance attendant. Standing near him was the other occupant of the apartment. He was still handcuffed and a uniformed cop held him by the arm. The prisoner watched the attendant work on his injured partner. He didn't seem to be showing much interest. Diluvio was obviusly waiting for the detectives to search their prisoners.

McKenna and White walked over to the standing prisoner. "What's your name?" McKenna asked.

"Jorge Chavez," he replied.

"What's your friend's name?"

"I don't know that man. I never saw him before in my life," Chavez replied with a straight face.

OK, thought McKenna. These guys are going to go the tough route. Smart. He leaned over the stretcher and asked the injured man what his name was.

"Francisco Torres," he replied.

"And who's your friend?" asked McKenna.

Torres closed his eyes and said, "I don't know him."

Two tough guys. They both know the system.

White searched Torres while he was being treated and found nothing, no wallet, no money. Then Chavez. He had a wallet with two twenties in it. White put the money in Chavez's pocket and gave the wallet to McKenna. Then McKenna went over to the dead gunman and lifted his head so that the two prisoners could see the gunman's face. "You guys ever see this man before?" Two defiant stares returned McKenna's gaze.

McKenna gave up on them. He asked the ambulance attendant, "Which hospital are you bringing Torres to?"

"Kings County."

McKenna turned to Rocco Diluvio. "Sarge, could you have Chavez brought to the Seven-one Squad office? And please, don't let him talk to anyone."

22

"OK." Diluvio relayed these directions to two uniformed cops and they prepared to leave with Chavez on the same elevator as Torres, the ambulance crew, and the cop who had been assigned to guard Torres in the hospital.

The elevator doors opened and out stepped Detective First Grade Timmothy D'Arcey and two detectives whom McKenna knew from the Crime Scene Unit. D'Arcey was the vice-president of the Detectives Endowment Association, the detectives' union. Expensively dressed and neatly groomed, he looked like he had just fallen off the cover of *Fortune* magazine. McKenna had figured that D'Arcey would be coming and he was glad to see him. D'Arcey pulled McKenna to the side while the Crime Scene Unit detectives started their task of photographing and measuring the hallway and the body.

"Looks like I'm becoming your full-time delegate, Brian. Did you tell them anything?"

"Nothing."

"How about O'Shaughnessy?"

"Nothing."

"Good!" said D'Arcey. "That O'Shaughnessy is a treacherous prick. He might love to hang you. We have to find a place where we can talk. I've got our lawyer coming and he'll meet us later at the station house. Until then, say nothing about this shooting to anybody unless I'm standing next to you. Got it?"

"Of course."

"C'mon. We'll go up to the roof to talk."

"Can't leave just yet, Timmy. The dead guy still hasn't been searched, and I've got to be a witness for that."

"OK. We can wait."

The Crime Scene men finished photographing the hallway and they asked Diluvio to have the body moved back to the place and position that it was in when he first saw it. White supervised two cops who made the final placement in front of 12G. Rogers went into the temporary headquarters and got the TEC-9 automatic pistol. He gave it to White, who placed it back down by the dead gunman's right hand.

Nice job, McKenna thought. Like he had never been moved.

The Crime Scene men took a series of pictures. When they were finished, White crouched over the body, ready to begin the search. Rogers stood over him, taking notes. White started by emptying the dead man's pockets. There was a good leather wallet in the back one. White opened it and found a Florida driver's license with a picture of the dead man. He was Raoul Camarena, with a Fort Myers Beach address, date of birth September 2, 1949, forty-two years old. There was also a Social Security card in the same name. In the rest of the dead man's pockets White found lots of cash. He counted out $1,461.26 and gave it to Rogers. Then White removed the jewelry, a gold horseshoe ring studded with small diamonds that had been on the right hand and a gold chain with a crucifix around the neck. Rogers got that too.

White pulled off the dead man's jacket, revealing a large leather shoulder holster. White started to take the holster off and stopped. He had felt something. He looked up at McKenna and said, "He's got something under his shirt."

The cops' interest was aroused. McKenna helped White unbuckle and remove the shoulder holster. White pulled the dead man's shirt over his head. Taped together to his back with surgical tape were a pink plastic rectangular box and a blood-stained envelope. White ripped the box and the envelope away.

Everyone was now leaning over the body. White opened the pink box and jerked back his head, startled. A finger with a ring attached fell out and landed on the dead man's back as the box snapped closed. Nobody moved. The finger had been recently and cleanly severed from its owner's hand. There was still some uncongealed blood visible at the spot where the finger used to be attached. The finger belonged to a white male. There was thick black hair on the knuckles. It was clean and the nail was neat and cut fairly short. The ring on the finger was a large, heavy gold ring with a crest cut into the face. It was old and the gold around the crest was worn.

D'Arcey broke the tension. "Well, there's something you don't see every day. A man with eleven fingers."

McKenna picked up the finger and examined it. He eased the ring off and handed it to Rogers, then took the pink plastic box and the envelope from White's hands and put the finger back inside. The box looked familiar to him. Then he remembered. Angelita, his girlfriend, carried an identical box around in her pocketbook. She used it to store her once-a-month necessities. He placed the box on the dead man's back and started to open the envelope. "This should be interesting," he said.

It was. The envelope contained two color Polaroid photos. The gunman's blood had not seeped through the envelope; the photos were undamaged.

The first was of a white male, about thirty years old. He was seated on a chair and holding a copy of a newspaper across his chest with his right hand.

The second was a close-up that showed the same man's right hand holding the newspaper. The pinky of his right hand had recently been surgically removed. There were antiseptic orange markings at the

24

base of the hand. Black stitches were visible where the wound was closed and the hand showed extreme swelling in that area. The ring finger of the right hand shown in the photo appeared to be the same severed finger that the detectives had just found, with the same gold ring on it. The newspaper in the photo was the *Boston Globe* and the main headline read MAYOR CAVES IN ON BUS STRIKE.

McKenna realized that the man in the photo was now minus at least two fingers.

Rocco Diluvio went to tell O'Shaughnessy. As soon as he left D'Arcey said, "Brian, I don't think that you have to worry about Dog Dick anymore. You just stumbled into a major case. Let's go talk."

McKenna said to White, "Tell anyone who might be looking for me that I went to look for a bathroom to wash up." McKenna and D'Arcey took the elevator to the top floor of the building, walking up the last flight of stairs to the roof. There was a fence along the edge of the roof and they went over to talk. McKenna told D'Arcey everything that had happened, leaving out nothing.

Below them on the ground the crowd had swelled considerably, and so had the number of cops. They could even see a cop in a white shirt, a captain, walking up and down the line of cops giving orders to sergeants to adjust the placement of their men. They must be miserable, McKenna thought. There was a lot of yelling going on, but from the roof the two detectives couldn't tell exactly what the yelling was about. July in the ghetto. There were now three television vans set up, and a fire-department engine company standing by. Two cops who were being closely supervised by a sergeant completed picking up the rocks of cocaine from the ground and placed them in two of the bags that McKenna had thrown from the window. The grass still had a white sheen to it.

Then things really got interesting. The captain waved to the fire trucks and the firemen started unrolling their hoses. The crowd then realized that the firemen were going to wash away the cocaine from the grass; they were about to be deprived of a potential free source of chemical happiness. The chant started, over and over, "Leave it! leave it!" It sounded like thunder to McKenna and D'Arcey. The crowd pressed against the line of cops, and the cops began to slowly lose ground. More sirens revved in the distance. The firemen started working faster, hurrying to finish. Some bottles thrown from the crowd landed close to the firemen, but they kept on hooking up their hoses.

The line of cops standing shoulder to shoulder against the crowd started to give in places. More police cars arrived. The cops ran from their cars and reinforced the line by pushing them forward from behind. The added police manpower made the difference. They held the line; the firemen turned on the water and quickly sprayed the grass. It was over.

The crowd stopped chanting and pushing, and the captain began directing police cars to leave. The mob had lost its cohesiveness and its reason for being. McKenna and D'Arcey watched as a large, disorderly crowd, seemingly intent on riot, turned into simply a lot of people on a crowded ghetto sidewalk.

McKenna finished his story and D'Arcey analyzed the pitfalls and trouble spots for him. "It seems that you shot him in the back without giving him any chance to surrender. That's not great when it's played on prime time."

"He was good. Maybe better than me. He already had tried to kill me three times. He had to go and I wasn't going to give him another chance."

"According to regulations, a nice 'Police, Don't Move' would have been better," said D'Arcey. "How well do you know Richie White?"

"Hardly."

"And how about the two cops who came up the stairs with him?"

"Not at all."

"Well, I know Richie really well. He's a stand-up guy and a hard worker. I'll find out who the two cops were and I'll talk to their PBA delegate. We'll fix it. Just remember, 'Police, Don't Move.' Now, I don't want you talking to anyone until Harry McCrystal gets here. He's the best lawyer we've got and he'll know just how to handle this. The DA and a few chiefs are going to be at the station house, so you're going to the hospital for now to be treated for your wounds and for trauma. Remember, you were just forced to take the life of a fellow human being in the line of duty and you're really shaken up. Got it?"

"You're right, Timmy. I'm really broken up and I've got to talk to a shrink. I just can't bring myself to talk to anyone else yet. I don't want anyone to see me crying. How am I doing?"

"Perfect! Let's get the ball rolling." They walked down the stairs and took the elevator down to the twelfth floor. When the doors opened there was O'Shaughnessy, looking right at them. He had been waiting for them. He seemed to be smiling as they stepped out. "Brian! Glad you're here. I need to have a couple of words with you. A lot's been happening."

McKenna and D'Arcey looked at each other. Brian? Did he say Brian? McKenna asked himself. I thought this man hated my guts. A lot must have been happening. Dog Dick has lost his mind. Brian?

D'Arcey was the first to recover. "If you don't mind, Inspector, I'd like to be there while you're talking to Detective McKenna."

"Of course, Timmy. Love to have you. Come on into the temporary headquarters." Timmy? There he goes again. Something's up.

The two detectives and McKenna followed O'Shaughnessy into the living room of the temporary headquarters. He was still smiling and he exuded goodwill. McKenna looked down to make sure that he wasn't standing on a trap door that would drop him into an alligator pit.

"Brian," O'Shaughnessy began, "it looks like you've stumbled onto something here. A kidnapping. A major case. A very newsworthy case. Stopping a dangerous armed felon and recovering a substantial amount of money and drugs. Good job. I just wish that you would've searched the body a little earlier. But, I understand that you were just following procedures. If I would've known a little more a little bit earlier, maybe we wouldn't have had to get so cranky with each other. Maybe I was a little wrong."

Wrong? McKenna thought. Deputy inspectors of police are never wrong unless a chief tells them that they are. So that's it. There's a chief in this picture somewhere.

O'Shaughnessy continued. "There's already been a lot of interest generated. We're going to try and keep the press in the dark until we know more about this case. We have no active kidnapping cases right now and Chief Brunette is checking with the Boston police. We'll know more in a little while. But until then, nothing to the press. I've already talked to my men."

Chief Brunette. Ray Brunette, the Chief of Detectives. He's got Dog Dick shaking, McKenna thought.

"The press won't get anything from me," McKenna said.

"As a matter of fact," O'Shaughnessy said, "I just talked to Chief Brunette. He told me that it sounded like great police work on your part, Brian. When I think about it, I have to agree with him. You've done a great job. He wants me to iron out any little wrinkles in this shooting matter before he gets here."

"Chief Brunette is coming here?" asked D'Arcey.

"Yes. We're going to meet him at the station house. He's not crazy about the Boston chief of police and he wants to embarrass him a little by solving one of his crimes for him. Plus get some good coverage for us."

D'Arcey thought over this new piece of information for a minute and said, "Before the chief gets here, Inspector, I'd like to take Detective McKenna to the hospital. He's been shot at, he's injured, and he's just killed a man. He's pretty shaken up. I even think that he should go sick."

"Of course, Tim. Get him treated. But Brian, if you do have to go sick, please stop by the station house before you go home. I think that the chief might want to congratulate you himself."

"Sure, Inspector. Whatever you say," McKenna answered. The two detectives turned and left O'Shaughnessy, both of them marveling at this dramatic turn of events. Popped out of the frying pan and into the Pot of Gold.

They had to wait at the door of the temporary headquarters, which was blocked by a collapsible stretcher. Two morgue attendants had arrived and had opened a black body bag on the stretcher in front of McKenna and D'Arcey. The attendants lifted the dead gunman onto the stretcher, leaving his head hanging over the end, and began to zip the body into the bag.

McKenna took a final look at the face of the loser. His eyes had glazed over and his mouth hung open. Then McKenna saw something. It looked to him like there was something white in the dead man's mouth. McKenna bent down and squinted. He was right. There was a crumpled, rolled-up piece of paper in the dead man's mouth.

Why would he try to hide or swallow something unless it was important? McKenna put in his fingers and pulled out the paper. The ball was chewed up and slimy with blood and saliva. The morgue attendants and D'Arcey were watching McKenna with interest as he unrolled the small ball of paper and spread it on the dead man's chest. There were seven numbers written on it. A telephone number. McKenna recognized the exchange code, 860, the code for Spanish Harlem in Manhattan, where McKenna had been assigned before his recent fall from grace.

McKenna took a handkerchief from his pocket, wrapped up the paper in the handkerchief, and put it back in his pocket. Then he walked into apartment 12G, past the Seven-one Precinct uniformed officer assigned to guard the apartment. D'Arcey followed him in. McKenna went to the bathroom and began washing his hands while he thought. By the time he finished drying his hands, he had reached a decision. He said to D'Arcey, "Let's keep this telephone number quiet for now, OK?"

"What telephone number, Brian? I didn't see anything and nobody talks to morgue attendants. Let's get to the hospital. You're the star of the show and your fans are waiting."

3

July 9   5:45 p.m.

McKenna and D'Arcey walked through the large waiting area of the emergency room. Kings County Hospital was a zoo, McKenna thought, a typical overburdened city hospital, where the care is free for those who cannot pay. People everywhere, people on chairs, people standing around, people on stretchers in the hallway. Cops all over, cops with prisoners, cops with crime victims, cops with accident victims trying to get all the information they needed for their reports. There were the homeless, the schizophrenics, the overdoses, and the working poor who just couldn't afford to go to a doctor, people who looked like they lived in the waiting area, people on crutches and people in wheelchairs, talking to each other or talking to themselves, kids playing and babies crying: the disposable flotsam of humanity seeking guaranteed medical care, minus dignity. No one is turned away.

D'Arcey and McKenna walked to the reception area. The receptionists were separated from the waiting area—probably to preserve their sanity—by a wall with a large rectangular sliding glass window in the center. A long line of people stretched from their window, waiting to be processed.

D'Arcey looked disapprovingly at the line. "I'll handle this. Hold up your hand and look like you're in pain."

McKenna held up his scraped right hand and imagined that someone was plucking his eyelashes, one by one. His face contorted and his eyes half closed. He followed D'Arcey to the window, being careful to limp on his scraped right knee. D'Arcey disregarded the line. He looked like the mayor, but acted with more authority. He knocked on the glass window. The two faces on the other side looked at him. *Bore me if you must,* their faces commanded.

"This is Detective McKenna," D'Arcey said, pointing to him. "He's just been shot."

Shot? thought McKenna. That's right. I have been shot.

One receptionist, a thin black woman with glasses sitting on the end of her nose, stood and looked McKenna up and down. "He don't look shot to me," she said in her West Indian accent. "Where's he shot?"

D'Arcey replied in an exasperated voice, "In the chest. Thank God he was wearing a bulletproof vest. The bullet hit him in the chest. Probably broke some ribs and caused some internal damage. He's suffering from blunt body trauma. And he's having a lot of trouble breathing."

McKenna started breathing heavily. The final touch.

The receptionist picked up the phone, dialed an extension, and spoke briefly. Then she said to D'Arcey, "Go to Triage. Make a right, end of the hall through the swinging doors, the room on your right. Doctor Patel. There's a wheelchair right around the corner, if you need it."

"Thanks, Miss. I know where it is," D'Arcey replied. "We'll be able to make it without the wheelchair." He grabbed McKenna by the arm and took him down the hall to the Triage room.

It was a large room broken down into small curtained booths along the wall. They were expected. A young black nurse met them at the door and guided them to one of the booths. The prevailing color was green. Light green walls, light green curtains, light green linoleum floor. Dark green oxygen bottles, and a dark green cushioned examining table in the middle of the booth with a large roll of white paper attached to the end of the table. The nurse pulled a fresh sheet of paper from the roll to cover the table and told McKenna to take off his shirt and pants. She left.

McKenna took his pistol from his holster and gave it to D'Arcey. He removed his jacket and tie. When he started to pull off his shirt, a 9-mm bullet fell from his shirt and rolled onto the floor. D'Arcey picked up the bullet, looked it over, and gave it to McKenna. The nose of the bullet was flattened from the force with which it had hit McKenna's vest.

"Not everyone gets to hold the bullet that had his name on it," D'Arcey remarked.

This gave McKenna something to think about while he finished. After he took off his shoes and pants, he sat on the examining table and loosened the Velcro straps of the vest. When he lifted it over his head, he found that it hurt to raise his arms. As he peeled off his undershirt he experienced the same pain in his chest. D'Arcey whistled. McKenna looked down and saw a large, purple bruise where the bullet had hit him.

"It looks worse than it feels," he said to D'Arcey.

The nurse returned and purfunctorily took McKenna's pulse and blood pressure. She asked some questions and wrote McKenna's answers down on a chart attached to a clipboard. Brian McKenna, address One Police Plaza, age forty-four, no allergies. She was in and out in a flash. "The doctor will be right with you," she said.

McKenna started to feel silly sitting in front of D'Arcey in his underpants. It got to D'Arcey, too. He started pacing around the small curtained room as he discussed the classic police textbook shooting, which McKenna's action would resemble after D'Arcey adjusted some facts.

D'Arcey said, "Let's talk about lying and maybe a little perjury. Just to make your shooting 'right.' "

McKenna raised his eyebrows and shifted his eyes from one curtain to the other on either side of him.

D'Arcey got the message. He peeked through the curtain to the adjoining room on their left. Nobody. Then he checked the area on their right.

"Hey!" he said. "Look who's here."

D'Arcey pulled the curtain back and McKenna stood up to see. Lying on a table was Francisco Torres, covered to his waist by a sheet and with tubes coming from almost every orifice in his body, looking as if he were caught in the middle of a spider web. His upper body was covered with scars, making his latest chest wound seem innocuous. Torres could have been a retired knife-fighter. He read a Spanish-version "Hulk Hogan" comic book, which he held over his face with one hand. His other hand had been handcuffed to the metal rail at the side of his bed. Sitting in a chair next to the bed, a young uniformed Seven-one Precinct cop looked very bored.

"Hi, McKenna," the cop said.

"Sorry you wound up with this job, buddy," McKenna answered.

"It's not so bad. Sure beats riding around the Seven-one."

The sight of Torres made McKenna feel like a sissy even bothering to complain about his small ailments.

Torres looked up from his comic book. His face lit up in recognition. "Hey, you're the one who shot me, aren't you?"

"I'm sorry, *amigo*. It was an accident," McKenna answered. "I didn't mean to shoot you."

Torres thought this answer over for a moment. Then he said, "That's all right, Officer. I've been shot more times by accident than on purpose. Accident is better. Then you only get shot once."

Torres saw the purple bruise on McKenna's chest and asked, "What happened to you?"

"He's been shot," D'Arcey told him.

Torres looked surprised and he asked McKenna, "Who shot you, Officer?"

"Raoul Camarena."

A blank stare returned McKenna's answer. "Who?" asked Torres, confused.

Torres doesn't know who Raoul Camarena is, McKenna thought. Which means that maybe the dead gunman wasn't really named Raoul Camarena. But Torres must know him. When I shot the guy, he was pounding on Torres's door and calling for "Paco." Paco is frequently the Spanish nickname for Francisco. The dead man said his name was Rico when he was yelling at the door of apartment 12G. I'll try that, McKenna thought.

"Just kidding, Paco. Rico was the one that shot me. He would've killed me if I didn't have a vest on."

Now he got it. "Oh, Rico. Yeah, that Rico was a bad mother. From what I hear about him, you're lucky to be here right now, Officer. It should be you in the morgue instead of him."

"Yeah, I got lucky, Paco. Tell me, what do you hear about Rico? I'd like to know more about him."

Torres's face changed. No expression at all. "I've got a lawyer, Officer. You want to know anything from me, you ask my lawyer. Maybe he can make a deal with you."

That stopped McKenna for a moment. Under the current rules of engagement he couldn't ask Paco another thing once he said that he had a lawyer. His lawyer had to be present for any questioning, and lawyers managed never to make themselves available. They knew that there was no percentage in having a client talk to the police, especially if the client is very guilty. Not unless a formal deal had been made. But lawyers don't make deals with the cops, they make them with the DA. McKenna decided to try anyway.

"You know we've got you good, Paco. Lots of guns, lots of money, and lots of drugs. You're facing some heavy time, pal, and you might be able to help us out. I just want to know a few things that can't hurt you, might even help you in the end."

Paco looked at McKenna incredulously. There was no goodwill in his answer.

"You think I'm stupid, Officer? What are you going to do with all that stuff you got? Give it back? I've been around long enough to

32

know that anyone who makes a deal with the cops without their lawyer is in jail. I'll let my lawyer tell me how good you got me. Then, if you want to make a deal, talk to him. Tell him what you want to know. He's the best. We'll see then what I'll tell you." Paco went back to his comic book. The interview was over.

He's right, McKenna thought. There really was nothing I could do for Paco. This case was going to get too much publicity for me to help Paco out with any lies. Any deal for information that could be made had to be between Paco's lawyer and the DA.

McKenna considered asking Paco who his lawyer was, but he decided against it. Paco might ask me to call his lawyer for him, he thought, and I don't want to have a lawyer involved yet. Not until I think some more and talk to the bosses. Besides, I already found out more than I knew before I talked to him.

"Have it your way, Paco."

D'Arcey closed the curtain.

"These guys are getting too smart. It's sure not as easy as it used to be. Does that sound like I'm getting old?" McKenna asked.

"No, it sounds like you need some new lines. That old stuff doesn't work anymore. It sounds like you've been watching too much TV."

"I only watch TV when I'm on the news."

Dr. Patel came in, accompanied by the nurse. He was a pleasant and smiling Indian and he even seemed happy to see McKenna. I don't know this guy, thought McKenna. What makes him so happy? Must be that he's not in India.

Dr. Patel solicitously asked McKenna what had happened to him and McKenna told him.

"Trouble breathing?" he asked McKenna.

"No, not now, Doctor. Maybe I was just worn out before. I did a lot of running. There was a lot of excitement."

The doctor listened to McKenna's heart with his stethoscope, then he took his pulse. "Slow pulse," he said. "Are you a runner?"

"Yes."

"Do you smoke?"

"Not for years."

He pressed the area around the purple bruise on McKenna's chest. He felt McKenna's ribs. Then he held McKenna's chest from behind while McKenna breathed deeply.

"I don't think any ribs are broken, but I'm going to send you for some X-rays, just to be sure. Now I'm going to treat those abrasions."

With the help of the nurse, the doctor cleaned the abrasions on McKenna's knees and hand, then applied a stinging antiseptic to both scrapes. He wrapped McKenna's hand with a gauze bandage and taped a bandage to his knee. "You can get dressed for now. If the X-rays are negative, I'll give you a prescription for pain. Then you should just stay in bed for a couple of days and you'll be fine. No lifting and no running."

McKenna started getting dressed. Another nurse came in and asked, "Detective McKenna?"

"Right here."

"The mayor's office is on the phone. The mayor wants to talk to you. You can follow me if you like. The phone is in the hall."

D'Arcey looked shocked.

"Angelita," McKenna said quietly. D'Arcey got it.

McKenna slowly finished dressing while he thought about what he was going to tell Angelita, his love for the past four years. Angelita had never been able to pull off a face-to-face lie in her life. But on the phone was different. She always managed to find him, no matter where he was. On the phone, she had been everyone from the police commissioner's secretary to Barbara Bush. She spent less time waiting on hold than anyone in the City of New York.

McKenna stood and followed the nurse into the hall. He took the phone off the hook, pressed the light that was blinking, and said, "Detective McKenna, Your Honor. How are you? So nice of you to call." The nurse was glued to his side.

Angelita sounded frantic. "What's happening? How are you? I heard you've been shot. It's even on the news. You couldn't even call me? Talk to me!"

"Yes, Your Honor. I'm fine. Nothing serious. They're treating me just great here. You were right. This is the best hospital. I'd like to give you my report now, but there's a nurse standing next to me."

"Get rid of her," Angelita said.

"Yes, Your Honor. I know that it's confidential." He turned around and caught sight of the nurse moving down the hall. Then he asked Angelita, "How did you know I was here?"

She began to calm down. "Ray called me. He told me that I should bring a new suit and a new shirt. You know him. His detectives always have to look *sooo* good. He's really silly sometimes. He told me this whole thing was nothing, but I never know when to believe him."

"Where are you?"

"In the Seven-one Precinct. I'm in Dog Dick's office right now. Ray threw everyone out so I could call you, so don't worry. I'm bringing your clothes over. Make sure you're there. I just hope you're in one piece and everything still works, or I'm going to have to go out and get me a young stud. See you soon."

"Bye, baby," McKenna said as he hung up the phone. God damn Ray, he thought. A great guy, but a real pain in the ass sometimes. Why did he involve Angelita in this?

34

The fact that Ray Brunette, the chief of detectives, was McKenna's "hook" was one of the most closely guarded secrets in the Detective Bureau. You never let anyone know who your hook was. That would be like showing your hole card in five-card stud. Keep them guessing. But Ray Brunette, the chief of detectives, and Brian McKenna, the pride of the detectives and the bane of the Bosses, had been best friends for fifteen years. They knew all of each other's strengths and weaknesses. There were few secrets between them.

Only a few people in the job knew of their friendship. One, of course, was Brunette's driver. The others were old First Grade detectives who had been trusted friends for years and were now above the politics of the police department.

McKenna walked back to the triage room. He explained to D'Arcey that Angelita was bringing some new clothes for him and that he wanted to talk to her for a while to calm her down.

D'Arcey understood. He gave McKenna back his gun.

"Why don't you go back to the station house and wait for me, Timmy? Angelita will drive me back."

"What about the X-rays?" D'Arcey asked.

"Timmy, I'm not going to sweat some possible broken ribs when my balls are gonna be thoroughly broken in about fifteen minutes."

McKenna ripped the bandage off his hand. No need to look too bad, he thought.

McKenna walked D'Arcey out to his car and then waited for his girlfriend on the ramp outside the emergency room. Ten minutes later she drove up in her 1977 multidented Ford Pinto. She got out of the car and waved at him. Angelita wore a bare-shouldered white flowered sundress that contrasted nicely with her tan. She had black hair that she wore in a French braid, and her sunglasses were on the top of her head.

Damn, she looks good, McKenna thought. I only wish she looked a few years older.

McKenna was careful not to limp as he walked down the ramp to meet her. She watched him carefully as he approached and she threw her arms around his neck when he reached her. McKenna felt her chest heave. She was crying. Before she let him go, she reached to the top of her head with one hand and pulled her sunglasses onto her nose to hide her tears. Then she pushed herself away from McKenna and looked him up and down, noting his scraped hand and the hole in the knee of his pants.

"Tore another pair of pants playing cops and robbers, huh?" Angelita admonished. "That's three this year. And a shirt, too? I can't take it anymore. If you keep this up, I won't have anything left to bury you in."

McKenna kissed her on the forehead. "It was an old suit. I was going to throw it out soon anyway."

He saw that Angelita didn't appreciate his attempt at humor. "Don't worry, baby. I'm fine."

"You were just lucky again," she said. Then she opened the door of her car, took a long clothing bag off the backseat, and said sarcastically, "Here's another old suit. About two months old."

McKenna took the clothes bag from her and went back up the ramp into the hospital. He found a men's room that had a STAFF ONLY sign on the door and went in to change. She had gotten good at picking out his clothes. There were socks, underwear, a suit, a shirt, a tie, a belt, and shoes in the bag. He put on the fresh underwear and socks, the white shirt, the blue patterned tie, the dark blue suit, and the black belt and shoes. He threw the old suit, shirt, and underwear in the garbage can under the sink, packed up his belt and shoes in the bag, and went back out to the car.

Angelita was waiting with the engine running. McKenna returned the clothes bag to the backseat and then climbed into the front seat beside her. There was a cold six-pack of nonalcoholic Kaliber beer between them. Looks like a long talk coming, McKenna thought. And I think I know what the main topic of conversation is going to be.

Angelita drove to the back of the hospital, to "G" Building, the psychiatric ward. She parked the car and said, "This looks like a good place to talk. Because one of us is crazy."

She opened up two of the cold beers and gave one to McKenna. He drank half of his in three gulps while Angelita sipped hers. Then he lowered the bottle from his mouth and looked at her. He knew what was coming.

Angelita stared intently at McKenna. "I want you out of this job. I want us out of this town. This time I'm not kidding."

Doesn't look like she's kidding, McKenna thought. He waited. The silence became an unbearable pressure building up inside the car.

Finally he said, "Or?"

Angelita answered calmly and quietly. "Or I'm leaving you, Brian. It hurts me to say it, but I swear I'll leave you."

McKenna said nothing and let her continue. "You were lucky today. You've always been lucky. But you're getting older and one day your luck is going to run out. You can't keep playing cops and robbers forever. You're not a kid anymore and this isn't a game you're playing. You have to grow up."

"I've heard this somewhere before."

Angelita ignored him. "Tell me! I want to know. What are you doing it for, anyway? Nobody cares. The public doesn't care if you

36

get killed. And except for Ray, the Bosses don't care. They hate your guts and they're going to get you sooner or later for something. They'd love to give you a big Inspector's Funeral. So what are you doing it for? First Grade? You know that Ray was going to get you First Grade before he retired, whether you wanted him to or not. All you would've had to do is take it easy for a while and stay out of trouble. Just go to a quiet squad and work your cases. But you'll never do that. It's too late now and I'm through dreaming. Do you know what you're working for?

"You already said it. First Grade. There are only ninety-nine First Grade detectives on this job and I want to be one of them. You know it means a lot to me."

"I know that it means a lot to you now. But take it from me. Once you get it, it won't mean anything. What you're working for now is *nothing*. I've done some figuring and I've got my facts straight. We would have more every month if you'd retire today. You have twenty-three years on the job. You'd retire with more than half-pay, with very little taken out. No union dues, no Social Security tax, no state tax, no city tax, and a lower federal income-tax bracket. You're out here risking your life to arrest some dirtbag and make me miserable for what? An extra hundred and fifty a month if you make First Grade. But remember this! If they fire you over one of your heroics, like they'd love to do, you get nothing. No pension, no benefits, nothing. You're risking everything, every day. Even Ray knows the score. He's thinking of retiring himself, and I know he wishes that you would too. He's just waiting for you to make the first move."

Persuasive argument, McKenna thought. I wonder where she's getting her information. Ray? Why would he give it to her? McKenna finished his beer and she automatically opened another one for him. He was surprised that it still tasted great going down. She gave him some time to answer her arguments, but he said nothing for a few minutes. Finally he said, "Is that all?"

It wasn't. "I'm alone most of the time. Baby, you can't leave Spanish women alone forever. I get lonely. You're either working your regular tour or you're in court. If you work at night, I don't see you because I'm working during the day. I go crazy worrying about you all the time. I'm already living like a widow. I want to have children. Your children. But I won't raise them by myself." She paused, then added, "They have to have a father who they see more than every once in a while. A live father. And I won't raise children in this degenerate city."

"We live in a good neighborhood," McKenna protested.

"No, Brian. We live in an expensive neighborhood. That's not always the same thing as a good neighborhood in New York. I bought an ice cream cone at Häagen Dazs today. Two blocks from our apartment. Then I made a mistake. I thought that it would be all right for a woman to walk down a street in New York City with an ice cream cone. Do you know what happened?"

"I'm sure I'm going to find out," McKenna answered.

"Six different degenerates tried to stop me and get me to talk to them. In two blocks! From Seventh Avenue to Hudson Street. Six degenerates. You know. Baby, can I have a lick? Baby, can we share some? Baby, where's mine? Baby, let me buy you another? Baby, can I watch you lick it? Baby, you're good. Can you lick this for me? Not to mention the three different panhandlers. Thank God I'm not on the Job anymore. If I still had my gun, I would have shot them all. Then I would have reloaded and shot them some more. This town has burned me out. I don't want to live here anymore and I sure don't want to raise our kids here."

Another good argument, McKenna thought. Greenwich Village was a great neighborhood for a man. They were living in the same apartment that he'd grown up in and he knew everyone. Probably even some of those degenerates and most of the bums. He loved it. If he had been with her, nobody would have said anything. But it's different for a woman. A woman walking alone is fair game. Say any filthy thing you want to her. The women just keep on walking. They get used to it. Thank God Angelita kept on walking this time. But he knew that she wouldn't always. She's got a mean temper and a powerful left hook, McKenna thought. Too bad the neighborhood doesn't have as many gays as everyone thinks we have; they're never any trouble.

"Where would we live?" McKenna asked.

"Jersey City, Upstate, Florida, South America. Anyplace that doesn't have Alternate Side Parking. I don't care. Anyplace but here."

Leave New York City? He had never seriously entertained the thought. He had assumed that he would die here. Not soon, necessarily. But eventually.

"What would I do?" McKenna asked.

"I don't care if you do nothing all day. I'll work. You've already crammed a lifetime of work into twenty-two years. You can golf, you can ski, you can fish, or you can just help me raise some kids. You can get a hobby."

"Hobby? You mean like model airplanes?"

"You can join some clubs. You can go back to school. You can even get a job if you want. Any job. I don't care if you pump gas, if you just want something to do. I can go on and on. But the point is, I don't care what you do, as long as you're with me. Please, Brian. I need you with me."

Yeah, I could get another job, McKenna thought. But then I

wouldn't be Detective Brian McKenna, NYPD, the best "gun man" around and "Master of All He Surveys." Just Brian McKenna, another retired cop from New York. Not the same thing. And what would happen when I get bored? Start drinking again and ruin both our lives?

The thought terrified him. Angelita had heard about that part of his life, but she could never really know what it was like, and McKenna hoped that she would never see it.

"What kind of time frame are we talking about?"

"You're going to think I'm unreasonable. I'm going to give you a day to think. Tomorrow you've got to promise me that you'll retire this week. That'll give you enough time to get this mess straightened out. If not, I'm gone. I love you, Brian, but I won't look back. I've got to have a life, too."

"Angelita, I need more time. This shooting is going to get big. One of the biggest cases ever. I'm going to try to get myself assigned to it. If everything goes right, I may even get First Grade out of it. By myself, without Ray's help. It's important to me. I want to go out as a First Grader, by myself."

Angelita stayed silent for a moment while she finished her beer. "I'll give you an extra day to tell me what you're going to do. I'll take you back to the station house now."

There was no conversation between them during the trip to the Seven-one Precinct. There never was when Angelita drove. She maneuvered defensively at her standard twenty miles an hour, constantly on the brink of disaster. But the terror that her driving ordinarily induced in McKenna wasn't as strong this time. She had given him too much to think about. He was occupied with a different kind of terror—the thought of life without Angelita, and the idea of retiring and leaving New York City.

McKenna believed Angelita. It was going to be one or the other, Angelita or the Job. He didn't know what to do.

They made it to the Seven-one. There was an uncomfortable moment of silence while they parked in front of the building.

"I know that you don't want to hear this, but I'm probably going to be working straight through to tomorrow night. I've got a lot to do on this case to get the ball rolling."

Angelita didn't look like she was taking that well, but McKenna needed the time to think without her pressure. She just shrugged her shoulders.

"So what else is new?"

McKenna kissed Angelita good-bye. As he got out of the car, he hesitated.

"How do you know Ray's thinking of retiring?"

"His wife told me. She's been putting up with this job for thirty years. He doesn't even know that he's seriously thinking about it yet. But he is. Ray's in the same boat you are."

McKenna stared at her a moment, then shut the car door. She drove off without looking back.

4

Ray Brunette and Brian McKenna had first met years ago, when things had been different in the police department. Then drinking was tolerated much more than it was now. The officers routinely pulled drunken stunts both on and off duty that would certainly have gotten them fired today; though there was a limit, you didn't get fired for drinking. You recovered.

The instrument of recovery was the God Squad, headed by a police chaplain known simply as the Monsignor. His power was almost limitless. The place of recovery was the Farm, Veritas Villa, located upstate in the Catskill Mountains. The process was simple. The Monsignor heard that you were getting out of hand and that alcohol was your problem. The God Squad—cops who had been there and back—watched you while you were on duty and monitored some of your off-duty activities. They examined your conduct and every complaint against you. Then one day you crossed the line of acceptable behavior and you disappeared—off to the Farm.

A drunken cop simply vanished from his post. At the end of the tour, when he failed to show up to sign out, someone would say, "Oh, he's been captured. He's at the Farm." And the response invariably was, "So they finally got him."

The Monsignor's proposition was simple. Go to the Farm, pay attention, do as you're told, and get cured. Otherwise, get fired.

In 1973 Ray Brunette was one of the youngest sergeants in the Bureau. He was assigned to the Hotel Squad, a great place to drink.

He was married and he thought that he was miserable. He later came to realize that his drinking made his family miserable, and then they made him miserable. So Brunette left his family as often as possible to drink some more. He accomplished this by convincing his family and himself that he was a fishing fanatic. But the fact was he just liked drinking on the water while he listened to his old-time rock and roll music. So he bought a nice fast boat, one of those runabouts that you stand up in while driving. He really didn't like fishing at all, too much blood on the boat and too much cleaning up to do.

One day in 1973 Ray Brunette planned to take one of his drinking buddies out fishing. He had heard that the fish weren't biting, which made him even more anxious to go. With some cases of beer for his cooler he drove to his dock in Suffolk County to wait for his buddy. The weather was getting bad and his accomplice didn't show. No problem. More beer for Ray. So Ray Brunette took his boat far out into the ocean, where he wouldn't be annoyed by fishermen. He blared his radio and almost finished both shares of beer. Then he started for home, standing and driving his boat while dancing to the oldies. He reached back to get just one more coldie from the cooler. At that moment, his boat hit a wave and Ray fell backwards. He reached for the wheel and barely grabbed it. The boat turned violently to starboard and he was thrown overboard.

Ray landed in the water and pulled himself to the surface, treading water while he helplessly watched his boat make ever-larger concentric circles around him. About two hours later, darkness was approaching and the circles were about a mile in diameter, with Ray in the center.

Fortunately, someone had reported the driverless boat and the Coast Guard came to investigate. They found the boat, but couldn't catch it to board it. Then they looked for Ray in the middle of the circle, found him, and pulled him in, still drunk and now exhausted. The Coast Guard boat remained in the center of the circle and waited for Ray's boat to run out of gas. During that waiting time, Ray couldn't explain to the young Coast Guard Reserve lieutenant's complete satisfaction exactly what had happened.

Finally, Ray's boat ran out of gas and the Coast Guard boarded it. Being a budding environmentalist, Ray had neglected to throw his empties overboard. When the Coast Guard lieutenant saw the number of empty beer cans on board, he assumed that there had to be at least two more drunks still in the water and he wanted to resume the search. Ray was forced to admit that he had drunk all that beer by himself. The Coast Guard turned him over to the Suffolk County Marine Police.

On that same summer day in 1973, young Police Officer Brian

McKenna went to a party at a friend's rented summer house in the Hamptons, also in Suffolk County. He was assigned to the Street Crime Unit and he loved the job. The unit worked citywide and the cops assigned to Street Crime were expected to average two felony arrests per month. This was no problem for young McKenna. He had a talent that he had developed into an art.

Brian McKenna was a "gun-collar" man. He had a gift for spotting whoever was wearing a gun on the street. The illegal possession of a firearm on the street was a felony under the New York State Penal Law, so every gun collar fit the bill.

McKenna developed his talent by watching other cops while they were off duty. He studied the way the constant wearing of a two-pound piece of metal changed their posture and the alignment of their clothes. Their bodies started to sag slightly on whatever side they carried their gun. The alignment of the buttons of their shirts with their belts and flies was off. The weight of the gun always shifted the belt buckle and the fly toward the side the gun was on, while the line of buttons on their shirts still pointed straight down. Jackets were no problem, either. He noticed that people seeking to conceal a firearm usually zipped or buttoned their jackets. The gun was always catching on the inside lining of the jacket, so that after a while the alignment stretched off. The downward line formed by the zipper or buttons of the closed jacket pulled away from the downward line of the buttons on the shirt, whether the gun was in a shoulder holster or worn on the belt. It made no difference.

McKenna practiced and further refined his techniques. He learned to look for persons who swung one arm slightly away from their bodies while they walked. The "stiff arm" usually meant that there was a gun in a shoulder holster under that arm. Then there were ankle holsters. Cops who wore them slightly threw out the leg that the gun was on, to keep the holster from hitting their other ankle as they walked.

Making gun collars became easier and easier for McKenna. He developed ways of making the bad guys show him the gun. Whenever he became suspicious of someone on the street, but wasn't quite sure yet, he followed that person and stared at him. Invariably, the bad guy would become nervous and either look down to the spot under his clothes where his gun was to make sure it wasn't showing, or he would discreetly pat the gun with his elbow while he walked. Then McKenna had him.

Once McKenna pointed out who had the gun and where it was to the other two officers in his team, the mechanics of the actual arrest were simple. It wasn't like TV or the movies. It never became a shoot-out. The bad guys knew that it was only a gun collar, an inconvenience, and few of them wanted to shoot it out with the cops over something like that. The two men in McKenna's team positioned themselves in front of and behind the gunslinger, so that he had nowhere to go. He knew the deal. Then they just removed the gun from him and quickly carted him off to Central Booking. It got easier and easier.

Next came cars. McKenna would get behind a drug dealer's car and follow him, waiting until he made eye contact in the drug dealer's rearview mirror. The slight lowering of one of the dealer's shoulders as he took his gun from his belt and placed it under the seat would give him away. Then McKenna radioed the police officers in the local precinct that he had a suspected gunslinger under observation. He would give his location, the direction of travel, and a description of the drug dealer's car. The ghetto precincts were heavily policed and it would usually be seconds before the suspect's car was intercepted and stopped by a marked car. The uniformed officers would ask the dealer to step out while they questioned him on his choice of auto insurance companies. Then McKenna would reach under the seat and take the gun. Case closed, on to Central Booking. All that was needed was some creative testimony when the case came up in court. No problem.

It got too easy. Two collars a month was a breeze; he did that by the first week in every month. He couldn't do too much more because he was young and new in the unit and he couldn't afford to make everyone else in his squad look bad. So he helped his two partners cover the sheet early in the month. They all had their collars by the second week. Then he helped his whole squad. By the third week of every month, and frequently before that, the whole squad was collared up for the month. Gun collars for everyone.

Then it was party time. The risks had been taken and the job had been done, just a little earlier in the month, thanks to McKenna. They drank their tour away and continued drinking after work. McKenna couldn't buy a drink; he was always the Squad Guest. He took full advantage and after a while whatever car he drove always looked like it had finished in first place in the Demolition Derby. His auto insurance was canceled and he started catching rides to work from other squad members. His girlfriend left him. He was no fun anymore. His entire social life became drinking and the Job.

Things got worse. McKenna started having blackouts in which he couldn't remember where he had been. He missed work, just didn't go. His sergeants covered for him because he was the star. They spent the first half of their tours looking for him when he failed to show up. They didn't want to go back to working the whole month, either.

Besides, when he was sober, he was still the best. But they knew that if he kept it up, he was going to get shot while working or kill himself in a car crash. He was too young to be so good, and he couldn't handle it.

Then McKenna went to that party in the Hamptons. He played cards at his friend's house and won. Of course, he was drinking. The drunker he got, the more he won. Then he decided to go out on the town for a while, just to celebrate.

McKenna awoke seated at the wheel of his car with the sun in his eyes. He looked up and saw a West Hampton cop tapping on his window. One of those summer cops, he thought. Probably a high school teacher during the rest of the year.

McKenna just wanted to get rid of him, so he reached down for his shield. No shield. No wallet. No money. No pants. As he tried to cook up an explanation, he looked around. He was parked in the Atlantic Ocean and the tide was coming in. Behind him a few bathers in swimsuits and many more people in street clothes had come to watch the show. His tire tracks led into the water. Then McKenna looked down and saw that his feet were covered with water. Which meant that this summer cop who was tapping on his window was standing in ocean up to his knees. McKenna knew that no explanation would be good enough this time.

The next day Police Officer McKenna of the Street Crime Unit woke up in the Detox Unit of the old Columbus Hospital, which was across the street from the Police Academy. In the bed next to him was Sergeant Ray Brunette of the Hotel Squad. They both had a few laughs together while they told each other their stories. It was all fun until the Monsignor came to visit.

So Ray Brunette and Brian McKenna spent the next six weeks in the Catskills. The Farm was packed: it was the summer season of drunks. Since Brunette and McKenna had arrived at the same time and since they were both cops, they were assigned to the same room.

They had a lot in common. Both had been born and raised in Manhattan. McKenna had grown up in Greenwich Village on the West Side and Brunette in Yorkville on the East Side. Both were from police families. McKenna's father had retired as a First-Grade detective and Brunette's father as an inspector. While their fathers didn't know each other personally, they knew of each other, which might have been more important. McKenna's father said of the senior Brunette, "Great boss, good reputation." Brunette's father said of the senior McKenna, "Great detective. Famous."

There was more. Both had attended Catholic grammar school and Catholic high school, played baseball for their high school teams, and were still avid baseball fans. In baseball, they found their only point of disagreement. McKenna was a die-hard Mets fan while Brunette followed the Yankees.

Then there was the Marine Corps. Brunette had spent the majority of his four years in the spit-and-polish peacetime Marine Corps guarding the U.S. Embassy in Reykjavik, Iceland. McKenna had put in a couple of years as a machine gunner in Vietnam. They laughed together for hours over boot camp stories and the similarities to their present situation.

But the thing that brought them closest together was their shared religion—the New York City Police Department. They worshipped in different ways and had different methods of spreading the message among the infidels to assure the salvation of the citizens. Brunette loved the challenge of a good investigation and the thrill of finally arresting a dangerous criminal, using all the available resources of the police department, if necessary. McKenna loved the street. He loved taking toys from the gunslingers and putting them in jail. They were both good at what they did. And they both fervently believed, despite whatever roadblocks were thrown in their way, that the citizens would be protected and the criminals would go to jail. Like all drunks, they were practiced liars. If lying was what it took to put the criminals in jail, fine.

The end result of all the group therapy and counseling sessions at the Farm was the realization that McKenna and Brunette drank for the same reason—the Job was so easy for them that they had become bored. Hard times had come for New York City, and the police department was about to shrink. No promotion tests were scheduled and grade promotions were increasingly rare. Brunette, who had fifteen years on the job, figured that he might retire as a lieutenant, at best, and McKenna wasn't even a detective yet. They had set long-term goals for themselves and they despaired of ever achieving them. So they drank to suppress their ambitions and their boredom.

After they left the Farm, Brunette and McKenna continued their cure together. They attended AA meetings together and started skiing and playing golf together. They bought adjoining condo apartments in Florida and shared vacations. They supported each other in every way and they quit just about every vice they had. No more gambling, no more smoking, no more womanizing. They resumed their memberships in almost every police fraternal and social organization, but drank only nonalcoholic beer, first Moussy, then Kaliber.

The informal organization of graduates of the Farm was the Club. Two of the rules of the Club were that you never repeated anything anyone said at the Farm and you never told whom you saw there. These rules were never broken and the group was close, although

46

most of the members did not even know each other. There were secret high signs by which Club members recognized each other. Get in a little scrape, some violation of the rules, and give the high sign. Go for an interview for some job and give the high sign. It frequently worked.

As Brunette advanced in the department, eventually reaching chief and earning a reputation for the increased number of convictions following arrests made by the Bureau, McKenna sometimes found himself working in units that were ultimately under Brunette's supervision. But on a day-to-day basis their professional lives did not mix. Off duty they constantly talked over the Job together and shared in each other's professional decisions. But during working hours, business was business. During the rare times that they saw each other at work, they exchanged the barest signals of recognition. They gave no one any reason to suspect the relationship that existed between the two of them. They couldn't afford to.

McKenna realized that common knowledge of their friendship would hurt them both professionally. McKenna had been assigned the reputation of the talented bad boy of the Bureau. He had been promoted to Detective Second Grade, and for his exploits with various gunmen—including a headline-making shoot-out that was the first and only time he had fired his gun in the line of duty—had become a media darling. On the side he picked up extra money as a celebrity bodyguard, developing a taste for good clothes and good food. Brunette had watched the growth of that reputation with amusement. McKenna was always doing something to infuriate the Bosses while he got the job done. For his sins he was frequently exiled to a squad in Brooklyn, but Brunette always quietly pulled him back to the "Bright Lights" that McKenna enjoyed. If word of their friendship got out, Brunette would have been expected to supervise McKenna directly to bring him into line with the image that the department had of its detectives. Brunette never wanted that assignment and he just wouldn't do it. Besides, he was having too much fun watching McKenna's antics from a distance.

While he was curing himself, Brunette returned to his family's good graces. He became a good husband and a good father. McKenna watched Brunette's children grow up as Brunette himself matured.

McKenna went through a succession of "true loves." He constantly seemed to be on the verge of marriage, but somehow avoided the final step. The sign to Ray that McKenna's latest girl was another one of his true loves would be a dinner date at the Brunette residence. There she would be entertained, scrutinized, and appraised by the entire Brunette family. Some passed and some failed. The failures quickly left McKenna's life. But even those who passed the Brunette family inspection were heard from less and less, and they all finally moved on to more promising ground.

Then came Angelita Morena. Pretty, with an athletic body, still looking like some kind of overgrown tomboy, she was outspoken, spunky, intelligent, fun-loving, and she mixed well with company. She was devoted to McKenna and he adored her. Angelita came as close to understanding McKenna and Brunette and their relationship as anyone could. She became one of Ray Brunette's best friends. For the first time in his life, McKenna wanted to get married. All the reservations about marriage he had experienced with the previous women were gone. Marriage was for him and Angelita was the one. But there was one major drawback. Angelita hated New York City and she loathed the New York City Police Department. She wanted McKenna to retire and move from the city.

When McKenna first met Angelita, she was a rookie police officer assigned to the 9th Precinct on the Lower East Side of Manhattan.

McKenna and his partner were working in the Manhattan Robbery Squad and they'd brought a robbery suspect into the 9th Precinct. Angelita had been assigned as the telephone switchboard operator that day. She noticed the tall, well-dressed Irish detective with the easygoing manner. He looked like a captain, and many of the older cops and Bosses in the precinct treated him like a returning hero. He knew everybody's name. He was much older than Angelita, but she found herself wishing that he knew her name. Then this detective started questioning his prisoner in colloquial Spanish and her heart was lost. He was so polite, even to the prisoner. During her lunch break she asked an older female cop about McKenna and received a short glorified history and No, she didn't think he was married.

Five minutes later in the Detective Squad office news reached McKenna that he was the object of some interest. McKenna had seen the pretty little switchboard operator on his way into the station house. No, she wasn't married. No known romantic involvements in the precinct, although she had been the object of many attempts.

When Angelita returned from her duties at the switchboard after her lunch break, she found McKenna waiting for her. Would she mind making some telephone notifications to complainants for him? He was conducting a lineup and he wanted as many robbery victims as possible to view the lineup. He gave her a pile of Complaint Reports in which the description of the robber matched his prisoner. No, she wouldn't mind at all. An obvious ruse to get to meet me so that I'll go out with him, she thought. She knew that it would work.

Angelita went all out to fulfill the assignment that McKenna had given her. Two hours later the Squad office was filled with about twenty of the robbery victims who had come to see if they could pick McKenna's prisoner out of the lineup. Angelita had done a great job and she managed to get herself assigned to the Squad office to help interpret for some of the complainants.

The next three months were a whirlwind of fine restaurants, Broadway shows, and Mets games. Many times McKenna made a date with Angelita that he had to cancel at the last minute because of an arrest, but she understood. Sometime during the second month, McKenna managed to literally charm the pants off her, something that few had been able to do in the past. One day they made a date for dinner at the house in Long Island of a special friend of Brian's, a chief. She was shocked. She had heard that Brian wasn't a particular favorite of the chiefs'. This dinner was a secret, he told her, never to be mentioned.

They went to Ray Brunette's house and Angelita passed the Brunette family inspection with flying colors. One week later Angelita changed her address. She moved from her parents' house in Queens to McKenna's large apartment in Greenwich Village. This move didn't make her traditional Colombian parents happy, and they cried and screamed as she packed up and left.

When she met McKenna, Angelita found herself frequently assigned to duties in the station house, for a number of reasons. She spoke Spanish, was a good typist and computer competent, and she tried hard. But the main reason was that she had a horrible driving record.

Before she joined the Department, Angelita had always prided herself on being a good, safe driver. She had worked as an airline reservation clerk at Kennedy Airport and she'd driven back and forth to her job from her home in Corona, Queens. She'd never had an accident and had never received as much as a parking ticket. She had never even been pulled over by a cop.

She did well in the Police Academy and graduated as the number one recruit with the highest academic average. Her instructors marked her as someone to watch, someone who would go far in the job. Angelita was ready to arrest bad people, help good people, and make New York a better place to live.

Then Angelita was assigned to the 9th Precinct, one of the busiest precincts in the city. Located on East 5th Street between First and Second avenues, the 9th Precinct covered the East Village, the Lower East Side, and the predominantly Hispanic Alphabet City. Only fifteen blocks from the Police Academy, the 9th Precinct was in a very different kind of neighborhood, a tough place for a rookie female police officer to break into the job.

The first day was orientation. A sergeant loaded all the rookies into a marked police van for the guided tour of the 9th Precinct. Angelita was in shock as they drove by Tompkins Square park, where the homeless lived in a ramshackle village and drug dealers operated without fear. She had never seen anything like it. She knew that she might have to work in a bad neighborhood, but this was a *bad* neighborhood. This was not the police department she had joined. She had joined the police department that patrolled neighborhoods like Corona, where she would write some parking tickets, give nice people directions, and ride around in an air-conditioned car waiting for those times when she could help people, and occasionally arrest a bad guy and bring him to justice. But this was different. Her first ride around the 9th Precinct convinced her that half of the population of the precinct needed help and the other half needed to be arrested.

Angelita felt overwhelmed, but she was determined to make the best of it and be a good cop.

Then the shortcomings in the makeup of Probationary Police Officer Angelita Morena began to make themselves known. These could not have been predicted by any entrance examination, by any personality profile, by any psychological screening test, or by any exercise in the Police Academy. They only showed themselves in the very real world of the 9th Precinct.

Naturally, as part of her duties, Angelita was expected to drive a police car on patrol. This meant driving in the frantic traffic of Manhattan, something she had never done before. While she was driving, she was also expected to see everything that was happening on the crowded sidewalks, and to be prepared to jump out of the car on a moment's notice to take police action. And something was always happening on the sidewalks of the 9th Precinct. At the same time she had to be constantly monitoring the police radio. Most of the rookie officers eventually adapted to this new way of driving. Angelita, trying as hard as she could with as much concentration as she could muster, could not.

One month after she arrived in the 9th Precinct she was known as "Crash Morena," and was sent to take the Defensive Driver Course. She passed without a problem, was grounded for ten days and put on foot patrol. No problem. Then one day she was again assigned to a radio car. Ten minutes later, five blocks from the station house, she sideswiped a parked car while responding to a radio call of a "Burglary in Progress." The whole corrective process had to be repeated again, with the same results. This time she was grounded for thirty days, the maximum.

Five times over the course of the next year she was grounded and sent to the Defensive Driver Course. The police cars in the 9th Precinct, which never looked great, started to show the signs of Angelita Morena's presence in the precinct. Then the 9th Precinct cops started writing on every little dent on their patrol cars, *Angelita*

50

Was Here. She was becoming famous and the object of many jokes.

The sergeants took pity on Angelita and whenever possible assigned her to duties in the station house, where she did a great job. But, unfortunately for Angelita, the police department was in the midst of another civilianization drive, replacing the uniformed officers who performed administrative duties with lower-paid civilian workers. Time after time, as soon as Angelita learned one job inside the station house, a new civilian worker replaced her.

There were not many assignments left for Angelita. Most of the foot posts in the 9th Precinct were being covered by male officers. So the sergeants started assigning her to guard DOAs, those persons who had died in their apartments or on the street. Some had died of natural causes, two weeks before the smell coming from their apartment prompted the deceased's neighbors to call the police. There were the suicides who used every bizarre method possible to terminate their existence. There were the homicide victims killed in the midst of life. There were the accident victims and the overdoses. These bodies had to be guarded by the police until they were attended to by the medical examiner and either sent to the morgue or released to a funeral parlor. There were always enough bodies in the 9th Precinct to ensure Angelita a fairly steady stream of assignments.

Because of this, Angelita learned something about herself she had never known, only because she had never experienced the circumstances unique to a ghetto precinct. She hated the sight of death and physical suffering. Many times she became violently sick at the scene of her assignments. She grew sullen and depressed. She lost her appetite and began to lose weight. Every time she raised food to her mouth, she imagined the smell of death. She sought counseling and went to see the police psychiatrist. She felt that if she could spend a couple of years in a slower precinct, she would overcome her deficiencies and adjust to the job. But her request was denied, and Angelita believed that she was going to be fired at the end of her probationary period. Her old job with the airlines started looking better and better to her. She checked with them and they told her that they would be happy to take her back.

By this time Angelita had been living with McKenna for six months. She knew that she could go to Ray with her problems and that he would have her transferred to any precinct she wanted. But Angelita had begun to feel like McKenna in this regard. Ray was a friend who just happened to be a chief. Don't ask your best friend for favors, don't take advantage of a special friendship. She decided that police work just wasn't for her.

One Friday Police Officer Angelita Morena walked into the 9th Precinct and turned in her guns and shield.

After a week, she felt fine. She went back to her old job and loved it, sending normal people to faraway places. She knew that she had done the right thing. But she always harbored a deep resentment for the police administration that had taken a nice girl from Queens who just wanted to do the Job and started her off in Hell.

5

July 9   7:30 p.m.

Angelita and her ultimatum were on McKenna's mind as he walked through the double glass doors of the modern Seven-one Precinct station house. He had two days to decide how he would spend the rest of his life.

There was the usual collection of victims sitting on the row of chairs just inside the front doors, waiting to tell their stories to the police. McKenna walked past them on his way to the Seven-one Detective Squad office on the second floor. A big, middle-aged black man seated on the center chair looked familiar and seemed to be staring at him as he passed. As McKenna reached the door to the stairwell, the man called, "Detective McKenna?"

He remembered the man. He was the guy McKenna had talked to on Empire Boulevard in Brooklyn three hours ago while they were both stuck in traffic, just before all this began.

"Yeah. How'ya doing?"

"You remember me? My name's Curtis Bradford."

The big man held out his hand and McKenna shook it.

"Sure I do. What can I do for you, Mr. Bradford. You here to invite me to a party?"

"Not this time, but I got something for you. Could you use the license plate number of the gypsy cab?"

"What gypsy cab?"

"The gypsy cab the man you was chasing got out of."

"Mr. Bradford, I think you're about to become my best friend. You got it?"

Bradford held up the palm of his left hand. License number T00573C was still visible.

"I wrote it down after you started chasing that dude."

"What made you do that, Mr. Bradford?"

"Well, I was still stuck in that traffic, and then the shooting started. I figured that you got yourself in some shit and I'm still looking at that gypsy cab that the dude got out of. It's right in front of me. I can't go nowhere yet, so I say to myself, maybe it's important. So I write the plate number down on my hand. Then I heard all these caps going off. Damn if one of them didn't break the window of the gas station right next to me, and that cleared up the traffic. Everybody started driving every which way to get out of there."

McKenna smiled at that. The best way to clear up any ghetto traffic jam is to let a couple of rounds go. Everybody goes in a hurry any way they can, on the sidewalks, in reverse, against traffic, or they'll just leave their cars. Not like in a white neighborhood, where people hang around to see what happened. In the ghetto, the people are smarter than that.

Bradford continued. "Now there's police cars coming from everywhere, and they're flying. I tried to tell them about the plate number, but they wouldn't stop. So I said, the hell with it. I just went home. I was about to wash up for dinner when I heard your name on the news. I go to the TV and there you were, Detective McKenna in trouble for shooting a man in the back in the Ebbets Field Houses. I tell my lady, 'Look at that! I was there. I know him!' I tell her the story and show her the number on my hand. So I tell her I'm going to the precinct and here I am."

"How long you been here?"

" 'Bout half an hour. The desk officer told me you'd be here soon, so I waited."

McKenna took his note pad out and wrote down the plate number that Bradford had given him. Then he said, "Mr. Bradford, I really appreciate this. There should be more people like you. Wanna give me your phone number? I want to take you and your lady out to dinner at the Plaza when this is all over."

"Fine by me. You gonna need me for court or something like that?"

"No. I'm gonna keep you out of this. I don't want you getting any trouble from these people down the road."

McKenna walked Bradford out to his car. Then he went back into the station house and asked the desk officer to run the plate through the Department of Motor Vehicles on the precinct computer. While he was waiting, he thought about the many times he had been helped out by people like Curtis Bradford. It pays to be nice, he thought.

The plate came back for a 1985 four-door black Chevy sedan owned by the Black Night Cab Company, 378 Fulton Street, Brooklyn. The desk officer gave McKenna the computer printout for the plate.

McKenna walked up the stairs to the Squad office. As soon as he walked in Lieutenant Schnieder yelled, "Go next door to Sex Crimes, Brian. Everybody's waiting for you."

McKenna walked down the hall to the Brooklyn Sex Crimes Unit office. He opened the door and immediately wished that he was someplace else. They were all there. D'Arcey and Harry McCrystal, the DEA lawyer; "Dog Dick" O'Shaughnessy; Assistant Chief Mike McCormick, the borough commander; Captain Dennis Sheeran, the commanding officer of the 11th Detective District; two Bosses from Internal Affairs; and a young man in glasses wearing an ill-fitting suit, who McKenna assumed was the Brooklyn assistant district attorney who was assigned to prosecute him, if he could.

O'Shaughnessy came right over. "Chief Brunette is waiting for you in my office downstairs. He wants me to finish this shooting investigation as quickly as possible so he can start working on the kidnapping case."

"That's sure fine by me, Inspector," McKenna answered.

McKenna looked over O'Shaughnessy's shoulder and saw D'Arccy beckoning to him from the empty office of the commanding officer of the Brooklyn Sex Crimes Unit. McKenna excused himself from O'Shaughnessy and joined D'Arcey and Harry McCrystal in the office. D'Arcey closed the office door; he and McCrystal were both all smiles.

"This one's almost over," McCrystal said. "The DA took statements from Richie White and the two cops who followed you into the hallway."

"What did they tell him?" McKenna asked.

"They all told him that they were following you up the stairwell. They said that they were on the tenth-floor landing when they heard you shout above them, 'Police, Don't Move!' Then they heard three shots and when they got to the twelfth-floor hallway they saw you standing over the dead man, who had an automatic pistol lying next to his right hand. IAD canvassed all the other apartments on the twelfth floor and nobody heard anything bad. A couple of tenants said they heard some shots, but that's OK. This one's all over."

"What do I tell the DA?" McKenna asked.

"Tell him nothing. The DA wants to give you Miranda warnings before he questions you so that anything you might tell him would be admissible in court. Then I'm going to jump up and, as your lawyer,

I'm going to evoke your constitutional rights under the Fifth Amendment and advise you not to answer any questions Period. Case closed."

It was simple. The young DA was mired in a Catch-22 situation. It used to be that a police officer had to answer any question that a DA or a Boss asked him about his conduct. If he didn't answer, he was fired. Then the Supreme Court decided that police officers were also citizens of the United States, and therefore were entitled to the same constitutional protections against self-incrimination as all citizens. District attorneys and police administrators were forced to agree. So police departments all across the country had to set up a system to deal with police officers who might be criminally prosecuted for something they did in the line of duty. The Bosses couldn't question the officer until the DA was done with him. If the DA gave the officer Miranda warnings so that he could use the officer's statement in court, the officer, usually through his lawyer, would refuse to make a statement. Then the DA had to decide whether he had enough to make a case against the officer without his statement. While he was deciding, the police department still couldn't question the officer. After all, not only were they Bosses, they were also cops, and therefore technically agents of the DA.

Because in most instances the DA never decided that the case was over, the Bosses could never question the officer. And they could not prosecute him for any violations of their rules unless they had enough to go on without the officer's statement. But if they had enough to prosecute him without his statements, then so did the DA and the DA would have prosecuted the officer first—Catch-22.

The DA's got nothing to go on, thought McKenna, except for a possible violation of the Noise Control Code when I blasted Rico. Richie White and the two Seven-one Precinct cops came through. Harry was right. This shooting investigation is all over except for the formalities, and I'll probably never have to tell anyone the circumstances leading up to Rico's death.

And that's the way it was. Harry took McKenna outside and introduced him to the young DA.

"Detective McKenna, you have the right to remain silent, and anything you say may be used against you in a court of law," the DA said.

Harry McCrystal jumped up and two minutes later McKenna said good-bye to everyone. He went downstairs to O'Shaughnessy's office to see what the chief of detectives was up to.

McKenna knocked and walked in. Ray Brunette and his driver, Bobby Johnston, sat at O'Shaughnessy's desk playing a game of gin.

Brunette was a tall, good-looking man. He was fifty-five, but he had a full head of black hair that made him look forty-five. The most striking thing about his face were the two dimples that appeared in his cheeks whenever he smiled. "They help to keep my dick wet," he used to say before he changed his ways. Women found him handsome and men thought he looked rugged. He was smiling when McKenna walked in.

"Come watch this, Brian," Brunette said. "I've got him this time."

McKenna walked over to the desk and looked at both men's hands. He could see that Brunette was wrong again. He could never beat Bobby.

Brunette threw a ten of clubs and Bobby picked it up for gin. Bobby knew that Brunette and McKenna wanted to talk alone.

"Sorry, Chief, but you lose again. We can do the arithmetic later. I'm gonna go gas up the car."

Bobby Johnston left and McKenna sat in the newly vacant chair.

"How'd it go with the DA?" Brunette asked.

"A breeze since you took Dog Dick off my back."

"I figured that would help. I heard that Richie White and the two uniformed cops really stood up for you. Don't tell me you really said, 'Police, Don't Move!' "

"Let's just say they stood up."

"I'm gonna take a look at White's record. Maybe it's time to put him on the Second-Grade fast track. What do you think?"

"It'd be the right thing to do. But we're gonna have to dress him up first. Did you see that jacket?"

"Yeah. He's no slave to fashion. How you feeling?" Brunette asked.

"A little sore, but I'm fine."

"I want you to go sick. When you come back, I'll put you in headquarters to count paper clips until this thing blows over."

"Not this time, Ray. Please. I want to work on this case."

"You just can't seem to stay out of trouble, Brian. I thought you were just supposed to lay low in Brooklyn for a couple of years until everyone forgot about your last caper. Instead, you put yourself on the front pages and everybody's going to be talking about you and your history again. Bad Boy Detective Brian McKenna still rides in Brooklyn. No way I can put you on this case."

"Ray, I need this one. This is my shot for First Grade. I can get it on my own if you can figure out a way to put me on it."

"Wrong. It's an interesting case, but not a First-Grade case. One drug dealer kidnapping another drug dealer is interesting, but that's all. The first day it's on page one. The second day it's on page nine. By the third day it's on the page with the obituaries, where the victim may wind up anyway. Nobody cares too much about dead drug dealers. And how can I put you on the case? This'll wind up with the

Major Case Squad, and you're in the Seven-one Squad and still officially under investigation. How can I do that?"

"Just gimme a minute, would you? I don't think that the victim is a drug dealer and I don't think the kidnappers are drug dealers, no matter how much money and drugs we took out of that apartment. I think that there's a possibility that they're terrorists and they're holding the victim in New York."

Brunette sat up straight in his chair. "Terrorists? What the hell put that idea in your head?"

McKenna laid it out, point by point. "That guy I killed was no run-of-the-mill crook. He was in excellent condition for a man his age and he was good—the best I'd ever seen. I'm lucky to be alive. He was a great shot and he was thoroughly familiar with the capabilities of his weapon. Just take a look at the small group his bullets made when they landed in the tree I was hiding behind. A group that small is hard to achieve at that range with a hand-held pistol firing full automatic. He was very resourceful and thoroughly trained. He even used the shoulder of one of the women in the lobby as a barrel rest to fire at me. How many rounds did he fire and how many bullets did we recover?"

Brunette rummaged through the papers on O'Shaughnessy's desk. Finally he found what he was looking for, a scrap of notepaper, and read, "Emergency Service and the Crime Scene Unit found twenty-one shell casings and a total of twenty spent bullets. Only one is missing."

"No, it's not," McKenna said. He put the bullet that had fallen from his shirt in the hospital on the desk and said, "This is the one that should've killed me. So he fired twenty-one rounds and we've recovered twenty-one spent bullets. How many times have we been able to do that?"

"Not many," Brunette said.

"Not many is right. Brooklyn will eventually sink into the Atlantic Ocean under the weight of the bullets we haven't been able to recover."

"OK, he was good with his weapon. So what? Maybe he was a vet?"

"He was better than good. In the stairwell I thought I almost had him and I gave him a chance to surrender. At the time he would've been facing the gun charge and Attempted Murder of a Police Officer. Let's face it, those are bad charges, but this is Brooklyn. He could've been out in five years, depending on his record. And he had bargaining chips taped to his back. He could have parlayed information he had on the kidnapping into a sentence reduction. But he was dedicated. Then he showed me something else. He fired one burst, which ricocheted off three walls and one of those bullets hit me in the chest. And he did that just firing at the sound of my voice. That kind of shooting falls into the range of advanced urban warfare training."

"What else?"

"I knew then," McKenna said, "that this *hombre* wouldn't be taken alive and that, no matter what happened, it was him or me. The end result, fortunately for me, is that I'm here and he's in the morgue. But it could have gone either way. If this guy is any indication of the general caliber of the kidnappers, we're facing a highly disciplined, highly dedicated, well-trained, and well-armed bunch. These boys are good and tough. They're either experienced terrorists or a group of drug enforcers who are so good that we don't even have knowledge of their existence. And they've got good resources."

"What kind of resources?" Brunette asked.

"Expertly forged or otherwise reproduced papers of identity, for one," McKenna answered. "It hit me in the project hallway that we hadn't found much in the way of ID on the body. Just a Florida driver's license and a Social Security card. No pictures, no business cards, no credit cards, no slips of paper that people write phone numbers on and put in their wallets. In short, this guy's wallet was missing most of the things we all carry. He had only what he needed to identify himself as Raoul Camarena, which made me think that maybe he wasn't Raoul Camarena."

Then McKenna told Brunette what happened with Torres at the hospital, that Torres didn't know who Raoul Camarena was.

"Torres knew that guy only as Rico," McKenna said, "not Raoul. He knows more, but we'll have to make a deal to get any information from him. I'm sure we'll know more about Rico when we get his fingerprints back. Have we checked out that address on his Florida license?"

"Schnieder called the Fort Myers Beach police to make a death notification at the address on the license, but I don't think they've called back yet. What else makes you think that Rico was a terrorist and not just a drug enforcer?"

"How about they got a doctor working with them? The victim's finger was surgically removed and so was the pinky shown in the picture. What doctor is going to slice off a finger for some drug enforcers? Not once, but twice. They have to have their own doctor in the gang. They're a self-sufficient, complete package. But the main reason is their victim. He's not a drug dealer. He's from old money."

McKenna paused for effect. Brunette had been listening. He wanted more. Finally he asked, "Why do you think the victim's not a drug dealer?"

I got him, McKenna thought.

"Because of the shirt he was wearing and because of the ring. He's wearing a Brooks Brothers shirt in the photo that Rico had taped to his back. I'm sure of it. This is a Brooks Brothers shirt that I'm wearing." McKenna touched his collar. "See the points on my collar? They're longer than the points of the collars on other shirts. Only Brooks Brothers makes this type of collar and the style never changes. When you look at the picture, you'll see the Brooks Brothers collar. I've been shopping there for years and I've never seen anything that looked like a drug dealer there. It's an old-money, father-and-son kind of place. It's very conservative and not for the nouveau riche drug-dealer type."

Brunette picked up the phone on O'Shaughnessy's desk and dialed the Seven-one Squad office.

"This is the chief. Get me Lieutenant Schnieder." A moment later Schnieder came on the line. "Lou, have somebody bring me down the ring and the photos we got from the dead man's body. Right away." He hung up and said to McKenna, "Go on."

McKenna continued, "The ring on the finger of the victim is about twenty-two-karat gold, which is very rare. Twenty-two-karat gold is very soft and very yellow. It's so soft that you can cut it with a knife. I put a good scratch on that ring with just my thumbnail. It means that the ring was handmade, not mass-produced. Nobody mass-produces jewelry using twenty-two-karat gold, it doesn't hold its shape. The ring is old, and it has to be the family heirloom of an old, rich family. Now, I bet that Rico was on his way to deliver the ring, the finger, and the photos to the victim's family when I ran into him. We can also assume they already delivered the poor guy's pinky to the family, and now they were just reinforcing their point. So it makes sense that it was something that his family would recognize immediately, something that had been in the family for years. Drug dealers generally don't come from old, rich families that have that kind of heirloom, even in Colombia."

There was a knock on the door and a Seven-one Squad detective came in with the ring and the photos, put them on the desk, and left. Brunette picked up the photos and stared at them. Then he stared at McKenna's collar. He put the photos down, picked up the ring, and scratched it. Then he said, "You've got me so far, Brian. What next?"

McKenna told him about the information that he got from Curtis Bradford. "If we can locate the cab driver who picked up Rico, we'll get an idea where the hostage is being held. That finger was really fresh. It was still attached to its owner a couple of hours before we found it. Besides, I've got something else."

McKenna took his handkerchief out of his pocket and unfolded it.

He took the piece of paper out of the handkerchief and handed it to Brunette.

"I took that out of Rico's mouth. I'm sure he was trying to swallow it when I shot him, but he didn't have enough spit because he was out of breath. I haven't had time to trace this number yet, but I know it was important to Rico and I know that it's in Spanish Harlem. Nobody knows about this except me and D'Arcey."

"You holding out on Schnieder, Brian?"

"Who, me? No! It's just that he left McKeever Place by the time we found it in Rico's mouth. I haven't had a chance to talk to him yet. I guess it's possible that I *am* thinking of myself, just a little. After all, *I* found the phone number, *I* found the gypsy cab company, and *I* started the case. This is all ammunition you can use to get me assigned."

"OK. What would you do next?"

"I'd go to Brooks Brothers. If the victim is as rich as I think he is, somebody at Brooks Brothers will know him. It's a starting point. That is, unless we're so unlucky that he was wearing his only Brooks Brothers shirt on the day he was kidnapped."

"What do you think about the *Boston Globe* the victim's holding up? Suppose he is being held in Boston?" Brunette asked.

"Can't be. The finger's too fresh. He's gotta be much closer than that. There's no way that Rico could have got from somewhere in Boston to Brooklyn at that time of day in under four hours, even if he was flying. And gypsy cabs don't hang around airports."

"I'll give you that," Brunette said.

"What the *Boston Globe* means is that the victim was either living in the Boston area or was kidnapped in the Boston area. So the bad guys want the Boston police, the FBI, and the victim's family to think that he's still being held there. It's just another indication of the resources of the kidnappers. They have somebody go up to Boston just to get a newspaper for their photo. Of course, it could be an out-of-town edition, but I don't think so. There must be some way to tell the out-of-town editions from the local editions. I think the kidnappers are too thorough to use an out-of-town edition in the photo. They'd take the trouble to get the local edition."

"But I called the Boston police," Brunette said, "and they knew nothing about a kidnapping in Boston. I had Schnieder call the FBI and they've got nothing, either. What I don't get is why didn't the hostage's family notify the police of the kidnapping?"

"Maybe the family has decided to meet the kidnappers' demands. They've probably been told that if they notify the police the hostage will be killed. Maybe they know the kidnappers. Maybe they believe that we're not good enough to find the victim, so what's the use. If we can find out who the victim is, then we'll call the family and find out why."

"There's one small thing, Brian. If this isn't a drug kidnapping, why was Rico going to apartment 12G when you killed him? That sure looks like drugs to me."

"I don't know yet. But I still think that I'm right. This isn't directly about drugs."

Brunette leaned back in O'Shaughnessy's chair and closed his eyes to think. After a minute, he sat up straight and said to McKenna, "Let's say you're right. It's more than just drugs. Let's say terrorists. A First-Grade case. If we can solve this one, everybody who works on the case will be in line for grade, not just you."

"That's right." This would be the first terrorist case in New York City since the FALN, and everybody got grade on that one.

"But this case is going to wind up with the Major Case Squad. You won't be in the picture if you're still in the Seven-one Squad after tomorrow morning. And I can't assign you to the Major Case Squad since I just transferred you to Brooklyn under a cloud."

"I've got to be assigned. I've never asked you for a favor before, but I need this one."

Brunette paused for a few seconds that seemed like hours to McKenna.

"OK, buddy. If I can do it I'll do it. Just give me a minute to think this one out."

McKenna relaxed. I'm in, he thought. Ray is the greatest plotter in the business. I can't wait to see how he's gonna do this.

Brunette stood up. Class was about to begin.

"Here's how we're going to pull it off. I'm going to make everybody so miserable that you're here that they won't question it when you're gone. Who're our candidates for misery?"

"It has to be Schnieder, Sheeran, and Dog Dick. That's my whole chain of command."

"OK. Schnieder first. He can assign you to the case for today, at least. I'm gonna call him down and tell him how important I think this case is. I'll tell him about the gypsy cab and the telephone number from Rico's mouth. Then I'm gonna tell Schnieder what a good job you did. Here's the good part. I'll give him a long list of things I want done immediately. I want the cab driver who picked up Rico located and interviewed as soon as possible. That's two detectives out. I want Torres fingerprinted at the hospital, that's three. Rico fingerprinted at the morgue, that's four guys out. And Chavez fingerprinted immediately. Then I want all sets of fingerprints hand-delivered to the Identification Section in Police Headquarters for a criminal-record check. Then I'll tell him that I want the detective who delivers the fingerprints to wait until the record search is complete and to bring the criminal records back to the Squad office. I'll tell him that I want twenty eight-by-ten copies of the photos taken from Rico's back made up at the Photo Section. You know what Schnieder says then?"

"Sure," answered McKenna, laughing. "He's got to say that he's out of manpower. He's only got five guys working tonight. That's just enough to work his usual cases. This will push him over the edge."

"That's right," Brunette said. "And all these chores have to be done anyway. Schnieder will suggest that maybe he could use you on the case. I'll tell him that he's got a great idea and suggest that you locate the gypsy cab driver and interview him. So it's his idea."

"One down," McKenna said.

"Then I'll call Captain Sheeran down. He's the one that's ultimately responsible for you now. Again, I'll say what a great job that Detective McKenna has done. I'll tell him that Schnieder requested that you be assigned to the case. Then I'll tell Sheeran that, since you've been such a bad boy in the past, I want detailed daily written progress reports on your activities. That extra work will make Sheeran very unhappy and not sorry to see you go."

"Two down."

"The last is the best. I love making Dog Dick miserable. I'll tell him that I want him to keep a very close eye on you since the Seven-one Squad is located in his station house, and that I'll hold him responsible if you screw up and he doesn't catch you. That'll make Dog Dick a nervous wreck."

"I love it," McKenna said.

"It'll work. By tomorrow everyone will be looking to get rid of you. Tomorrow morning, after you've done a lot of work on this case, you'll give Sheeran your terrorist theory. You'll also tell him that you want to keep on working on the case and that you want to be transferred to the Major Case Squad. Then at about eight-thirty tomorrow morning, I'll come back to the Seven-one Precinct to check on the progress. Sheeran and Dog Dick will both be exhausted by then because they'll probably have spent the whole night working on the Unusual Occurrence Report to explain your shooting. Sheeran will tell me about your theory and your request. I'll think it over and tell him that it sounds like a good theory to me. Then I'll ask Sheeran and Dog Dick what they think of your transfer request. They'll tell me that it's a great idea, but what they'll really mean is that they'd do anything to get rid of you. So I'll be a nice guy and transfer you to the Major Case Squad, at about nine o'clock tomorrow morning. And the best part is that it all looks like their idea. How's that?"

McKenna was in awe. It all sounded so simple when Brunette

explained it. "Ray," he said, "you are the greatest lying, conniving con man I've ever met. I'm proud to know you."

"Why, thank you, buddy. Now we'd better get to work. Send Schnieder down and see if you can locate Bobby. I want to get home soon. We're going to have a big day tomorrow. Get a couple of hours' sleep yourself, if you can."

McKenna got up and walked to the door. Then he turned and said to Brunette, "Ray, one more thing. Did you hear that both of us might be retiring soon?"

Brunette looked shocked. "No," he answered. "Where'd you hear that?"

"From Angelita. She got it from your wife. I just got an ultimatum from Angelita. I've got two days to retire or she's going to leave me. She said that she was talking to your wife and she has the same plan for you."

"I've been hearing some noise at home, but nothing like an ultimatum, yet. Do you think that Angelita means it? Will she really leave you if you don't retire?"

"I'm sure she means it."

"Then what are you looking to be assigned to this case for? What are you, nuts? Retire, keep her, and enjoy life. I would if I were you."

"That's because you've already got everything you want out of this job. I haven't, yet.

"What if this case takes more than two days? Will she come back to you when it's over?

"I hope so, but I really don't know. In her mind, this is a test of my love. I could conceivably wind up as the most miserable First Grader on the Job."

McKenna left Brunette sitting at O'Shaughnessy's desk, scratching his head.

6

McKenna left Brunette in O'Shaughnessy's office, feeling better than he had when he went in. He went upstairs to the Seven-one Squad office. It was busy, as usual, with a row of victims sitting on chairs waiting to talk to a detective. They've got a long wait, McKenna thought, unless they've got something to do with this case.

In a holding cell built into one wall of the room McKenna saw Jorge Chavez, the industrious destroyer of evidence, sitting on a bench with three male black teenagers.

Three Seven-one Precinct detectives were seated at three different desks. Each detective was talking to a complainant on an adjacent chair.

Bobby Johnston was reading a copy of the latest Department Orders, which detailed the transfers within the department, doing his job as Brunette's eyes and ears.

"Bobby," McKenna said, "the chief's gonna be ready to leave soon. He wanted me to let you know."

"Great. I'll go wait in the car."

Johnston left and McKenna walked into Lieutenant Schnieder's office. Schnieder's desk was covered with the money from apartment 12G. The bags of drugs, the guns, the scales, and the notebooks swamped a small table next to the window. Richie White and Property Officer Rogers were counting out the bills in the wrapped stacks of currency taken from the blue canvas bag. Captain Sheeran watched them count while he tabulated the totals. Schnieder had pulled a small typewriter stand to his chair next to the wall and was busy typing out the property vouchers for the money.

McKenna was amazed. In his twenty-three years in the police department he had never seen a lieutenant touch a finger to a typewriter key. The Seven-one Squad must be very shorthanded already, McKenna thought. He stared at Schnieder and knew that, as miserable as Schnieder looked, that moment would be the high point of his evening. Things were going to get worse.

"Lieutenant Schnieder," McKenna said, "Chief Brunette is looking for you."

Schnieder's fingers froze over the typewriter keys. Then he appeared to gather his courage. Without a word, he got up and started his trip to the first floor. A good Christian going to feed the lions, McKenna thought.

Nobody gave McKenna a polite word; they were too busy with numbers running through their heads, trying not to lose count.

"How much?" McKenna asked.

Without looking up from his note pad, Sheeran said, "One hundred and seventy thousand and still counting, thank you."

McKenna, feeling slightly unwelcome in the office, asked, "Anything I can do?"

Sheeran looked like he had a few ideas, but he kept them to himself.

Richie White finished counting a stack of hundreds and said, "You can fingerprint Chavez, if you don't mind."

Good, thought McKenna. Something for me to do while Schnieder is being tortured downstairs. I want to look busy when he returns to the office after his chat with the chief.

He closed the door of Schnieder's office behind him. McKenna took his pistol out and handed it to one of the detectives typing at his desk in the outer office. He put McKenna's pistol in his top drawer and turned around to watch the fingerprinting process. Department procedure mandated that police officers be unarmed when they fingerprint prisoners, and that another officer must be present to assist the fingerprinting officer in case the prisoner tried anything aggressive. Everyone recognized the validity of these procedures and knew that they were written over the bodies of some careless police officers.

McKenna took the holding cell key from its hook on the wall and opened the door.

"Let's go, Chavez."

"It's about time, Officer," said Chavez, rising. "If you don't get me printed soon, I'll never make Night Court."

Chavez knew the procedure, and had an air about him as if he were attending a party thrown in his honor. McKenna took him over to the fingerprint board and took the required three sets of prints—federal, state, and city. It was easy. Chavez was an experienced customer and probably could have fingerprinted himself.

Then McKenna walked Chavez over to an unoccupied desk and sat him down in a chair. He handcuffed Chavez to the arm of the chair and took a Booking Report from the top desk drawer.

"Name?"

"Jorge Chavez."

"Address?"

"417 Sterling Place, Brooklyn."

"Date of birth?"

"January 1, 1964."

"Place of birth?"

"Brooklyn."

"Have you ever been arrested before?"

"What do you think, Officer?"

Let me try this, McKenna thought. "What do you know about Rico?"

"Nothing."

"What about Raoul Camarena?"

The same blank stare as Torres. "Who's he?"

McKenna became more convinced that Rico was not Raoul Camarena. "What were you doing in Apartment 12G?"

"Talk to my lawyer."

"Anything you'd like to tell me to help your case?"

"I wanna go to the bathroom."

Another experienced veteran of the system, McKenna thought. He finished filling out the top part of the Booking Report. He left the narrative section for White to complete since he was the arresting officer and it was his story that mattered. McKenna had Chavez sign his fingerprints, took him to the bathroom, and then returned him to the holding cell. He was typing up the fingerprint cards when Schnieder returned.

Schnieder hadn't looked good when he'd left and he looked worse now. He scanned the busy office and knew that he had to perform the loaves and the fishes trick with his available manpower. Then he focused on McKenna.

"How do you feel, Brian?"

"Fine, Lou."

"I'm short manpower," Schnieder said. "Can you help me out in this case?"

"Sure."

"Good," Schnieder said. "Go locate that taxi driver and find out where he picked up Rico. Report back to me when you're done. I'm sorry, I can't spare a partner for you right now."

"Don't need one, Lou."

Schnieder went back into his office. "And find out who that phone number belongs to," Schnieder said as he closed the door.

So far, so good, McKenna thought. He finished typing up the fingerprint cards and gave them and the Booking Report to the detective who had his Glock. He took back his pistol.

Then McKenna called the Identification Section and gave them the telephone number he had removed from Rico's mouth. The 860 number belonged to a pay phone located on the street at the corner of East 115th Street and Park Avenue in Spanish Harlem.

McKenna was confused by the information. Why had Rico tried to eat the piece of paper that only had the number of a pay phone written on it? Just so we don't get the general location where their hostage is being held? That might be it, McKenna concluded.

Before he left the Squad office, McKenna went over to the Telephone-Message Log. The message to the Fort Myers Beach police requesting a death notification to the family of Raoul Camarena had been entered. There was still no reply. McKenna knew that the Seven-one Squad would be needing all their cars that evening, so he went next door to the Sex Crimes Unit, took a set of car keys from the row of hooks on the wall, and logged out a car.

McKenna drove through two miles of urban jungle, past the drug dealers, the prostitutes, the working people on their way home, and the children whose only playground was the street. In ten minutes he was at the Black Night Cab Company office.

Gypsy cabs in various states of disrepair were double-parked outside the office. He eased his car in the line and walked in. The room was partitioned by a wall with a door and a glass window. All McKenna could hear was the sound of the gypsy cab radio network. The dispatcher sat behind the window in the wall. Three cab drivers stood outside the window.

McKenna spotted a pistol concealed under the shirt of one of the drivers. Not now, he thought. Besides, in his occupation in this neighborhood, he probably needs his gun more than I need mine. McKenna knew that there had been a recent rash of cab robberies, with the bodies of cab drivers turning up behind the wheels of their cabs in deserted parts of town.

The three cab drivers left as McKenna walked up to the window and tapped on the counter with his shield. He didn't need the shield; the pretty young black girl seated behind the window knew who he was. She was on the phone and writing down an address. She held up her hand, indicating to McKenna that he had to wait until she was finished with the customer, hung up the phone, and talked into the microphone on her desk. Then she looked at McKenna with a great smile. "They're moving the cabs now, Officer. I'm sorry about the double-parking."

"I don't care about double-parking, dear. That's not why I'm here. I'm investigating a series of cab robberies," he lied. "I think that one of the Black Night cabs picked up my suspect at about three-fifteen this afternoon. I'd like to talk to that cab driver to find out if he noticed anything suspicious about the guy. I think he was looking for another driver to rob."

She was interested and eager to help. McKenna gave her the license number and she went to a book and looked it up.

"That's the license number for cab 346," she said. "Ronald Bronson is the regular driver for that cab." She went to her dispatch log and looked for the jobs assigned around three-fifteen. She found it. "I remember that one. A man called the cab office at three o'clock and said he wanted a cab to pick him up at Tilden Place and Flatbush Avenue in Brooklyn for a trip to Kennedy Airport. I told him we could do it and that the fare would cost twenty-two dollars."

"Did he give a call-back number?"

The dispatcher consulted her sheet. "Yeah, 729-1870. I assigned Ronald Bronson's cab to the job." She read from her dispatch sheet, "At three-ten Bronson radioed that he had picked up the fare. At three-thirty he radioed again and said that the fare wanted to leave the cab at Empire Boulevard and Bedford Avenue and that he needed a price. I told him six dollars. Then I gave him another job."

"Is Mr. Bronson still working?" McKenna asked.

"Officer, Ronny Bronson is always working. Twelve hours a day, seven days a week."

"Can I talk to him now?"

"He's got a fare in his cab now, going to Utica Avenue and Eastern Parkway. He should be there in about fifteen minutes."

"Great. Can you radio Bronson and ask him to wait there for me?"

"Sure, Officer."

McKenna took her name and walked to the door. "Hope you kill that cab robber, Officer," she called to him as she left.

All the cabs that had been double-parked were gone. McKenna drove to the busy intersection of Utica Avenue and Eastern Parkway, which was about halfway between the cab-company office and the Seven-one station house. He made it in five minutes and cab 346 wasn't there yet. McKenna wanted to look as unmenacing as possible, so he bought a newspaper and sat behind the wheel reading. He saw cab 346 drop off a fare on the corner. Bronson got out of his cab to look for him. McKenna kept on reading. Bronson spotted McKenna's unmarked car. He got back in his cab and backed up so that his car was next to McKenna's. Then he honked his horn. McKenna looked up from his paper at a very black man, about fifty years old, wearing an old plaid shirt and a Kango cap. McKenna yelled through his open window, "Are you Mr. Bronson?"

"All the time, Officer."

McKenna got out of his car and into the front seat of Bronson's cab. McKenna gave him the cab-robber story.

"I knew it, I knew it!" Bronson said. "That man was really strange."

"Tell me everything you remember about him."

"Sure. I got the job at three o'clock and I went to Tilden Place and Flatbush Avenue. He was a Spanish dude, which surprised me a little. Not many Spanish in that neighborhood. He was dressed all in green. Reminded me of a green snake, especially when I saw his shoes. They was green snakeskin. Pretty, you don't see shoes like that every day. They shine at you."

"Where'd he say he wanted to go?"

"The Intercontinental Hotel at Kennedy Airport, but he tells me that he didn't want to take the parkway. I was surprised because the parkway would have been the quickest way. He was a pleasant guy, but he started making me jittery after he got in the cab. He was always sticking his head out the window. He kept looking up and looking behind us. I started talking to him about the weather."

"Did he have an accent?"

"He spoke good English with a small Spanish accent. When I turned onto Empire Boulevard from Flatbush Avenue, he asked me if there was a public men's room close by. Now I get really suspicious. That'a fare-beating trick. So I told him that he could use the men's room at the precinct at Empire Boulevard and New York Avenue. I said I would wait for him outside. On Empire Boulevard the traffic was a bitch. When we got to Bedford Avenue, he told me that he knew where there was a bathroom. He said he was gonna go and asked how much he owed me. I radioed the dispatcher and she told me six dollars. He gave me ten dollars and told me to keep the change. Then he split."

"Did you see anybody chasing him?"

"No. I never looked. I was busy talking to the dispatcher. She gave me another job right away and I was writing it down on my trip sheet."

McKenna thanked Bronson for his cooperation and took down his address and phone number. As he left the cab, Bronson said to McKenna, "Hope you get the guy."

"Already did," McKenna replied.

McKenna headed toward Tilden Place and Flatbush Avenue. He passed the station house on the way and he saw that Brunette's car was gone. When he got to Bedford Avenue and Empire Boulevard, he started timing the trip. Almost two miles in ten minutes with no traffic. There was a phone booth on the corner. McKenna parked his car and went to the pay phone. The number on it was 729–1870, the same number the dispatcher had told him. There was a sticker for the Black Night Cab Company glued to the side of the phone. Then he walked around the neighborhood, which was virtually 100 percent black. In ten minutes he didn't see another white or Hispanic face, except for one motorist, and he looked lost.

McKenna noticed that just about everyone he passed on the street stared at him. He didn't belong. What was Rico doing here? he wondered. He got back in his car and drove to the Seven-one station house.

When McKenna walked in the door, the desk officer told him that O'Shaughnessy wanted to see him.

Inside the office O'Shaughnessy was laboring over the Unusual Occurrence Report. He looked up.

"McKenna, if you fuck up anytime, anyplace, I'm going to get you, every time."

"Inspector, no offense, but I've been chased by the best, and even they only get me some of the time."

There it was. Red right to the top of his head. Countdown resumed. "Get out of my office, McKenna!"

McKenna left and started up the stairs to the office. Classic paranoid schizophrenic marked by extreme mood swings, he thought. Obviously Ray had spoken to Dog Dick. McKenna made a mental note to make sure that O'Shaughnessy received a steady stream of applications for the Dale Carnegie Personality Development Course.

Things looked different in the Squad office. The chairs inside the door were still occupied with victims, but none of the detectives working there were Seven-one men.

Ray's plan is working so far, McKenna thought. All the Seven-one guys are on Brunette missions and Schnieder had to borrow detectives from other squads to keep his daily operation going.

McKenna knew a few of the replacements and he introduced himself to the rest. There were boxes of pizza everywhere, a sign that they were busy. Even Brooklyn detectives normally don't have to order plebeian pizza into the office.

"Have a slice. There's plenty," one of the replacements said. McKenna opened a box and saw a hot pie covered with anchovies. Real men, he thought. He took two slices and went to the coffeepot to pour himself a cup of used motor oil.

Then he got back to work. He checked the Telephone-Message Log and found that someone had written in a return message from the Fort Myers Beach Police Department. It was from an Investigator

Miguel Montoya. He had tried to make a next-of-kin death notification at the residence of Raoul Camarena at 137 Beachview Drive, but no one was home at the time. Montoya had checked the telephone listing for Raoul Camarena and found that the number was unpublished. A 1987 Ford Bronco had been parked in the driveway, Florida registration number WW 1274. Montoya had run that plate through Florida DMV and found that it was registered to Rosa Figueroa of 2938 Pelican Drive, Fort Myers. The Fort Myers Beach police would make an additional notification attempt in the morning.

The Telephone-Message Log also recorded an inquiry made to the office of the *Boston Globe* concerning their headline for that day and whether out-of-town editions of the *Boston Globe* were sold in the New York metropolitan area. The reply was that the day's headline was MAYOR CAVES IN ON BUS STRIKE. There were eleven locations in the New York area where out-of-town editions of the *Boston Globe* were sold.

McKenna went into Schnieder's officer. White and Rogers had finished counting the money and they were now weighing and packaging the drugs that had been recovered. Sheeran was still taking notes as they finished weighing each package. Schnieder was still typing property vouchers.

McKenna told Schnieder about his interview with Ronald Bronson, and that the telephone number that he had found in Rico's mouth was for a pay phone in Spanish Harlem.

"Good," Schnieder said. "As long as it's not in the Seven-one Precinct, I don't have to worry about it."

"Lou, why don't you let me do that typing?" McKenna asked.

Schnieder smiled for the first time that day. "You got the job, kid. Sit down."

McKenna relieved Schnieder and finished typing the property vouchers for the money, using the information in Sheeran's notes. Three hundred and fifty thousand dollars even had been taken from the blue canvas bag. Then McKenna typed the vouchers for the drugs. The total was 12 kilos, 102 grams. Sheeran telephoned the Narcotics Division and found that the drugs had an approximate wholesale value of $266,000 and an uncut retail street value of $726,000.

There was nothing left for McKenna to do. He gave the completed vouchers to Schnieder and sat at his desk in the Squad office. He couldn't get Rico off his mind. Then he had an idea. He dialed the Fort Myers Beach information operator and got a telephone listing for Rosa Figueroa. McKenna looked at the clock on the wall. Eleven o'clock, not too late. He dialed and after a couple of rings, a man answered the phone. McKenna identified himself and asked for Rosa Figueroa. After a minute, she came on the line.

"I'm afraid I have some bad news for you, Miss Figueroa. Do you know a Raoul Camarena?"

"Yes," she answered.

"There's been an accident here. I'm sorry, but he's been killed."

McKenna knew he was breaking police protocol. Death notifications were supposed to be made in person. They had tried to do that, but now time was important.

Rosa Figueroa didn't seem to mind. She started to laugh. "You better get yourself together, Officer. Raoul Camarena is sitting right next to me."

McKenna wasn't surprised to find that the man he had killed was not Raoul Camarena. "Can I talk to him, please?"

"Sure. He wants to talk to you now anyway."

Raoul came on the line. He had a slight Spanish accent. McKenna told him that they had the body of an accident victim in New York who had Camarena's driver's license and Social Security card in his wallet.

"Impossible, officer. I've got my license and Social Security card in my pocket."

"Can you give me your Social Security number and then read me the numbers off the license?" McKenna asked.

While Raoul read the numbers, McKenna wrote them down. Then he asked Raoul to wait on the line for a minute. He went into Schnieder's office and got the envelope containing Rico's personal belongings. He took out Rico's wallet and compared the information on the license and Social Security card against the information that he had just gotten from Camarena. The numbers matched. He went back to the phone and asked, "Mr. Camarena, you ever lose your wallet?"

"That must be it. Somebody broke into my car and stole my wallet last year sometime. I think it was in November."

"Where'd this happen?"

"Fort Myers Beach."

"Did you report it to the police?"

"Yes sir."

"There might be some connection between yourself and the dead man. We don't know who he is, but if I can figure out the connection it might help. When was the last time you were in New York?"

"Never been there, Officer."

"I'm going to send you a picture of the dead man. Maybe you'll recognize him."

"Sure. I'd be interested to see what he looks like." Camarena gave McKenna a Miami address to send the photo to.

"When are you getting to Miami?" McKenna asked.

"I'm in Miami now, with Rosa. She's in real estate and she hates to miss a call. She's got call forwarding, so she had all her calls forwarded here to my brother's house. That's the address I gave you."

McKenna thanked Camarena for his cooperation and interest, and hung up. He felt better knowing that he had been right about Rico.

While McKenna was congratulating himself, a Seven-one detective returned from headquarters with the enlarged photos of the hostage and the criminal records of Torres and Chavez. Both men had long records.

Chavez had five arrests. He was twenty-eight years old. His last arrest was in August 1988 for Attempted Murder Second Degree and Criminal Possession of a Loaded Firearm. He had pleaded guilty in October 1988 to Assault Second Degree and the gun possession and was sentenced to serve three to five years. He was released to parole in June 1990 and his parole would expire in October 1993.

Torres's record was even worse. He was forty-two years old and his record listed eleven arrests. His last arrest was in February 1990 for Murder Second Degree. He was found guilty after a jury trial and was released on $50,000 cash bail for sentencing in January 1991. Torres never showed up for sentencing. His bail was forfeited and a bench warrant was issued for his arrest. He was never located until this arrest.

Rico had no record. Unusual, McKenna thought. Maybe they'd get a record for him from the federal set of his fingerprints, but not for a couple of days. The criminal records and the photos were brought into Schnieder's office.

Just as McKenna thought about the Feds, John Weatherby, the new special-agent-in-charge of the FBI Brooklyn office, walked into the office. Although McKenna was sure that this was Weatherby's first time in the Seven-one Squad office, his nonchalant air of superiority made it apparent that he considered the office part of his domain. He was young and cocky. Too young for his job, McKenna thought.

McKenna intensely disliked Weatherby, and the feeling was mutual. Weatherby's composure sagged a bit when he saw McKenna.

"Where's Lieutenant Schnieder?" he asked McKenna with his midwestern twang.

McKenna remembered his last run-in with Weatherby and decided that he would try to avoid a confrontation this time, since it was possible that Weatherby would also wind up having something to do with the kidnapping case. He pointed to Schnieder's office door. The agent walked in without knocking and McKenna followed.

White and Rogers busily stamped the money with the NYPD evidence stamp while Schnieder and Sheeran watched them.

Weatherby introduced himself, saying, "I'm John Weatherby. I'm now in charge of the Brooklyn office of the FBI."

McKenna looked at Sheeran and Schnieder and read their minds. It wasn't hard. Their faces said, So what?

Weatherby didn't get it. "I understand you've stumbled on a kidnapping case. I need to know what you've got."

Schnieder matter-of-factly told him about the shoot-out, the finger, the photos, and what McKenna had learned about the gunman's movements immediately before the shooting. Schnieder also told him about Torres's and Chavez's criminal history, that he had learned from the *Boston Globe* that the newspaper the hostage was holding in the photos was that morning's edition, and of the attempts to notify Camarena's family in Florida.

"Can I see Camarena's personal effects?" Weatherby asked Schnieder. "I'd also like to see his gun, the ring, and the photos."

Schnieder gave him the items that he had asked for and Weatherby looked them over, one by one.

McKenna decided not to mention to Weatherby that the dead gunman was not Raoul Camarena. Weatherby went through the gunman's wallet and wrote down Camarena's information in his note pad. Then he said to Schnieder, "The FBI is going to assume responsibility for this kidnapping investigation, Lieutenant. I'm keeping all these items."

There was complete silence in the room until Captain Sheeran walked over to Weatherby and took the wallet out of his hand. Weatherby looked shocked.

"Does the FBI have anything to add to this investigation?" Sheeran asked him. "Do you know something we should know?"

Weatherby tried to regain his composure. He didn't make it. "No, we have nothing on this kidnapping yet. But I'm sure we'll develop something."

"So will we, Mr. Weatherby. But first, let me give you the ground rules. You are standing in an office of the Detective Division of the New York City Police Department and I am a captain of detectives. You, Mr. Weatherby, are not in my chain of command unless the chief of detectives puts you there. Which means that you're not going to come into this office and take my evidence unless the chief approves it. Or unless you get a court order for it. How we doing so far?"

Weatherby was burning. After a few seconds he opened his mouth to say something, but Sheeran ignored him and continued. "The New York City Police Department started this investigation and, as far as I'm concerned, the New York City Police Department is gonna finish it. The FBI is welcome to assist us in any way you can, of course, but the investigation is going to stay the responsibility of this police department, unless we find the victim is not being held in New York City. The indication so far is that he is."

"Kidnapping is a federal offense, Captain."

"Try that someplace else, Mr. Weatherby. Kidnapping is also a violation of Section One-thirty-five of the New York State Penal Law. It's one of the crimes that makes us real cranky. I hope you understand me."

"Where's this evidence going to be?"

"I am going to give you the courtesy of sending it to Chief Brunette's office tonight. You can go talk to him tomorrow morning. If the chief wants to give you the evidence, that's fine with me."

Weatherby turned to leave.

"One more thing, Mr. Weatherby," Sheeran said, stopping him. "In this police department, we observe some courtesies." He walked over to Schnieder's door. "This is how we usually go into a lieutenant of detective's office unless we're related to him." Sheeran knocked twice on the door.

Weatherby stalked out. His humble exit was a sharp contrast to his grand entrance.

McKenna was beginning to like this Captain Sheeran. McKenna then told Schnieder and Sheeran what he had just learned from Raoul Camarena.

"Glad you didn't tell Farmer Weatherby about that, McKenna. Good thinking. It never hurts to know a little bit more than the FBI," Sheeran said.

"It's no great feat to know more than Weatherby. I know you told Weatherby that everything was going to the chief's office, but I want to send Camarena's license and Social Security card to the Police Lab Document Section to find out how they were forged."

"Do it," Sheeran said.

McKenna left Schnieder's office with the license and Social Security card. He sat at a desk outside and typed out a Request for Laboratory Examination and addressed it to the Document Section. He requested specific information on how the license was forged. Then he typed his Investigation Report, form DD 5, on his interviews of Ronald Bronson and Raoul Camarena. Just as he finished, Schnieder's office emptied out. They had finally finished stamping the money. Sheeran and Rogers were ready to leave with all the evidence.

"What are you going to do with all that, Captain?" McKenna asked.

"I called the chief and told him about Weatherby's visit. He gave me the combination of the evidence safe in his office. Everything goes there until tomorrow."

"Can you do me a favor and drop Camarena's identification at the lab?"

"Sure."

McKenna gave him the paperwork and Sheeran and Rogers left with their bundles.

White finished filling out the Booking Report on Chavez. Then he took Chavez out of the holding cell and handcuffed him. Schnieder assigned one of the other detectives in the office to drive White and his prisoner to Central Booking. McKenna knew that it would be some hours before White got any sleep.

It was midnight. McKenna gave Schnieder the Investigation Reports he had just finished and said, "If it's OK with you, Lou, I'm signing out. It's been a long day. I've been going since eight this morning."

"Fine. Why don't you go sick or take a couple of days off?"

"No thanks. I'm sleeping over. This is getting interesting and I want to see how it turns out."

"Suit yourself."

McKenna was tired. He called the switchboard operator, told her that he would be sleeping in the Squad office, and asked that someone wake him up at five A.M. He signed out, went to his locker, and took out his frequently used emergency stay-over kit and two fresh sheets. He thought of calling Angelita before he went to bed, but decided against it. No reason to aggravate each other now, he thought.

McKenna went to the small bunk room in the rear of the Squad office, made one of the bunks, got undressed, and lay down. He had a lot to think about and he didn't fall asleep for another hour.

7

July 10   5:00 A.M.

McKenna woke with a start. He had been too excited to sleep well. He got up, put on his pants, and went to the locker room on the fourth floor, where he showered, shaved, and shined his shoes. Then he went back to the Squad office, made a pot of coffee, and sat down to arrange his thoughts and answer the one question that perplexed him most about this case—what had Rico been doing at Tilden Place and Flatbush Avenue?

McKenna was sure that the hostage wasn't being kept near there. The kidnappers and the hostage would be too conspicuous in that black neighborhood. He examined and discarded every possible reason for Rico being there. The more he thought about it, the more convinced he became that he was right. And if he was right, this case was going to have him working back in Manhattan.

The thought made McKenna smile. Now he had to spend the morning following Ray's plan to the letter to get officially assigned to the case.

McKenna was ready to advance his terrorist theory to Sheeran and officially request assignment to the case. Because of what he had learned about Rico last night, that theory seemed even stronger than ever. He was intrigued by the sudden interest of the FBI in the case and their desire to exclude the NYPD from the investigation. Weatherby knew more than he was telling.

McKenna knew that Sheeran and O'Shaughnessy would still be working on the Unusual Occurrence Report for the shooting, especially since the case had become so complicated. He didn't want to bother

78

Sheeran yet, but he wanted to check on their progress, so he went down to the commanding officer's clerical office on the first floor.

Police Officer Betty King was there, sitting at her word processor while it printed a report. She was in civilian clothes and looked like the grandmother everybody wished they had. She was a good friend, one of McKenna's favorite people in the world. She was delighted to see him.

"Morning, Brian. I'm so glad that you weren't hurt too bad yesterday. That was some job you did."

"Morning, sweetheart. What are you doing here so early?"

"I'm not here early. I'm here late. I've been working all night on the Unusual for your shooting. It's printing up now and it looks real good."

"What time did you start?"

"Ten o'clock yesterday morning. But I still feel OK."

Twenty hours and still ticking without complaint, thought McKenna. She's the best.

Betty King had been in the police department for thirty years, at least. She had joined the department in the days when women were relegated to the roles of cell matron, the Youth Division, the Pickpocket and Confidence Squad, and little else. Rumor had it that she had left a high-paying job as a legal secretary with a big law firm to join the department, and the Job quickly became her life.

Betty was competent to the point of boredom. She was considered the authority in the police department on what form had to be filled out in any situation, what obscure office or hidden unit had to be notified in each unusual event, and she was an expert in writing exactly what the chiefs wanted to hear. After bad news was passed through her word processor, it always emerged looking like a welcome event that her boss, the Seven-one Precinct commanding officer, had astutely anticipated and meticulously planned. She was, and had been for the past twenty years, the real commanding officer of the precinct.

McKenna knew that Betty was the main reason commanding officers arrived in the Seven-one as captains and left as deputy inspectors. As the years went by, her protégés, using the lessons they learned from her, rose within the department after they were promoted out of the Seven-one. And they remembered how they got where they were. She was the most sought-after clerical police officer in the department. She could have any clerical assignment she desired in any unit she chose, but she refused all offers. If she wished, she could be a detective tomorrow in a quiet investigative unit. It was common knowledge at police headquarters that Betty King was going to retire from the police department as the captain's clerical officer in the Seven-one at the mandatory retirement age of sixty-three.

Betty King's greatest strength or greatest weakness, depending on your viewpoint and the situation, was that she loved cops. At any party, after a few cognacs (her drink of choice when she drank at all), they became "her boys and girls." She was the precinct den mother and she especially loved police war-stories and the "stars" of these stories. To hear her say about a particular police officer, "He's one of my heroes," meant that bad things could not happen to that officer in the Seven-one Precinct. She smoothed the path between the Bosses and the cops.

The printer stopped. Betty tore the pages from the word processor and gave them to McKenna. In twenty-seven pages the report covered the incident and McKenna's entire police career, absolving him of any wrongdoing in shooting Rico and Torres. It took McKenna half an hour to read it.

"Thanks, Betty. You make me look like a hero."

"You'll always be one of my heroes, Brian."

McKenna was a little embarrassed. He saw that Betty had a vase full of carnations on her desk. "Where'd you get the flowers?" he asked.

"From Inspector O'Shaughnessy. He's such a nice man and he brings me flowers every day," she answered.

Dog Dick's smart, McKenna thought. Then McKenna thought of a way to antagonize O'Shaughnessy and reward Betty at the same time. He had an elaborate brass vase in his locker that he had been meaning to give to Angelita for some time. But Betty needed it more this time.

McKenna told Betty that he would be right back and left. He went up to his locker for the vase and then checked out a car. He drove three miles to the Brooklyn Bridge approach and bought two dozen roses from one of the street vendors. Then he stopped at a restaurant on the way back to the station house and bought two breakfast specials. He presented the flowers to Betty and she absolutely beamed. She placed the flowers and the brass vase on her desk next to O'Shaughnessy's flowers.

They were just finishing breakfast when Sheeran and O'Shaughnessy came into the office. Both of them looked exhausted. Sheeran seemed happy to see McKenna, but all O'Shaughnessy could see was the vase with McKenna's flowers standing next to his carnations on Betty King's desk. His flowers looked like weeds in a rose garden.

Without saying a word to McKenna, O'Shaughnessy took the report and began to read it over. McKenna saw his chance and said to Sheeran, "You got a couple of minutes, Captain? I need to talk to you."

"Sure, Brian. What is it?"

"It's kind of private."

O'Shaughnessy looked like he wanted to object, but he evidently decided to keep quiet. Sheeran brought McKenna to his office on the third floor of the station house, sat at his desk, and gave McKenna a look that said, *Tell me something interesting.*

McKenna began his pitch. "I've got a few ideas on this case that I want you to hear, Captain."

He outlined the case as he saw it. He explained that a wealthy man was kidnapped in the Boston area and presumably, demands had been made by the kidnappers to the victim's family. To show that they were serious, the kidnappers surgically removed the victim's pinky and sent it to the victim's family with a list of ransom demands. The family could not or would not give in to the kidnappers' demands immediately. So the kidnappers cut off the victim's ring finger and were in the process of taking this additional reminder to the victim's family or representative at Kennedy Airport. Then the New York City Police Department got lucky and discovered the crime. Halfway to Kennedy Airport, the messenger's taxi got stuck in traffic and the messenger had to go to a bathroom. A lucky break from Mother Nature. He had to go bad and he knew there was a bathroom at 277 McKeever Place, apartment 12G. McKenna said, "I don't know how yet, but somehow Rico knew Francisco Torres."

As he had told Brunette, he now explained to Sheeran the things about Rico and the victim that made him think that Rico was a terrorist and the hostage was from a rich family and not a drug dealer. Sheeran looked halfway convinced.

Then McKenna said, "I think the hostage is being held in Manhattan, not Brooklyn."

That went a long way toward making Sheeran a happy man. If the hostage was not being held in Brooklyn, then Sheeran would not be the one primarily responsible for the case. He had enough to do already. But he needed more convincing.

McKenna was ready. "Rico definitely wasn't from Flatbush Avenue and Tilden Place, where he ordered the taxi from the Black Night Cab Company. That part of Brooklyn is one hundred percent black and Rico would have stood out like a nickel in a jar full of pennies. That's not the kind of neighborhood that a bunch of Spanish kidnappers would choose to hide out in with their victim. They would choose a neighborhood that they knew and where they would blend in. They would hide with their victim much easier in Manhattan, which has the biggest Latin communities and neighborhoods in the world outside of Latin America."

"Why not Corona or Williamsburg?" Sheeran asked. "Those are big Spanish neighborhoods, and they're not in Manhattan."

"Aside from the fact that, when Rico died, he was trying to eat a piece of paper that had a Spanish Harlem telephone number on it, I just think that Rico looked like a Manhattan guy," McKenna answered. "He was sharp, well dressed, and he had money in his pocket. He'd probably be embarrassed that he got killed in Brooklyn. He must have asked himself the same question I've been asking myself recently—Why should I be anyplace but Manhattan? Rico was an uptown Manhattan guy. I spent a lot of time up there and I know the look and the fashion. Take his shoes, for instance. Green snakeskin. They must have cost at least four hundred dollars. You don't buy shoes like that at Macy's or A&S. You buy them on upper Broadway in Manhattan. And you don't wear them in Corona. Too ostentatious. And you sure don't wear them in Williamsburg, where you could get shot and robbed for a pair of shoes like that."

"So what was he doing at Flatbush and Tilden?" Sheeran asked.

"Being careful," answered McKenna. "Put yourself in his head for a moment. You've had your guy for at least a couple of days. You've delivered at least one ransom demand and a pinky to his family. Now you've got another of his fingers taped to your back and you're going to somehow deliver it with a second message for the family. You must think that the full resources of the police and the FBI are being directed toward finding you. You think that they might even know where you are already. So what do you do? The first thing to find out is if the police know where you are. So when you leave your hideout, you make sure that you aren't being followed. You walk around a little to see if there's anyone following you or if there's anything unusual in the neighborhood. You assume that, if you're under surveillance, the police will use Spanish or Spanish-looking officers that would blend into the neighborhood for their surveillance operation. Then you go to a corner and call a taxi to take you to a neighborhood where a Spanish cop would stick out so far that you'd have to notice him—Flatbush, Brooklyn. On the trip there you constantly check for a tail. You also look for police helicopters. When you get to Flatbush and Tilden, you take a little walk around to make sure there're no other Latinos around who might've followed you. Once you're satisfied you're in the clear, you call your buddies at the hideout and tell them everything's OK. Then you take the telephone number of a local taxi company that's on a sticker glued to the phone and call for another taxi to take you to the Intercontinental Hotel. You tell the taxi driver not to take the parkway to the airport, because you know that aerial surveillance would be easier on the parkway, so you're still being careful and still looking around."

"Why wouldn't he have driven himself to Flatbush and Tilden?" Sheeran asked. "They must have access to a car if they're in the kidnapping business."

"Too risky. On the chance that the police might suspect where they are, they figure that the police would have planted a transmitter on the car. These boys are too careful for that. I assume that any car that they would've used during the kidnapping, or to transport the victim to New York, was stolen, or at least had stolen license plates. Why would our boy take a chance on getting stopped by some cop for a red light when he's in a stolen car with a finger taped to his back? No, he took a taxi from their hideout. That way he could give his surroundings his full attention to see if he was being followed while he was sitting in the back of the taxi. Besides, we didn't find any car keys on the body. Which brings us to another unusual point. Rico had no keys of any kind on him. That's another indication of how careful they are. No keys to be found by the police which could be traced back to their hideout."

McKenna gave Sheeran some time to digest this theory. Then he made his request. "I want to be assigned to this case. I should be. I started it and I've already done a lot of work on it. I want to go with it, wherever it takes me, but you're the one who'll have to assign me."

"I can't do that. The chief of detectives sent you to Brooklyn and the chief is the only one who can get you out. How long did he tell you that you'd be staying with us after your last Manhattan adventure?"

"Two years or forever, whichever comes first. But your recommendation that I be assigned to this case would mean a lot."

Sheeran disregarded McKenna's plea. "Two years?" he said. "Well then, it wasn't as bad as I heard. What were the conditions?"

"Stay out of trouble and follow you like a god," answered McKenna. For the first time in a long time, McKenna, who had become accustomed over the years to being on the carpet, felt uncomfortable. He knew that it was beginning to show on his face.

"I see," said Sheeran. "Well, so much for the conditions. I don't feel like a god when you're around. I should be home right now hitting the snooze button on my alarm clark. Instead, I'm here documenting your exploits. I can't take too many more nights like last night."

McKenna sweated while Sheeran sat back in his chair and thought. Then Sheeran smiled. Two down, McKenna thought.

"OK. For what it's worth, I'm going to recommend to the chief that you be assigned to the case. I think you deserve it and I think you'll do a good job. But mostly because I'm selfish. The chief told me yesterday that he wants me to do daily evaluations on you, and if you're gone, I get a chance to get back to a normal routine. Your presence in Brooklyn is starting to make me miserable. You're even starting to make O'Shaughnessy more miserable than he already was, and nobody would've thought that was possible. I think you can pack up."

That's all I need, McKenna thought. Sheeran's recommendation and back to the Bright Lights. Then McKenna thought about Angelita and her plans for the rest of his life, and things still didn't seem quite so good after all.

Sheeran got up. "Don't get ecstatic yet. It's not a done deal till the chief says *yes.* Meet me in O'Shaughnessy's office in a few minutes. I want you to read the Unusual over before we disseminate it worldwide."

They both left Sheeran's office. Sheeran went back to O'Shaughnessy's office and McKenna decided to wait with Betty.

Betty had already found other things to do after working all night on the Unusual. She had a pot of coffee going and she was humming as she opened the morning's batch of department mail. She glanced at each new order or directive and separated the ones she thought important enough into two piles. She threw about a third of them into her wastepaper basket. "Chief Brunette's on his way here from headquarters," she said to McKenna as soon as he entered her office.

How did she know? thought McKenna. Then he figured it out. Of course, someone in headquarters would call Betty King as soon as they found out that any chief was headed for the Seven-one. McKenna knew that Betty had told O'Shaughnessy of the impending visit. He reflected that he would hate to be the one in charge of trying to surprise Betty. McKenna had a cup of coffee with Betty. Then he went to O'Shaughnessy's office, knocked on the door, and went in.

O'Shaughnessy was behind his desk and Sheeran sat facing him.

"Sit down, Brian," O'Shaughnessy said.

Brian! There he goes again, McKenna thought. Apparently Sheeran has explained my theory and request. And O'Shaughnessy is in a mood to agree. Anything to get rid of me.

McKenna took a seat next to Sheeran and O'Shaughnessy pushed the Unusual Occurrence Report across the desk.

"Tell us if we told any lies," O'Shaughnessy said sarcastically.

McKenna picked it up and began to read. He had to pretend that he was reading the report for the first time and he found it hard to concentrate. He spent fifteen minutes faking it. He handed the report back to O'Shaughnessy and said, "A masterpiece. Exactly what happened."

Brunette walked in.

O'Shaughnessy, Sheeran, and McKenna stood up. All three men tried to look surprised by the unannounced visit.

"Sit down, gentlemen," Brunette said. "There's been a lot happen-

84

ing in this kidnapping case and we have a lot to talk about." Brunette gave McKenna a look that seemed to say that he should excuse himself while the Bosses talked, but Sheeran said, "I think that Detective McKenna should stay, Chief." Brunette looked at Sheeran quizzically.

Sheeran took a few minutes to tell Brunette about McKenna's theories on the case and McKenna's request to be assigned.

"That's funny. I've been doing a lot of thinking and I've reached the same conclusions. What do you think of McKenna's request?" Brunette asked Sheeran.

"Good idea," Sheeran hurried to answer.

Brunette turned to O'Shaughnessy. "What do you think?"

"I agree, Chief," O'Shaughnessy answered just as quickly.

Brunette appeared to think the matter over for a couple of minutes. Then he said to McKenna, "If I were to assign you to the case, you would be working with the Major Case Squad, McKenna. You would have to promise to stay in line, get along with the FBI, and keep everything out of the papers. Got it?"

"Yes sir," McKenna answered. "That would be no problem. What's going on with the FBI?"

"I smelled a rat in my office when I got in at seven this morning. Weatherby was waiting with a request for the evidence on the case. He told me that he was here last night and that Sheeran had been uncooperative. I got suspicious, so I told Weatherby to go get some coffee. Then I looked at the evidence and reached some conclusions. Next I thought about Weatherby. He lives about sixty miles upstate, in Brewster. So I ask myself, why would the agent in charge of the Brooklyn office of the FBI leave his home in the middle of the night to make a request for evidence? He could've sent someone else to do that. The only answer has to be that they know more than they're telling, they have something to hide, and they want to keep the whole thing a secret."

Makes sense, McKenna thought, but he didn't have a reason yet. Why keep it a secret from us?

Brunette continued. "After Weatherby returned from his coffee break, I told him of my suspicions. I said that I thought the FBI was withholding information from *me* on a kidnapping case. Do you know what he did?"

McKenna answered. "He looked you straight in the eye and lied."

"That's right," Brunette said. "He told me the only thing that he knew about this case is what the New York City Police Department told him. But I made him nervous. So he told me that he would have to check further and he would let me know what he found out this afternoon. Then I told him that if he didn't give me some answers, I was going to go straight to the Director and, if that didn't work, I would go to the press. He looked like he was ready to go back to his cornfield by the time he left. But I did give him everything we had at the time. I'm not going to be so generous the next time unless they start filling us in very fast."

"What would they have to hide?" O'Shaughnessy wondered.

Brunette answered, "They have to have a reason to keep this kidnapping from going public. They know that they're much better at keeping secrets than we are. They're more tightly controlled than us regarding information given to the press. It's my guess that the secrecy has something to do with the victim. I think he's a political figure and that the kidnappers have been identified by the FBI as terrorists. I could work out some pretty good reasons to keep it a secret if that's the case."

At that moment Betty King knocked perfunctorily on the door and entered the office with four cups of coffee on a tray. She smiled at Brunette and said, "I was wondering when you were going to get here, Chief."

"Hello, Betty," said Brunette. "I don't know how you do it. Have you given my proposal any thought?"

Betty King giggled and said, "You're already married, Chief."

"Not that proposal, Betty. I mean will you come work for me and teach my detectives about old-fashioned police work? However, since you spilled the beans, let me state for the record that if you would marry me, my wife and kids would have to find someplace else to live."

Betty King smiled at the chief, gave him a wink, and said, "I guess they all know about us now. But honestly, Chief, just leave me here. I like working with Inspector O'Shaughnessy and he's teaching me a lot."

Brunette looked at O'Shaughnessy and said, "I bet he is. But he might have to lose you. Detective McKenna might be assigned to this case and he would need you more than Inspector O'Shaughnessy. Besides, you've already gotten O'Shaughnessy promoted once. Give McKenna a chance."

Betty King looked at McKenna and said, "Well, that's different. I'd love to help Detective McKenna."

"That means you might have to be a detective," said Brunette. "Is that all right with you?"

"Whatever you think is best, Chief. I'll just leave you gentlemen to your work now." She left and closed the office door behind her.

While they were drinking their coffee, Brunette asked McKenna, "What needs to be done?"

"Find out who Rico really is and find out who the hostage is. Find out who Rico was going to meet at the Intercontinental Hotel. Get an opinion from the medical examiner about exactly when the finger was removed from its owner, just to rule out the possibility that the hostage was being held in Boston. Talk to Torres and Chavez's lawyer to find out more about Rico, but that means bringing the DA in. I'd like to go to the morgue to find out about the finger, and then on to Brooks Brothers to see what I can get on the hostage. You have to squeeze the FBI to see what they know."

Brunette thought it over and said, "Let's see how much the FBI really does know. We know that Rico is not really Rico Camerena, but do they?"

Brunette picked up the telephone from O'Shaughnessy's desk and got the number for the Fort Myers Beach Police Department. He dialed the number, explained who he was, and asked to speak to their chief. When he was connected he asked if they had made any progress in their attempt to notify Raoul Camarena's relatives at 137 Beachview Drive. He smiled when he got his answer, thanked the Florida chief, hung up, and said, "We know more than they do. The FBI is really busy down there right now. They got a search warrant signed by a federal judge and right now they're in the process of searching the home of Raoul Camarena. Once they find out about their mistake, I'm sure that we'll be hearing from them again. The cat has to come out of the bag, and for now, we've got the bag."

Brunette finished his coffee while he seemed to be thinking over McKenna's case plan. Finally he turned to McKenna and said, "I hope I'm not writing my professional epitaph, but here it is. McKenna, you are assigned to this case. It's the only way that I can think of to get Betty King promoted before her age forces her to retire. You'll work in the Major Case Squad directly under Deputy Inspector Tavlin. I am going to arrange for a command center to be set up in the Two-five Precinct in Spanish Harlem. Captain Sheeran will direct the Brooklyn end of this investigation. We have a lot of planning to do here, so why don't you and Tommy Pacella go down to the morgue and see what the medical examiner can tell you about the finger. Pacella came here from headquarters with me and he's waiting in the Squad office."

McKenna wondered if he should thank Brunette in front of Sheeran and O'Shaughnessy. That might be pushing it, he decided. So he got up and turned toward the door. As he glanced over his shoulder, he saw that Brunette's award-winning dimples showed for a second, and then vanished.

8

Detective First Grade Tommy Pacella was one of the most knowl-
edgeable and respected detectives in the Detective Bureau, and one
of McKenna's best friends. They had worked together on many cases
in the Manhattan Robbery Squad and in the Career Criminal Apprehension Unit. It used to be said that McKenna and Pacella were a
first-rate song-and-dance team.

Last year, Pacella had retired from the police department with close
to thirty-five years of service. But retirement didn't agree with him.
He missed the Bright Lights, he missed the action, and he missed his
friends. He lived in the Long Island suburbs and got bored just staying
home or, as he put it, "I wasn't meant to spend my twilight years
mowing lawns in Massapequa." So Pacella came back to the Job after
six months of retirement and was assigned to the Major Case Squad.

McKenna found Pacella filling a chair in the Squad office. He was
reading a newspaper that looked like a paper napkin in his hands.

He's starting to show some years, McKenna thought. Losing some
hair and showing some wrinkles. But he looks better with the added
years. A few pounds too many, but I still wouldn't want the job of
throwing him out of that chair. Pacella seated in the Squad-office
chair reminded McKenna of a father sitting at his child's first-grade
desk on Open House Day. The whole scale was wrong.

Pacella looked up from his newspaper. "Hi, kid! It looks like you're
the new man of the hour. You're front page in the *Post* and the *News*

and page twelve in the *Times*. I brought two copies of each for you. One for framing and one for your scrapbook."

"Tommy, my favorite Ginzo. It's good to see you, and I'm glad to hear that I'm still a 'kid' to our senior officers. But remember what they say... when the cops and your doctor start looking like kids, that means you're getting old."

"They're right. I'm lucky that everything still works on this body."

Pacella rose from his seat and the two friends shook hands. McKenna picked up the stack of newspapers from the floor next to Pacella's seat and asked him, "Am I good news or bad news?"

"Mostly good. The tabloids love these police shoot-out stories, as long as only bad guys or cops get hit."

"Anything about the finger and the kidnapping?"

"No. That's still under wraps. They think it's just drugs. But there's an editorial in the *News* about the Glock. They question the wisdom of giving our police a pistol as powerful as the fourteen-shot nine-millimeter Glock. They're worried that we might accidentally shoot some grandmother through a steel door."

"What's wrong with those slimeballs. The good guys don't need to be as well armed as the bad guys? Gimme a break! I would've loved to have had one of those liberal dirtbags with an old police revolver in his hand standing between me and the bad guy yesterday when I was getting the TEC-9 version of 'Vietnam War Story.' I bet he'd write a different editorial today."

"I don't think so, kid. An editorial writer will never sacrifice his ideals in the face of experience or sanity. If he did, it would make him just an ordinary person, not a Philosopher to the People. What he'd probably write is that you should have stopped chasing the bad guy when he went full automatic on you, using their theory that we can always safely get our man sooner or later anyhow."

"Not that guy, Tommy. Taking him could never be done safely. Just between you and me, if I didn't have a Glock yesterday when this guy was putting bursts all around me, I would've let him get away. I've been around too long to still think that I can win on a lucky shot."

"You can give the press your theory on your way out," said Pacella. "They're all waiting on the front steps for their follow-up story."

"I can't do that right now. Ray just informed me that he was my new press agent and I don't want to disappoint him on his first day in his new position. We're going to have to sneak out the back door. Once we're outta here, we can radio back and someone can tell the Fourth Estate we're gone."

"Where we going?"

"To the morgue."

"That's great," said Pacella. "I've wanted to see how good a nine-millimeter Glock works. But we'll have to pick up some breakfast on the way. I've been thinking bacon and eggs all morning."

"Please, Tommy. New Rule Number One . . . no breakfast before morgue visits. That place is one of my incomplete digestion factors."

"I'm surprised to hear that, kid. Weren't you in the Manhattan Homicide Squad?"

"Yeah. When I was in Homicide, I lost ten pounds, mostly during morgue visits, and mostly on my shoes. So let's just skip breakfast and I'll buy lunch in a couple of hours, OK?"

"Sure. It warms my heart to see that you kids still fall for the Morgue-Breakfast scam. A nice business lunch in Midtown will be just fine."

"It'll be my pleasure. Let's go."

The two detectives left the station house by the back door, took the unmarked car assigned to Pacella, and left for the Bellevue Morgue, which is located next to Bellevue Hospital in Manhattan. McKenna filled Pacella in on the progress in the case during the ride. It was ten o'clock as they finally approached the block before the blue brick building. McKenna felt the familiar queasiness in the pit of his stomach.

McKenna had never been able to get used to these morgue visits. Of course, he had long since become accustomed to the sight of death during his police career, but the difference between a body at a crime scene and the same body at the morgue was more than just a matter of setting. At the scene of a homicide, the dead were surrounded by the living. A body as evidence of a violent death at a crime scene always evoked feelings of rage and horror in McKenna as he reconstructed the motives of greed or senseless passion that led to the untimely ending of life for the victim. Death at those scenes was still a unique event and McKenna saw each body as more than just evidence of the former existence of a person.

In the morgue, however, the living were surrounded by the dead. There, where the signs and smells of death were pervasive and where the many bodies of victims were regarded as commonplace work tasks, death seemed too impersonal for McKenna's constitution. It made him sick.

The two detectives entered the building through the side loading door on East 30th Street. As they pushed through the swinging double doors, McKenna nearly gagged at the familiar overpowering stench of disinfectant. His stomach reminded him of how he had felt when, as a child, he was seated in the first car of the roller coaster at Coney

Island as it approached the first big hill. Things did not get better after that.

The two detectives walked into the main room of the morgue. They saw two bodies covered with sheets lying on rolling stretchers along the wall as they entered. A giant floor-to-ceiling refrigerator chest of stainless steel drawers that contained the bodies of persons to be autopsied or identified dominated the middle of the room. At the end of the room, a middle-aged female clerk sat at a desk filling in the blank spaces on a form with information from a police report.

McKenna identified himself and asked to speak to the doctor in charge of the autopsy of the person tentatively identified as Raoul Camarena. She reacted with such a show of annoyance that McKenna thought he might have asked her if she minded if he squeezed her breasts for a while. She reached over and picked up a clipboard that hung on the side of the desk and rustled through the pages until she found the information—"Raoul Camarena, July 13, 1992, 71st Precinct." She examined the entries next to the name on the chart, gave McKenna a smug spider-to-the-fly grin, and said, "You're in luck, Detective McKenna. Doctor Lee is assigned to that case and he's doing the autopsy right now." She pointed to a door to her left marked AUTOPSY ROOM and said, "Just go right in."

Some luck, thought McKenna. The roller coaster reached the top of the big hill. Pacella grabbed McKenna's arm and they both went through the door.

The room was large and well lit and contained four autopsy tables spread in a line. There were teams of doctors performing autopsies on the first and last tables to the detectives' right and left. The detectives saw that the body being autopsied on the right was that of a female black, so they walked to the table on the left.

Rico lay on the table. The doctors had cut a Y-shaped incision on the front of his torso and had pulled the skin back in such a way that his internal organs were exposed.

Two doctors bent over the body. One was an oriental man who appeared to be about twenty-five years old. He had a small tape recorder on his belt and he spoke into the microphone which was attached with a headset that left both of his hands free. The other doctor, a tall, slender, bearded white man, looked to be about fifty years old. The oriental doctor held Rico's heart in his hands while the other doctor examined it with a scalpel and a forceps. Both looked up as the detectives approached.

"Doctor Lee?" asked McKenna. The oriental man nodded.

"I'm Detective McKenna and my large friend is Detective Pacella. We're from the Major Case Squad and we're assigned to an investigation that stems from this man's death. We're hoping that you can give us some information regarding the finger that was taped to his back."

"Not the same Detective McKenna who shot this subject, is it?"

"Yes, sir, it is."

"Well, this is very unusual. We seldom get a chance to talk to the people responsible for our work."

"This is a very unusual case, Doctor. Naturally, I'm not investigating the death of this man," McKenna said while pointing to Rico's body. "That investigation will be done by the Brooklyn Homicide Squad. I'm just assigned to get any information that you can give us about the finger."

"OK, but you'll have to wait until we're done with this case you sent us. This guy is really unusual."

"Unusual?" asked Pacella.

"So unusual that I've asked Doctor Stienner here to observe the autopsy and assist me in cataloging the wounds carried by the subject. Doctor Stienner used to work as an investigative pathologist for Amnesty International and this subject has obviously been subjected to some of the most extensive and systematic torture that he has ever seen. We don't often get a chance to examine a case like this where the body has not been extensively decomposed."

"Torture? When?" asked McKenna.

Doctor Stienner answered, "I'd say at least fifteen years ago. Let me show you." He picked up Rico's left hand and said, "All of his fingernails have been ripped out. He had fake fingernails glued to the damaged nailbed. Most of his teeth have also been forcibly removed at about the same time during torture. Look at these scars on his chin."

A set of dentures lay on the table next to Rico's head. Doctor Stienner parted Rico's beard in two places to reveal four puncture scars and continued, "I'd say that his jaw was forced open and held open using a device that punctured the skin on his jaw and pierced the jawbone. There are scars on the roof of his mouth consistent with this analysis."

Doctor Stienner moved down to the dead man's midsection and said, "There is also extensive scarring of the penis that indicates that the shaft was slit and acid was applied."

McKenna looked at Rico's scarred and misshapen penis and felt a wave of sympathy for the man pass over him. You've been worked over by experts, pal, he thought. I guess there was no way I was ever gonna make you tell me anything you didn't want to.

McKenna noticed that as his interest in the medical aspects of Rico's past piqued, his stomach began to settle.

Doctor Stienner continued, "We have so far counted a total of thirty-three burn scars that were made at about the same time as the other scars." He pointed to a circular scar at the top of Rico's left leg. "These scars were caused by the application of intense heat to the subject's body, probably with a cigar. There are burn scars on the subject's feet and lower legs of a type that indicate that a high-intensity torch was used to cause these wounds."

McKenna glanced over at Pacella and saw that his partner was now experiencing the same feelings of sympathy and revulsion.

"From your experience, could you make a guess about where he could have received these wounds, Doctor?" asked McKenna.

"Wait until we're finished here and I'll do some research and then I might be able to give you a guess. As I've said, these wounds are more extensive than any we've seen. We're going to continue now."

Doctor Lee placed Rico's heart on the platform of a scale that was hanging next to the autopsy table and said to McKenna, "From the examination that we've conducted on the subject so far, it's clear that you could have saved at least one bullet and probably two if your intention was to kill him."

"I just wanted to stop him, Doctor."

"Everybody we see here is stopped. All of your bullets entered his body from the rear in close proximity. There is one exit wound on his chest. The bullet that caused this exit wound followed the same general path of the other two bullets, but, incredibly enough, hit no bone. We have recovered two bullets from the body cavity. Both wounds caused by these two bullets caused fatal damage. We have already described the damage caused by the bullets for this report, but suffice it to say that the heart was pierced, the left lung was pierced, the spinal cord was damaged, and a total of four ribs and the scapula were broken. I'd say the subject probably expired within fifteen seconds after these wounds were inflicted." Doctor Lee turned toward McKenna and asked, "Am I right?"

McKenna stared at the recorder on the doctor's belt. Doctor Lee understood and shut the recorder off. McKenna then replied, "You know your business, Doctor. It wasn't long. From what you've shown me on this poor guy's body, you'd think he was almost impossible to kill."

Doctor Stienner interjected, "None of the wounds he suffered before yours were designed to kill. They were inflicted to cause intense pain, not death, probably in connection with an interrogation he was undergoing. But thank you for your information on the time lapse between infliction of his recent wounds and death. I'd have thought that fifteen seconds was too long an estimate considering the damage your bullets caused."

"May I see those bullets, Doctor Lee?" asked McKenna.

Doctor Lee gave him two small, brown evidence envelopes. McKenna opened them one at a time, examined each bullet, and returned each to its envelope. Both of his bullets had been deformed during their trip around the dead man's chest cavity. He handed both envelopes back to Doctor Lee, who then turned his tape recorder back on. Both detectives waited silently while the two doctors continued their autopsy.

After a while the doctors turned the body over. Doctor Lee measured and diagrammed the bullet-entrance wounds in Rico's back while Doctor Stienner continued his count of burn scars on the rear of the body. When he reached the rectal area, he called Doctor Lee over to consult with him on his findings.

Doctor Stienner then said to the detectives, "In addition to his other injuries, the subject also bears burn scars on the muscles of his anal sphincter. It appears that the wounds that caused these scars were inflicted at about the same time as the other old wounds which we have cataloged. Later, we will examine the lower digestive tract to see if any internal damage was caused by these wounds."

The doctors finished their examination of the rear of the body and again turned the body over. Doctor Lee then pulled out Rico's colon and both doctors examined it. Doctor Lee slit open the lower end of the colon and examined the inside tissue. The smell was terrible and McKenna could see that it was even getting to Pacella.

When Dr. Lee was finished, he said to McKenna, "This man lived with pain. There is scarring caused by burn damage on the inside tissue wall of the colon. Due to this damage, I'd say that the subject was not far from being incontinent."

"Would it be safe to say that when he felt the urge to defecate, he'd have to find a bathroom in a hurry?" McKenna asked.

"Yes. He wouldn't have much time."

That's what he was doing at the Ebbets Field Houses, McKenna thought. He had to go in a hurry. "What could have caused this damage?"

"I'd say that a heated circular rod had been inserted in his anus as a form of torture," answered Doctor Lee. "Let's get to the finger now."

Doctor Lee walked the detectives to a refrigerator in a corner of the room, opened it, and took out a plastic bag containing the finger. He noted the series of numbers written on the bag, then went to a file cabinet next to the refrigerator and took out a file that matched the numbers on the bag. He read the Serology Report in the file and said to the detectives, "The finger is from a male, probably Caucasian, blood type O positive. It was severed in a surgical procedure shortly

94

before it came into the custody of the Medical Examiner's Office. There is evidence of a Novocain-class drug in the blood, indicating that the owner of the finger received a local anesthetic before or during the procedure. There is also evidence of sodium phenobarbitol in the blood, leading me to conclude that the owner was heavily sedated when the finger was removed. There is no evidence of any narcotic drug in the blood. Anything else?"

"Yes, Doctor," said McKenna. "A number of things. It's vital that we find out when this finger was removed from its owner." McKenna then handed the doctor an enlarged photo of the hand of the kidnap victim and said, "We also need your best guess on how long before this photo was taken was the pinky of this man removed."

Doctor Lee studied the Serology Report, checked on the time that the finger was first refrigerated at the morgue, and then examined the finger. He took a pencil from his pocket, wrote some calculations on the side of the refrigerator, and then stopped to think for a minute.

Finally he said to McKenna, "This finger was first refrigerated after examination at six forty-five last night. Doctor Greene, who checked the finger in last night, concluded in his report that the finger had been removed from its owner at approximately two P.M. yesterday, which was approximately three and a half hours before he first examined the finger. Based on my examination of the finger and on the information we now have in the Serology Report, I'd say that Doctor Greene was right on the money. This finger was removed at two P.M. yesterday, give or take an hour."

"Thank you, Doctor. And the wound on the hand in the photo?"

Doctor Lee held the enlarged photo up to the light and examined it for a minute. Then he said to McKenna, "I'm not the best person to give a judgment on this. These photos should be shown to a practicing surgeon. But I would say that the pinky had been removed between three and five days before this photo was taken. The manner in which the wound was closed indicates to me that the operation was performed by a doctor or someone with extensive medical training. The stitching technique used in closing the wound is old and no longer in general use in this country. If you like, I'll show this picture to a surgeon friend of mine and get his opinion."

"Please do that," answered McKenna. McKenna took a business card from his wallet, scratched out *71 Detective Squad* and the Brooklyn telephone number that was under his name, and wrote *Major Case Squad* with the telephone number of the 25th Precinct Detective Squad. He gave the card to Dr. Lee and said, "Please contact me as soon as you speak to your friend. Time is real important in this case."

McKenna then approached Dr. Stienner, who was busy examining

Rico's jaw while an attendant stitched up the incisions made during the autopsy, and said to him, "Doctor, please call me as soon as you can with your ideas on when and where this guy was tortured. We have no idea who he is right now, and any information that you could give us on his possible history or origin could be instrumental in saving a life. Doctor Lee has my number."

Dr. Stienner answered, "If it's so important, I'll call a friend of mine who's still affiliated with Amnesty International, give him the information that we have, and ask him to do some research. But off the top of my head, and based on the age of the scars and the fact that the subject is of Hispanic origin, I'd guess that he was tortured in either Argentina or Uruguay in the late seventies. Those were the Amnesty International torture 'hot spots' fifteen years ago, at about the time this man's wounds were inflicted. He was probably captured after he was identified by the secret police of either of those two countries as being a member of the *Montoneros* in Argentina or the *Tupamaros* in Uruguay. They were guerrilla groups who were engaged in a violent insurrection against the Argentine and Uruguayan military governments at that time. The atrocities committed by both sides during those insurrections were horrible. He obviously escaped after he was tortured, because the secret police of either country could not have afforded to let him live to document their methods. If he hadn't escaped, he simply would have become another of the many thousands of *Desaparecidos,* the 'Disappeared Ones.' He couldn't have been a member of the secret police or military who was captured because he would have become a military hero after his escape and we would know who he was. In any event, I'll call you with any information I can get."

The detectives thanked both doctors for their help and started for the door. As they left the room, McKenna saw that the body of the black woman that was being autopsied when they entered was gone. An attendant washed down the autopsy table with a hose. The adjoining table was now occupied by the body of a black man; a doctor and an attendant were busy measuring their new customer before they began working in earnest.

On their way out of the building they passed once again the female clerk. She still sat at her desk, munching on a sandwich while filling in forms with information about the sorry residents of her institution.

There were now three covered bodies lying on stretchers along the wall.

As they left the building, both detectives simultaneously reached into their back pockets, extracted handkerchiefs, and blew their noses. They both took deep breaths as they walked to their car. McKenna thought to himself that New York never smelled so good.

Not until they were seated in their car were words exchanged. "I'll never get used to that place," said McKenna.

"Nobody should. Where to for lunch?"

"Lunch? Please, tell me you're not that tough and I won't tell a soul. You make me feel like a sissy. Let's do one more chore before lunch while my body shakes that place off."

"OK, kid. You've got me. I'm not that tough. Where do you want to go from here?"

"Madison Avenue and East 44th Street. Brooks Brothers."

9

Brooks Brothers, established 1818, is recognized as the world's bastion of "preppie" men's clothing. Its square-cut, conservative shirts, suits, and shoes, as someone once said, are never quite in style, but never out of fashion. The clothing is expensive, well made, and lasts forever. Traditionally, the rich and elite of the world are fitted for their first suits at Brooks Brothers before they progress to boarding school, and they go on to become lifelong customers.

Persons who find it necessary to generate trust by their conservative and solid appearance, such as successful bankers, stockbrokers, and high-priced lawyers, are regular clients at Brooks Brothers. McKenna had long since noticed that people tend to believe a person who is dressed in a blue or tan Brooks Brothers suit, which was why McKenna was numbered among the firm's clientele. McKenna bought his "testifying clothes" at Brooks Brothers.

McKenna was convinced that in order for a person to be convicted of any serious crime in New York State, a cop had to tell at least one lie somewhere along the line in the case. Under the Exclusionary Rule of Evidence, which holds that evidence illegally obtained by the police is not admissible, the rights of persons accused of crimes had become a formidable barrier to justice. Conviction of a guilty person who chose to fight a charge had become improbable if the police officer played strictly by the United States Supreme Court's rules, and impossible under the even more restrictive rules of evidence prescribed by the New York State Court of Appeals.

McKenna reasoned that if a person committed a crime, if the police went to the trouble to investigate it and were able to arrest the person who committed the crime, and if the state went through the expense of prosecuting this person, then this accused person should not be acquitted or his case dismissed because of a technicality of law.

So McKenna frequently lied in court. He regularly committed perjury, exposed himself to prosecution, and felt good about it. He never lied as to fact in a case, just as to the circumstances in which evidence was obtained. Like when, exactly, he gave a suspect Miranda Warnings, or when he first saw a gun, or if he ever momentarily lost sight of a suspect or vehicle he was surveilling. Under the Exclusionary Rule of Evidence, the question of "when" is the primary factor that determines whether evidence that is obtained by the police and that connects a person to a crime will be admitted in court.

McKenna figured that if he was going to go to the trouble to lie under oath, then he might as well be believed. Brooks Brothers suits were a prop he used in court; they fit the bill, making him look like a college professor at Harvard. Taken together with other techniques of testimony that he had learned over the years, he was able to project a cursory professional interest in any case in which he testified. He could sell the jury on his absolute honesty. For real whoppers, he found that the addition of argyle socks and horn-rimmed glasses further enhanced his credibility.

McKenna was a busy cop and he testified often. He was considered a good customer at Brooks Brothers.

McKenna drove from the morgue up Madison Avenue to East 44th Street. He couldn't believe his luck when he found an open parking meter directly across the street from the store. "This is the first time I've been legally parked in Manhattan in years," he remarked to Pacella.

"Unbelievable!" answered Pacella. "This must be your lucky day. I'm even gonna take care of the meter. Parking's on me today, kid."

The two detectives got out of their car. Pacella made a show of putting a quarter in the meter, and then both men walked across the street to the solid old building that housed Brooks Brothers. McKenna carried a manila envelope that contained enlarged photos of the kidnap victim holding the newspaper.

When they entered, McKenna received the familiar impression that the entire sales staff was waiting for them, but nobody wanted to bother them. The staff at Brooks Brothers was always attentive and helpful, but never pushy.

On the first floor of the store various styles of dress shirts were displayed in large mahogany islands of counters with a salesman in the center of each island. The walls were also mahogany and the floor was carpeted. The shirts were in rows under glass, and for a customer to examine a shirt the salesman had to remove it from his side of the counter and give it to the customer. No prices were visible anywhere in these sales islands. In the center of the first floor rose a large escalator that led to the store's other departments.

Pacella went over to one of the sales islands while McKenna looked around. Brooks Brothers was quiet at this early hour, with only three customers on the main floor. McKenna beckoned to a well-dressed man whom he recognized as the floor manager, who instantly came to life and approached him.

"Yes, sir," the floor manager said. "How can I help you?"

"Victor is the salesman that usually helps me. Is he working today?"

"Of course, sir. Victor is working upstairs in the Men's Sportswear Section. Would you care to go up or should I call him down?"

"Please call him," answered McKenna. "I'm interested in shirts today."

"Of course, sir. I'm sure that Victor will be down in a few moments."

The floor manager left and went to a telephone behind his desk. McKenna joined Pacella, who was examining the rows of shirts under the glass of the sales counter. The salesman assigned to counter had not approached Pacella but waited attentively for any sign from him that he was interested in a particular shirt.

"There's no prices on any of these shirts," Pacella said to McKenna.

"People who shop here find an open display of price gaudy, offensive, and unnecessary," McKenna said, conscious of sounding a little pompous. "Looking for a price on a shirt here is like asking what kind of gas mileage a Rolls-Royce gets before you buy one. They pick what they like and a salesperson takes it to his register for them. As long as it's Brooks Brothers, they know it's expensive, but they want it. Brooks Brothers is the only place to get Brooks Brothers clothes. See anything you like?"

"Sorry kid. I can't know if I like it if I don't know how much it costs."

"You're never going to make the Brooks Brothers mailing list with that attitude."

McKenna saw Victor coming down the escalator. He was in his thirties, trim, and neatly dressed in the Brooks Brothers fashion. He smiled when he saw McKenna and he hurried down the aisle to the detectives. He held out his hand. "Mr. McKenna. It's so good to see you. I read about you in the paper this morning and I'm glad to see that you're OK. I didn't expect to see you again so soon. How may I help you gentlemen?"

McKenna shook Victor's hand. "It's good to see you again too, Victor. We're hoping that you can give us some help in shirts. This is my partner, Tommy Pacella."

McKenna saw that Victor was looking Pacella over and he knew the salesman was hoping that his giant partner wasn't searching for a shirt to fit him. Pacella definitely fell into that hard-to-fit category.

"Relax, Victor," said McKenna. "I'm not going to send you to the basement to look for a shirt for this guy. This is an official business visit. I want to show you a picture of a man who was kidnapped and is being help for ransom. We don't know who the victim is yet, but I think that he's wearing a Brooks Brothers shirt in the picture that I'm going to show you. I'm hoping that you know who he is and that you can tell me whether he's wearing a Brooks Brothers shirt or not."

"Of course. I'll be happy to help, if I can."

"There's one more thing, Victor. This man in the picture is in extreme danger, and I'll have to ask you not to repeat anything that I've told you. Secrecy is very important at this stage of our investigation. Is that all right with you?"

"You can count on me Mr. McKenna. I'm glad that you think that I can be trusted."

McKenna took one of the enlarged photos of the kidnap victim out of the envelope and handed it to Victor. Victor studied the photo for a few moments and said, "He looks familiar, but he's not one of my regular customers. I can ask the other salesmen, if you'd let me keep the photo."

"And the shirt?" asked Pacella.

"Definitely Brooks Brothers or a good imitation. Is that a hand-crafted gold ring that the man is wearing?"

"Yes, it is," answered Pacella.

"Then it's a Brooks Brothers shirt. I'll show you one of these shirts, probably in the size that the gentleman is wearing. He looks to be about a sixteen collar and a thirty-three sleeve length. Please step this way."

Victor led the two detectives to an area along the wall where shirts were arranged on shelves according to size. He stopped in the middle of the display and picked out a blue shirt, which he compared against the photo of the kidnap victim. "This is the style of shirt your victim is wearing in his size."

Victor handed the shirt and the photo to McKenna, who compared them for a few seconds. He saw that the collar style matched exactly. "What do you call this particular line of shirt?" asked McKenna.

"That's a Pima Oxford button-down cotton dress shirt. It's been one of our better sellers over the years."

"How long has it been in production in this cut and color?" asked McKenna.

"I'll have to check to be certain, but off the top of my head, I'd say since 1935. It's very conservative and we don't change much at Brooks Brothers. It's an old-money type of shirt."

"I'll take this shirt, Victor. Please have it wrapped up for me."

Pacella interrupted. "Just to satisfy my curiosity, how much is that particular shirt, Victor?"

"Fifty-eight dollars, sir." Turning to McKenna, Victor continued, "Please let me speak to the floor manager about this. I'm sure it won't be necessary for you to actually pay for this shirt, and Mr. Schmidt would be very helpful in finding out who this customer is. He's been with the firm since 1953 and you can count on him to be discreet."

"Whatever you think is best, Victor. If you and Mr. Schmidt are able to identify the gentleman, I'll need all the information that you have on him, including a list of the dates and times of his purchases, his address, and any billing information that the store possesses. I especially need to speak to someone who knows him."

"Then we certainly must speak to Mr. Schmidt. I'm sure that you understand that the release of any information on our customers is highly irregular for this store."

"Then let's go talk to him," said Pacella.

The three men walked over to the counter where Mr. Schmidt was standing. McKenna reached into his pocket so that he could identify himself with his shield.

Mr. Schmidt stopped him by saying, "That won't be necessary, Mr. McKenna. Of course I know who you are."

McKenna began to explain the situation and Mr. Schmidt again interrupted him and brought the detectives and Victor to his office at the rear of the first floor. He directed the two detectives to two chairs in front of his desk while Victor remained standing. McKenna continued explaining his case and when he finished, Mr. Schmidt asked, "May I see the photo?"

McKenna handed it over. Mr. Schmidt studied it for a moment, then said to Victor, "You were correct in coming to me. The shirt is definitely a Pima Oxford." Mr. Schmidt turned to McKenna. "This is a photo of one of our valued customers. His name is Rodrigo Oxcalo Guiterrez. He's been a customer since he was a boy and I fitted him for his first suit myself. He comes to the store infrequently now, but I believe that he was last here in March. His account is now serviced by Mark Bremmen, who, unfortunately, is off today. His father has also been a customer for many years and I imagine that his grandfather was also a customer."

"Then he's American?" asked Pacella.

"No. He's from Peru. Before I give you the other information you've asked for, I would like to check with his family to get their authorization."

"I would prefer that you don't do that," asked McKenna. "We have reason to believe that Rodrigo's family has known of his kidnapping for some days now and, to the best of our knowledge, they haven't informed the authorities of the crime. I'm sure that they have good reasons for not doing so, but I hope that you'll be able to give us the information we need without informing the family of what we know. Rodrigo's in extreme danger right now, if he's not dead already, and I'm sure that you understand that time is of the essence."

"I will try to respect your request, Mr. McKenna. Please give me a little time to allow the store management to consult with the firm's attorneys before I give you the information. It will take a little time to gather everything you need anyway. Is the FBI involved in this investigation? Mr. Shields, who I'm sure you know is in charge of the New York office of the FBI, is a customer of ours."

"I believe they're becoming more involved every moment," answered McKenna. "I anticipate that we'll be working with the FBI on this case, but at the moment we're a little ahead of them. I can assure you that the information you give us will be shared with Gene Shields. How much time are we talking about before you'll be able to give us this information?"

"I would say by sometime tomorrow, if I can."

"Tomorrow's too late. We can get a subpoena for what we need, but by the time we do Rodrigo could be dead, especially if Brooks Brothers decides to fight the subpoena. We really are not ready to bring this case into the courts yet, where the cooperation or non-cooperation of Brooks Brothers would be a public record. I'd hate to think that Brooks Brothers would ever impede an investigation and cause the death of one of their customers by their reluctance to cooperate with the police in such an extreme and important situation."

"I'm sure that a subpoena won't be necessary, Mr. McKenna," Mr. Schmidt answered rather testily. "As I explained to you, I'm confident that the approval of our attorneys in this case will be perfunctory and expeditious. Where would you like the information you require delivered?"

"The Two-five Precinct. That's on East 119th Street between Park Avenue and Lexington Avenue."

"Isn't that in Spanish Harlem?" Mr. Schmidt's distaste for the location was apparent in his voice.

"I can come and get it, if you like. But I would rather spend my time working on other aspects of this investigation."

"I see," said Mr. Schmidt. "I'll call Mr. Bremmen into work and arrange to have him bring the information to your office as soon as I get approval. Now, can I help you with that shirt? I assume you require it in connection with your investigation," he said, pointing to the shirt that Victor had given McKenna.

"Yes, I need to show this shirt to my superiors. Of course, I'll want to pay you for it."

"Of course, Mr. McKenna. I'm aware of the current exaggerated state of ethics of the police department. We'll charge your account for the shirt. I believe that the price is one dollar. Please return the shirt for credit to your account when you no longer have use for it."

"That might be some time. This case could drag on for a while, especially if we're successful in freeing Rodrigo and capturing his kidnappers," answered McKenna.

"It doesn't matter. I believe that particular style of shirt will be sold by Brooks Brothers for the next twenty years, at least. Please feel free to call me if you think I might be of further assistance in this case."

McKenna shook the floor manager's hand and thanked him for his help. Both detectives walked out of the office with Victor as Mr. Schmidt reached for the telephone on his desk.

"Wow!" said Victor. "You really shook Mr. Schmidt up."

"That was shook up?" asked Pacella. "I felt like I was sitting in my high school principal's office with a cigarette on my ear. That man's as cool as ice."

"He's just doing his job," said McKenna. "It's because of people like him that Brooks Brothers has been around so long. We put him in a difficult position. He's just trying to do the right thing and he needed a little guidance. I'm sure that after our request gets kicked around a little bit, we'll get everything that he has. And soon."

Both detectives thanked Victor for his help and left the store. As they crossed Madison Avenue on the way to their car, McKenna said to Pacella, "Well, I'm hungry now. What do you feel like, partner?"

"How about a good steak?"

"Perfect!" McKenna answered. "Churchills on Third Avenue between 74th and 75th. You'll like it. It's on the way to the Two-five, and we can call Inspector Tavlin from there and tell him how we're doing."

10

McKenna felt like he was sitting in a hole as he drove the unmarked car uptown to Churchills from Brooks Brothers. Pacella's bulk had made a definite and very negative impression on the springs that supported the driver's seat of his car. It was noon when they reached the restaurant. There were no available parking spots anywhere near the entrance, so McKenna double-parked in a line of other double-parked cars and trucks and put the Police Vehicle Identification Plate on the dashboard.

Churchills was a bar and restaurant that specialized in good food in large portions at moderate prices. The decor was reasonable authentic Old English Pub. Churchill's clientele consisted mainly of construction workers, businessmen, local residents, and many detectives. Most customers were regulars.

The bartender, known to all only as Chipmunk, was an old friend of McKenna's. He was busy making a couple of drinks for two of the many customers at the bar when the detectives entered and he didn't see them until McKenna and Pacella were standing directly in front of him at the bar. When Chipmunk finished mixing the drinks he looked up, saw McKenna, lunged across the bar, and gave McKenna a kiss on the top of his head while holding McKenna's face immobile with both of his hands.

Pacella jumped back in shock, but none of the other customers, including McKenna, expressed the slightest surprise at Chipmunk's unorthodox greeting. Chipmunk said, "Brian, it's so good to have you working in Manhattan again. You're back even quicker than usual this time. How's it feel?"

"How'd you find out so fast that I got transferred back? I just found out myself three hours ago."

"Whatta ya think?" answered Chipmunk. "Nobody talks to me? I keep my ear pretty close to the ground. There's no secrets in the police department. I hear you're working on a big case." Chipmunk then turned to Pacella, held out his hand, and said, "You must be Tommy. It's a pleasure to meet you."

Pacella warily shook Chipmunk's offered hand while McKenna formally introduced the two men. "Don't worry, Tommy. You don't rate a kiss yet," McKenna said. Then he asked Chipmunk, "Got any Kaliber left?"

"Who else do you think drinks that stuff?" answered Chipmunk. "We've got cases of it. When you got transferred to Brooklyn, the boss thought that we'd have to throw it away. I told him you'd be back sooner or later, and probably sooner. Two bottles?"

"Why not?" answered Pacella. "I always wind up drinking the stuff when I'm with the kid. Clean living is one of the drawbacks of working with this donkey."

After they finished their first beers, they ordered two more bottles and took them to a rear table, where they ordered steaks for lunch. While waiting to be served, Pacella went to the pay phone at the end of the bar, called Inspector Tavlin at the 25th Precinct, and told him what they had learned at the morgue and at Brooks Brothers. He then rejoined McKenna at their table and during lunch they talked about the case. After finishing the steaks, both detectives ordered coffee and, at McKenna's recommendation, pecan pie.

While they were eating dessert, Pacella said, "I never found out exactly how you landed in Brooklyn this time. Something to do with a diplomat, right?"

"That's right," said McKenna. "I'll give you the unofficial version. Remember Laura Jimenez?"

"Sure. The pretty little girl who works as a barmaid at Raggs. What about her?"

McKenna answered, "She's a friend of mine. Nothing romantic. I just like her and I think that she's a sweet, hardworking girl. Well, when I was working in the Career Criminal Apprehension Unit, she started going with a guy who used to rough her up a bit. One day I'm in Raggs after work and she tells me about this guy and asks my advice. He appears to have a good job with lots of money and he dresses well, but he won't tell her exactly what he does. He's the jealous type and he doesn't like her working as a barmaid."

"It just means he's smart. I'd get a little crazy if she was my girl and worked at Raggs," Pacella said.

"Not like this guy. One day he gets a little loaded and goes over to her place and smacks her around. She doesn't like it, tells him to get out, and says that she's gonna call the police. He tells her he's not worried about the police and shows her that he's got a gun on his belt. She doesn't want any trouble in her apartment because she lives with her little girl, so she calms him down and lets him stay the night. But now she doesn't want any part of him and she's afraid. She doesn't want him arrested, she just wants him gone. I agree with her, he sounds like big problems. I told her that if she was serious about breaking up with him, she should fill out a Complaint Report on the assault just to get some leverage on him. She tells me she'll do that."

"Let me guess," said Pacella. "I'll bet she does nothing and he tunes her up again."

"Partly right. The next day she goes to the Two-five and makes out the Complaint Report. She gives his name, but tells the cops that she doesn't know his address or phone number. The report is going nowhere, but at least she's on record. I talk to her a couple of times after that and she tells me that he keeps calling her and that he came by her apartment once, but that she wouldn't let him in. Everything's fine."

"Everything's never fine," said Pacella. "How'd you screw it up?"

"I'm coming to that. A little while later Laura's working at Raggs and in he comes. He's a loud, obnoxious douche bag, giving Laura a hard time. Vinnie, the owner, can see that the guy's wearing a gun under his jacket and assumes that he's a cop. After all, the place is full of cops, but now everyone's starting to get uncomfortable. All the cops think that he's a cop too. Vinnie asks him to leave and the guy gives everyone a round of 'mother-fuckers' and walks out. One of the cops at the bar is Joe Flaherty, the Two-five PBA delegate. He's a little embarrassed by this guy's conduct, so he follows him outside to give him a lesson in police courtesy. They get into a little tussle and Flaherty comes to discover that the guy's not a cop. He takes the guy's gun and then this fella gets really snotty and shows Flaherty his credentials. He's a Cuban diplomat. Some kind of attaché at the Cuban Mission to the UN. Flaherty takes him back into Raggs and Vinnie takes the guy's picture with his Polaroid camera for his 'No Longer Welcome' file. Flaherty takes down all the information from the diplomatic credentials and then—"

"Gives him his gun back and throws him out again," interrupted Pacella.

"No. Vinnie throws him out. He's really mad at Laura for not letting him know that the guy wasn't a cop, but she's just scared. Vinnie calls the patrol sergeant and he makes out a complete report with all the correct information so that Laura's previous Complaint Report can be updated. That should be the end of the story. The patrol sergeant's report should go to the precinct CO, who should forward it to the Intelligence Division. The Intelligence Division should then send the report of this guy's conduct to the State Department, who should declare the guy *persona non grata* and revoke his diplomatic credentials. The guy should be quietly recalled to Cuba within a couple of days. Right?"

"That's the way it's supposed to work."

"Not this time. A couple of days later Laura gets a visit from two immigration agents who tell her that it might be time for her to leave. She's an illegal alien, but her little girl was born here. She lies and tells them that she was married to an American citizen and she shows them the kid's birth certificate, which shows that the baby was born in Metropolitan Hospital in New York. The immigration agents seem confused, but leave her with the impression that they'll investigate further. They tell her to stay out of trouble and Laura gets the message. She's terrified. She doesn't say anything to anyone. About a week after Vinnie threw the Cuban out of the bar, I'm sitting in Raggs and Laura comes into work. She's wearing sunglasses to cover up a shiner. I ask her what happened and she tells me that the Cuban surprised her outside her apartment and popped her in the eye for telling the police about him. She apologizes and he tells her that he loves her and he forgives her."

"Her boyfriend is a spy," said Pacella.

"That's what I figured," answered McKenna. "He's feeding information to either the CIA or the FBI and they don't want to lose him over some incident with an illegal alien. So, of course, the State Department doesn't tell the Cuban Consulate anything about their boy's extracurricular activities because the Cubans would just ship him back to Cuba to avoid any embarrassment. Somebody from our side must have had a little chat with him, but he's 'in love.' He can't help himself. So here's Laura getting tuned up every once in a while and she can't even go to the police. She figures that if she says anything else, she'll be deported. She doesn't know what to do."

"Enter Hero Detective McKenna," said Pacella. "Always the soft-hearted right guy in the wrong situation."

"Make that Stupid Detective McKenna. I can see that Laura is in trouble and that nothing is going to be done for her. I decided to interview the Cuban myself, unofficially of course, and see if I could talk some sense into him. Nothing else seemed to be working and I figured that the worst that could happen was that we drop a Cuban spy from the Fed's payroll. Anyway, what do the Cubans know that we need to know? Not even the Russians talk to them anymore. So whenever I have nothing to do after work, I go sit in front of Laura's apartment on 111th Street for a couple of hours. Sure enough, a couple of nights later I catch him walking down 111th Street. I can see that he's got a gun under his jacket, so I follow him into the hallway of Laura's building. But he gets scared when he hears me behind him in the hallway and he puts his hand on his gun under his jacket and turns around to face me. I didn't want to take a chance on this guy, and I sure couldn't explain shooting him. So I popped him in the mouth with my gun, and a couple of his chiclets dropped out. I had his full attention and I explained to him exactly what I thought of his chauvinist attitude. I thought he'd be ready to listen to reason, but he wasn't."

Pacella interrupted him. "Next he tried to show you his diplomatic credentials and told you that he'd have your job. So you ripped up his credentials, took his gun, put the cuffs on him, and took him under arrest to the Two-five. Right?"

"Right. On the way to the station house I told him that if myself or Laura had any more trouble from him, I'd denounce him to the Cuban Consulate as an American spy. I said that I'd tell his comrades all about Laura and the strange way our government reacted to his misdeeds, just because I was curious to see how they'd react. That shook him up. When I bring him into the station house he doesn't say a thing. By this time he's having a hard time talking anyway. I try to pass the whole incident off to the desk officer as just a routine off-duty gun collar, which I made on my way home from work. Unfortunately, the desk officer was Lieutenant Bradley."

"And he doesn't buy a word of it."

"Of course not," continued McKenna. "By the book, he calls the Duty Captain to investigate the off-duty arrest, and this captain happens to be another shaky, nervous, by-the-book type. He sends the Cuban to the hospital with one of the uniformed cops to have his mouth treated. By now every cop in the Two-five, except Lieutenant Bradley, knows who this guy really is and I'm starting to draw quite a crowd in the Squad office while I'm doing the paperwork. Then the Duty Captain interviews me, and while I'm being interviewed in the Squad office, the Cuban is brought back from the hospital and he asks Lieutenant Bradley if he can make a phone call to notify his wife of his arrest. Bradley gives him a phone and the Cuban makes his call and talks in Spanish. Bradley has no idea what he said."

"Enter the FBI," said Pacella.

"About an hour later. In comes John Weatherby, who at that time was the assistant special-agent-in-charge of the Manhattan office. He tells Lieutenant Bradley and the Duty Captain that the Cuban is a diplomat and that I robbed his diplomatic credentials. When Bradley hears that he just booked a diplomat, he clutches his chest, has one of his better seizures, and hits the ground. After the excitement clears up, the captain turns the Cuban loose. But it's too late. Everybody knows that a Cuban diplomat was arrested. There's no way to put a lid on it. So I'm in the box."

"Exactly where you put yourself."

"So me and Weatherby have a talk and we call each other assholes a few times. I tell him what I think of his organization and how the Laura thing was handled and he tries to tell me about national security and diplomatic protocol and things like that. In the end, although nobody said it, the general consensus was that the United States of America might have recruited a better class of spy. Weatherby's not stupid, so he wakes some chiefs up and we both go downtown to Headquarters."

"Which chiefs?" asked Pacella.

"Brunette, Martin from Internal Affairs, and Imundi from the Intelligence Division. I hammer out my best deal. The end result is that I have to take a good administrative beating for unjustifiably violating the rights of an esteemed diplomat from the People's Republic of Cuba so that our government can keep on using this guy. That way everyone looks good except me. The Cubans get a little mileage out of the unjustified, imperialistic conduct of the fascist, warmongering, running-dog Yanqui police, our government issues an apology, and I go to Brooklyn under a cloud."

"That's not as bad as I heard," said Pacella. "You could still go to the papers with how the FBI screwed up their handling of the whole Laura incident and how they abused their authority with her when she didn't do a thing wrong. That Immigration play was dirty."

"I never say that to them, but they know that it's in the back of my mind. They can give me a few shots, but they know that they can't knock me out."

"Greater love hath no man than to go to Brooklyn for a barmaid. I'm impressed. But why do you dislike Weatherby so much? It seems that you got the best deal that you could get, and you're back already," said Pacella.

"Because if he would have handled this Cuban right in the first place, none of this ever would have happened. He screws up his job and gets promoted and I wind up in Brooklyn with a black eye. But that doesn't matter. Part of the deal was that the Cuban never bother Laura again, and he hasn't, so I'm happy. Anyway, I'm back now, so let's just keep this between us. I'm still on some shaky ground and I don't want to embarrass Ray in any way."

"You've bought my silence and unending loyalty with this dinner, kid. It only goes to show that, as soon as I let you out of my sight, you get into trouble. It won't happen again."

"You're a cheap buy, Tommy."

McKenna gestured to the waiter for a check, who brought it immediately. "How much is it? I'll take care of the tip," said Pacella.

"Don't worry about it. Dinner, beers, and tip are all on me. Let's get back to work before Tavlin thinks we went on vacation together."

McKenna took five dollars from his pocket and left it on the table. Then he took the check to Chipmunk at the bar, who looked at it, whistled, and rang up fifteen dollars on the register. McKenna gave him the fifteen dollars and left another ten dollars on the bar, but Chipmunk yelled at him, "Are you crazy, Brian? Keep it. You bring enough good business into this place. See ya soon."

"All right, Chipmunk. But remember, that's another one I owe you."

Chipmunk grabbed McKenna again and kissed him on the head. Then he said to Pacella, "Pleasure meeting you, Tommy. Drop in again. Any friend of McKenna's who can read and write is always welcome here."

Pacella shook Chipmunk's hand again and the two detectives left the restaurant and got into their car. It was one-thirty, the traffic was bad, and the heat was oppressive.

11

McKenna felt exhilarated as he drove up Third Avenue to the 25th Precinct. Pacella was employing all his detective skills on the *Times* crossword puzzle during the drive.

Manhattan, with a resident population of close to two million diverse souls crammed into twenty-two square miles, is one of the most densely crowded places on earth. On weekdays the population of the borough swells to four million as people from the outer boroughs, from the suburbs, and from the rest of the word travel onto the tiny island to work and play. Almost anywhere in Manhattan, one is completely surrounded by people. Observing the obvious bustle of life on the sidewalks and streets, it is important to remember that life also exists a thousand feet above in its tall buildings and a hundred feet below ground level in its subways, basements, and tunnels. It is possible to learn almost everything there is to know about human behavior, including all the common neuroses and psychoses, just by standing on a street corner or observing from a window for a day. Almost nothing goes unnoticed; with so many people crammed into so little space, the odds are that someone is always watching.

Although geographically and administratively it is a part of New York State, Manhattan has very little in common with the rest of the state or, some think, with the rest of the country. Everyone in Manhattan seems to be from someplace else. It is cosmopolitan to the extent that people who live in Manhattan consider everyone else from every other city to be no more than varying degrees of bumpkins.

The line between privilege and poverty is clearly marked in Manhattan, and McKenna crossed this line on Third Avenue at East 96th Street, the acknowledged boundary of Spanish Harlem. Driving north from East 96th Street, the pricier high-rises vanished and, except for the numerous New York City Housing Authority projects, the tenements dominated.

Life is lived at street level in Spanish Harlem. The neighborhood is vibrant with the sights, the sounds, and the smells of the Caribbean. The small grocery stores, the storefront churches, the tire-repair and auto-parts stores, and the appliance-repair shops dominate Third Avenue in this neighborhood. The impression of poverty is pervasive, with people in wildly colored clothes hanging around the streets with nothing better to do than to drink beer out of cans "disguised" in brown paper bags. Among these people walk those of purpose; the janitors, doormen, city workers, factory workers, and small entrepreneurs who are the lifeblood of the city.

It was the type of neighborhood where a good cop could make a difference, and McKenna loved it and the opportunities it held for him.

McKenna made a left turn on East 119th Street and drove one and a half blocks to the 25th Precinct station house. The large, four-story building dominated the block. It appeared to be one of the newer structures in the neighborhood, but it was aging fast. Just as a runner's sneaker that gets pounded for ten miles a day in all kinds of weather soon looks old, this station house, which was used heavily twenty-four hours a day, showed its constant use.

A long row of marked and unmarked cars were parked diagonally, almost perpendicular to the front of the station house. The 25th Precinct also enjoyed the luxury of its own large, unpaved, fenced parking lot. This lot occupied the northern third of the block and was used for the police officers' private cars and to store the large number of stolen cars that were invoiced as arrest evidence.

In addition to the nearly 250 uniformed officers assigned to police the roughly one-square-mile area of the 25th Precinct, a number of other police department units were also housed in the large station house. The 25th Detective Squad office and the Manhattan North Public Morals Division office were located on the second floor, and the Manhattan Homicide Squad office and the Career Criminal Apprehension Unit office were on the third. An additional large office on the third floor was used by the detective district captain, who supervised detective operations in the 19th, the 23rd, and the 25th precincts. Locker rooms and a gym occupied the fourth floor.

113

McKenna parked the unmarked car in an open spot across the street from the station house and both detectives got out. McKenna held the shirt from Brooks Brothers as he stood outside the car for a moment and took in the familiar neighborhood.

There were children everywhere, being watched by their mothers and grandmothers from the windows of their tenements. Curtains were tied in knots at these windows so that any available breeze could enter freely while the guardians leaned on pillows placed on the windowsills as they watched the youngsters. Across the street from the station house a group of young children in various states of undress beat the heat by running through an open fire hydrant that had been fitted with a sprinkler cap, while four boys played a New York reduced-space version of handball against the wall of the station house.

Park Avenue was at the western end of the block on which the station house stood. This was the same famous Park Avenue that was synonymous with wealth and privilege. From the old New York Central building at East 46th Street to East 96th Street ran a mall down the center of Park Avenue that was well kept and decorated with massive displays of flowers at each corner. Along that stretch of Park Avenue stood grand, old prewar apartment buildings whose occupants had long since purchased their large apartments, most of which had space for servants' quarters. But at East 96th Street, about one mile south of the 25th Precinct station house, the character and complexion of Park Avenue changed dramatically, for there the flowered mall vanished and was replaced by the elevated tracks of the New York Central Railroad. At that point, these tracks left their hidden tunnel under Park Avenue and rose to dominate the neighborhood. The trains that ran these tracks sped commuters antiseptically from Grand Central Station in midtown through Spanish Harlem to the wealthier northern suburbs of the city.

McKenna knew that most of these commuters would say that they had never been in Spanish Harlem, although they traveled through the heart of it twice a day at sixty miles an hour. And most of the residents of Spanish Harlem had never even considered boarding one of these trains, which went to places where they wouldn't be welcome. The noisy trains were just a fact of life that they accepted much in the same way that they accepted poverty, crime, uncaring landlords, and occasionally, the indifferent police officer who had been burned out by the neighborhood.

In the shade under the elevated tracks of Park Avenue, McKenna saw that a thriving car-wash business was being operated by a few of the more enterprising residents. The city, an unknowing partner in the business, provided the water from another open fire hydrant.

114

Con Edison, the power utility for New York City, also contributed to the business, as the operators used electric power hijacked from a streetlamp to run their vacuum cleaner and electric buffing machine. The entrepreneurs supplied the soap and elbow grease to professionally wash and wax the cars of the neighborhood. As a tribute to the job done there, many of the police officers assigned to the Two-five used the service, forsaking the uncaring and indifferent car-wash business of the suburbs. As a further demonstration of the virtues of the capitalistic system, this car-wash business spun off customers to a few other ancillary neighborhood businesses. Operators of portable stands sold hot dogs, ices, barbecued ribs, and cold soda and, McKenna was sure, even cold beer to customers of the car wash who waited on the sidewalk while their cars were being washed or waxed.

The stoops of the tenements and apartment buildings on the block were crowded with seated people, many of whom were drinking beer and simply talking the day away. Some had radios tuned to one of the many Spanish stations. From almost anyplace in the Two-five, it was possible to hear the rhythmic beat of salsa music.

As McKenna happily took in the neighborhood, he thought to himself that this was the best place to be a cop. There was plenty of police work to be done, many of the neighborhood residents were friendly, the women were good to look at, and best of all, he was in Manhattan. He was only a five-minute drive away from some of the best restaurants in the world. And all good police work done in Manhattan seemed to be more important than the same quality of police work done in the other boroughs. The newspapers and the police brass just seemed to notice good police work more in Manhattan.

From where he stood, McKenna could see at least ten violations of the Administrative Code that would never be enforced in Spanish Harlem. For minor infractions of law here, the policy of the police in the Two-five was "Live and let live." As long as people were doing something productive and not bothering or hurting anyone else, who cared? Just don't bother us. We've got more important things to do.

And the police were busy in the Two-five. Serious crime was commonplace here and drugs were the engine that pulled crime through the neighborhood. Drugs bred murder, robberies, burglaries, and auto thefts. The motto of the user was "Anything for money to buy the drugs," and the motto of the pusher was, "Do anything you can to control the flow of drugs. Cut down the competition and increase your share." For these reasons, the neighborhood was heavily armed with guns intended for both offense and defense. Life was cheap in the Two-five, and the police, while working hard to prevent or solve

115

many violent crimes, always seemed to be on the verge of losing the struggle.

In the distance from where he was standing in the middle of the block to either corner, McKenna was sure that there had to be at least ten illegal guns and two or three persons wanted for serious crimes. He was anxious to get to work. He looked over at Pacella and was surprised to see that his partner stood with his arms folded, smiling at him.

"You finished yet?" Pacella asked.

"Sorry. It's just that I'm home, home, home at last. I've been gone too long."

"How long have you been working in Brooklyn this time?"

"Two weeks, a lifetime. Don't forget, I was facing two years there before I got lucky and this case came up. So let's roll."

The two detectives crossed the street and walked into the station house. They showed their shields to the civilian police receptionist and walked past the seven crime victims or witnesses who were seated in the foyer waiting for a typist to take their complaints, past the four kids standing in line at the water fountain, and past the always out-of-order elevators to the stairwell. They climbed the stairs to the third floor and entered the Career Criminal Apprehension Unit office. Sal Catalfumo and Joe Mendez, two old friends of McKenna and Pacella, were fingerprinting a prisoner.

"Hey, look at this," Catalfumo said. "Don't tell me they got you two working together again."

"Yeah," said Pacella. "Life was getting a little dull."

"Did you know they assigned us to your case?" Mendez asked.

"No. Who did it?" answered McKenna.

"Roberti."

"Do you mind?" asked Pacella.

"No. Sounds interesting," said Mendez. "We're getting bored locking up the same skells over and over."

Lieutenant Roberti came out of his office. He was the commanding officer of the unit and the detectives' former boss. "C'mon in," he said to them.

McKenna and Pacella followed Roberti into his office and he motioned them to two chairs.

"Welcome back to the Bright Lights, McKenna," Roberti said. "Didn't expect you back so soon."

"I got lucky," McKenna said.

"I heard. The chief and Inspector Tavlin were here already. They set up an office for your operation in Captain O'Connell's office. He's on vacation anyway."

"Who's O'Connell?" asked Pacella.

"He's the district captain," said Roberti. "He's got a big office next door. The chief is raiding everybody for this. I had to give him Mendez and Catalfumo."

"We heard," said Pacella. "They're not too unhappy."

"Yeah, they're good. They both speak Spanish, so the chief is happy too," said Roberti.

"What else is going on?" asked McKenna.

"A lot," answered Roberti. "The Two-five Squad had to assign two detectives, and Inspector Tavlin has a conference scheduled for four o'clock. The chief has gone ballistic on this case and he's got everyone coming to the conference."

"Who?" asked Pacella.

"The commanding officers of the Hostage Negotiating Unit, the Emergency Service Unit, and Joint Terrorist Task Force, and the Two-five Precinct will all be there. And me. You, McKenna, are billed as one of the guest speakers. That enough for you?"

"Too much, I think," answered McKenna. "Anything else I should know?"

"Yeah, one more important thing. Inspector Tavlin asked me about your stability. I think your reputation has him worried. I told him that you could always be counted on to do the right thing, even in the wrong situation. This didn't make him much happier, so be careful. Keep your mouth shut, play by the book, and stay out of trouble." Roberti then turned to Pacella and said, "Keep your eyes on him, Tommy. Try to slow him down a bit and keep a copy of the *Detective Guide* under your seat. When he starts to speed up, sit him down and force feed him a chapter."

Pacella answered, "He'll be fine."

"OK," said Roberti. "But remember what I said. I'm sure Inspector Tavlin wants to talk to the both of you, so you better get next door."

The three men rose and shook hands. When the two detectives were at Roberti's door, he said to them, "If it's any consolation, I think that you two working together probably make the best detective team in the department. You're both welcome back here anytime. Just don't screw this one up. See you at the conference."

The two detectives left the office, said good-bye to Mendez and Catalfumo, and walked down the hall to Captain O'Connell's office.

It was a large office consisting of two rooms, and McKenna and Pacella were both surprised at the high level of activity there. There were five desks in the outer office with a four-line telephone and a typewriter on each desk. A copy machine, a computer, and a fax machine crowded a long table against the wall. Six detectives were working in the room, and McKenna knew two of them, Detectives

Eddie Morgan and Caesar Gonzalez from the Two-five Squad. The other four worked with Pacella in the Major Case Squad. Pacella already knew Morgan and Gonzalez, and he introduced McKenna to Detectives Joe Sophia, Adam Saaks, Ernest Ford, and Sara Walden from the Major Case Squad.

"The inspector's waiting to see you two," Joe Sophia said.

"In a minute," answered Pacella. "Which one of these desks is ours?"

Sophia pointed to an empty desk in the corner of the room. McKenna placed the Brooks Brothers shirt in a drawer of the desk and then asked Pacella, "Ready?"

"Sure," answered Pacella while adjusting his tie.

McKenna and Pacella went to the inner office and knocked on the door. Inspector Steven Tavlin opened it and told them to come in. He was tall, thin, about fifty years old with thinning hair, and dressed like a banker. Already in the room was Sergeant Barry Goldblatt from the Major Case Squad, whom both detectives knew. The office was large and, besides a desk, there was a small conference table with eight chairs in the center of the room. Tavlin motioned McKenna and Pacella to the table and the four men sat down. McKenna thought to himself that he hadn't sat at so many tables listening to so many lectures in one day since he was changing classes every period in high school. He set his mind for another lesson.

Tavlin started by saying, "It seems you two have done well so far today. If the information from Doctor Stienner and Brooks Brothers comes through, we'll be in good shape. Keep after them. After we get more information on exactly who Rodrigo Guiterrez is, and who the guy in the morgue is, I'll have plenty of work for you two to do. When do you expect to hear from the doctor and the manager?"

"Sometime today, sir," McKenna answered.

"Let's hope so," continued Tavlin. "Meanwhile, we've been busy here. The chief thinks you're right. The victim is being held somewhere in Manhattan, probably Spanish Harlem, and we're operating under that assumption. We're also assuming that Rico took a gypsy cab from here to Brooklyn."

"Suppose he took a yellow cab?" asked Goldblatt.

"Yellow cabs just don't operate in this neighborhood," said Tavlin. "There's not enough money up here and there's too much of a chance that they'd get robbed. They avoid this neighborhood. Rico must've took an unlicensed gypsy cab to Brooklyn or used one of the marginally licensed car services."

"So we've got to find the driver who picked him up yesterday and took him to Brooklyn. And find out where he picked him up," said McKenna.

"It's not gonna be easy," said Tavlin. "I've got two men checking with the gypsy cab companies that operate in this neighborhood. According to the records of the Taxi and Limousine Commission, there are twenty-one cab companies in the Spanish Harlem and Washington Heights area. That's twenty-one licensed companies. I figure there's at least twice that many smaller, unlicensed companies, which leaves us sixty cab companies to check, if we can even find them all."

"Big job," said Pacella. "How many they get to so far?"

"Ten. It's taking too long. The dispatchers had to go through all their records for yesterday and search for Brooklyn destinations. Main problem is that their records are incomplete. Lots of times the drivers pick up fares on the street and only call the dispatcher if they need a price to a destination. The drivers don't necessarily turn their trip tickets in every day, only when they go by the office to turn in money. Naturally, they don't like turning in the money, so the drivers have to be called into the office so we can look at their trip tickets and interview them."

"So you need more men," McKenna said.

"Lots more," Tavlin answered. "The way we're going, we'll find the cab driver eventually, but 'eventually' will probably be too late for Rodrigo Guiterrez, which means that this'll be a murder investigation instead of a kidnapping investigation. So I talked to the chief and he arranged that all available Spanish-speaking detectives working in the city tonight would be reporting to the Two-five. I'm hoping to get about twenty men. I understand, McKenna, that you speak Spanish?"

"Yeah, I learned," answered McKenna.

"Tell me," asked Tavlin, "Where does a guy with a name like McKenna learn to speak Spanish?"

"Back in 1973, before the Job started hiring so many Hispanics, they sent a couple of hundred people to a private school. It was thirteen weeks, eight hours a day. I've been practicing ever since with our local *señoritas.*"

McKenna wanted to change the subject, so he said, "I think that twenty men should be enough for tonight."

"I hope so," said Tavlin. "Sergeant Goldblatt will run that part of the investigation, but I've also requested available sergeants and lieutenants from the chief to help out. The extra help should start arriving here at about five o'clock. I want that cab driver found by midnight."

"If we do, we need better photos of Rico for positive identification by the cab driver," said Pacella.

"I've already thought of that," said Tavlin. "In the Crime Scene Unit photos he looks too dead and his clothes are a bloody mess. Right now there's a team from the Photo Section at the morgue. They're going to dress Rico up and give his face a 'Maybelline Makeover.' We'll have these pictures sometime tonight. How's that?"

"Good," said Pacella. Both McKenna and Pacella knew that the things Tavlin described could probably be done by a professional undertaker, but the two detectives had just seen the cut-up body of Rico lying on a morgue autopsy table three hours before. It was going to be a very tough job to make him look alive and healthy, but they didn't tell Tavlin what they thought of his idea. Both men had been around long enough to know that the best policy for a detective in the police department was, "Inspector's ideas are always good ideas."

"Next," continued Tavlin, "I've sent Rogan and Gilroy from the Major Case Squad to Boston to speak to the editors of the *Boston Globe.* They left at eleven o'clock, so I should be hearing from them by six o'clock tonight. They're going to show them the picture that we have of Rodrigo Guiterrez holding their newspaper. Then they're going to bring back some copies of yesterday's editions of the *Boston Globe,* including the out-of-town editions, and they're going to find out for sure if the newspaper that Rodrigo is holding in the picture is an out-of-town edition."

"Isn't involving a newspaper, even a reputable one like the *Boston Globe,* a little dangerous?" asked Pacella. "All they have to do is print what we know and Rodrigo Guiterrez becomes a corpse. It'll be very hard for them to resist making an exclusive story of this case."

"I thought of that," said Tavlin. "That's why I sent Rogan. He sells used cars part time and he could even sell snow to the Eskimos. He's been told to sell the editors on the extreme sensitivity of this case and the danger that any publicity generated by them will probably result in the death of the victim. In return for their cooperation, Rogan has been authorized by the chief to offer the *Boston Globe* 'special consideration' by the department when this case goes public. This is a big case and I think it'll work on them."

"That'll also make the local papers scream bloody murder," said Pacella.

"We'll have to live with that. We need this information from the *Boston Globe* and we have no other choice. We're just going to have to explain the difficulty of our position to the local papers when all this is over and hope they understand."

"That's a lot to hope for," said Pacella.

"Unfortunately, we're going to make the press even less sympathetic than usual. We have to pull a scam on them and they're not going to like it when this is over. We're going to plant a false story in the New York papers to make the kidnappers think that Rico got rid of the victim's finger and ring before you killed him, Brian. We want the kidnappers to think that the New York Police suspect noth-

120

ing about a kidnapping. Otherwise, they might get nervous and either move the hostage or kill him. So tonight we're going to arrange for a 'homeless' person to find the finger in the pink case somewhere in the Ebbets Field Houses. And we're going to make sure that this 'find' gets a lot of publicity as a human-interest story. What do you think?"

"If the 'homeless person' is Reggie Boyd, then it has to work," Pacella said.

McKenna agreed. Detective Reggie Boyd fit the bill for this mission exactly. He always looked like a bum and he was a born actor. He had spent ten years in the Street Crime Unit as a decoy officer. There his mission was to get robbed so his partners could arrest the robbers, and he was good at it. He loved his reputation as the most frequently victimized person on the planet and he'd love to ham it up for the cameras as the bum who found the finger.

Tavlin agreed. "I'm going to have Reggie get dressed up, or dressed down, whatever. Then I'm going to give him the ring and send him to the morgue to pick up the finger. I'll set it up with O'Shaughnessy. I want Reggie to be on the evening news tonight with the finger. That should keep the kidnappers guessing."

"What about the pictures of Rodrigo holding the newspaper?" McKenna asked. "How are we going to get around that?"

"Maybe we can have somebody else find the pictures tomorrow," Pacella said sarcastically.

Tavlin ignored Pacella's pessimism. He said, "Can't do anything. They'll just assume that Rico got rid of the pictures and somebody threw them away."

Tavlin turned to McKenna. "You've been right on everything else so far, and I just hope that you're right on the most important thing. I hope Rodrigo's being held close to where we're sitting, and that we can find him before Rico's pals kill him and get out of town. Can you think of anything else we should be doing?"

"Nope. You've got all the bases covered so far, Inspector. All we can do is wait. I'm sure that Brooks Brothers is going to tell us everything they know about Rodrigo, and I hope that Dr. Stienner will be able to give us something on Rico. If this is an international case, and everything we've learned so far points in that direction, we're gonna have to get more cooperation than we've been getting from the FBI."

"That's already being taken care of. John Weatherby from their Brooklyn office is meeting the chief at his office downtown at four o'clock. The chief had already scheduled a conference here on this case at four o'clock, but the FBI meeting seemed more important, so he's going to meet with Weatherby instead. I'm going to run the conference here with your help, McKenna. The chief is really hot on this case and he's assembling a lot of talent and equipment here."

There was a knock at the door. Joe Sophia came in and said to Tavlin, "There's a Mr. Bremmen here to see McKenna."

Tavlin turned to McKenna and asked, "Who's he?"

"The salesman from Brooks Brothers who handles Rodrigo Guiterrez's account."

"Good. Go find out what he has to say and let me know. I'll see you two later."

McKenna and Pacella got up, leaving Tavlin and Goldblatt to go over their notes and plan for the conference. Seated next to an empty desk outside, looking as comfortable as if he owned the place, was Mark Bremmen. Dressed in a tan poplin suit, blue shirt, red tie, and brown penny loafers, Bremmen looked about thirty-five years old with an athletic build. His hair was blond and cut short. His legs were crossed and an expensive brown leather briefcase lay across his knees. He could have been a mannequin in the window at Brooks Brothers, even down to his brown horned-rimmed glasses.

Bremmen stood up as McKenna and Pacella approached. "Detective McKenna? It's a pleasure to meet you."

McKenna shook Bremmen's hand and introduced him to Pacella. McKenna sat in the chair behind the desk while Pacella took a chair from another desk. Bremmen remained standing until McKenna asked him to sit down. Bremmen made himself comfortable and placed his briefcase on the desk. McKenna got the impression that he was seated at Bremmen's desk in Bremmen's office. McKenna opened the top desk drawer, found a pad, and handed it to Pacella, who took a pen from his pocket and prepared to take notes.

"Mr. Bremmen, I hope you've got the information we requested," said McKenna.

Bremmen's composure didn't change at all. "Detective McKenna, I've been instructed by the management of Brooks Brothers to cooperate fully in your investigation and to place all records in our possession at your disposal. I've also been instructed to tell you that, even though it's against your wishes, the management feels compelled to notify the Guiterrez family that we are divulging this information to you. However, this notification to the Guiterrez family will be in the form of a letter to their residence in Peru that will be posted at the close of business tomorrow. We estimate that the letter will reach them in about two weeks. The management hopes that you will appreciate their position and that this arrangement will be satisfactory to you."

"That's fair enough," answered McKenna. He knew that there was an attorney's hand somewhere in this arrangement and he thought it was a very clever way for Brooks Brothers to keep both the Guiterrez family and the police happy. Two weeks was certainly enough time, considering that the police department probably wouldn't be able to keep this case out of the newspapers for much longer. "Now, who exactly is Rodrigo Guiterrez?" he asked Bremmen.

"Rodrigo Oxcalo Guiterrez is the second son of Hernan Oxcalo Guiterrez. The senior Mr. Guiterrez is a man of wealth and power in Peru. They're an old aristocratic family, and I believe that they trace their lineage in Peru directly to the conquistadors in the fifteen hundreds. The family has always been involved in politics and dip-lomatic efforts of their country. In New York, they used to maintain an apartment on Fifth Avenue, where they lived while the senior Mr. Guiterrez represented Peru as a diplomat at the United Nations. They sold the apartment in 1985 when Hernan Guiterrez took a seat on the Peruvian version of the Supreme Court, and he hasn't visited Brooks Brothers in a couple of years. Members of the family have traditionally been extensively educated in the United States, generally at Harvard. I know that when they stay in New York now, they generally stay at the Harvard Club at 27 West 44th Street. The family's account with Brooks Brothers dates back to 1923 and they've been good customers. Rodrigo's older brother, Hernando, is a senior official in the Peruvian army and I believe that he must be a general by now. Rodrigo was last in the store in March, when he selected a number of apparel items for himself and other members of his family. Brooks Brothers forwarded some of these items to the family residence in Peru, and we forwarded other items designated by Mr. Guiterrez for his immediate personal use to his address in Cambridge, Massachusetts."

Bremmen paused and waited while the two detectives digested the implications of the information that he had just given them. Pacella gave McKenna the notes he had made on the pad and McKenna read them. He made a few notes of his own on the pad and read the notes again. After a few moments, he looked up from the note pad and asked Bremmen, "Do you know why Rodrigo was living in Massachusetts?"

"He told me in March that he was either attending or instructing at the John F. Kennedy School of International Relations at Harvard. I don't remember which it was."

"Is he married?" asked Pacella.

"I don't believe so."

"Do you have the other information that I asked for?" asked McKenna.

"Please be more specific, Detective McKenna."

"I asked Mr. Schmidt to provide us with Rodrigo's present address in the United States, his address in Peru, any telephone numbers relating to him that you might have, his credit card numbers, and the amounts and dates of his purchases."

"Yes, I have all that information," answered Bremmen. He opened his briefcase and withdrew three files marked HERNAN OXCALO GUITERREZ, HERNANDO OXCALO GUITERREZ, and RODRIGO OXCALO GUITERREZ. He opened Rodrigo's file, took out a completed Brooks Brothers customer information profile, and handed it to McKenna. The form was obviously a printout from a computer file and, after glancing at the form, McKenna thought that it was possible that the Brooks Brothers file contained almost as much information on Rodrigo Guiterrez as a police department personnel file might contain on a new rookie coming onto the job. Then he remembered that Brooks Brothers must have a similar file on himself, and the thought made him uneasy.

The file contained all the information that McKenna had requested and much more. It gave Rodrigo's date of birth as March 21, 1957, along with two addresses for Rodrigo, one in Lima, Peru, the other in Cambridge, Massachusetts, and telephone numbers for each address. Rodrigo's size for any particular item of clothing that Brooks Brothers sold was listed and McKenna found that Victor was right on Rodrigo's shirt size, a sixteen collar with a thirty-three-inch sleeve length. A box near the top of the form captioned "credit limit" was filled in with the letter *D*.

"What does *D* mean under credit limit?" McKenna asked Bremmen.

"It signifies 'discretionary,' which translates roughly into 'no limit' in the case of customers such as the Guiterrez family who have been established Brooks Brothers customers as long as they have. It also means that there has never been a problem in prompt payments over the years."

McKenna continued reading the form and noted that there were credit card numbers for American Express and Diners Club, along with expiration dates. "Does he charge items on American Express when he buys anything at Brooks Brothers?"

"No, Detective McKenna. Items that customers such as the Guiterrez family might care to charge would be charged directly to their account."

McKenna found a box captioned "Update," filled in with "03-18-92." McKenna asked Bremmen, "Why was this form updated in March?"

"That was the last time that Mr. Guiterrez came into the store. As I told you, he made some purchases at that time for himself and for his father. Mr. Guiterrez selected some shirts, ties, and belts for himself, which he took with him. He also purchased two suits, which required some alterations, so we sent the suits to the address that he provided for us in Massachusetts when the alterations were com-

124

pleted. It was a new address, so his customer profile was updated at that time."

"Do you have a complete list of the items that he purchased at that time? I'm especially interested in whether or not he purchased a Pima Oxford buttton-down shirt the last time he was in the store."

"You have the list of that purchase in the file," answered Bremmen. "May I see it?"

McKenna shoved the file back across the desk to Bremmen, who went through it and extracted the sales record of Rodrigo's last purchase. He examined it and said, "He purchased nine Pima Oxfords. Five in white and four in blue. I see that there is a size discrepancy on two of these shirts. They are size seventeen and a half neck and thirty-five-inch sleeve. I recall now that he bought those two shirts for his bodyguard."

"Bodyguard?" McKenna and Pacella asked in unison.

"Well, I'm just assuming that he was a bodyguard. He was with Mr. Guiterrez and he appeared to be wearing a gun in a holster on his belt under his jacket."

"How do you know he had a gun under his jacket? Did you see it?" asked Pacella.

"No, Detective Pacella. I didn't have to see it to know that it was there. I am in the business of measuring men for good suits and when I first saw Mr. Guiterrez's companion, I looked him over closely because I assumed that he would be purchasing some suits and I wanted to get his size right as soon as possible. That was when I noticed that he appeared to be wearing a gun under his jacket and thought that he probably was an employee of Mr. Guiterrez, not a customer. My second impression of him was that he was some kind of a policeman."

"Why a policeman?" asked McKenna.

"Because he wasn't properly dressed. Detective McKenna, I hope that you'll excuse me for saying this but, with the exception of yourself and Detective Pacella, he was dressed like most of the men who surround us in this room. He just looked like a policeman."

McKenna glanced around and was forced to agree that there didn't appear to be any fashion plates among them. He thought this over for moment and asked, "Was this the first time that Rodrigo was in the store with a bodyguard?"

"To the best of my knowledge, yes."

"And how did Rodrigo treat his bodyguard?" asked Pacella.

"The same way that he treats everyone else. Rather imperiously, like he was an employee."

"Are you telling us that Rodrigo Guiterrez isn't exactly a nice guy?" asked Pacella.

"He's a good customer."

"This is just between us, Mr. Bremmen," said McKenna. "We'd just like some insight into the guy whose life we're trying to save."

Bremmen answered in his same conversational tone, "He's a first-class scumbag."

Pacella dropped his pen and looked up from his notes. He laughed and said to Bremmen, "Thanks for that news. You've reinforced the Pacella view of the world. I didn't expect that anyone as rich as Rodrigo would be a nice guy. But I didn't expect to hear it from you, Mr. Bremmen. This is like the Pope telling me that Mother Theresa is really a Tenth Avenue hooker."

"Let's get back to the bodyguard," said McKenna. "Could you describe him for us?"

"He was a large man. About six feet two, maybe two hundred and twenty pounds. He had black hair and a rather angular face. He spoke English with a slight Spanish accent. I'd be able to recognize him if I saw him again."

McKenna thanked Bremmen for his cooperation and shook his hand, and Pacella walked him to the door of the office. Pacella returned to the desk where both detectives went over the Brooks Brothers files.

"Whatta ya think about the bodyguard?" McKenna asked Pacella.

"Rodrigo must've known something was up. He never had one before."

"Where do you think he is?"

"Either dead or a prisoner, unless he's in on it," said Pacella.

All of the other detectives assigned to the case, with the exceptions of Joe Sophia and Ernest Ford, had left the Squad office to begin interviewing taxi drivers and cab-company dispatchers. Sophia and Ford were left to man the phones and maintain a log book on the investigation. The phones rang constantly as the detectives already assigned to the investigation reported their locations and their lack of progress in finding the taxi driver who had picked up Rico in Manhattan yesterday and driven him to Brooklyn. There were at least ten calls from squad commanders in detective squads all over the city who wanted to know what was going on in the Two-five, and why they were being stripped of men in the middle of July, the busiest time of year.

Sophia's and Ford's answer to these inquiries was always the same. "I can't tell you now, sir, but that's what Chief Brunette wants."

To the squad commanders, this simple answer was enough to end the conversation. In the New York City Police Department, one doesn't remain a squad commander for long by questioning the wisdom of the chief of detectives.

126

Then Joe Sophia called over, "McKenna! Doctor Lee from the morgue for you on line two."

McKenna picked up. "Thanks for getting back to me so soon, Doctor Lee. What'd you find out?"

"I showed the close-up photo of the man to a friend of mine, Doctor Crane from Bellevue Hospital. He agrees that the finger was surgically removed about three days before the photo was taken. He said that the wound from this operation was closed with an old stitching technique. Today we use staples, not stitches like that. Whoever closed that wound hasn't received recent medical training in the United States."

"Thanks, Doctor. Did Doctor Stienner get anything on Rico's identity?"

"He's come up with some possibilities. He went to see some of his former associates at Amnesty International to learn more. He said he'd call you later."

McKenna gave Dr. Lee his home telephone number and asked him to have Dr. Stienner call him at home or at the Two-five as soon as he could. Then he said, "Anything else?"

"Nothing, except that some other detectives were here. They dressed up Rico's body and took a lot of pictures of the corpse. They left about an hour ago."

McKenna thanked Dr. Lee for his help, then went into Tavlin's office and informed him of what he and Pacella had found out from Bremmen and Dr. Lee.

After McKenna filled in Tavlin, he and Pacella went about the routine tasks of documenting their existence. The Complaint Follow-Up, known as a DD 5, was the form used by the Detective Bureau to document investigative work performed during an investigation. Procedurally, every interview of a witness, every discovery of evidence, every lineup conducted, every request from the Identification or Photo sections for the criminal history or photos of a suspect, and the circumstances surrounding almost every arrest by the Detective Bureau needed to be documented on a DD 5 by the detective performing that particular aspect of the investigation. These DD 5s would then be reviewed and signed by a detective supervisor and kept on file in the case folder.

The DD 5s in a case are frequently admitted as evidence in court and are used by both the prosecutor and the defense attorney to follow the progress of an investigation as it leads to the arrest of the suspect. The prosecutor would use the DD 5 to prove that the police were legally and procedurally correct in their investigation that produced the arrest of the defendant. The defense attorney would use the DD 5s to discover potential witnesses and to discover any legal or procedural defects in the police investigation that could lead to the suppression of evidence or to the dismissal of the charges against his client.

Both McKenna and Pacella had been detectives for so long that they could quickly bang out DD 5s while simultaneously eating lunch, watching TV, and participating in a high-stakes card game. They followed the Simple Detective's Rule Number One, "Fill in the boxes on top and keep the story short and simple." If you don't type it in on a DD 5, it can't be a mistake and you can fill in the jury while testifying on the stand.

"Which ones you wanna do, kid?" Pacella asked.

"I'll do the interviews of the doctors and the Brooks Brothers visit. You can do Bremmen and the voucher on the shirt. How's that?"

"It's your case. Just point me in the right direction."

McKenna and Pacella were in the process of completing their paperwork when an old friend, Detective Roquefort from the Photo Section, came in with the photos of Rico that had been taken at the morgue.

"Howya doing, Cheese," McKenna said.

"Fine. Got your work here," Roquefort said, handing the photos to McKenna.

While McKenna looked at the photos, Pacella leaned over his shoulder. They were surprised at how well the detectives from the Photo Section had done.

The photos were eighty-by-tens, fifty copies total, and they showed Rico sitting on a chair in clothes that were almost identical to what he was wearing when he was killed. He looked a little sick, but very alive. There were front and profile photos of him smiling, laughing, and looking straight ahead. He might have been someone sitting on the subway.

"You guys did a great job on this one," said McKenna. "He looks really nice. You should all be working for Walter B. Cook at one of his funeral homes."

Roquefort appreciated the compliment. "We did our best. We used mannequin braces from a clothing store to keep him propped up. Then we had to use a lot of makeup and some pretty unusual lighting. We even had to glue a wig to the top of his head, right over his brains, because after the autopsy the top of his head kept falling off. After a while, we got a little crazy at the morgue, so we decided to make up a couple of wallets for your scrapbook."

Roquefort then took a smaller photo from his pocket and gave it to McKenna. It showed Rico seated with his right arm extended. The middle finger of the right hand was raised in a customary greeting of salutation and written in ink at the bottom of this photo was *Fuck you, McKenna.*

McKenna laughed and put the photo in his pocket. "You're sicker than ever, Cheese."

He took six of the eight-by-ten photos of Rico and handed the rest back to Roquefort. "You'd better give these to Inspector Tavlin. I'm sure they'll make him happy," said McKenna.

By this time it was three forty-five and Sergeant Goldblatt came out of Tavlin's office with a large stack of papers. He gave Pacella the stack and said, "The conference is gonna be downstairs in the Sitting Room. There's not enough room up here. Go downstairs and make sure that everyone coming to the conference knows where it is and give them each a copy of these reports. And get ready to shine, McKenna."

12

McKenna and Pacella went downstairs and stood on the front steps of the station house, looking over the reports that Goldblatt had given them to distribute. Each packet contained a map of the 25th Precinct, O'Shaughnessy's report on the shooting, a list of telephone numbers for the task force assembled at the Two-five, and copies of the photos of Rodrigo holding the *Boston Globe.*

The Bosses began arriving at ten to four. Lieutenant Crosby from the Technical Assistance Response Unit (TARU), Lieutenant Hargrove from the Hostage Negotiating Team, and Captain Flynn from the Legal Bureau all came in the same car. Next came Captain Sheeran, who greeted McKenna warmly, shook his hand, and said, "Congratulations. I'm beginning to think that either you have ESP or that you're in with the kidnappers. I've always suspected you of being some kind of terrorist."

"Who, me? What do you mean, Captain?"

"Just going to have to pay close attention at the conference. Wanna go in?"

McKenna accepted Sheeran's suggestion and with Pacella they went back through the station house toward the Sitting Room.

The large rear room on the first floor of every station house in the city is the Sitting Room, where the outgoing police platoon receives its assignments and instructions by the patrol sergeant before going on patrol. The walls of the Sitting Room were crowded with bulletin boards bearing WANTED posters, descriptions of persons and vehicles wanted in connection with crimes committed in the precinct, orders from the commanding officer, positions available in other precincts and units, flyers detailing upcoming social events, and letters from the various police unions.

McKenna saw that Captain Delaney, the commanding officer of the Two-five, was there. Delaney had fulfilled his responsibility for the hospitality of the conference by having a coffeepot set up in the back of the room.

Sheeran, Pacella, and McKenna went over to the pot and talked about the case while they waited for the other Bosses to arrive.

Roberti came down from his office and joined in the discussion. Pacella had given everyone a packet of reports, but they were already familiar with the contents and used them to mark their chairs in the room.

Captain Keller of the Emergency Service Unit made his entrance. He was the only one in uniform, wearing medals over his shield that reached past the top of his shoulder. The impression he created was that John Wayne had wasted his whole life in a futile attempt to look just like Captain Keller.

The last to arrive were Lieutenant Wrynn of the Joint Terrorist Task Force and Captain Schaeffer from the Motor Transport Division.

Inspector Tavlin was nowhere in sight and everyone present continued talking, clustered in small groups of three or four. Finally, at four thirty Tavlin and Sergeant Goldblatt came down. Tavlin stood at the lectern and was generally ignored for a few moments until he said, "Gentlemen, please take your seats. I just got off the phone with Chief Brunette and I've been directed by him to chair this conference in his place. We've got a lot to go over, so let's begin."

McKenna thought he saw a number of knees begin to bend in genuflection at the mention of the chief of detective's name. All conversation stopped as everyone except Captain Delaney took their seats. The Two-five commanding officer closed the doors of the Sitting Room and yelled an order to the desk officer to permit no one to enter the room. Delaney then took a seat in the front of the room.

Tavlin began the conference. "The chief has us gathered here today to discuss a unique kidnapping case which has the potential to generate a lot of credit or embarrassment to the department and especially to the Detective Bureau, depending on how we handle the case. We have reason to believe that a Peruvian national of some political influence has been kidnapped in the Boston area and is being held in New York City until the kidnappers' demands are met by the victim's family or by the Peruvian government. We think that the

131

victim is being held very close to where we are meeting right now. There's a strong possibility that the kidnappers are part of a terrorist organization."

Tavlin paused for effect. The word *terrorist* caused the assembled Bosses to lean forward in their seats. He continued, "This group has already shown itself to be well armed and resourceful. Its members are dedicated and ruthless. As I'm sure you all realize, unlike the rest of the world, this country has not suffered through any successful terrorist attacks, with the exception of the Puerto Ricans from the FALN, which our government considered an internal matter. What I'm talking about in the case of this present kidnapping is foreign terrorists using the territory of the United States of America as their area of operations. Now we can't do too much about anything that these people might do in the rest of the country, but they're in New York City right now holding a hostage. The chief is determined that, if terrorists ever do operate successfully in this country, New York City will not be the place they get their start. He asked me to particularly emphasize to you exactly how he feels about this case and to instruct you that the full resources of this department are to be directed toward the successful conclusion of this case. Are there any questions on this?"

Lieutenant Wrynn of the Joint Terrorist Task Force, the unit that works closely with the FBI and which normally should have been given the assignment of this case, stood up. "What's been the involvement of the Feds in this case? This sounds like something that they'd be in charge of. What you've told us about this case so far has all been news to me, and that's not the way it's supposed to work."

Tavlin answered, "We have not, as yet, received any cooperation or assistance from the federal authorities in this case. Lieutenant Wrynn, since you're already personally acquainted with so many federal agents, you'll be in charge of coordinating the assistance of the federal authorities. You're to report to me what they uncover in this investigation without waiting to go through normal channels. Understand?"

"Sure," answered Lieutenant Wrynn. "I'm assigned as the chief's spy."

"That's right. I'm gonna turn the lecturn over to Detective McKenna, who's responsible for initiating this case. Detective McKenna was assigned to the Seven-one Squad in Brooklyn, but now he's with the Major Case Squad. He'll explain how this case came about and he'll fill you in on the progress we've made so far in Manhattan. After Detective McKenna is done, Captain Sheeran of the 11th Detective District in Brooklyn will address you. The chief placed him in charge of the Brooklyn end of this investigation. Captain Sheeran will tell you about the progress he's made so far. I'll conclude by telling you exactly what the chief expects from each of your units in the way of assistance. Then I'll open up the conference for suggestions and discussion. Sergeant Goldblatt of the Major Case Squad will take notes on this discussion and your suggestions for inclusion in my report to the chief."

As Tavlin motioned for McKenna to take his place at the lectern, McKenna suppressed a sudden and almost overwhelming urge to pee in his pants. He cleared his throat, put a smile on his face, and walked to the lectern. As he started to relate the events of the day before in Brooklyn, he saw that many of the Bosses were following his narrative by reading the Unusual Occurrence Report.

McKenna told them of his encounter with Rico, of Rico's refusal to surrender, and of the large amounts of currency, weapons, and drugs recovered from the apartment in the Ebbets Field Houses. Then came the criminal records of Francisco Torres and Jorge Chavez. He explained why he believed that the kidnap victim was being held in New York, and concluded by detailing what he had learned so far on the identity of Rico and the victim, Rodrigo Oxcalo Guiterrez.

By the time he was finished, McKenna had a real case of cotton-mouth; he felt like he had just run five miles along the equator. He had spoken for about half an hour and he was glad that his part in the conference was over. McKenna left the lectern and took a seat in the back of the room next to Pacella, as Sheeran took his place with a cup of coffee in one hand and a pile of notes in the other.

Sheeran began, "We know that Rico was on his way to the Intercontinental Hotel in Kennedy Airport when he felt the urge to relieve himself and was subsequently killed by Detective McKenna. Rico was carrying Rodrigo's ring finger and photo when he was killed. We can safely assume that he was on his way to deliver these things to a confederate for delivery to Peru or to a member of Rodrigo's family who was staying at the hotel. Rico wasn't going to Peru himself because he didn't have a passport or luggage with him. We checked the Intercontinental Hotel and found that no one named Guiterrez was registered there, so we proceeded under the assumption that the finger and photos were being delivered to a confederate at the Intercontinental Hotel, who would then hide these items on his body and deliver them to Rodrigo's family in Peru. He would have to hide them on his body just like Rico did, because he would have to sneak them through customs in Peru. He couldn't put the finger on ice in his luggage. And he had to get the finger to Peru before it began to stink. So he must've planned to leave either last night or this morning at the latest. When Rico failed to show up at the hotel yesterday, we

133

figured that the contact must've gotten pretty nervous, but thought that he would stay put and await further instructions."

Sheeran turned a page in his notes and finished his coffee. Tavlin yelled over to Pacella, "Do me a favor and get Captain Sheeran another cup of coffee."

Rank sure has its privileges, McKenna thought. Five minutes ago I was drying up like spit on the sidewalk and nobody seemed to notice, but when a captain looks a little thirsty, the call goes out for Gunga Din.

Sheeran went on. "We checked with all the airlines that fly to Peru from Kennedy Airport. After some difficulty, we obtained a list of persons who had made reservations for flights to Lima yesterday and today who did not board that flight. That covered six airlines, two days. There were ninety-three people on the list. Then we matched this list against the guest list at the Intercontinental Hotel, and I think found our man. There was a Flavio Asturo who was booked to fly to Lima, Peru, on Lan Chile flight number 141, which left JFK yesterday at 6:05 P.M. Flavio registered in the Intercontinental Hotel the day before yesterday. He was booked into room 639 and he's still registered there. However, we have learned from the maid that he has not been in his room since last night. The bed hasn't been slept in, but his luggage is still in the room. I've got three men at the Intercontinental Hotel right now. They're waiting for Flavio to return to the hotel so we can identify him. We don't have enough to arrest him, we're just interested in seeing where he goes and who he talks to. I'm also in the process of trying to arrange that female detectives who know how to make a bed take over the housekeeping duties on Flavio's floor, but so far I haven't been successful in finding suitable people or in convincing the management at the Intercontinental Hotel that this'd be a good idea. Having our people on the floor would come in handy when it's time to search Flavio's room, and I don't want Flavio speaking with any talkative maids. I requested surveillance equipment so we can really watch Flavio, but I don't have the necessary court orders yet to really set it up."

McKenna, along with everyone else in the room, glanced over at Captain Flynn from the Legal Bureau and Lieutenant Crosby from TARU. Both men looked very uncomfortable. It was the mission of Flynn's unit to draw up the applications for eavesdropping warrants and Crosby's unit was responsible for installing wiretaps and surveillance devices once the warrants had been obtained. Sheeran's brief allusion indicated that their units were fumbling the ball on his requests for court orders and surveillance equipment. McKenna couldn't wait to hear what they had to say.

Pacella brought Sheeran his cup of coffee and resumed his seat next to McKenna. Sheeran took a sip and continued, "Unofficially, my detectives found out that Flavio made a number of telephone calls from his room. They were listed on his bill. Because of the way they got this information, what we know at this point won't be admissible in court, so there won't be a DD 5 on this yet. Once we get the necessary court orders, we'll officially learn what I'm about to tell you."

Sheeran, relishing the moment, played his audience well. Every Boss in the room was straining forward in his seat, waiting for the next word.

McKenna knew that "unofficially" in the police department meant that a procedural violation had occurred in this case and that the violation would be denied by those present right down to their dying breath. Someone's constitutional rights, as interpreted by the Supreme Court or the New York State Court of Appeals, had been stepped on, but this could never be proven. For a captain of detectives to admit to this violation in public emphasized the importance of the time factor in this case, and this emphasis wasn't lost on the other Bosses. But McKenna knew that they had nothing to worry about. Bosses are not called upon to testify. It was the detectives who would do the lying in court, and that was just fine with the Bosses, as long as the detectives were competent liars.

Sheeran took another leisurely sip of coffee and placed his cup down. "Flavio made two telephone calls to Lima yesterday, one at twelve fourteen, and the other at four twenty-one. The calls were to the same number and took a total of thirteen minutes. The important thing is that Flavio made one local call yesterday. It was made at four thirty-three P.M. to a telephone booth located at East 113th Street and Lexington Avenue. That's six blocks from where we're sitting right now. I think that call gives us some reason to think that Detective McKenna was right about the general location of where Rodrigo is being held, especially since it's the second time a pay phone in Spanish Harlem figured in this case."

Sheeran looked directly at McKenna, smiled, and gave him a thumbs-up sign. Everyone in the room followed Sheeran's gaze to McKenna. I guess there's some hope for me in this job after all, McKenna thought. How am I going to make best use of my moment in the sun? He considered standing up to take a bow, rejected that idea, and finally said to Sheeran as everyone watched him, "Thank you, Captain. I'm always trying to do a first-grade job, sir. And having some good luck didn't hurt."

Unfortunately for McKenna, all the Bosses in the room seemed to agree with him about his luck. They missed the implication that McKenna was a Second-Grade detective doing a first-grade job.

Pacella leaned over and whispered, "Look's like it's not your time yet, kid. You're the main reason that everyone's here, and this doesn't look like an especially happy group to me."

Sheeran resumed, "This information is also unofficial. Flavio gave the Intercontinental Hotel an American Express credit card so that he could make long-distance calls and charge them to his room. The card is under his name and is a business credit card. The business is *Laxthaca Importadors y Exportadors, S.A.* and they have a Lima billing address. We're waiting for a court order to be served on American Express to obtain information on where Flavio's been lately and I think that this information will be very enlightening. I've had Flavio Asturo and *Laxthaca Importadors y Exportadors* checked through the Narcotics Division, and they have no record of any past or present investigations on them."

Sheeran took another sip of coffee and turned to the next page in his notes. "Next we come to our efforts in Brooklyn to determine who Rico really is. The only thing that we've got to go on is Francisco Torres and Jorge Chavez, the people who were arrested in the apartment yesterday. They're both represented by attorney, so we can't talk to them. Both have long records and we have them good on the narcotics and weapons charges, and we know that they couldn't possibly object to some 'special consideration' from us in their present case, otherwise they're facing a lot of time. Chavez is on parole until 1993. We could ensure that he finish up that time before he even begins serving time on his present charges, which could get him eight years. He's twenty-eight now, so that would make him thirty-eight before he had any possibility to see daylight again by the time we got finished with him. Torres's case is even worse. He's forty-one years old now. He's been convicted of murder and jumped fifty thousand dollars' cash bail while awaiting sentencing. I think that indicates how reluctant Torres is about going to jail. He has to do at least eight years four months on the murder. Now add the eight years he could get on the present charges, and Torres could be fifty-eight years old before he gets out. That has to be the same as 'never' to him. Not to mention the fact that these boys are probably in deep trouble with whoever they work for. They would say that it's not their fault, but they lost three hundred and fifty thousand dollars in cash and two hundred and sixty-six thousand dollars' worth of drugs. If they worked for me, I'd be a little mad at them. Even in jail, the life expectancy of out-of-favor drug dealers isn't spectacular. I talked to the Brooklyn district attorney about cutting a deal for these two. At first he was less than enthusaistic. He's got two easy convictions here and he sees no reason to make a deal with them. So I had to tell him what we've got, and he jumped. He thinks that he should have some input in this case with his District Attorney's Squad, which really means that he thinks that he should be in charge. I know that would certainly rub Chief Brunette the wrong way, so I told him that I'd get back to him."

Everyone in the room smiled at the improbable thought of the Brooklyn DA taking a case away from their chief of detectives. That was about as likely as Lech Walesa declaring that Berlin is the new capital of Poland.

"I know that I was a little out of line," continued Sheeran, "but I called Torres and Chavez's lawyer, Murray Plenhiem. I used to know him fairly well."

Murray "Don't Worry" Plenhiem was a high-priced lawyer whose specialty was defending rich drug dealers. They liked to brag that Murray "Don't Worry" was their lawyer and being represented by him had become something of a status symbol among them. Murray had disturbed McKenna a few times in the past with a display of competence. He was good and his clients got their money's worth. McKenna disliked Murray, but respected him.

Sheeran continued. "I told Murray that we needed information on the man who was killed at the door of apartment 12G, and that we believed that his clients could help us out. I told him that, if his clients could provide us with real information on the identity and business of the dead man, then we were prepared to help his clients as much as we reasonably could. Murray was very glad to hear about our problems. But he's tough. For openers, he suggested that his clients be permitted to plead guilty to reduced charges. He also suggested that, if his clients feel that they are placing themselves in any danger because of the information they may provide to us, they should be transferred to federal custody, serve their time-of-state, and be considered for inclusion in the Federal Witness Protection Program when they finish serving their time. Of course, I couldn't give Murray any answers on my own, but if the chief can't talk any sense into the DA, and if Torres and Chavez won't play ball with us, we might have to go to the Feds for help and drop this whole thing in their lap. Meanwhile, Murray is talking to his clients to see if they have anything useful. That's all I have for now, so I'm giving the floor back to Inspector Tavlin."

Sheeran's stock was soaring as he left the lectern; McKenna could feel it in the room. He was very impressed at the amount and quality of work Sheeran got from his detectives in such a short period of time. Captain Sheeran was going to be invited to a lot of exclusive social events where captains from Brooklyn aren't normally found, and his dance card would always be full.

Inspector Tavlin returned to the lectern. "The chief has given me specific assignments for the members of each unit involved in this conference. I'm not throwing stones at anyone, but he instructed me to tell you that he considers this to be a very important case and that the failure to adequately perform these assignments would be looked upon unfavorably."

You could hear a pin drop in the room. Tavlin had said the "F-word," which in the Detective Bureau is "failure." He didn't say "unsuccessful" or "unsolved," but "failure." The "F-word" conjured up immediate images of captains leaving the bureau, giving up their take-home department autos, and working around the clock in the provinces. To the lieutenants, the "F-word" meant losing their captain's pay and working in uniform at the Precinct Desk of someplace far removed from the Bright Lights. Tavlin had their full attention as they took pens from their pockets and began to write.

"First of all," Tavlin began, "everyone assigned to this case is off the normal working chart. There will be no days off until this case is successfully resolved. Commanding officers are authorized, at their discretion, to grant cash overtime to all members of their command below the rank of captain. Captains will, of course, work overtime in return for nothing but the affection of the chief of detectives. Commanding officers will ensure that my office is kept informed of their locations when they are not actually working."

McKenna heard some almost imperceptible groans at this announcement, but he couldn't tell from which lips these offending noises had emanated. Everyone in the room looked accusingly at the person next to him as the originator of this involuntary expression of disloyalty, so McKenna decided to look at Pacella. He was a little unsettled to find that Pacella was already looking at him. That's why he's a First Grader, McKenna thought. I'm just not fast enough.

Tavlin took a moment to glare at everyone before he continued. "The commanding officer of the Legal Division will ensure that a department attorney is always present at the Two-five to draw up and expedite the processing of applications made by members of this unit for eavesdropping warrants, search warrants, material witness warrants, and court orders for records and information. The Legal Bureau will also supply a competent typist to assist in drawing up these orders. The Legal Bureau will make arrangements through the Bureau of Criminal Justice to ensure that a judge be available twenty-four hours a day to review these applications and grant these warrants and orders. I suggest that the Legal Bureau install a fax machine in the home of whatever judge is assigned in order to save time in the granting of these warrants. As we've just learned, the Legal Bureau already has a full work load with the information that Captain Sheeran has just given us, so I suggest that Captain Flynn get

138

together with Captain Sheeran to get his Brooklyn show on the road, legally speaking."

Captain Flynn was furious and red as a new fire engine as he rose. "In my own defense, until I came to this conference, I didn't know anything about this case except what I read in the Unusual. I even thought that the purpose of this conference was to figure out the best way to finish McKenna off. I see that I was wrong, but everything about this case was a secret until now. I was aware of Captain Sheeran's request for legal assistance, and these requests were being dealt with. Naturally, now that I am informed of the facts of this case and the importance that the chief of detectives correctly attaches to it, my office will expedite every request for legal assistance made by members of this unit."

Nice recovery, thought McKenna. But probably still a dead man. McKenna and many of the others in the room immediately conjured the same mental picture of Flynn chasing ambulances to make his living after his impending retirement.

"Thank you, Captain Flynn," Tavlin said. "Next, TARU will assign all equipment and personnel necessary to complete work on wiretaps authorized in connection with this case. This equipment and personnel will be assigned to the task force at the Two-five station house so that the necessary work can be performed quickly. TARU will provide all equipment necessary for surveillance, including vehicle-location transmitters, binoculars, night-vision devices, and surveillance vans. Once the apartment where Rodrigo is being held is located, TARU will provide and operate all equipment necessary to monitor activities inside that apartment. In addition, TARU will supply twenty-five radios tuned to a secure frequency for use by members of this unit. While I understand that these assignments will stretch the resources of your unit, Lieutenant Crosby, I suggest that Captain Sheeran's needs in Brooklyn on this case also be attended to immediately."

Lieutenant Crosby remained extremely composed during the assignment of these arduous chores to his unit. He merely answered, *"Jawohl, mein Kapitän."* His response set the tone for the remainder of the conference.

"The Hostage Negotiating Team will assign a team to the Two-five station house for possible use when the kidnappers' apartment is located."

"Of course," answered Lieutenant Hargrove.

"The Emergency Service Unit will supply two truck units should it be necessary to forcibly enter the kidnappers' apartment to rescue the hostage."

"No problem," answered Captain Keller.

139

"The Motor Transport Division will supply ten nondescript vehicles for members of the task force. These vehicles are not to look like police department unmarked cars. The Motor Transport Division will also supply a telephone company truck, a Con Edison truck, a postal service truck, and a moving van. This will be done as soon as possible."

"Yes, sir," answered Captain Shaeffer. "I'll have the nondescript vehicles here tonight and I should have everything else by tomorrow."

That's all? thought McKenna. Just "Yes, sir" and "I'll have the rest of the stuff tomorrow"? McKenna could remember waiting years for an old, worn out, unmarked car to be replaced by the Motor Transport Division. But then, he remembered, he wasn't the chief of detectives.

Tavlin wasn't done yet. There were still a few happy people left in the room, so he went back to work. "The commanding officer of the Two-five is responsible that the secrecy of this operation is maintained. He is to ensure that the third floor of this stationhouse will be a restricted access area. A police officer from the Two-five will be assigned to the third floor to challenge the identity of all persons seeking entry. This officer will maintain a log book documenting the arrival and departure of authorized visitors and of all persons assigned to the task force. The commanding officer of the Two-five will also place his Anti-Crime Unit at the disposal of the task force. I suggest that the first place we put under surveillance is that telephone booth at East One-thirteenth Street and Lexington Avenue. Make sure that all persons answering that phone are followed until we can get the proper surveillance equipment and wiretaps in place."

"I understand," said Captain Delaney.

"Captain Delaney, I've been asked to convey to you that the chief of detectives understands that he has no authority over you in these matters and that his requests for your manpower would normally be routed through the Chief of Patrol's office. However, he suggests that there's no reason for you to forward his request through channels."

"I understand completely," said Captain Delaney.

"Lieutenant Roberti, you will make as many members of the Career Criminal Apprehension Unit available as this task force may require to successfully solve this case."

"Sure," said Lieutenant Roberti. He was the commanding officer of the largest detective squad in the Detective Bureau, and he was accustomed to his manpower being used for anything special that came up.

"That's all the assignments that the chief wanted me to make. The floor is now open for discussion and suggestions," said Tavlin.

There was a lengthy and embarrassing silence before Captain Flynn

140

said, "What's to discuss and what's to suggest? We've all been around long enough to know what we have to do. So I suggest that this conference be ended and we get to work."

Maybe there's some hope for you after all, Flynn, thought McKenna.

Tavlin ignored Flynn and said, "Before we go, I have just one more thing to tell you. The lid is on regarding this investigation. That means nothing to the press. The chief feels that any coverage of this investigation by the press would endanger the life of the victim. He ordered me to say that if any part of this investigation finds its way into the papers, he will not rest until he finds the person responsible for the leak. All press releases in this case will go through the Office of the Chief of Detectives, and not through Public Information."

This was a very unusual order, put in a way that couldn't be mistaken. No press leaks meant friends in the press ignored, or worse, avoided. It also meant some free dinners missed, during which they would explain to the press how their unit was instrumental in breaking the case. This order effectively eliminated the competition between units to exploit their parts in the investigation on the front pages.

Inspector Tavlin finally dismissed the conference and returned to his new office. On his way to the stairwell, he noticed with some satisfaction that all of the Bosses had started searching throughout the station house for available telephones so that they could relay the bad news to the subordinates in their units. The sky was falling, the earth was shaking, and nobody was going home for a while.

13

McKenna and Pacella hung around on the ground floor of the station house, amusing themselves by talking to old friends from the Twenty-fifth Precinct, while the Bosses lit up the switchboard. Even Captain Flynn, whose nickname was "Flynnskint," was using the pay phone on the wall.

"That's a new one," Pacella said. "Never saw a captain use a pay phone in a station house."

"Shake, rattle, and dial," answered McKenna.

When they figured that they could avoid it no longer, the two detectives went to their new office on the third floor. A security desk had already been set up, manned by Police Officer Joe Flaherty, the Two-five PBA delegate. He laughed when he saw them and said, "Advance and be recognized. Are you friend or foe?"

Pacella answered, "Hiya, Joe! Well, since you're doing it, this must be the softest job in the station house. Where are the coldies being kept?"

"Fourth-floor locker room, locker number one twenty-nine. There's a refrigerator hooked up and hidden in the locker. The combination's written on the back of the door of the locker room." Flaherty turned to McKenna and said, "Sorry, Brian. No Kaliber yet. I'll give Vinnie a call and have him send some over."

"That's all right," said McKenna. "We'll pass for now and go see Vinnie later. We just want to see what's doing."

142

"Suit yourself. But you have to sign the Sacred Book before entry to the Secret Command Center is permitted."

McKenna and Pacella opened the log book and were surprised to see that they had to sign in on the second page. Twenty-nine detectives and supervisors had already come in during the last half hour. Many of the names were familiar.

The task force office was the scene of controlled bedlam. Just like the chief wanted. Hispanic detectives from all over the city had reported to the office to look for the gypsy cab driver who had taken Rico to Brooklyn for his date with destiny. Making sense out of chaos was Lieutenant Hardcass of the Chief of Detectives Office. He was painfully competent and his disposition sounded like his name.

When McKenna and Pacella entered the office, Hardcass was busy assigning detectives to their tasks. He told them to call in by telephone with the results of each interview, not to use their radios. The press regularly monitored the police frequencies, and the idea was not to give them any indication that there was something unusual happening in the Two-five. Joe Sophia and Ernest Ford still manned the phones and cataloged the results of each interview as they were called in. It took McKenna and Pacella roughly ten seconds to take in the scene and pick up the disgruntled attitude of the detectives who were assigned for the evening.

As soon as he saw McKenna, "Cisco" Sanchez from the 34th Detective Squad left the assignment line and sarcastically said, "Make sure that you don't tell me anything, Brian. Let me tell you, this whole thing sucks. They're giving us assignments on an investigation without telling us what it's all about. What do they think we are? Kids?"

"I'm sorry, Cisco. That wasn't my idea. Not to mention that it's a waste of time. Anyone who calls himself a detective will find out on his own exactly what's going on here in half an hour. I'll talk to the boss about it."

"It's stupid. I'll find out what this is all about by myself, just for my own satisfaction. But this is no way to run an investigation. We'll do our best and get whatever you need, but this no-trust shit ain't right."

McKenna didn't know what else to say. He could see both points of view, but in the end he felt that a bad management decision had been made. If you don't trust your people, don't use them. These detectives were going to spend at least half the night complaining and that much less time working.

Lieutenant Hardcass looked up from his assignment sheet in the crowded room, saw McKenna, and yelled over to him, "Where've you been? The inspector wants to talk to you."

That's just great, thought McKenna. McKenna left Pacella to listen to Cisco's bellyaches. He want to Tavlin's door, knocked, and entered. Tavlin was on the phone and he motioned McKenna to a seat in front of his desk. McKenna waited while Tavlin read the Riot Act to some foolish squad commander who had tried to get out of sending a detective to tonight's assignment in the Two-five. The conversation ended with Tavlin saying, "I'd better see one genuine Spanish-speaking detective from the Seven-two Squad in my office in less than an hour." Tavlin slammed down the phone and took a moment to compose himself after he sat down. He adjusted the placement of papers on his desk while he thought. Finally he said, "Brian, I need a little favor."

McKenna was beginning to feel like the seat of his chair was upholstered with flypaper; he tried to wiggle, but he couldn't seem to move. When a deputy inspector uses your first name and asks for a favor, what he really means is, "McKenna, I need a big favor, and you've got to do it." McKenna had no choice except to answer, "Sure, Inspector. Just name it."

"It seems that I've jumped on my cock a little bit and it's starting to hurt. I thought that it would be a good idea to restrict the information that we've got on this investigation. I told Lieutenant Hardcass to assign detectives for this investigation tonight, but just to tell them what they needed to know to do the job. Of course, Hardcass is a German soldier, and he follows orders to the letter. He got a lot of resistance from the Hispanic detectives, but he held the line. Nobody found out anything from him. It was just, 'Here are your orders. Now go to it.' Ten minutes ago I got a call from the president of the Hispanic Society. He wants to know why I don't trust Hispanic detectives. He said that every donkey and guinea detective in the place probably had the whole story, while the Hispanic detectives who were doing the job were operating in the dark. I told him that it wasn't prejudice, I was just trying to restrict access to information on a very sensitive investigation. He halfway understood, and told me that everything would be all right as long it got fixed. Now I can't have Lieutenant Hardcass go back and fill them in after he spent so much time on the battlements, so I thought of you."

"That's an easy one, Inspector. It'll be my pleasure. I wanted to talk to you about that anyway."

"OK. Now, back to the real business. I heard from Rogan and Gilroy in Boston. They talked to the editors of the *Boston Globe* and laid our deal out for them. They went for it. They won't reveal anything about our investigation until we give them the word or until some other newspaper prints it. Then they get their 'special consideration' when we give out the story. The editors looked at the picture of

Rodrigo holding their paper and they said that it's definitely a local edition. Know what that means?"

"Yeah! It means that Rico and his boys went to an awful lot of trouble to make Rodrigo's family believe that Rodrigo was being held in Boston."

"Or he's in Boston after all, and we're wasting our time here."

"No way. The finger was too fresh. One of them bought the paper in Boston yesterday morning. Then he came down here, gave the paper to Rodrigo for his photo session, then sliced off his finger. They're smart enough to know that someone could tell the difference between a local edition and an out-of-town edition. It means that their gang is big enough to have an extra man to use as a courier. How can they tell it's a local edition?"

"The local edition is thicker because of the advertisements. And there was a slight difference between yesterday's local edition and the out-of-town edition on the alignment and placement of the stories on the front page. But now for the bad news. Two agents from the Boston office of the FBI visited the *Boston Globe* this morning. They had the same questions and got the same information as us. And they didn't even have to make a deal. They just appealed to the *Boston Globe*'s journalistic ethics. I didn't even know that there was such a thing. What do you make of this now?"

"Well, the FBI showing up doesn't surprise me. They're in this, one way or the other. We just don't know how deep they are and whether they're holding out on us for some reason. But they had the pictures from Rico's body last night and they probably put two and two together to figure out the same things that we have. But they still don't know that much. They went to the trouble to get a search warrant to hit the wrong house in Florida, and they have to be suffering from a black eye on that one. I'm anxious to hear what they had to say to the chief. They won't be able to lie to him for much longer."

Tavlin stood up and said, "I hope you're right. Now, get to my favor before my phone starts ringing again."

"Sure thing, Inspector." McKenna walked to the door and was about to leave when Tavlin called to him, "One more thing. Betty King is assigned here starting tomorrow morning, eight o'clock. She would have been here today but—get this!—she had to pass a urine test today before she could be assigned to the Bureau. If she's not drug-free, this whole job's in trouble."

"This puts her in line for the Shield, right?"

"Let's see how we do. Now get outta here. I have to write this report to the chief on today's conference, and I'll be busy for a while. Let me know how you make out," said Tavlin.

McKenna left Tavlin's office and found Pacella seated at a desk outside. He looked thoroughly bored as he pretended to read the assignment sheet for the evening. The effectiveness of the air conditioning was dampened by the presence of so many people in the room, and Pacella was sweating. He looked at McKenna quizzically and McKenna simply nodded.

Pacella got up and they both headed for the door. Lieutenant Hardcass saw them leaving, but didn't say anything since he knew that McKenna had just left the inspector's office. He made a practice of never questioning anyone who might be engaged in a higher mission. As McKenna and Pacella were passing Flaherty at his desk, Pacella said to him, "You didn't see us leave, Joe."

"Then I guess I won't see you when you get back either."

"Right. Need anything?"

"Yeah. Tell Vinnie to send a sandwich over and to put it on my tab."

"I'll take care of it," answered Pacella.

McKenna and Pacella walked down the stairs and out the front door of the station house. They crossed the street and strolled casually up East 119th Street toward Park Avenue, which was always in darkness because of the shadows cast by the New York Central elevated tracks. As they walked into the shadows, they disappeared. They were in. If you blinked your eyes twice, you might swear that they had never been there in the first place.

Virtually every station house in the City of New York has a bar nearby where the officers assigned to the precinct go after work to talk over the events and traumas of their day. Some of these places are famous even among police officers assigned to other precincts. Generally speaking, once a police officer is transferred or promoted from one precinct to another, he doesn't frequent the bar of his old precinct. But that was not the case of the bar frequented by police officers and detectives assigned to the 25th Precinct. They always came back to Raggs. Raggs was a tradition, and traditions, once started, are not easily broken.

It might be the magical cast of the lighting, but Bosses who entered Raggs never seemed to notice anyone on duty drinking there. Raggs was a sanctuary. That is, of course, unless another tradition was being violated. If your Boss came in while you were working, tradition had it that you quickly finished your beer and left your Boss free to hide from his Boss.

There were a number of reasons for the success of the "Whitest Bar in Harlem." Primary among them was the owner. Vinnie was a retired detective of some renown who knew absolutely everyone. The bar generated a good business, and Vinnie's secret was that he treated the bar as a hobby. His real business was a successful midtown restaurant, so Vinnie just bought the place where he would probably be anyway. There was always food left over from some party or other, and the eats usually came with the beer.

Another reason for the success of the bar was location. Raggs was just nine blocks from the Triboro Bridge, and most of the cops partying in Manhattan stopped at Raggs either before or after their festivities. Parking was plentiful along Park Avenue under the El, in the large middle space between the girders, among the stolen and stripped cars that always seemed to be there.

Finally, there was the ambience, or more correctly, the complete lack of ambience. Although Vinnie could always be counted upon to tell you how much work he'd put into the place since he bought it, the surprising thing was how he got away with it while you were standing next to him in the middle of the dump. But nobody seemed to notice.

Not that the bar didn't have atmosphere; Jack London, Ernest Hemingway, or Damon Runyon would have been very much at home here. There were white bars, there were black bars, there were Spanish bars, and then there was Raggs, where every type of character felt in tune and not the slightest bit out of place. Two white men drinking together at the bar at the same time qualified Raggs for its "white bar" title. But there was something there for everyone, regardless of race, color, creed, or sexual orientation.

There were neighborhood people who knew every cop in the precinct, along with an assortment of either very good-looking or tremendously ugly girls enjoying a drink at the bar. The only discernible difference between the attractive girls and the ugly ones was that the latter told better jokes and occasionally found it necessary to place money in front of their position at the bar. There never seemed to be any average-looking girls in Raggs. When you saw an average girl at the bar at Raggs, it meant you'd been drinking too much and you were about to make a mistake that your friends would laugh about in the morning. Meet Harry He-She, the most average-looking transvestite around. But all women at Raggs, including Harry, were treated with some degree of decorum, and they all got asked to dance late at night to all types of music in both Spanish and English. Everyone had fun at Raggs. Guaranteed.

McKenna and Pacella walked down the bar and took a spot at the end. Laura Jiminez was working and she blew McKenna a kiss as he passed. McKenna was relieved to see that she wasn't wearing sunglasses. The place was crowded and McKenna said hello to some of the Hispanic detectives he knew who had been assigned by Lieutenant Hardcass to the case. Their return greetings were perfunctory and they seemed less than happy to see him. They were in and out after a beer. McKenna picked up the routine. Finish an interview, come into Raggs, order a beer, call in the results of your assigned interview, and receive another assignment from Joe Sophia or Ernest Ford. Finish your beer and get back to work again.

Laura came over and asked Pacella, "You drinking with McKenna tonight?"

"Sure," he answered and Laura went to the freezer under the bar and returned with two bottles of Kaliber.

"Hear any more from your old pal?" McKenna asked her as he put a twenty on the bar.

"No, *Gracias a Dios.* Thank you so much for that favor, Brian. I'm sorry you got into so much trouble. I really owe you."

"Relax, Laura. I'm back already, no harm done."

The bar was busy, so Laura left to get some beers for other customers, most of whom were engaged in the pastime of watching Laura bend over in her low-cut blouse to get their beers from the freezer under the bar. The view was great from both ends, and it kept the customers ordering. During one of her trips to the freezer, Pacella asked McKenna, "Would you, kid?"

McKenna feigned shock as he answered his partner, "Tommy, is nothing sacred with you? Laura and me are just good friends. Besides, I'm getting too old. Angelita doesn't let me out of the house unless I'm exhausted, and I'd better have some energy when I get home if I expect to feel safe enough to go to sleep. She's made me into a one-woman man."

McKenna's answer didn't suit Pacella. He thought for a second and said, "What I meant was, would you ever?"

"Four years ago, in a minute, partner. But I'm kind of glad to get all that behind me. It's just the thrill of the chase for me now. Sometimes I just want to see if I've still got it. I guess it's an ego thing. So I wander around and talk some trash to whatever ladies will listen. The problem is that sometimes I get lucky and I have to wiggle out. So when they say no, I say thank you, and I'm just as happy to go home."

Tommy finished his beer in one gulp, put down the empty bottle, and said, "Brian, please don't tell me any more or I'll have to stop calling you 'kid.' You're getting wise beyond your years."

Laura brought them another two beers as Vinnie approached them at the bar. Vinnie signaled to Laura that these two beers were on the house, which didn't seem to make much sense, as McKenna's twenty still lay on the bar untouched. Vinnie put his arms around both detectives' shoulders and said, "Good to have you two working together again. Welcome back. I'm glad you came in 'cause I've got a few ideas about your case. Wanna hear?"

"Let's hear the solution, Vinnie. That's why we came in," McKenna lied with a straight face. "If you can do it, I'll throw my First-Grade promotion party here."

"McKenna, my kid in high school will be a First Grader before you. Besides, I can't afford any of your parties. They leave me broke. But here's the answer."

The fact that Vinnie probably knew most of the details of this supposedly secret investigation surprised neither McKenna nor Pacella. Whatever Vinnie knew would never be repeated to anyone who wasn't supposed to hear it.

Vinnie continued, "I understand that you're worried that the kidnappers are getting nervous since you shot Rico and he didn't appear at his meeting with Flavio at the Intercontinental Hotel. You think they might kill Rodrigo and get out of town. I've been thinking and the answer is, don't worry. These guys aren't going to kill him. They went to too much trouble to get him."

"They still might kill him if they think we're on to them," Pacella said.

"No they won't. Not unless they think you're close."

"Why not?"

"Because of what they are. Put yourself in their heads for a few minutes. You're a terrorist. What do you do all the time in your own country? Kidnap people and hold them for ransom. You have to maintain a certain degree of credibility. You can't just blast your hostage every time something goes wrong. It's bad business. You're dealing with the hostage's family, and there has to be an understood guarantee that the family has to be given a chance to pay before you do anything like that. Otherwise, you might as well go out of business. Nobody will pay the next time. Besides, you've just spent a lot of time, trouble, and money to get yourself a trophy-class prisoner. Why kill him just because you've had a little trouble?"

"Your messenger getting killed is more than a 'little trouble,' Vinnie," Pacella said. "It should make them real suspicious that the police might be on to them. They seem to be a very suspicious bunch as it is."

"If it's not handled right by the police," Vinnie said, "of course they'll get more suspicious. But it is being handled right, so don't worry."

Vinnie was watching the cash register behind the bar. The bar was busy, but the cash register wasn't ringing too often and might as well have been in the basement. He looked concerned. "I'll see you guys

149

later," he said. "I've got to circulate or my girls won't charge any cops for their drinks." But as he left he motioned for Laura to bring McKenna and Pacella two more beers on the house. Vinnie was never going to get rich here, McKenna thought.

"Vinnie's right," Pacella said. "They're in no hurry to kill him. The papers made Rico's shooting seem pretty random, and he probably already called his pals from Brooklyn to tell them that he wasn't followed. That has to be the pay phone number that you took out of Rico's mouth. Now, keep yourself in their heads. There's no reason for you and the rest of your gang to think Rico's killing wasn't random. It seems like it was just bad luck. Besides, nobody's been knocking at your door, so there's no reason for you to think that Rodrigo's family is trying to double-cross you. They wouldn't. They're from your country, they know your reputation, and you've already proven to them how serious you are. But you still want to play it safe. So what do you do?"

"You're the First Grader. I'm listening."

"Fall back," said Pacella. "Tie Rodrigo up real tight, gag, him, and leave the apartment. Go to a place where you can watch the apartment where Rodrigo is, just to see if anyone is interested in the place. You watch for a couple of days, just to make sure. Then you go back and clean Rodrigo up, because by this time he's a mess. Two days is a long time to hold it when you have to go. Then you take another picture of Rodrigo holding another newspaper, cut off another finger, and send the package to his family to let them know that you're still in business. Time is no problem for you. You've got a doctor to keep Rodrigo alive. Rodrigo's still got at least eight more messages left on his hands. You just have to keep him healthy enough to look alive."

"How did they get him into whatever place they're holding him without anybody noticing?" McKenna asked.

"That's easy. They've thought this out good and they're prepared. They're just rented an apartment for the express purpose of holding Rodrigo. So they moved him in, probably in a trunk, along with a whole lot of other furniture. What we have to find out is exactly what day Rodrigo was kidnapped and then we have to find out who moved into an apartment in Spanish Harlem that day or the next day. And we have to find that out in this neighborhood where everyone moves once a year. Simple, huh?"

"Why'd they do it in the United States instead of in Peru? They're operating on unfamiliar ground here," McKenna asked.

"For the same reason that people try to cross the Atlantic Ocean in a bathtub. Because it's never been done. You get the added benefit, if you're successful, of giving the imperialist dogs a kick in the pants by embarrassing the United States government."

150

"Maybe it has been done before," said McKenna, "and nobody's telling about it. There has to be some reason why Rodrigo has a bodyguard all of a sudden. Know anything about terrorist groups in Peru?"

"Just what I read in the papers. I know that the country is loaded with them, but there's two main groups. The Shining Path and the Tupac-Amaru. One of them is communist and the other one is Indians. I think that the Shining Path ones are the commies."

Laura brought the beers. After she left McKenna asked Pacella, "What else do we have to figure out?"

"How'd they take him without anybody noticing? Especially a guy with a bodyguard."

McKenna took a sip of his beer while he thought that one over for the tenth time. Pacella looked at him expectantly. McKenna put his beer down and said, "Romance. Rodrigo had to get rid of his bodyguard for romance. They had to set him up in Boston in a private place where they could operate. Then they had to deal with his bodyguard. This means to me that there had to be a lover involved somewhere to set Rodrigo up. Otherwise, they couldn't have taken Rodrigo quietly and we would've heard about the kidnapping."

"Interesting theory, kid. Suppose Rodrigo is gay?" asked Pacella.

"Makes no difference. But let's say the lover is a woman. She's part of the gang, but she has to have some class to attract a guy like Rodrigo and not get the bodyguard suspicious. Probably a couple of dates around town to get him feeling secure. Someone in Boston or Cambridge must have seen them together."

"Say you're right, she'd have to be some package, dedicated, sophisticated, good looking, and hard as nails."

McKenna looked past Pacella at the women present in the bar and said, "I've got some good news for you, Tommy. From your description of her, I can see that she's not here right now. Let's work the lover angle some more. What should we do next with it?"

Pacella had the answer instantly. "Have somebody go to Massachusetts to find out who Rodrigo's been romancing lately and then find out exactly when he disappeared from the scene. That's the only way we can narrow it down to the date when they moved into a new apartment in this area."

Just then, Cisco Sanchez slipped into the bar and McKenna motioned for him to join them. Cisco talked briefly to a few of the other Hispanic detectives at the bar, and then walked over. McKenna caught Laura's eye and indicated to her that he wanted to buy Cisco a drink. Laura brought over a bottle of Dos Equis beer and McKenna pushed his twenty-dollar bill forward on the bar to pay, but Cisco said, "I'd rather pay for my own beer, if you don't mind."

151

Laura sensed the tension between the two men and looked at McKenna for guidance. "I guess this isn't my night to spend money here," McKenna said as Cisco took ten dollars from his pocket and pushed it across the bar.

Laura looked at Cisco's bill for a second and resolved the situation by saying, "That's all right, Cisco. This one's with me." With that, she leaned forward, stuck out her tongue at Cisco, then turned and slapped her own behind as she walked to the other end of the bar. All three men laughed at her and the tension was broken.

Cisco took a long pull on his beer as McKenna said, "I wanna tell you whatever you wanna know about this case, Cisco."

"McKenna, I already know all about your case. But I want Lieutenant Hardcass to tell me about it."

"He can't do that, Cisco. He's just following orders, and you know that Hardass always follows orders."

"Whose orders?" asked Cisco.

"Tavlin's."

"Then I want Tavlin to fill me in on the case. The way this whole thing is being handled is a disgrace."

"That's why I'm here. Tavlin asked me to fill you in. As a matter of fact, I went into his office to talk to him about it, but he brought it up first. He said he received orders from some knucklehead in headquarters to keep this whole investigation as secret as possible. Only detectives working full time on the case were to be given complete information. Tavlin thought that the orders were wrong, but he followed them anyway. He told Hardcass not to give any of the detectives working tonight any more information than they needed to know. Tavlin knew that you guys would be working on this case for only one night, and he was afraid of press leaks with so many men from so many different commands working it."

"That was wrong," said Cisco, indignantly. "We can't be trusted?"

"He knows it was wrong. He started thinking about it and he started to feel bad. He thought to himself that this was one of those orders that should be violated. Now he couldn't ask Hardcass to do it, because Hardcass already took a lot of heat on this from you guys. If he had Hardcass tell you, Hardcass would be embarrassed. And you know how these Bosses are. One Boss never embarrasses another Boss in front of the men?"

"Yeah," said Cisco. "We all know. Right or wrong, they always stick together when it comes to fucking the troops."

"Usually, but not with Tavlin. He plays straight and he's not afraid to admit when he makes a mistake. He wanted to fill you guys in on this case himself, but he was afraid that headquarters would find out that he violated a direct order. They'd transfer him and then blame any press leaks on him and your guys. So he asked me to tell you that he's sorry. He wants to fill you in on everything. He figures that you can unofficially tell the story to everyone else working tonight and explain his position. He wants to make it up to you. So we make the deal, and then, right while I'm sitting there, somebody calls from the Hispanic Society and tells Tavlin that he's prejudiced and that he doesn't trust Spanish detectives. Can you imagine that?"

Cisco looked astonished, which made McKenna absolutely certain that he was behind the phone call to the Hispanic Society. "I never would've said that Tavlin is prejudiced," Cisco said.

"Of course not," McKenna said. "I know that Steve Tavlin personally requested that as many Spanish detectives as possible be assigned to work full time on the case. We've already got Joe Mendez and Caesar Gonzalez, and they know all about the case. And Tavlin wants more Spanish detectives than that."

Cisco thought this over for a while as he finished his beer. Then he asked, "Tavlin's Jewish, right?"

"I think so," answered McKenna.

"That's what I thought. He's not afraid to bend the rules to get the job done. Everything is just like business with the Jews in this job. We're not interested in all the silly rules, just in getting the job done."

"Wait a minute, Cisco," interrupted Pacella. "Don't tell me that you're one of the Christ killers?" he joked.

"What's the matter? Haven't you ever heard of a Spanish Jew? Ever hear of the Sephardics? What about Christopher Columbus? Of course I'm Jewish. I'm upwardly mobile, *amigo*. A Second-Grade detective on the sergeant's list. Haven't you ever noticed that you see lots of Jewish Bosses and detectives, but very few Jewish cops?"

Cisco was on a roll and he didn't wait for Pacella to answer his question. "It's because we don't waste a lot of time hanging around on the bottom of the heap. And once we start going up, we don't stop. That's because we know how to bend the rules, do the job, and go home. We're not like your donkey Bosses who have memories like elephants. They spend all their off-duty time drinking while trying to figure out how to stab some other donkey Boss for breaking one of your rules ten years ago. Not us. Bend the rules to get the job done, and never be afraid to say that you made a mistake and you're sorry. Besides, that whole Christ thing was an internal matter. He was a Jew who broke the rules and he had to go. He was bad for business, preaching during Passover and drawing the crowds away from the stores. That used to be one of our busy seasons before we targeted the goyim as a viable market and invented Christmas."

Pacella could take it no longer. "Cisco, are you sure of all of this? Where do you get your facts from?"

153

Cisco and McKenna had a good laugh and finally Cisco said to Pacella, "Well, that's the way it could've been. But I am Jewish, so it's time to make a deal for my men." Then he said to McKenna, "Tavlin just wants to find out who the taxi driver was and where he picked Rico up, even if it takes all night. Right?"

"As I understand it," answered McKenna.

"And he wants to make this whole top-secret mess up to us, right?"

McKenna knew what was coming next. But he wanted to correct the mistakes and get his case solved, so he answered, "He sure does!"

"Well, I was thinking. Suppose it doesn't take all night to get the information? That would mean that we would get sent back to our commands early to finish working there. There's no percentage in that for us. After all, it's not our case. I was thinking that, since Tavlin owes us, maybe we could solve our part of the investigation a little sooner, and then we could finish our night here with nobody bothering us."

McKenna thought this proposition over and knew that he had to give Tavlin's answer while the mood was perfect. What would Tavlin say? he asked himself. Well, as Cisco says, he is Jewish and it's results that count. "I think that Tavlin would say that was fine, as long as you cover all of your time on paper and as long as you say that nothing on this investigation will get into the papers."

"Not from us, *amigo*," answered Cisco. "It's a done deal."

McKenna and Cisco closed the deal with a handshake and finished their beers. Cisco left to talk it over with the other Hispanic detectives in the bar. Pacella said to McKenna, "Kid, you were born in the wrong time and place. You should've been born in Italy about four hundred years ago and you could've taught Machiavelli how to really be a prince. You would've ruled the place."

"Well, the prince is getting hungry and we don't know when we're gonna get home again. Whatta ya say we walk over to Dante's. We can split a pie with some anchovies."

"They make me thirsty, but lead the way, kid."

McKenna called Laura over, gave her the twenty-dollar bill, and asked her to have Vinnie send Flaherty his sandwich. The two detectives left the bar.

14

When McKenna and Pacella returned to the office, Lieutenant Hardcass was supervising the placement of the radio chargers for twenty-five newly arrived secure-frequency radios. Space was getting tight and he was forced to put them on the table that used to hold Captain O'Connell's coffeepot. Ford and Sophia were hanging a key rack for the nondescript autos assigned to the unit. McKenna noticed that there were already five sets of auto keys on the rack and five Police Vehicle Identification plates on Sophia's desk. Pacella, never one to look idle, picked up the Radio Log that had arrived with the radios and began writing the radio numbers in the log.

McKenna walked through the outer office to Tavlin's door, knocked, and went in. Once again, Tavlin was on the phone, but he seemed happy to see McKenna. He motioned for him to sit down, cradled the phone between his shoulder and his ear, and handed McKenna a list of ten detectives. "Look it over. They're gonna be working the case," he said.

McKenna looked at the list. He knew most of the men and women, and it was a good crew. Most were Hispanic, and Cisco Sanchez was at the top of the list. Among the two or three non-Hispanic names was Richie White. Brunette always remembers. McKenna thought.

Tavlin finished his phone conversation. "That's good news, Sheeran. I'll keep in touch." Then he turned his attention to McKenna. "How'd you make out?"

McKenna told Tavlin about the deal that he had made with Cisco

155

Sanchez and explained that Sanchez had promised to find the taxi driver tonight, but that he wanted some time off for his men in return. McKenna waited while Tavlin thought this proposal over. Finally Tavlin said, "Are they going to cover their time on paper if they find him early?"

"He said they would. Also, he promised there'd be no press leaks from them."

"Then what's the problem? I don't want to hear any more about it. In fact, I never heard a thing. It's results that count. I'll just have to find something else for Lieutenant Hardcass to do so he don't break their balls. Captain Sheeran is doing big things over in Brooklyn and he's been working straight for days. I'm gonna send the good lieutenant over to Kennedy Airport so Sheeran can get some sleep. Which reminds me, you've been working for days, McKenna. Go home. I'll see you in the morning."

"OK. Inspector. But don't keep me hanging. What's Captain Sheeran got?"

"OK," he said. "It's your case and I guess I owe you. Your name goes at the bottom of every report anyway. They got Flavio at the Intercontinental. He got there in a yellow cab, but Sheeran's men didn't know what he looked like then. They only knew it was him when he went to his room. Sheeran's men had been taking down the license numbers of all cars and cabs delivering people to the Intercontinental, and they got the license number of the yellow cab that delivered Flavio. It's a fleet cab registered to a company in Jackson Heights. Sheeran's men went to the company and found that the cab driver doesn't get off until midnight and there's no way to get in touch with him right now. So we can't find out where Flavio was picked up until then."

"Sounds like Captain Sheeran should be running out of men by now," said McKenna.

"I'm sure it's a problem for him, but he hasn't been complaining. He's scoured all his Squads in Brooklyn for manpower and he's got everybody on overtime. Everybody's making money and nobody's squawking. Apparently Sheeran's well liked."

"Yeah, I'm getting more impressed with him every minute."

"Everyone is. By midnight he'll have plenty of people. At eleven o'clock he's gonna get two Spanish female detectives from the Manhattan Sex Crimes Squad. They're gonna be Flavio's maids. We've got a couple of yellow cabs outside the Intercontinental in case Flavio decides to go anywhere. TARU has installed locating transmitters on the cabs, so it'll be no problem following them. The Photo Section has taken pictures of eight of Sheeran's men and they're going to have Hack Licenses with an old date of issue made up for them. That way, if Flavio takes our yellow cab, whoever is driving will have his hack license in the holder on the dashboard and Flavio won't get suspicious."

"How you been making out on the warrants?" asked McKenna.

"Captain Flynn's been on top of that. He's got applications for eavesdropping warrants for Flavio's hotel room and for the pay phone at East 113th Street and Lexington Avenue. He's getting a search warrant for Flavio's room and a court order for American Express for records on Flavio's card and court orders for the airlines that fly from Peru to Kennedy Airport. We wanna find out when Flavio arrived. Flynn says he's got a sympathetic judge and that he'll have the warrants and orders by ten o'clock. TARU is ready to install the wiretaps as soon as Flynn gets the orders signed."

McKenna smiled at hearing this piece of information and Tavlin was forced to smile back at him. Appearances must be maintained. Both men knew that the wires were already installed and that the eavesdropping warrants just made them legal. What they got from the wires before the warrants were signed was just information that would never appear on a DD 5, and would never be introduced as evidence in court.

"How are you going to handle East 113th Street?" McKenna asked. "It seems to me that's our most important location. That's the place Flavio made the phone call to from the Intercontinental and I think that he'll probably try to call the kidnappers there again, probably at the same time of day."

"We've got a telephone company truck between 113th Street and 114th Street on Lexington Avenue. They've opened up a manhole cover in the street and set up a telephone company tent over the manhole. Sara Walden and Adam Saaks from Major Case are in the hole. Sergeant Goldblatt drove by them and he says that they look like the real item. Telephone company hard hats, a boom box playing the Grateful Dead, and drinking beer from brown paper bags. They got the corner under photographic surveillance and we've got men from the Street Crime Unit waiting to put a tail on anyone who answers that phone. We had a small problem there already with one of the local drug dealers. He was using that pay phone for his office and Walden saw the garbage can where he stashed his drugs. I talked to Captain Delaney about it, and he had the Two-five Anti-Crime Unit lock him up, just to keep the phone free. The wiretap of the pay phone is run right from that hole, so we're ready to go. We've just got to replace Walden or Saaks with somebody who speaks Spanish to monitor the wire. But everything is recorded anyway. Did I forget anything?"

"Equipment?"

"Got everything we need," Tavlin answered. "We've got five non-descript autos and another five are being delivered to Captain Sheeran. There are two-door wrecks, Toyotas, pickup trucks, new Buicks, gypsy cabs, and whatever else you can imagine. None of them look anything like police cars. They all have confidential license plates registered to fictitious owners, like most of the other cars in this precinct. They're hidden deep in the parking lot. We've got twenty-five radios set at a frequency way beyond our normal ones. They operate outside of the usual scanner ranges, so we don't have to worry about the press or bad guys listening. I'm gonna send ten of these radios to Captain Sheeran with Lieutenant Hardcass."

"It sounds to me like you've covered all the bases, Inspector."

"That's what worries me. I'm spending a bundle of the taxpayers' money watching Flavio. I hate to think of the overtime bill. If he's legitimate, we're done for. I might have to get a real job."

"You spoiled it for me, Inspector," McKenna said, "just when I was feeling good. I'm ready to go home. What about Pacella?"

"Tell him to go home too. Everybody back at eight in the morning, OK? Sign out and give me your overtime slips in the morning. You guys are both making more than me with this operation you've started. Good business sense, McKenna. Good night."

McKenna left the inspector's office and gave Pacella the good news. Both detectives signed out at nine o'clock.

When they left the office, Joe Flaherty said, "Cisco wants you to stop by before you go home."

The street outside was clogged with gypsy cabs stretching to the corner of Park Avenue. "It looks like Cisco's been thinking," said Pacella. They crossed the street and walked up the block into Raggs.

The place was jammed, standing room only. Spanish cab drivers and Spanish detectives occupied every available square foot of space. The jukebox was blaring "El Rey" and Vinnie was behind the bar helping Laura serve drinks and beers. Pacella, who had the advantage of size and was able to see over the crowd, said to McKenna, "Cisco's holding court in the rear."

McKenna could see nothing but the back of the head of the cab driver in front of him, so Pacella grabbed McKenna's arm and cleared a path to the back of the bar, where Cisco was seated at a small table, talking to another man. He looked up as McKenna and Pacella got close. "Hey, McKenna! I've got your driver right here, just like I said. Where do you think he picked Rico up yesterday?"

"Not here?" said McKenna.

"You're close. Right down the block, corner of East 119th Street and Lexington Avenue. At two o'clock right on the corner of the station house!"

158

I was right, McKenna thought. They're here. Thank God. I knew it, but it sure feels good hearing it. Rico getting picked up near the station house makes sense. They're sharp. He must've left his hideout and walked around to make sure he wasn't being followed. Then, just to be sure, he walks to the corner of the station house where cops are passing all the time on their way in and out. If someone is following him, the tail would probably be known to the uniformed cops in the precinct, and they'd see him, maybe even wave to him. Then Rico would see him. Good sense. That's the place for Rico to get a cab."

"Where'd he take him?" McKenna asked.

"Right to Tilden and Flatbush."

McKenna turned to the cab driver. He was a small man, about fifty years old, and the cares and worries of a hard life were etched in his face. "Do you speak English, *Señor?*" he asked.

"Un poco."

"Do you want me to translate, McKenna?" asked Cisco.

"Thanks, Cisco, but I think I can handle it. Let's go out to your car. I can't hear myself think in here."

Once outside, Cisco led them to his unmarked car, parked in the shadows of the El on Park Avenue and East 120th Street. McKenna got into the rear seat with the taxi driver, who was obviously nervous, while Pacella and Cisco filled the front. Cisco took a pad from the glove compartment and prepared to take notes.

McKenna slipped easily into Spanish, introduced himself and Pacella, and said to the cab driver, "You got nothing to worry about. You won't have to go to court. You just might have to sign some papers if we need a search warrant later on. That OK with you?"

"Sí, Señor."

"What's your name?"

"Pablo Quinones."

"Got any ID?" McKenna asked.

The driver reached into his back pocket, took out his wallet, and gave McKenna a New York state driver's license in the name of Pablo Quinones. McKenna noted that the license indicated that Pablo was forty-one years old and that he lived in Spanish Harlem. He gave the license to Cisco to copy the information and asked, "Got any more ID?"

Pablo took the registration for a 1986 Pontiac from his pocket and gave it to McKenna. McKenna noted that the car was registered to Pablo, but the address was different. He gave it to Cisco and asked Pablo for his real address. Pablo gave him a third place on East 123rd Street in Spanish Harlem and his telephone number, which Cisco wrote down. Cisco then returned Pablo's papers to him and McKenna continued his interview. "You take somebody to Flatbush yesterday, Señor Quinones?"

"*Si, Señor.* A man. At two o'clock."

"Where'd you pick him up?"

"On the corner, over there," Pablo said, pointing down East 119th Street.

"Describe him for me."

"He was dressed in green clothes. He had a beard."

"How old was he?"

"Maybe forty."

"Tell me about the trip."

"I was driving down Lexington and the man waved to me. I pulled over and he got in. Said he wanted to go to Flatbush Avenue in Brooklyn, but he wasn't sure exactly where on Flatbush Avenue. He said he would recognize the place when he saw it. He told me to take side streets to East 96th Street, and then get on the East River Drive at 96th Street. I was driving and he told me to pull over at some green lights. I did, and he looked out the back window."

"He made you nervous?"

"*Si, Señor.* Very nervous. I thought he was a drug dealer. He told me, 'Don't worry.' He said he had a fight with his girlfriend's brother and father, and he wanted to make sure that they weren't following him. When I got to the corner of East 96th Street and Second Avenue, he asked me to pull over again. I did and he got out of the car and looked all around. Then he was looking at the sky before he got back in the car. Then I took the East River Drive to the Brooklyn Bridge."

"Did he talk during the trip?"

"About baseball. He knew a lot about the Yankees and the Yankee players. He told me he had bet the game."

Cisco's partner came over to the car with four beers and asked him how long he would be. Cisco told him about ten more minutes. There were two Dos Equis bottles and two of Kaliber. Everyone had a few sips before McKenna said, "Go on."

Pablo said, "I took the Brooklyn Bridge into Brooklyn and then went down Tillary Street to Flatbush Avenue. When we were on Flatbush Avenue, I saw that the man got really nervous. He had his hand under his jacket. I looked in the rearview mirror and saw there was an unmarked car behind us. I got nervous too. I thought he had a gun under his jacket. I was happy when the police turned off Flatbush Avenue at Atlantic Avenue. But the man was nervous for the rest of the trip."

"Did you see a gun?" McKenna asked.

"No. But I thought he had one."

"Go on."

160

"I went down Flatbush Avenue to Tilden Avenue. Then he told me to stop the car at Tilden Avenue and he got out. He asked me how much and I told him twenty dollars. He gave me thirty dollars and told me to keep the change."

"How was he when he left the cab?" McKenna asked.

"Still nervous. Still looking all around. He left the cab and walked down Tilden Avenue. I was happy he was gone."

"What kind of shoes was he wearing?"

"Expensive green shoes. Snakeskin."

"Did you fill out a trip ticket?"

"No. I was on my lunch hour and the whole trip was my money. I didn't need no trip ticket."

"Where you from, Mr. Quinones?" McKenna asked.

"Panama."

"How long you been here?"

"Since 1979 off and on."

"Where do you think the man was from?"

"At first I thought he was Cuban, but later he sounded like a rich South American, maybe from Argentina or Chile. His Spanish was different, like he lived in Queens. You know how they talk."

McKenna said to Cisco in English, "Show him the photos yet?"

"Net yet."

Cisco reached into a folder under his seat, took out the photo of Rico, and gave it to McKenna. McKenna showed the photo to Pablo. "That him?" he asked Pablo in Spanish.

"Si, Señor. That's him. What's this all about, Officer?"

"You got nothing to worry about. He was a rich drug dealer, but he's dead now."

"Too bad," Pablo said. "You take your chances when you deal drugs, but he seemed like a nice guy."

McKenna switched back to English to talk to Cisco. "Did I miss anything?" he asked.

"Nope, *amigo.* I've got everything I need for my DD 5. Pablo is going to be our guest at Raggs until eleven o'clock, when he can officially tell me the whole story again. That way we cover our time. Care to join us? I want some of my guys to hear you speak Spanish. In fact, I want to officially induct you into the Hispanic Society. I was impressed, gringo."

"Sorry, Cisco. Another time. I'm beat and we're signed out already. We'd feel pretty stupid being the only two detectives in the place who weren't getting paid to drink. Besides, check your records. I've been a member for years. Now tell me how you found Pablo so fast."

"That was easy. I asked myself, Why should we waste our night chasing gypsy cab drivers all over Harlem when we can make them

161

come to us? So I collected fifteen dollars a man from my guys and I called a *señorita* I know who works as a dispatcher for a cab company. I asked her to broadcast over the Spanish gypsy cab radio network that there was a two-hundred-dollar cash reward for the right cab driver who picked up a fare in Spanish Harlem yesterday afternoon and dropped him off in Flatbush. I had her say that they should go to Raggs to pick up the reward, and if they had a trip ticket for Brooklyn yesterday, they were guaranteed two free cold beers. She broadcast the message, and it was picked up and passed on by every Spanish gypsy radio net in the city. Two minutes later we were up to our asses in gypsy cab drivers and it became a job sorting out all the bogus trip tickets. The easy thing was that they didn't know what kind of shoes Rico was wearing. There isn't a Latino in the world who wouldn't remember those shoes once he saw them."

"But Pablo said he didn't list Rico on his trip ticket," said McKenna.

"Of course not. He came in with a bullshit trip ticket just like everybody else. But he knew about the shoes. So my partner knew that he was the one we were looking for and he brought him over to me. It was just that easy."

"It looks to me like fifteen dollars a man isn't going to cover the tab. That's a real drinking crowd in there."

"I know. I called my *señorita* to cancel the message as soon as we found Pablo, but it seems that a lot of these guys didn't get the word. Vinnie donated five cases of beer to the cause and it looks like he's gonna make a fortune tonight. These guys don't look like they're set to leave after only two beers. They're here for the duration. My advice is, don't take a gypsy cab anywhere tonight. I didn't notice any designated drivers among that group in Raggs tonight."

"Did you pay Pablo yet?" asked Pacella.

"Are you crazy? Not till eleven o'clock when I officially take his statement, if he can still talk by then. But he's our guest and we'll take care of him."

"Tavlin likes your style, Cisco," McKenna said. "I know he's requested that you be assigned to the Major Case Squad for this case. How's that suit you?"

"Just fine. Change of pace for a while."

Everyone finished their beers and Pacella and McKenna walked Cisco and Pablo to the front door of Raggs. After they went in, Pacella said, "I felt like a dumb shit sitting in that car, kid. I'm going to start studying that language. How hard can it be?"

"Just get yourself a *señorita*, Tommy."

"Then I guess I'll never learn. Those hot-blooded Latin women would kill me. I'm getting too old. Can I drive you home?"

"That's all right. I'll take a cab. You must be tired. Go home."

162

"A cab? Didn't you hear Cisco? Besides, it's not out of my way. I have to take my department car down to our office in headquarters to pick up my own car."

Just then Vinnie came out of the bar with an envelope in his hand. He gave it to McKenna and said, "Bobby Johnston dropped this off for you."

McKenna took the envelope, opened it up, and read the message scribbled on a piece of paper inside. It read, *See you home, buddy* and it was signed *Ray.*

McKenna folded up the paper and put it in his pocket. He thanked Vinnie and then said to Pacella, "Take me home, partner."

15

The trip downtown went fast. It was a good time to travel in Manhattan and the detectives arrived at the corner of Bleecker Street and Perry Street in Greenwich Village at ten o'clock. Pacella spent most of the trip talking about the problems of commuting to Manhattan every day from Long Island. They each came to the conclusion that the other was crazy to live where he did.

When McKenna got out of Pacella's car he said, "I'm nuts to live here? You still got an hour to drive. Go home and mow your lawn, buddy. See you tomorrow."

Pacella gave him a wave and drove off.

The neighborhood was still jumping and McKenna took his usual walk around the block before entering his apartment building. It was a habit he had developed in the days when Internal Affairs used to follow him from his apartment to try and catch him working off duty in violation of the department rules. Instead, he used to catch them while they were waiting for him to come out. It always gave him a silly sense of satisfaction to bring a couple of containers of coffee to their car while they were straining their eyesight watching the door of his apartment building.

It was hard for IAD. Because of frequent arrests and court appearances, McKenna kept an irregular schedule with the police department and they never could seem to figure out exactly when he was working. They would spend hours sitting outside his apartment house when he was in court, and hours sitting outside his station house when he was home. McKenna enjoyed the game and was a little disappointed to find that there was no one waiting for him tonight. It had been six months since they were last there and McKenna felt a slight loss of importance and prestige.

McKenna stood outside his building. He was glad to be home. He couldn't imagine having quite the same feeling anyplace else. This old building in Greenwich Village had always been home. It was home before the gays came, before the real estate speculators came, before the Yuppies came, before all the apartment houses went co-op, before the neighborhood became rich and fashionable. McKenna was still living in the same apartment in the same building that he had grown up in. And because he had stayed in the neighborhood in his parents' old apartment, and because he had managed to scrape together enough money to buy his apartment years ago when his building went co-op, he might now even consider himself rich and fashionable. After all, he owned a five-room apartment in Greenwich Village.

But it wasn't the money. He just loved it. He loved the neighborhood and he even managed to stay on good terms with most of the people who now lived there. He also loved the convenience. Everything was close here: the stores, the movies, the restaurants. He never really had to walk more than couple of blocks for anything. McKenna took a certain perverse pride in the fact that he didn't even own a car. Angelita did, of course. For the first time since he had met her, the thought of Angelita brought him down. He had never considered that he would ever live anywhere else, until now.

McKenna tried to cheer himself up as he entered his building. At this time of night years ago there would have been people sitting on lawn chairs watching their older kids play, mothers and grandmothers trying to beat the heat. It used to take him fifteen minutes to get into the building. He would have had to chat with everybody. Now there was nobody. The grandmothers were dead and everyone else was in their air-conditioned apartments watching cable TV. And there weren't very many kids in this neighborhood now. Maybe it wasn't so good anymore.

The halls of the building were freshly painted. It seemed to McKenna that they were always freshly painted nowadays. He saw by the indicator that the new elevator was on the sixth floor. He remembered that when he was a boy, if the elevator was on the sixth floor, he could walk to his apartment on the fourth floor long before the elevator managed to get down to the lobby. McKenna pushed the elevator button and one minute later he had his key in the lock of his apartment door.

Angelita unlocked and opened the door while his key was still in the lock. She had been waiting for him. She gave him a peck on the cheek and said, "Ray's here."

Brunette was sitting in his usual chair, drinking a Kaliber while watching CNN. He frequently stayed over at McKenna's apartment in the summertime while his family stayed at their summer home upstate. The apartment was convenient for him, only ten minutes from his office at headquarters. Besides, McKenna had plenty of room and he and Angelita had come to refer to their second bedroom as Ray's room. Ray would just move the weights to the wall, pick up the skis, and help Angelita fold the wash that she always seemed to have on the bed, and then he was right at home. Ray had a mobile phone, so he could always be reached and no one knew where he was. It was perfect for him.

Whenever Ray came to stay, he always brought the dinner. If he brought three steaks, a quart of milk, and two six-packs of beer, that meant that he was there just for the night. If he brought a roast and a case of beer, they knew that he would be there for a couple of days. He kept enough clothes at the apartment to stay a while, in any event. But it didn't matter to McKenna and Angelita. They always enjoyed his company.

"We've been waiting for you to get here before we put the steaks on, Brian. I'm starving," Brunette said.

Steaks, McKenna thought. Just one night. He was glad to see Ray and he immediately sat down on the couch and started talking about the progress in the case, while Angelita went into the kitchen to cook.

"How'd the conference go?" Brunette asked.

"Tavlin petrified them. They're all hopping to do their sacred duty."

"That's what I wanted him to do. This case'll fall apart unless every unit pulls its weight."

"We found the cab driver," McKenna said.

"I know. I just got off the phone with Tavlin. He told me he's not supposed to know yet, but he's sharp. Sheeran's doing some good things too. I hope we're on the right track with Flavio or we're going to wind up looking as bad as the FBI."

"What'd you get from them?"

"Plenty," Brunette said. "Weatherby was in my office right on time. He's an obsequious little prick. He was shaking. The FBI is in this to their eyeballs and in deep shit. Turns out that this is the third time that a rich, politically connected Peruvian has been kidnapped by a guerrilla group in this country in the past eight months. They're afraid that this's a new trend and that they're going to wind up losing their reputation over this one."

"Three? Not three in New York?"

"No. This is the first one here. Their first one was in November in Miami. They found the body of a male Peruvian student after an anonymous call to their local office in Miami. The kid was a student at the University of Miami, cause of death, three nine-millimeter bullets to the head. They tortured the kid and cut off four fingers from his right hand. The autopsy concluded that one finger was cut off every three or four days. He also showed signs of malnutrition and they think they fed him intravenously while they had him."

"Who was the kid connected to?" McKenna asked.

"Turns out his father is the military governor of Ayacucho province in Peru. There's a lot of fighting in Ayacucho province between the government forces and a guerrilla group called *Sendero Luminoso*. Ever hear of them?"

"Yeah. Pacella mentioned something about them today. *Sendero Luminoso* means 'the Shining Path' in English. I never paid too much attention to what's going on in South America."

"You're gonna know a lot more about them. I got a CIA report on them from Weatherby. You can read it later. It's just background stuff. They don't have much information on the leadership."

"OK. I'll read it later. Get back to the father. What did he say?"

"He refused to be interviewed by the FBI, but they say that the military operations in Ayacucho province against *Sendero Luminoso* were intensified after the murder. The military got a little crazy. A number of suspected members or sympathizers of the group disappeared, along with some members of their families. The rumor the CIA got was that some of their bodies were found later, minus fingers. The State Department got nervous, but the Peruvian government denied there was any connection between the kid's death in Miami and the disapperance in Ayacucho province."

"This is starting to get strange," McKenna said.

"It gets worse. The next case occurred in March. The son of a military official in the Peruvian Ministry of Prisons was attending UCLA when he disappeared. This official had been implicated in the deaths of two hundred and forty-six members of *Sendero Luminoso* who were being held in three prisons in Peru. There was a prison uprising in 1982 and the military stormed the prisons, killing everyone. Nothing happened and Amnesty International went public and charged that lots of the prisoners were executed after the prisoners were recaptured. In the end, the father wound up being charged with ordering the executions of thirty prisoners. He was cleared of any wrongdoing by the Peruvian Supreme Court in 1986."

"It's getting pretty clear. Rodrigo's father is on their Supreme Court and Rodrigo is a student."

"It gets clearer. In April the smell led them to the kid's body in an East LA apartment. The LAPD investigated the disappearance and found that this kid had been dating a South American waitress he met at a Mexican restaurant; she also disappeared. LAPD found that the waitress was the same woman who had rented the apartment. She used a Florida driver's license in the name of Tricia Flint as ID when she rented the apartment. They checked the license out and found that it was stolen in a purse-snatch from Tricia Flint by a male Hispanic in November of last year. The real Flint couldn't give much in the way of identification."

"Another stolen Florida license? Stolen in November, just like Camarena's license," said McKenna.

"Some coincidence, huh? The body of the kid in LA was in bad shape when they found it, but their medical examiner concluded that he had been killed shortly after his disappearance. The cause of death was four nine-millimeter bullets to the head. What do you think he was missing?"

"Four fingers from his right hand," McKenna answered.

"That's right, but the ME said that the fingers were removed after his death. Just a little message for the father, I think. Because the killing might've been linked to a kidnapping and because the victim's father was a Peruvian government official, the LAPD notified the FBI on the case. They sent another agent to Peru to talk to this kid's father, and he talked. He said he didn't get any ransom demands, but he assumed the death of his son was a revenge killing by *Sendero Luminoso.*"

"So the Feds know they got a real problem."

"Right. They linked the Miami killing and the LA killing. They found that different guns were used to kill each one, but that the gun used in each case was—"

"A TEC-nine automatic pistol," McKenna interjected.

"Right. They took Rico's TEC-nine and did a ballistic comparison with the bullets in the other two cases. Three different guns, but all TEC-nines."

"How about the crime scenes?" McKenna asked.

"Nothing. No fingerprints, no garbage, no literature, nothing. Both apartments had been wiped clean. They questioned the owners of both apartments, and it got interesting. In both cases the apartments had been rented a month before the killings by an English-speaking woman in her thirties. She rented the apartment with one month's rent and a two-month security deposit, all in cash, so she wasn't closely questioned. In East LA she had black hair and in Miami she had blond hair. The FBI had their artists get together with neighbors, the real estate agents who rented the apartments, and the apartment owners to draw composite sketches of the woman."

168

Brunette picked up his briefcase, which was alongside his chair, and took out a folder. He opened the folder and handed McKenna two FBI composite sketches.

McKenna put the two sketches side by side on his lap and compared them. There were some differences in the faces. The dark-haired sketch had a beauty mark or mole on the left cheek. The hairstyles were completely different. The blond sketch showed the woman in glasses. Both sketches depicted a good-looking woman. They were very similar.

Just then, Angelita came out with the steaks and set them on the small table in the front part of the dining room. She said, "Let's go, boys."

The two men got up and went into the kitchen. Brunette got the butter, the ketchup, the sour cream, and three fresh bottles of Kaliber from the refrigerator. McKenna picked up the three baked potatoes from the counter next to the stove and two plates of hot vegetables. Angelita brought the glasses, the silverware, and the napkins. They all carried their goods to the dining room table and sat down. Then McKenna got the two sketches from the sofa and gave them to Angelita. "Which one do you like better?" he asked.

Angelita looked at both sketches. Then she said, "I like her better with the black hair. But she could lose the beauty mark. She looks much better without the glasses. She probably got contacts."

"You think both sketches are of the same woman?" McKenna asked.

She looked at him like he was blind. "Was there ever any doubt?" she asked.

Any doubts that Brunette and McKenna might have had they kept to themselves.

While they were eating, Brunette continued. "In Miami the FBI found one of the neighbors who saw the woman in the sketch in the company of a man she introduced as her husband. This guy spoke to the neighbor in Spanish and the FBI managed to make a sketch of him, too. I'll show it to you after dinner. You might find it interesting."

"It's Rico, right?"

"Wait. The FBI questioned everybody again in both neighborhoods in LA and Miami and showed them the sketch of the man. They got a surprise. The man had also rented apartments in LA and Miami, very close to the apartments where the killings took place. In LA he rented an apartment across the street and in Miami he rented an apartment down the block. He used the same scam as the woman to rent them—cash and a Florida driver's license. In both LA and Miami, the driver's license was in the name of Eduardo De Soto of Tampa, Florida. The FBI located the real Eduardo De Soto in Tampa and . . ."

"His wallet was stolen in November."

"Right. Is this too easy for you? It was a street robbery. De Soto said that he was knocked to the ground by a couple of men who approached him from behind, and he couldn't identify the people who robbed him."

McKenna thought this information over. He had never worked on a kidnapping case like this one before, but he thought he knew why the kidnappers rented an apartment close to the place where they were holding their hostage. "I think that they must live in one apartment and keep the hostage in the other," he said to Brunette. "They probably use only one person at a time to guard the hostage, and they can see if anyone is showing any interest in that apartment where they keep him. They might even have it booby-trapped in case the police find the hostage."

"Maybe," Brunette answered. "We'll have to be careful when we find the place they're keeping Rodrigo, if we do."

"How's the Peruvian government been taking all this?" McKenna asked.

"Hardly a squawk from them. In April they made an unofficial request through the State Department that the American government take some steps to safeguard Peruvian nationals while they were in the United States. The State Department assumed that the request was 'unofficial' because the Peruvian government, which is armed and supported by us, is in a very dirty war against *Sendero Luminoso*. There are kidnappings, assassinations, reprisal killings, and atrocities on both sides. According to the FBI, the government seems to be winning now because the rebels used to get their arms supplies from Cuba. But the Russians cut the Cubans off, so their supplies are drying up. So the Peruvian government sees no reason to give *Sendero Luminoso* any free press in this country by making an official request that would attract attention to a civil war that they're winning anyway. Nobody in the United States seems too interested in what's happening in Peru, and the government wants to keep it that way."

"What happened to the 'unofficial' request?"

"The State Department passed it on to the FBI. The FBI did a survey on the number of possible targets they would have to protect, and what they found made them shit their pants. It seems that anyone with any money in Peru is in the United States as much as possible. Conditions in Peru suck. There's the political kidnappings and *Sendero Luminoso* is constantly knocking out the power lines into the cities. It's too uncomfortable there for the rich. So they're spending a good part of the war here. They have houses here, they send their children to school here, they shop here, and their military is trained here. There's hundreds of them here on student visas and thousands more who have resident alien status. Weatherby told me that the job of protecting all these possible targets was just too big for them, so instead they decided to attack *Sendero Luminoso* with every resource that they had, for a number of reasons."

"Reasons like kidnapping and murder?" asked McKenna.

"Not exactly. They don't think like us. Their primary reason is that *Sendero Luminoso* is a foreign terrorist group operating in the United States in defiance of American interest. It's happened a few times before. In 1976 agents of the Chilean military government blew up the car of the former ambassador to Washington of the Allende government, killing him and his secretary. Also, some anti-Castro groups managed to kill a few officials of the Castro regime. But those were all isolated incidents, and the FBI eventually identified or captured whoever did it. Know why this one is different?"

"Because the FBI's got nothing on this one. They're afraid that *Sendero Luminoso* is about to expose the 'myth' that the FBI spent years cultivating," said McKenna.

"You got it," answered Brunette. "The myth that the FBI is ever vigilant and that a series of successful terrorist attacks on American soil would be so difficult and costly that it would seem almost impossible. It's protected the United States from the terrorist groups that operate in Western Europe. *Sendero Luminoso*'s going to blow it by being successful. And the reason they were successful is geography."

McKenna looked perplexed. "How'd geography help them?"

"It used to be that terrorists couldn't get here without the FBI knowing about it. The FBI had the advantage of shared intelligence with the security services of the Western European nations. They knew what to look for and who to guard against. Almost unlimited funding was available to them and the CIA to watch these Arab and anarchist terrorist groups, and they couldn't put their people here. They tried, but they were never successful, and the myth got stronger."

"I see," said McKenna. "The FBI and the CIA have virtually no intelligence on *Sendero Luminoso*."

"Right. And it can't be too hard for *Sendero Luminoso* to slip their people into this country. All they have to do is get them to either Mexico or the Dominican Republic, which is no great feat. Just look at the number of illegal immigrants here from these two countries. From the Dominican Republic, it's just a short boat trip to Ponce, Puerto Rico, American soil. Then they just climb on a plane for the mainland, no questions asked, just like flying from Boston to New York. And getting here from Mexico is even easier. They just walk across. They look like everybody else coming here from those two

171

countries and they speak the language. Once they're here, they can go from one Latin community to another, and nobody'll bother them."

By this time they had finished dinner and everyone took their plates to the kitchen sink. Angelita started scraping the dishes and putting them in the dishwasher while Brunette finished clearing the table and McKenna wiped the table. Then McKenna put coffee into his old espresso coffeepot and plugged it in. The two men returned to the living room and sat down while Angelita stayed in the kitchen to finish the dishes.

"It looks like we might be solving all the FBI's problems for them. Why didn't they come clean with us right away? We're gonna get these guys, or at least get closer than they did," said McKenna.

"That's not what's worrying them. Once we started to get close, they sat down and did some thinking, and now they're really worried."

"Why? Because we make them look bad?" asked McKenna.

"No. It's bigger than that. The FBI feels it was *Sendero Luminoso* that called their office in Miami to tell them where the body was located. They didn't call the Miami police, they called the FBI, which the FBI thought was a direct challenge. They can't let *Sendero Luminoso* get away with it, or every guerrilla group in Latin America would find a reason to extend their operations to the United States to pursue their goal. But then they thought some more and now believe that *Sendero Luminoso* feels they can't lose, even if they get caught. If they get caught, they get the publicity for their cause that they haven't been able to generate so far in this country. Which is the thing that the FBI fears most—prisoners of an active and capable guerrilla army being held for trial in this country for killing nationals of their own country. They envision a wave of destruction of American property abroad and the taking of American hostages to get us to release their comrades. We'd be in the position of France, Germany, Italy, and even Israel, of being pressured to release terrorists to save American lives and property. It's something the Feds didn't have to worry about before."

Brunette paused for a few minutes while McKenna thought over the implications of finding Rodrigo and capturing his kidnappers. Finally Brunette asked, "You know what that means, Brian?"

"I know the sensible thing. No prisoners when we find them," McKenna answered.

"Weatherby didn't exactly say that, but I'm sure that was his intention," Brunette said. "I think that's one of the reasons he wanted to make this a total FBI operation. That and the fact that he didn't want the press in on this at all so that the *Sendero Luminoso* operations in this country wouldn't be publicized. But thanks to you, it's our game now. The FBI is just going to be our assistant on the sidelines."

Angelita brought out the espresso and they sipped it in silence. Then McKenna said, "Maybe we should give this back to the FBI. I think they might be right. Maybe there should be no prisoners, and they must be prepared for that. I don't enjoy killing people. Besides, we need too much. We have to find out exactly where Rodrigo was kidnapped from, we have to get in touch with his family, we have to talk to Raoul Camarena to see how Rico got his license, and we have to find out who Rico is. The FBI is better equipped than us to do all those things."

Angelita was bringing out the cheesecake when Brunette said, "Speaking of Rico, have you heard from Doctor Stienner?"

Angelita stopped short and said, "There was a message from a Doctor Stienner left on the answering machine. I was out earlier and I didn't think it was important, so I forgot to mention it. Sorry."

McKenna played back the answering machine that was on the table next to the sofa. The message from Dr. Stienner only listed a number to call. McKenna looked at the time. Eleven thirty. He dialed the number and Stienner answered. McKenna identified himself and then took notes on a pad next to the phone for ten minutes while Stienner talked. McKenna didn't say a word, he just wrote. Then the thanked the doctor and hung up. McKenna told Brunette, "You'd better keep the FBI heavily involved in this case, Ray. It's getting worse."

"How much worse?"

"A lot. We're dealing with some real professionals here," McKenna said. He read from the notes he had just made. "Doctor Stienner took a picture of Rico, along with his height, weight, a description and age of his scars, and his approximate age to the United Nations office of Amnesty International. He talked to some friends there and the UN office faxed the photo and information to Amnesty International's Buenos Aires office and to their Montevideo, Uruguay, office. They heard from the Buenos Aires office. Rico is Doctor Carlos Mendosa, one of the twenty thousand Argentines who disappeared after they were kidnapped by the Argentine military during their "Dirty War" with the leftist Argentine groups. The war lasted from 1972 to 1983."

"So he's their doctor," said Brunette. "When did the military kidnap him and why's he in New York? I thought they were all dead?"

"There's more. Doctor Mendosa's brother, Alfonso Mendosa, had been identified by the Argentine secret police as 'Ali,' a former leader of the *Montonero* guerrilla army. Alfonso's wife, Isabela, had also been identified as a member of the *Montoneros* and in 1978 the group attacked and destroyed a number of Argentine military and police installations. Lots of losses on both sides. Shortly after these attacks, Carlos Mendosa was kidnapped as he left his office in Rosario, Argentina. He became one of the *Desaparecidos,* the 'Disappeared Ones.' Doctor Stienner said it's now known that Carlos Mendosa was taken to the secret-police headquarters in Rosario for questioning before execution. That's where he must have got all those scars. You had to see them."

"Yeah, I heard that they were bad. Go on."

"Two days after Carlos was kidnapped, the *Montoneros* successfully attacked the secret-police headquarters in Rosario. All the officers that weren't killed during the attack were summarily executed by the guerrillas before they left. The *Montoneros* also freed all the prisoners being held in the headquarters by the secret police. Doctor Stienner said that during the next three years, every secret-police official of the Rosario barracks was hunted down and killed by the *Montoneros*. 'Ali' was identified as the leader of many of these assassination squads and he led a few ambushes against the Argentine army. But the Argentine army eventually won. Neither 'Ali' nor Isabela were ever known to have been captured or killed."

"That was a long time ago. How can Stienner be sure that Rico is Carlos Mendosa?"

"He's sure. In 1983 the military government was thrown out in Argentina after they lost the Falklands war. There was a big movement to account for the *Desaparecidos* and Alfonso's mother, Carmen Mendosa, became one of the major leaders of an influential organization, the Mothers of the Disappeared Ones. They got some press here years ago. She couldn't protest over Alfonso and Isabela because there are still active arrest warrents for them in Argentina for crimes like bank robbery and kidnapping. But she wanted to know about her son Carlos. In 1985 she left the organization. Doctor Stienner assumes she had found out that Carlos was still alive. Doctor Stienner said that she identified his picture today. The Doctor Carlos Mendosa of 1978 is the Rico of 1992."

Neither Brunette nor Angelita said a word for the next few minutes as they digested the information that McKenna had just given them. Then Brunette said, "I have the sketch that I forgot to show you before. It was interesting then, but now I think it's very important."

Brunette pulled an FBI sketch out of the folder and handed it to McKenna, saying, "This is a sketch of the man in Miami. It's the man who the woman who rented the apartment there identified as her husband."

McKenna looked at the sketch. It looked like it could be a sketch of Rico, except the man in the sketch didn't have a beard. And he didn't have the ugly scars on his chin that the beard concealed. "Alfonso Mendosa," McKenna guessed.

174

"And the woman who rented the apartments must be Isabela," Angelita said. "We're getting out of here. This man hunted down and killed everyone who had anything to do with torturing his brother, Brian. And you just killed his brother. You're getting off this job and we're going to start having a normal life."

Brunette and McKenna just stared at Angelita. She knew that she was talking to herself. Finally she came to the same realization that Brunette and McKenna already had. She shrugged her shoulders and hid her face in her hands. Then she said it. "I know that they've got to be killed. But not by you, Brian. Please get out of this."

McKenna didn't answer her. Each person kept their own thoughts for a while. The silence started to become uncomfortable. Then Brunette asked McKenna, "Are you in or out, buddy."

"I don't see any other way for me, Ray. I'm already in too far to get out. I don't want to have to be looking over my shoulder for the rest of my life. I'm in till this is over." Then he turned to Angelita and said, "I need more time, Angelita. I have to stay with this case till the end."

Without saying a word, Angelita turned and walked into the kitchen. Once again, the silence started to get uncomfortable. Then Brunette said, "They don't have a doctor anymore. You killed him yesterday, Brian. If Rodrigo is going to lose any more fingers before we find him, it's not gonna be easy for him."

Silence again. They were thinking of Rodrigo, thinking of Rico, and thinking of themselves. Brunette made a number of decisions and he spoke with authority. He wasn't Ray the friend anymore. He was the chief of detectives. He was talking from years of experience and McKenna was ready to listen.

"We're gonna use the FBI as much as we can. They'll talk to the CIA and to the security forces in Peru and Argentina to find out what they know about Alfonso and Isabela Mendosa. We're gonna know whatever they know. When we learn the location where Rodrigo's being held, only you and other people I trust will be there. I'm not gonna have you and Angelita worrying about these people for the rest of your lives. We're gonna do it right. We'll use our people and it's gonna stay our show, not the FBI's. Agreed?"

"I've got no choice," said McKenna.

Brunette continued. "Tomorrow Pacella and Sal Catalfumo are going to Massachusetts to guide the FBI on their investigation there. I want them to find out the location where Rodrigo was kidnapped and I want to know what happened to the bodyguard. But most of all, I want to know if the kidnappers overlooked anything. If they did, Tommy'll find it."

"Why is Tommy going without me?"

"Because tomorrow you're going to Fort Myers Beach to talk to Raoul Camarena. The Documents Section said that Rico's license was an excellent forgery made by using a color photocopy of Camarena's license with Rico's picture superimposed over it. Camarena won't talk to the FBI since they tore his house apart with their search warrant. Maybe he knows something about the Mendosas, even if he doesn't realize it. You find out. Bobby'll drive you to the airport in the morning. I'll take care of the tickets."

"But Camarena's in Miami."

"Not anymore. Someone called and told him when the FBI searched his house and he went home."

"What'll Tavlin say about me and Pacella disappearing for these assignments?"

"Don't worry about Steve Tavlin," Brunette answered. "He's one of my trusted men. I promoted him and I put him where he is. He won't ask any questions."

Angelita returned from the kitchen. McKenna and Brunette could both see that she had been crying. "Anybody need anything else?" she asked.

"Yeah, about ten hours of sleep," Brunette answered. "Why don't we end this party and get to bed. Tomorrow's gonna be a big day."

Bed sounds like a good idea, thought McKenna. Maybe I can soften Angelita up a bit.

16

McKenna was awakened by the sound of the door buzzer. He looked at the clock on the nightstand. Too early, he thought. He got up and passed by Ray's room on the way to the intercom. Empty. Ray had made the bed before he left. McKenna answered the intercom. It was Bobby. McKenna yelled for Angelita to get up and he waited by the door. He still felt tired. It had been a hectic night.

Angelita had been very upset and McKenna knew from experience that he couldn't talk sense to her when she was in that mood. He wasn't sure if he had anything to say that made much sense, anyway. He knew that she had slept very little during the night. McKenna himself had been awakened a few times during the night by the sound of Ray's mobile telephone ringing in the bedroom next door. Each time, he had found that Angelita was still awake.

McKenna opened the apartment door for Bobby before he had a chance to ring the bell. Bobby looked beat.

"Morning, Brian," he said. "I'm taking you to the airport. You got an eight-thirty flight outta La Guardia."

"Got time for breakfast?"

"Sounds good."

"Where's Ray?" McKenna asked.

"Just dropped him off at his office. He called me at one this morning and told me to pick him up at six. He was outside when I got here. Mind if I catch a nap while you get ready? This twenty-four-hour job is killing me."

177

"Hit the couch, pal."

Bobby headed right to the living room and collapsed on the sofa. Angelita came out of the bedroom in a robe and began making breakfast while McKenna went into the bathroom to shower and shave. At least Ray's absence this morning alleviated the usual line for the bathroom, McKenna thought.

Breakfast was almost ready by the time McKenna got out. He quickly dressed and then packed a small bag. He put the photos of Rico, his pistol, and his case notes into the bag. McKenna figured that he wouldn't need a change of clothes, but he wanted a bag to put his gun in and check as luggage. It would save the trouble of notifying the airline that he would be traveling on official business with a gun on board. They'd become so touchy lately. Then he woke up Bobby and sat him down at the table for breakfast. Angelita brought the bacon and eggs in and also sat down.

After Bobby had had his first gulp of coffee, McKenna asked, "What's Ray doing in his office at six thirty in the morning?"

"Beats me. Said he had to talk to the commissioner and he wanted to get his thoughts together."

Bobby and McKenna were ready to leave for the airport by seven thirty. Angelita gave McKenna a look that said she wanted to speak to him in private, and he followed her into the bedroom while Bobby waited awkwardly by the front door of the apartment. In the bedroom, Angelita turned and said, "I've been thinking all night. Remember what I said about giving you two days to decide. Two days are up and you've evidently decided that this job is more important than me and our happiness together. I won't be here when you get back from Florida."

"Where you gonna be?"

"At my folks' house for now."

"Aren't you being a little hasty and close-minded about this, baby? You know that I love you. I just need a little more time. That's not a lot to ask."

"It's too much. I'm not here to watch you get killed. I've got to get away, Brian. I'm just not up to this anymore. I'm sorry, but this is it."

"Don't do this. Let's talk when I get back."

Angelita didn't answer. Her eyes started to fill with tears. Then she ran from the bedroom to the bathroom and closed the door.

Well, that's that, for now at least, McKenna thought. He joined Bobby at the front door. "Let's go, buddy," he said.

They made good time and got to La Guardia Airport just after eight. It was a quiet trip. Bobby could see that McKenna didn't feel much like talking. As McKenna was leaving the car, Bobby gave him a folder that he had under the seat. "Ray told me to give you this," Bobby said. "It's some light reading for your flight."

McKenna opened the folder while he was still standing at the curb. It was a classified report from the National Security Agency addressed to the director of the Federal Bureau of Investigation. The title of the report was "Confidential Assessment of *Sendero Luminoso.*" McKenna was glad to get it. He needed something to occupy his mind. He said good-bye to Bobby and headed into the terminal.

There was a ticket for Fort Myers waiting for him at the Delta ticket counter. He checked his bag and still had twenty minutes before his flight, so he decided to call Camarena to let him know that he was coming. He didn't have Camarena's phone number, so he dialed Rosa Figueroa. She answered on the third ring.

McKenna told Rosa that he was on his way to Fort Myers Beach to see her and Raoul and that he would be there at about two that afternoon.

"Raoul won't be here then," Rosa said. "He owns a fishing boat and he decided to work today. But you can go to his house and wait till he comes home. I'll meet you there. You heard what the FBI did?"

"Yeah, they're not too sharp. I had nothing to do with that."

"They messed up the house and I'll probably still be cleaning when you get here. Raoul is real mad at them. I hope he doesn't mind that you're coming."

"I'll be nice, not like the FBI," McKenna said. "I just need to show him a picture and ask him some questions. He shouldn't mind that. I'll see you at two."

McKenna hung up and then called the Fort Myers Beach Police Department. He asked to speak to Investigator Miguel Montoya, the investigator who had initially responded to the NYPD notification request for Raoul Camarena. Montoya came on the line, and McKenna asked if he would pick him up at the airport at 1:30 and bring him a copy of the police report that Camarena had filed on the theft of his wallet in November.

"No problem," Montoya answered. "I don't have much to do today, anyway."

Maybe I took a wrong turn in life, McKenna thought. Maybe I would've been better off working in a suburban Florida police department with not much to do. McKenna told Montoya that he would buy lunch and hung up. He was the last one to board the plane. There were many empty seats. The smart money doesn't head for Florida in July, he thought.

As soon as they were airborne, McKenna opened up the folder and began reading the report. It was difficult and loaded with statistics. What McKenna got from it was that Peru was a mess. The population was estimated at twenty million, with 10 percent white, 55 percent *mestizo,* or persons of mixed blood, and 35 percent Indians. About four million people primarily spoke one of the two dominant Indian languages. There was 40 percent unemployment, triple-digit inflation, a 15 percent illiteracy rate, and 70 percent of the population had no electric service to their homes.

The resources of the country were disparately divided, with the whites owning most of the resources, and the top 2 percent of the population was enormously wealthy, having profited in the last century from the now depleted export of guano as an agricultural fertilizer. This 2 percent tended to exercise behind-the-scenes control of the politics of the country. One of the main problems facing Peru was the lack of investment capital, as the deteriorating economy and the huge inflation rate made foreign investment more attractive to rich Peruvians than investment in their own country.

Again this background, McKenna learned, two major guerrilla groups operated in Peru. One was the Tupac Amarú, a predominantly Indian group that operated in the northeast part of the country. *Sendero Luminoso* was the other group.

The report stated that *Sendero Luminoso* operated in the mountains and, increasingly, in the urban areas of the country. Their philosophy was Maoist, calling for the total redistribution of wealth. Their tactics were violent confrontation with the government, coupled with attempts to disrupt life in the cities by acts of sabotage, bombings, assassinations, and kidnappings. Their creed was to tell no lies in their dealings with the government and to exact certain revenge against the individuals they considered responsible for every act of repression by the government. *Sendero Luminoso* was in partial or absolute control of 25 of Peru's 180 provinces.

The report showed that the contest between the government and *Sendero Luminoso* was a no-mercy, no-quarter war. Fifteen thousand people had been killed during the course of the conflict, and a 1989 Amnesty International report stated that government forces had executed three thousand members of the group and that another three thousand had disappeared while in police custody. Many of the acts of terrorism that Amnesty International attributed to the government were carried out by a secret paramilitary group known as the *Comando Rodrigo Franco.* The government also held about fifteen thousand prisoners suspected of belonging to *Sendero Luminoso.*

Sendero Luminoso had answered each round of government operations and arrests with terror and assassinations. During a national election in November 1989, the group murdered so many of the candidates and incumbents that some provinces had no slate of contestants for the election.

180

According to the report, *Sendero Luminoso* was previously thought to be armcd by Cuba. Recently, these arms supplies had dried up and *Sendero Luminoso* had extended its control to the coca-producing regions of Peru. There was increased evidence that the group was preparing to enter the international narcotics trade in cocaine to finance its war against the government.

In 1989 the United States government placed itself in indirect confrontation with *Sendero Luminoso.* In cooperation with the Peruvian government, they initiated Operation Snow Cap, which entailed spraying the coca fields controlled by *Sendero Luminoso,* further depleting the group's ability to purchase arms on the international arms market. In April 1990, the United States government stationed Special Forces troops in Peru to train the Peruvian army to combat *Sendero Luminoso.* The United States provided $35 million annually in military aid to the Peruvian army.

The report stated that the operational leadership of *Sendero Luminoso* was uncertain, since most of the old leadership had been captured by government forces and subsequently killed in a prison uprising in 1982. There were reports that foreign nationals had been operating in some positions of leadership in the group since that time, and that many of these new leaders had received training in Cuba or in Lcbanon. Leadership was now based on a cell structure, with members of one cell having knowledge of no more than one member of the next higher cell in the organizational structure.

By the time McKenna had digested as much of the report as he cared to, the plane was landing in Atlanta, where he had to change. He left the plane and paused long enough at a window in the connecting corridor to watch his bag leave the Miami-bound plane and get loaded on the Fort Myers—bound plane, which was parked at the next gate. McKenna boarded and saw there were even fewer people on this flight.

McKenna thought over the things that he considered important in the report, the things that affected his investigation and his life. He found it interesting that *Sendero Luminoso* was preparing to traffic in cocaine. There was already cocaine involved in this case. What was the connection among a fishing-boat operator in Florida, two drug dealers in Brooklyn, and an Argentine doctor fighting in the United States for a Peruvian guerrilla group? Then there was the fact that when and if they finally located the place where Rodrigo was being held, the police department would be facing a military organization trained in reprisals, bombings, urban warfare, and assassination. Quite a lot to handle.

One of the things that disturbed McKenna was *Sendero Luminoso*'s documented policy of seeking revenge against specific government officials involved in confrontation with them. That policy seemed to fit right in with Alfonso Mendosa's own philosophy. He felt certain, just from the little he knew of Alfonso Mendosa, that "Ali" would seek personal retribution for the death of his brother.

Which brought McKenna to the thing that disturbed him most. Last night, sitting in the living room of his home, he had tacitly joined a death squad. Maybe not a death squad in the style of the *Comando Rodrigo Franco,* for he was not going to drag anyone out of their home and summarily execute them. But the result was the same. To protect his own life, he was going to ensure the death of others, using whatever means he could. He had placed himself above the law he had sworn to protect.

How did I get into this mess, McKenna wondered. He knew little and cared less about Peru and its problems. He had never intended to go there, and the country was now certainly scratched off his list of places to see. McKenna didn't care what was happening in New Jersey, much less Peru.

McKenna realized that he was in this mess because two days ago he had been bored in Brooklyn and had decided to take another gun off the street. He became interested in an unusual case, and that interest might have saved his life. Otherwise, he was sure, he would have been gunned down on the street or killed in a bombing of his apartment without ever knowing why. If it happened now, at least he would know why. Crazy reasons, but reasons that *Sendero Luminoso* and "Ali" lived by.

McKenna remained lost in thought until the plane landed. He looked at his watch. Right on time, 1:30. McKenna got off the plane and was waiting at the baggage carousel for his bag when he saw a man looking around. He was straight out of "Miami Vice." Beige cotton suit, white shirt, no tie, white loafers, large automatic on his belt under his jacket, two-day growth of beard, great tan, and I-can-see-you-but-you-can't-see-me mirrored sunglasses. Investigator Miguel Montoya of the Fort Myers Beach Police Department, an uptown pimp, or a moderately successful drug dealer, McKenna thought. McKenna picked up his bag and went over to Mr. Flash. "Hello, Miguel," he said. "I'm Brian McKenna."

"How'd you know who I was?" Montoya asked.

"Easy. You just look like a cop to me," McKenna lied.

Montoya brought McKenna out to his car, which was parked right on the curb outside the terminal. The Florida heat hit McKenna like a fist in the face. He took a couple of seconds at the curb to adjust to the change in the environment while he looked at Montoya's car in amazement. Not only was the car clean, but it had also been waxed. Life was good for those who preserved the peace in the Sunbelt,

McKenna thought. He got into the car, took his pistol and holster from his bag, and put them on.

Miguel Montoya turned out to be a pleasant enough fellow. He gave McKenna the Fort Myers Beach police report on the theft of Camarena's wallet. On November 24 Camarena had walked into the police headquarters and said that his wallet containing his driver's license and his social security card had been taken from under the front seat of his 1991 Oldsmobile while he had been fishing on his boat. The place of occurrence listed was the Fort Myers Beach town-dock parking lot. The report mentioned no damage to Camarena's car.

"Know anything about Raoul Camarena?" McKenna asked.

"I checked him out. He never had any dealings with us before, cxccpt for the theft report. Until the FBI decided to search his house, that is. He called me last night and told me that he was suing me, the Fort Myers Beach Police Department, the City of Fort Myers Beach, the State of Florida, the FBI, and the United States government because we violated his rights. I don't think he'll be happy to see me. Maybe I should wait in the car while you talk to him."

"Fine by me. What did the FBI get on the search?"

"I don't know. I wasn't in on the actual search. I'm getting sued just because I represented the Fort Myers Beach Police Department. I sat outside the house the whole time talking with one of our uniformed guys while the FBI was inside. It was their warrant and they never invited me in, thank God."

"How long did it take them?" McKenna asked.

"Four hours. They made a big job outta it. They brought a locksmith to open the doors, vacuum cleaners, fingerprint technicians, and photographers. I don't think they got anything. I didn't see them take anything big out and they didn't seem too happy."

It took half an hour to drive to Camarena's place. It was a small corner house, but the nicest one on the block. Everything on the outside was meticulously cared for. A bright green lawn contrasted with the brown lawns of the neighbors. McKenna saw that Camarena had an underground lawn sprinkler system. The driveway was new concrete and without the small oil stains of the other driveways on the block. The windows and the red-tile roof looked new. There were flowers everywhere and an in-ground pool in the backyard. A late-model Ford Bronco was in the driveway and McKenna remembered that Montoya had run the plate when he was trying to make the next-of-kin notification for the NYPD and found that it was registered to Rosa Figueroa. There wasn't a dent or a speck of dust on it.

McKenna left Montoya in the car, took the folder with Rico's picture from his bag, went up to the front door, and rang the bell. Rosa Rigueroa answered. McKenna could see that she would have no trouble selling real estate or anything else. She was beautiful and her smile lit up the doorway. Rosa was about thirty years old with large eyes, long black hair worn wrapped up on the top of her head, and a great tan. She was dressed for business in the Florida fashion, wearing shorts, a loose-fitting halter top, and sandals. McKenna introduced himself and he shook her offered hand. He felt a large rock on her finger. McKenna saw the diamond engagement ring as he released her hand. More than a carat, he thought. Raoul obviously thought quite a lot of Rosa, if the ring was real.

Rosa invited McKenna in and he was instantly chilled by a blast of air conditioning. About seventy-two degrees, he thought. Raoul wasn't worried about his electric bill.

McKenna noted the signs of the FBI's visit. Rosa watched his face as he looked around the living room. The walls showed the black or white smudges of the fingerprint technician's dusting powder at all the corners. The rugs were no longer snug against the walls; the FBI had obviously lifted them. There were indentations on the rug that showed that the furniture hadn't been replaced in the exact spots the pieces had previously occupied. The place was a neat mess. McKenna said to her, "The FBI's got some nerve. I'd sure sue them myself if this was my place. I hope you get them good."

McKenna thought that he just made a friend out of Rosa Figueroa. "Why'd they do it?" she asked.

"They just made a mistake. They make lots of mistakes," McKenna answered, but as he looked around the living room, he wasn't so sure. He would now bet that Rosa's diamond ring was real. Everything in the small simple living room was quality. Antique Spanish furniture in excellent condition, a Hitachi projection TV, two Sony VCRs, an elaborate stereo system, and a collection of bronze statues of bull fighters and bulls in a display case. The fishing-boat business must be better than I imagined, McKenna thought. He noted that the top of the display case was filled by a row of fishing-tournament trophies.

"Can I get you something to drink?" Rosa asked.

"Maybe later. I wanna show you a picture now, if you don't mind."

He pulled the picture of Rico from the folder and handed it to Rosa. While she was stared at it he said, "I'm sorry, but I lied to you yesterday. The man in the picture wasn't killed in an accident. He was killed by the New York Police during a gun fight two days ago. He was carrying a forgery of Raoul's license and Raoul's Social Security card in his wallet. That was the mistake the FBI made. They thought Raoul was the dead man because he had Raoul's ID. Honest mistake, but still stupid."

184

McKenna pointed to the photo. "Have you ever seen him before?"

She handed the photo back to McKenna and said to him without a trace of emotion, "Don't tell me another lie. Aren't you the one who killed this man, Detective McKenna?"

They did their homework, McKenna thought. They went to the trouble to read a New York newspaper, or somebody told them something. "Yes, it was me," McKenna said. "I didn't want to tell you because I didn't want you to be afraid of me. That's why I'm on the case. My boss wants me to try and find out who the man I shot really was. At least I got a trip to Florida out of it."

His answer seemed to satisfy her. He had her confidence. Rosa said, "I don't think that I've ever seen that man before in my life. What else do you need to know from me?"

"Nothing, really. I just hope that Raoul will recognize him, since he used Raoul's license to make the forgery he was carrying."

McKenna decided to extend his position a little. There was more that he needed to know from Rosa about Raoul. He said, "I know that Figueroa is a Spanish name, but I can't hear a trace of a Spanish accent when you talk."

She laughed at him and said in an exaggerated Spanish accent, "Maybe you tink you like me better if I talk like dees, Seenyor."

McKenna laughed with her. "Sorry. I wasn't trying to be insulting," he said.

"That's all right. I'm not insulted. I'm Cuban, but I was born in the United States."

"Do you speak Spanish?"

"Of course."

"How about Raoul?" he asked.

"Yes, he does," she said. "He was born in Cuba. Raoul is one of the good *Marielitos,* the ones that you don't read about in the newspapers."

"*Marielitos?*" McKenna asked. McKenna knew who the Marielitos were, but he thought that this was a good time to look stupid.

Rosa said, "The *Marielitos* were the last wave of Cuban immigrants to arrive in this country. They came here in small boats in 1978, mostly from the port of Mariel in Cuba. Lots of good people came here then, but so did some bad ones. Castro played a little joke on Uncle Sam. He emptied his prisons and mental institutes onto small boats and pointed them in the direction of the mainland. 'Good luck and don't come back,' he told them. He sent some spies too. Some of the *Marielitos* are in jail in this country now, but most are good citizens. But it's the bad ones who got the publicity. Not the good ones, like Raoul."

"You said that Raoul is a fisherman?"

"Yes. He was a fisherman in Cuba too. When he got to this country he worked hard on his brother's boat in Miami. He saved his money and his brother helped him to buy his own boat. Now he owns the best for-hire sport-fishing boat in Fort Myers Beach. He's always working and never does anything wrong. He's even a citizen now and he loves this country."

Rosa was obviously very proud of her man, so McKenna said to her, "He sounds like quite a guy."

Rosa seemed to like McKenna's opinion. Dumb old Detective McKenna is doing real good, he thought.

"Can I make you a sandwich or something?" she asked.

"No thanks. I've got a local cop in the car outside and I promised to take him to dinner. What time does Raoul usually get home?"

"Four o'clock, but his car is in the shop. I'm gonna pick him up at the dock and we were supposed to go out to dinner. Why don't you just eat something light and meet us at the town dock at four? Your friend will know where it is. Then you can come to dinner with us. Raoul knows the best restaurants in town."

"Thank you. I'll be there at four. See you then." Rosa opened the door for him and he said as he left, "I hope Raoul doesn't mind."

McKenna rejoined Montoya in his car. "Let me buy you lunch in a good restaurant for your troubles," he told Montoya as soon as he got in.

Montoya didn't need to hear any more. He drove down the coast road to a restaurant called The Fisherman's Cove. The back of the restaurant was right on the beach. They went in and McKenna was a little disappointed. Montoya didn't seem to be recognized by the staff of the restaurant. What kind of a detective is he? McKenna thought. They took a table facing the beach and sat down to study the menus. A large seafood selection, McKenna noted. Moderately priced by New York standards, but probably considered exorbitant in Fort Myers Beach. The cocktail waitress came by and Montoya ordered a frozen margarita, McKenna a Coke. While they were having their drinks, McKenna asked, "How's the crime here?"

"Getting worse all the time. We got two homicides already this year, which is a lot for us. Last year at this time we didn't have any. And the burglaries are keeping us busy. In the summer the snowbirds leave their homes here and head north. They never know what they're gonna find when they get back."

"Many robberies here?" McKenna asked.

"Twelve robberies of convenience stores alone this year."

McKenna maintained a sympathetic ear. Times were tough. He didn't want to burst Montoya's bubble by telling him that more crimes were reported in the Two-Five last week than happened in his entire Fort Myers Beach crime wave.

"You got any problems with drug smugglers?" McKenna asked.

"Nothing I'm aware of. Of course, the DEA and the Coast Guard are always catching them at sea, but we don't get involved in that. We got enough to do."

McKenna had an idea. He excused himself from the table and went to the row of pay phones against the wall next to the bar. There was something else he needed to know about Raoul, and he knew that he would have to break a few rules and laws to find out. He wanted to know something about Raoul that all the police computer networks in the country couldn't tell him, so he called Bob Hurley in New York. Bob was an old friend, a retired detective who now ran a private investigating service that specialized in debt collection.

Hurley answered the phone and McKenna told him that he needed to know someone's outstanding debts and credit rating. "A little risky, Brian. But for you, I'll do it. Give me his information."

McKenna offered Raoul's Social Security number, his date of birth, and his address. "Call me back in half an hour," Hurley said.

McKenna hung up and was returning to his table when he saw a man at the bar who seemed to be staring at him. As soon as McKenna looked at him, the man looked away. He was white, about thirty years old, wearing tan slacks, a white shirt, and a blue blazer. The alignment of the buttons on his shirt was two inches to the left of his belt buckle. Maybe a gun on his right side, McKenna thought. It seems he's trying very hard not to look at me now.

The waitress returned to the table as soon as McKenna sat down again. He ordered the baked grouper. Montoya ordered the surf 'n' turf and another drink. Without looking at the menu, McKenna knew that Montoya's order would be the most expensive dish served by the restaurant. I'm having a tough day, McKenna told himself. Buy dinner for the kid and he orders the best. Time to have some fun with him. "I think I fixed things for you with Raoul Camarena," he said to Montoya.

"Great. How'd you do that?"

"I just told them that you agreed with them. The FBI was a bunch of dumb rednecks and they should have to pay for being so stupid," McKenna answered.

When Montoya heard this, he started to dribble his drink on his beige suit. Hardly noticeable, McKenna thought. You should have ordered a frozen strawberry daiquiri. Something with color for contrast.

"Why'd you do that?" Montoya protested.

187

"Don't worry, Miguel. Only kidding. I've got a feeling that the lawsuit is going nowhere. I think that Raoul Camarena is about to see the error of his ways."

"What makes you think that?" Montoya asked.

"I'll tell you when I know a little more. But I think Raoul's dirty. He's making more money than the average for-hire boat owner."

The waitress returned to ask if everything was all right, and McKenna answered, "Just fine. Has Raoul Camarena been in yet today?"

"No," she replied. "Mr. Camarena usually comes in on Wednesdays."

McKenna was gratified by that information. The most expensive restaurant in town, and Raoul comes here every Wednesday. There was a lot of cash floating around in Raoul's life. McKenna knew a retired cop who owned an open fishing boat on Long Island. He was good and he did a great business. But he wasn't living anywhere near as well as Raoul, even with his pension.

McKenna and Montoya finished their dinners. The grouper was good and well worth the price. McKenna picked up the check when it came and Montoya left the tip. Ten dollars. Not such a bad guy, McKenna thought. On their way out, McKenna again stopped at the phones. The man in the blue blazer was still at the bar and still trying not to look. McKenna took out his note pad and pen and called Bob Hurley again.

"Your boy's in excellent shape," Bob said. Raoul had borrowed $100,000 on a business loan for a boat in 1988. It was a five-year variable-rate loan with monthly payments averaging $3,200 a month. He'd bought his home with a $40,000 home-mortgage loan in 1988. The monthly payments were $417 a month. Raoul had taken a $10,000 three-year auto loan in 1991. The monthly payments for that loan were $485 a month. Raoul had a total of thirteen credit cards with a total credit limit of $24,000. He had never owed more than $3,000 on his cards. Raoul's credit rating was excellent. He always paid on time. McKenna did some quick calculations. Raoul had a $4,100 nut to crack every month before he could live and breathe. Fishing had to be great at those figures.

"Thanks Bob. I owe you. I'll return the favor sometime."

"I'm not worried, Brian. You always do."

McKenna hung up and said to Montoya, "Don't stare, but do you know the guy in the blue blazer at the bar?"

Montoya was good and casual. He took a quick look around the place and then walked out with McKenna following. On the way to his car he said, "Never saw him before. Why?"

"Probably nothing. Don't worry about it."

188

"What did you find out about Camarena?"

"It's like I said. He's spending a lot of dough and everything's not straight with him. I'll keep you posted."

They had an hour before Raoul's boat put in, so Montoya showed McKenna a bit of the town. It was beautiful. Large condo apartment buildings everywhere, most on canals with boat slips in the back. There were restaurants all along the coast road. They passed what looked like a pretty good golf course with lots of water holes. Everything was clean and the traffic wasn't too bad. McKenna liked this place better than West Palm Beach, where he and Ray owned adjoining condos. Maybe retiring here wouldn't be so bad, he thought. I'll have to tell Ray about it. Living in a place where the cops don't have much to do might be nice.

At 3:45 Montoya pulled into the parking lot by the town boat dock. Rosa's Bronco was already there.

"Want me to pick you up later and drive you back to the airport?" Montoya asked.

"Thanks anyway. I'll take a taxi when I'm ready to go. I appreciate your help and I'll give you a call when I find out what's going on with this guy."

"OK. Good luck. I'll be at the station if you change your mind."

Montoya drove off and McKenna walked over to the dock, carrying his overnight bag.

The for-hire boats were starting to put in. None of them were crowded, and McKenna thought that owning a for-hire boat here in July was more like a hobby than a job.

He saw Rosa. She was standing on the dock talking on a pay phone. The phone was located right under the sign for the *Pescador II,* which stated that the *Pescador II* was the best and fastest for-hire sportfishing boat in Fort Myers Beach. The price was $400 a day. Raoul's boat hadn't put in yet, but McKenna saw a big sport-fishing boat coming through the channel.

Rosa waved when she saw McKenna. A few seconds later, she hung up the phone. It was getting a little cooler, and she had changed for dinner into a pink cotton sleeveless dress with matching pink high heels. She had let her hair down and looked like a real class act. When McKenna was next to her she asked, "Where did you go for lunch?"

"Had a couple of burgers at McDonald's," McKenna lied.

"McDonald's?" she said, disdainfully. Then she turned and pointed at the big boat coming in. There were three big fish hanging from the rear of the boat. Raoul did know his business, McKenna thought.

The *Pescador II* pulled into the dock. Raoul's mate jumped off the boat and secured it to the dock. It was a fifty-foot fiber glass Bertram, which McKenna knew was an expensive boat. Like Raoul's house, the boat was spotless. It was the prettiest boat around, and McKenna figured that it was also the fastest, just like the sign said.

When the boat was docked, the captain came down from the topside bridge and shook the hands of the four paying passengers. The passengers then jumped to the dock and the mate helped them carry the fish to their cars. Raoul was having a good day so far, McKenna thought.

Raoul waved at Rosa from the bridge and then he and the mate began cleaning the boat. They used fresh water from a hose on the dock to wash away the fish blood and salt water. Raoul was dressed in an old pair of blue jeans and a T-shirt that had PESCADOR II printed across the front. While Raoul and his mate were hosing down the boat, McKenna caught Raoul stealing a couple of glances at him. McKenna waved each time their eyes met. The mate left after they finished and Raoul went into the main cabin.

Ten minutes later Raoul came out dressed in Miguel Montoya fashion. When Raoul stepped off the boat, Rosa introduced McKenna to him. Raoul was polite but reserved. McKenna ignored his aloofness and said, "That's the most beautiful boat I've ever seen."

Raoul couldn't help himself. He had to show off his boat, his first love. "C'mon aboard. I'll show you around," he said.

"I'd love that."

Raoul showed McKenna the navigation equipment on the bridge, the twenty-five-mile Furuno radar, the LORAN, the depth finder, and the sophisticated fish finder. There was a galley where lunches were prepared for the paying customers. Then came the engine room. Twin Detroit Diesel 1200s with matched Allison transmissions. "This boat will do thirty-five knots all day," Raoul said proudly. McKenna made a mental note of everything.

At the end of the tour McKenna asked, "What does *pescador* mean?"

"Spanish for 'fisherman,' " Raoul replied.

As they were leaving the boat, McKenna heard Raoul ask Rosa in Spanish, "Why did you bring him to the boat? Aren't we having enough trouble with the police here?"

She appeared to be annoyed with his question, but replied in Spanish, "Don't be like that. He's a nice man and he had nothing to do with searching the house. He doesn't even like the FBI."

"What does he want?" he asked her, again in Spanish.

"He's just trying to find out about the man who was using your name. Don't you care about that? Try to be polite. I invited him to dinner with us."

Raoul didn't look too happy while McKenna concentrated on trying to look as dumb as he could. He just followed behind while they talked. He noticed that Raoul spoke excellent Spanish, not the Spanish of an uneducated Cuban refugee fisherman.

When they got to Rosa's car, Raoul asked McKenna, "Want to show me the picture now?"

"I'll show you later, over dinner. If you don't mind, I'd like to ask you a few questions then. I'm sorry you've had so much trouble over this, so why don't you let me buy?"

"That's not necessary. I know you're just trying to do your job. You can ask me whatever you want whenever you want."

Rosa slid behind the wheel of her car and Raoul got into the front passenger's seat. McKenna sat in the back. As they left the parking lot, McKenna caught a glimpse of the man in the blue blazer again. He was sitting behind the wheel of a cream-colored old Chevy parked in the rear of the lot.

While Rosa was driving, Raoul asked her in Spanish, "Did you make reservations anywhere?"

She replied in kind, "No, I didn't make reservations anywhere. But you're being rude and I don't like it. Speak English."

Raoul turned to McKenna and said, "I'm sorry. We were just trying to decide which restaurant to go to. I'm thinking of the Red Lobster."

"How about the Fisherman's Cove? One of your local cops told me that it's the best restaurant in town."

"Too expensive," Raoul said. "We hardly ever go there." Rosa looked at Raoul, but said nothing.

"Don't worry. I really insist on paying. But go to whatever place you want."

"Let's stick with the Red Lobster," Rosa said.

Five minutes later Rosa drove into the parking lot of the Red Lobster. The front of the restaurant faced the highway and the rear faced the beach. McKenna saw the old Chevy pass the restaurant just as they walked in.

The place was nice, but no Fisherman's Cove. A cocktail waitress came by and Rosa and Raoul ordered sea breezes, McKenna a Coke. Rosa and Raoul looked at McKenna when he ordered his drink, so McKenna explained that he was on duty, even if he was enjoying himself in Florida.

McKenna ordered oysters all around for appetizers. When the oysters came, he asked for another round of drinks. From then on, whenever Rosa's or Raoul's drink got close to empty, McKenna called the cocktail waitress over for refills. McKenna was drinking more Coke at one sitting than he ever had in his life. After a while the cocktail waitress picked up on the routine. Raoul didn't seem to mind. He wasn't paying. Rosa stopped drinking after her second sea breeze. She just sipped at her third.

Over dinner and always more drinks for Raoul, McKenna kept the conversation directed at the fishing business. "Do you have to work seven days a week?" he asked Raoul.

"I try to, but there's no telling when customers will show up to hire the boat. But I'm at the dock at five every morning, unless the weather is really bad. Me and my mate have to get there early to try and lure customers. No customers, no work."

"Sounds tough," McKenna said sympathetically.

"It's not that bad," Rosa said. "He doesn't mind too much when customers don't show up. It gives him time to work on his real love . . . his house, his lawn, and his flower beds."

"I saw the house. It's beautiful," McKenna said.

Raoul beamed with pride until Rosa said, "Yeah, the worse the fishing business, the better the lawn."

You've got a great lawn now, Raoul, McKenna thought. I guess the fishing business isn't too good.

After Raoul offered a dissertation on grass and flowers in Florida, the conversation shifted to McKenna's case. McKenna gave them the story of the gunfight, the money, and the drugs, but left out the finger taped to Rico's back.

Raoul and Rosa were interested and McKenna said, "I know it sounds bad, but the New York City Police Department isn't too concerned. The FBI seems to be taking it very seriously, but they overreact to everything. We only want to find out who we got in our morgue. It's pretty routine for us."

McKenna reached down into his bag and gave Raoul the picture of Carlos Mendosa. "Mind looking at this now?"

Raoul stared at the photo intently. Then he gave it back to McKenna and said, "I don't know the man."

"Mind telling me how your wallet was stolen?"

"Not at all. One day last November I parked my car by my boat at the town dock and I left my wallet under the seat. I took some customers out fishing and when I got back to my car the wallet was missing."

"Was the window broken?"

"No, nothing was damaged."

"What did you do then?"

"I reported it to the Fort Myers Beach Police Department and went to the Department of Motor Vehicles office the next day to get a duplicate license. I also wrote away to the Social Security office and they sent me a new Social Security card."

"Didn't you have any credit cards in your wallet?" McKenna asked him.

"No, I usually keep my credit cards at home unless I'm gonna use them."

192

"Can I see your license?"

Raoul reached into his wallet and pulled it out. McKenna could see a number of credit cards in Raoul's wallet, but said nothing. McKenna looked at the license and noted that the date of issue was November 26, 1991. He reached into his case folder and took out a photocopy of the license that Carlos Mendosa had been carrying. He compared Raoul's license against the photocopy. Everything was the same except the picture. McKenna thanked Raoul and gave him his license back.

"It looks like I just wasted a day in Florida," McKenna said. "But I don't mind. I learned a lot about fishing and flowers, which used to be two of my weak points."

The rest of the dinner was uneventful. As soon as they ordered dessert, McKenna excused himself to go to the men's room. He walked to the rear of the restaurant, past the men's room, and out the back door onto the veranda facing the beach. Three tables were occupied by patrons and McKenna went past them toward the beach. When he got to the water's edge he made a left and ran for a minute, then made another left and ran back toward the highway. There were beach houses along the highway and he slowed down. He walked between two houses to the road, crossed it, and started back toward the Red Lobster. He took his time. Three minutes later he stood across the highway from the restaurant.

The old Chevy was in the parking lot, close to the highway and in the shadows, facing the front door of the restaurant. A man sat at the wheel, watching the entrance. The lot was deserted.

McKenna crossed the highway and took his pistol out. The driver still watched the front of the restaurant. The back of the Chevy was ten feet in front of him when McKenna began running to the driver's door. The man heard him coming and reached for his gun in his holster. It was Blue Blazer and he was too late. McKenna reached through the window with his left hand and grabbed Blue Blazer's hair while he put his Glock in Blue Blazer's ear with his right hand.

"Looking for me?" McKenna said.

Blue Blazer tried to turn his head toward McKenna, but McKenna gripped his hair and pulled his head back. "Not yet, pal, unless you wanna hear your last loud noise," McKenna said while he watched Blue Blazer's Adam's apple run up and down his throat a few times. He was searching for spit with his eyes opened wide. Then in a hopeful voice he said, "McKenna?"

"That's me. Who are you?"

"FBI."

"That's nice. But I didn't ask your occupation. I asked your name."

"John Cortes."

"You mean Juan Cortes?"

"OK. Juan Cortes. Let me go. This is a mistake. We have another team here."

"Whose mistake?" McKenna demanded.

"Ours. Mr. Weatherby didn't tell us you were coming. We didn't find out who you were till after you saw me at the Fisherman's Cove."

"Who's in charge of the New York field office?"

"Mr. Shields."

"Where's your ID, Juan?"

"Inside coat pocket, right side."

"Take it out and hand it to me."

Cortes slowly reached into his coat pocket and pulled out his FBI identification case. McKenna released his hair and took the case from him, still keeping the Glock in his ear. He flipped the case open. Special Agent Juan Cortes. He took his Glock out of Cortes's ear and put it back in his holster. "Gonna talk to me, Juan?"

"I can't. Ask Mr. Weatherby."

"I sure will. Where's the other team?"

"Down the highway. I just tell them when Rosa leaves."

McKenna dropped the ID case on Cortes's lap. "Goodnight, Juan. Talk to you again sometime," he said as he turned toward the Red Lobster. He walked along the side of the restaurant to the back veranda, shook the sand out of his shoes, and went in.

Rosa and Raoul were halfway through with dessert.

"Sorry I took so long. Those oysters aren't agreeing with me," McKenna said.

"That's what we figured," Raoul said. "I was just about to start on your dessert."

"I wish you would. Dinner was good, but I'm not too hungry anymore."

"You going back to New York tonight?" Raoul asked.

"I'd like to stay, but I got to get back. I'll get a cab to the airport from here."

"Nonsense," said Rosa. "We'll drive you."

Sure enough, Raoul did finish off McKenna's dessert. McKenna picked up the tab and Raoul left a twenty-dollar tip. They left the restaurant in good spirits. The Chevy was gone.

During the drive to the airport, Raoul offered to give McKenna a free day of fishing if he ever got to Fort Myers Beach again. He was in a great mood. McKenna said that he would give him a call if he was in the area. It was seven o'clock when they dropped McKenna off at the airport.

McKenna went into the airport bathroom and put his pistol back in his bag. Then he bought a ticket for a flight that left at eight o'clock and checked his bag. It was a nonstop flight getting into New York at 10:30. He sat down in the airport lounge with a pen and paper and did some figuring on Raoul's finances while he was waiting. First he tried to estimate how much Raoul made on each fishing trip. He figured about $450 each day, $400 for the boat and $50 profit on meals and drinks. Take away $50 for the mate, $20 for the food and drinks, and $20 for bait. Then he figured that the fastest boat in town must use a lot of fuel, about $80 a day to feed the twin Detroit Diesel 1200s. That left Raoul with $280 for every day he sailed. Still not bad. If he sailed thirty days a month, that was $8,400. Take away dock fees and boat insurance, he could still clear about $7,000 a month if he sailed every day.

McKenna then subtracted the $4,100 a month that he knew Raoul needed to pay for his boat and his house. He thought that Raoul's car was probably registered to his business, so everything was still tax deductible. That left him with about 3,000 pretax dollars a month to live on, if he sailed every day. But he doesn't sail every day, McKenna thought. And he's spending a lot more than $3,000 a month with his life-style. McKenna did some more figuring. If Raoul only sailed twenty days a month, he was barely breaking even, if he lived like a miser. Raoul wasn't living like a miser. The best restaurants, the best things in his very well maintained home, and the best things for his very nice girl.

McKenna concluded that Raoul was dirty. He looked perfect on the surface if you didn't look at his life-style. But he was dirty. He was spending much more than his business indicated he should be able to. And he wasn't borrowing to maintain his life-style. He had the cash. Raoul had to have another large source of income. Now, what was it? McKenna asked himself.

Drug smuggling was the obvious answer. The fastest for-hire sport-fishing boat in town could go out every day, even without customers on a particular day. Nobody would be suspicious. The *Pescador II* had excellent navigation equipment on board, and Raoul's LORAN was probably accurate to within five feet for determining location. Another boat could drop drugs off the coast, maybe secured to some kind of anchor or submerged ten feet below the water with a flotation device. Raoul could pick the drugs up as long as he had the LORAN coordinates. He could then resume his fishing and take the drugs off the boat concealed in whatever fish he caught, or even in his bait locker.

But there was more about Raoul that bothered McKenna. His Spanish, for one thing. He didn't sound like a poor Cuban fisherman. And where did he learn to be such a trophy-winning sport fisherman? Not in Cuba. Fishermen in Cuba fished for food, not sport. It was an entirely different kind of fishing. Not to mention that even with the huge loans that Raoul had on his boat and house, he still needed sizable down payments to get those loans. Where did he get that money?

McKenna had the feeling that the FBI knew something about Raoul even before this investigation. Why had they searched his house so soon? McKenna wondered. Was it a mistake? Most important, why does Weatherby have Camarena's house under surveillance? They didn't know I was coming, so they weren't following me specifcally, he thought. They were following whoever left Camarena's house. But Cortes said they were following Rosa. How can that be?

McKenna kept thinking. He needed to see the search warrant application for Camarena's house that the FBI had submitted to the federal judge. That would tell him a lot. The application would have to list the specific items for which they were searching, along with whatever probable cause the FBI had to believe that those items were in Raoul's house. The FBI still hadn't come clean in this case, McKenna thought. Why not?

McKenna went to a pay phone and called Brunette's mobile phone. Brunette answered and McKenna said, "Get ready to make me a Third Grade again, Ray. I'm gonna put Weatherby's lights out."

"I heard about it already," Brunette said. "You really should be more gentle with those good old boys."

"Word travels fast. Who told you?"

"Gene Shields. I just got off the phone with him. You made his day. He hates Weatherby and he says you gave him a ton of ammunition. Shields will hold him while you smack him. He's gonna find out exactly what Weatherby is up to and give it to me. Find out anything else?"

"Raoul's a nice guy, his girlfriend is a doll, but he's dirty. He's mixed up in this somehow."

"We'll talk about it when you get home. I'm sitting in your best chair, watching your TV, and drinking your beer. Want me to have Bobby pick you up at the airport?"

"No. Give him a break. I'll take a cab. Is Angelita there?"

"Sorry, pal. She's gone."

"I didn't think she was kidding." McKenna felt a lump forming in his throat. He searched for something else to say before it got too bad. Finally he asked, "Should I call Tavlin and let him know what's going on?"

"I'll take care of it. Sleep on the plane and I'll see you later. I've got a big day planned for you tomorrow."

McKenna hung up and boarded his flight. He was asleep five minutes after the plane took off.

17

July 11   8:00 A.M.

While McKenna was arriving at La Guardia Airport for his trip to Florida, Pacella was entering the task force office, right on time for work. He liked to get in at least half an hour early, but traffic on the Long Island Expressway was even worse than usual this morning. Every day as he drove onto "The World's Longest Parking Lot," he had to remind himself that this was what he wanted to do. He loved the Job, but he hated getting to it. Pacella had left his house in Long Island at 6:05 to travel thirty-seven miles and arrive at 8:00.

The office was crowded with at least twenty other detectives when Pacella walked into the room. Five of them were women. Most were Spanish and dressed for their parts in the neighborhood. They looked no different than any group hanging around on any corner in Spanish Harlem. Pacella knew many of them and it seemed that they all knew him. Two detectives from TARU nodded and Detective Clayton Grey, an attorney assigned to the Legal Bureau, raised his hand. The rest were from the Major Case Squad or recruited from squads all over the city. Everyone in the group had one thing in common. They all knew Spanish Harlem, had either grown up there or worked there at one time or another. Pacella saw a lot of talent in the room, and he knew that many of them already had Grade.

A large coffeepot was set up on a table by the wall and five dozen doughnuts had been provided by some thoughtful soul. There were twenty ceramic coffee cups next to the coffeepot. This is going to be a class act, Pacella thought. The coffeepot was the center of activity

197

in the office and it seemed to Pacella that all conversation in the room focused on the case.

Then Sergeant Goldblatt came out of Tavlin's office and started giving out the assignments for the day. Seven detectives were assigned to the surveillance of the pay phone at East 113th Street and Lexington Avenue. The two detectives from TARU would work in the phone-company truck and monitor the wiretap on the pay phone, while the other five detectives stationed themselves near the pay phone and waited for the signal to follow whoever answered the phone call from Flavio. Goldblatt said, "I'm gonna run the surveillance and I'll be in an apartment we managed to get at East 113th Street and Lexington Avenue. I can see the pay phone from there. I got a phone if you need me for anything, so stay off the radio as much as possible."

Goldblatt gave them the address and phone number of the apartment and then showed them the surveillance radios that TARU had rigged up. They looked just like Sony Walkmans, complete with headphones. "The nice thing is that you can play a tape on them. The radio messages just cut out the music. The problem is they can't transmit, so each team's got to check out a regular radio and keep it close by so you can transmit during the surveillance."

He assigned two detectives as relief men for the people working the surveillance. Then he said, "Everyone assigned to the pay phone surveillance will be working till ten tonight and you gotta be back here at eight tomorrow morning."

The moans and groans in the room that followed this announcement were loud and undisguised. After the noise died down, Goldblatt assigned Cisco Sanchez and Wilfredo Gomez. "I want you two to get all the New York newspapers, including the Spanish ones, from June twenty-sixth to July fourth. Go through the classified sections and make a list of every apartment advertised that's between East 110th Street and East 120th from Park Avenue to Third Avenue. Then check with all the real estate offices in the neighborhood and get a list from them of all the apartments they rented in that area during that time."

Goldblatt assigned Joe Sophia and Ernest Ford as the investigation coordinators. "Stay in the office," he said, "take all the phone calls, check out the cars, radios, and equipment, plus do whatever else Inspector Tavlin wants you to do. Sophia, your first mission is to go to Betty King's house and pick her up."

Five more unassigned detectives, three male and two female, were to meet Captain Sheeran at room 739 of the Intercontinental Hotel at Kennedy Airport. Goldblatt told them, "Captain Sheeran is running out of manpower, so you'll be assigned to the airport with him as

198

long as he needs you. Everyone hang around for a few minutes. The inspector wants to talk to you."

Goldblatt went over to Taviln's door and knocked.

Pacella noticed that he and Sal Catalfumo from the Career Criminal Apprehension Unit were the only two detectives in the room who weren't yet assigned. Where was McKenna? McKenna had told him last night that he would see him in the office this morning. He decided to just sit tight. He figured that Tavlin must be working on something else for him and Catalfumo to do.

Tavlin came out of the office a minute later, followed by Goldblatt. In fifteen minutes he outlined what had been happening in the investigation. He told them that they were dealing with *Sendero Luminoso,* an extremely competent and dangerous guerrilla group from Peru. He briefly outlined the history of *Sendero Luminoso* and told them of the killings in Miami and East LA. While Tavlin was talking, Goldblatt gave to each detective copies of the FBI sketches of the persons thought to be Isabela and Alfonso Mendosa.

Then Tavlin said, "For the people assigned to the surveillance, the important thing is to follow whoever answers the pay phone at East 113th Street and Lexington Avenue without being seen. The group we're dealing with is very careful and they'll be looking for a surveillance, so it's gonna be difficult. If you think that you're spotted, check with Sergeant Goldblatt and then grab whoever answered the phone. But that's the worst-case scenario and not what we're trying to do. We want to find out where they go. You should know by now that these people are killers. They're ruthless and well armed, and they won't hesitate to shoot a cop. They shoot cops in their own country all the time. You should expect that the person who answers the phone will have a backup person nearby, so be very careful."

Tavlin paused for a minute to let his warning sink in. Nobody seemed too impressed so he continued, "When you find out where they go, the Legal Bureau will get the warrants and TARU is gonna set up an electronic surveillance on the building. It's possible they're using two apartments close to each other. That's what they did in Miami and LA. They might be using one to hold Rodrigo and another apartment as their main base of operations. One apartment building can probably be seen from the other. That's why I have Cisco and Gomez making that list of apartments. When we find the apartment building they're using, we'll use the list to find the other."

Then Tavlin gave them the bad news. "Raggs is off limits to anyone working this case. *Sendero Luminoso* is close, and I see no reason for them to find out what we're up to by sitting on a barstool and listening to you people. Secrecy must be maintained, so don't talk about this case with anyone who's not assigned, including wives and girlfriends. And especially the press. Any questions?"

There were none. Tavlin said, "Good luck and be careful. I don't want any dead heroes." Then he returned to his office.

Pacella saw that Eddie Morgan from CCAU was the first one to take off his bulletproof vest. Morgan was assigned to the surveillance and knew from experience how difficult it would be to successfully follow a wary subject while wearing a bulky bulletproof vest. When the bad guys look for cops, they watch for the three things: vests, radios, and guns. The radios had been taken care of. The Sonys were good enough. Guns can be hidden. But not the bulletproof vests that are so easily visible under a shirt in July. There's nothing to do with the vest except take it off. One by one the other detectives assigned to the surveillance, including the three female detectives, took turns in the bunk room taking off their vests.

Pacella liked it. They were assigned to a job with a great potential for danger, and they were taking the risks necessary to get the job done, starting with the vests. He felt good about the people Tavlin had picked.

The office cleared out quickly and Ernest Ford started to take apart the coffeepot to clean it. Pacella and Catalfumo were left there just looking at each other. Then Tavlin poked his head out of his door and called them into his office. He said, "Sit down. I've got a special mission for you."

They took two chairs in front of Tavlin's desk and Tavlin said, "You're wondering where McKenna is, right?"

"Yeah," said Pacella. "I was supposed to meet him here this morning."

"The chief sent him to Florida to find out what he could about Raoul Camarena. You two are going to Cambridge, Massachusetts, right now to help out the FBI and keep an eye on them."

"How long we going for?" asked Catalfumo.

"A day or two. You're gonna meet the FBI at the Cambridge police station at one o'clock. They used the information that we gave them on Rodrigo. They went to Harvard and found out that Rodrigo Guiterrez was enrolled in a doctoral program at the Institute of Politics, which is part of the John F. Kennedy School of Government at Harvard. He started in January and had registered for some summer courses. His last day in class was July second, before the Independence Day break. He didn't show up for his classes on July seventh. On July eighth the registrar got a letter from Rodrigo saying he had a personal emergency at home and he had to resign from his classes. The registrar still had the letter and the envelope it came in. The envelope was postmarked in Boston on July sixth."

"So Rodrigo was kidnapped sometime between July second and July seventh," Catalfumo said.

"Probably before July seventh," Tavlin answered. "McKenna killed Rico on July ninth, and when the ME looked at the pictures of Rodrigo that Rico had, he said that the pinky was taken off about three days before."

"Rico is Carlos Mendosa, right?" interrupted Pacella.

"Right. So figure July second to July sixth. The FBI's got a search warrant for Rodrigo's house in Cambridge. The chief worked out a deal with them and they're gonna wait for you before they do the search. They're not happy with that, but we supplied Rodrigo's name and address in the first place, so they had to go along. The chief still doesn't trust them. He thinks they've got some secrets and he wants you to make sure that he isn't part of the confused public. Help them out as much as you can, but keep an eye on them. When you're there, don't tell anyone you interview that you're New York City detectives. We don't want *Sendero Luminoso* to find out that we're investigating the kidnapping in New York. They've gone to a lot of trouble to make everyone believe that Rodrigo is being held in Boston, and we don't want to upset them."

"We'll be cool," said Catalfumo. "That it?"

"That should be enough." Tavlin took an envelope off his desk and handed it to Pacella. "The directions to the Cambridge police station and two hundred dollars cash are inside. Get receipts for anything you spend. Get a car from Sophia. He's got a new Olds gassed up and waiting. Good luck and stay in touch."

Pacella put the envelope in his pocket and checked his watch. Eight forty-five. Four hours to get to Cambridge.

Pacella and Catalfumo got up and left Tavlin's office. Sophia gave them the keys to the car and said, "It's parked in the lot. It's a green Olds. I left some Frank Sinatra tapes in the glove compartment so you can get some culture on the trip."

They found the car outside, just like Sophia said. Catalfumo climbed behind the wheel, which made Pacella happy with their mission. He loved to travel, as long as someone else was doing the driving. And he liked Sal Catalfumo.

Pacella considered Sal to be one of the most talented and hardest-working young detectives on the Job. Sal had been born in Malta with a Spanish mother and an Italian father, and he spoke both languages. How he came to be living in New York was still a mystery, but Pacella had found that Sal fit in anywhere and could get information from anyone.

A couple of blocks from the station house they stopped and picked up the New york papers and Pacella went through them while Catalfumo drove. He found what he was looking for on page fourteen of the *News* and page eleven of the *Post*. Both stories stated that the police in the 71st Precinct in Brooklyn were investigating the circumstances surrounding a severed finger found by a homeless man in a garbage can in the Ebbets Field Houses. The unusual part of the story was that this homeless person turned the finger in with a valuable gold ring attached. He was interviewed by a *Post* reporter and said that he thought that it had something to do with voodoo and that he wanted nothing to do with the ring. Both stories reported that the police requested that anyone who could help with the investigation call the 71st Detective Squad.

There was some traffic and it took them two hours to get to New Haven on I-95. Then the road opened up and Sal brought the Olds to eighty and kept it there, which enabled them to meet a Connecticut state trooper near New London. Professional courtesies were observed and by the time they got to Cambridge at one thirty they had also managed to meet members of the Rhode Island and Massachusetts highway patrols.

They found the Cambridge police station on Western Avenue without a problem. They were expected. Four men were waiting for them on the front steps of the station house. Pacella and Catalfumo met Detectives John Hoyt and Joe McMahon of the Cambridge police and Special Agents Roger Ervast and Charles Tennant of the FBI. They were well received by Hoyt and McMahon, but Pacella thought that the FBI agents didn't seem particularly thrilled with the presence of the two detectives from the big city. Tennant said, "We talked it over before you got here and decided that, since it's our search warrant, we'll be in charge. Is that a problem?"

"Of course not," Pacella said. "We're just here to help in any way we can. It's your show."

Tennant and Ervast looked satisfied while Hoyt and McMahon seemed bored.

The FBI agents took their car, the Cambridge detectives took another car, and Pacella and Catalfumo brought up the rear of the procession. The address belonged to a large, two-family house on a stately tree-lined street two blocks off Massachusetts Avenue, about half a mile from the JFK School.

They all got out of their cars and Tennant rang the bell. An elderly white man answered the door. He walked with a cane. Tennant introduced himself and showed the man the search warrant. The owner said his name was Bill Dunn. He wasn't thrilled with the search warrant.

"Does Rodrigo Guiterrez live here?" Tennant asked.

"I've got a Rodrigo Oxcalo who lives on the second floor," Dunn answered.

"That's him. Does he live alone?"

"No. He lives with his friend, Oscar Barbero."

"When did you rent to them?"

"January of this year."

"What do they do?"

"They're students at Harvard."

"They good tenants?" Tennant asked.

"The best. They keep to themselves and never cause any problems. And they always pay the rent on time. They're great tenants as far as I'm concerned. What's this all about?"

"I'm sorry. I can't tell you, Mr. Dunn. It's a national security matter."

Tennant's answer somewhat mollified Mr. Dunn. I'll have to remember that line, Pacella thought.

"When was the last time you saw them?" Tennant asked.

"The July fourth weekend sometime."

"That was more than a week ago. Didn't you think that was strange?"

"No." answered Dunn "They travel all the time. Besides, their car is gone and their rent is paid, so I got nothing to worry about."

"What kind of a car do they have?"

"It's a new one. I think it's a Chrysler. It looks a little like a limousine. You know, big and black."

"Know the license plate number?"

"No."

"How do we get to their apartment?"

"It's on the second floor. They got their own entrance in the backyard."

"You got a key for the apartment?" Tennant asked.

"I got one key. But they put another lock on as soon as they moved in. They put in a burglar alarm, too. They're real careful."

That's just great, Pacella thought. Let's see how the FBI handles this one.

Everyone followed Mr. Dunn to the rear of the house. The door leading up to Rodrigo's apartment was heavy wood with no windows in it.

John Hoyt asked Mr. Dunn, "Got a ladder?"

"In the garage. What're you gonna do if the windows are locked?"

"We'll have to break one to get in."

"Who's gonna pay for it?" Dunn asked nervously.

"The FBI," Hoyt said, pointing at Tennant.

"Don't worry, Mr. Dunn," Tennant said. "We'll pay for any damages."

"OK," Dunn said. "C'mon, I'll show you where the ladder is."

Hoyt followed Dunn into the garage and returned in a minute with a long extension ladder. Hoyt climbed up the ladder to a second-floor window and tried to open it. It was locked. He broke the window with the butt of his gun and a loud burglar alarm sounded from a box located under the eaves of the house. Hoyt rushed down the ladder and moved it until the ladder was directly under the alarm box. Then he climbed back up, knocked the box off the eaves with the butt of his gun, and pulled the wires from the interior of the box. The noise stopped. He then repositioned his ladder under the window he had broken and he climbed in. One minute later Hoyt opened the rear door to the apartment from the inside and everyone went up the stairs to take a look at Rodrigo's place.

Rodrigo's apartment was large with two bedrooms, two baths, a modern kitchen, and a large living room. The place was immaculate. The investigators decided to break up into two three-man teams for the search, with each agency represented on each team. Tennant, Hoyt, and Pacella were one team and Ervast, McMahon, and Catalfumo formed the other.

Pacella's team took the larger bedroom first. He knew it was Rodrigo's room. The closet was filled with Brooks Brothers clothes and there was a bookcase loaded with political treatises in English, French, and Spanish. Everything was neat, and they tried to leave it that way. A jewelry box on the dresser contained $6,400 in traveler's checks. In the top drawer of the dresser Pacella found a checkbook for Citibank New York along with statements and canceled checks for the past six months. Rodrigo's last statement indicated that he had over $14,000 in the checking account. Rodrigo was meticulous in his record keeping. He kept every paid bill, neatly stacked in the top drawer of the dresser. There was a stack of paid telephone bills. Pacella noticed that Rodrigo generated a huge phone bill every month with calls to Peru, Europe, and New York. There was a paid bill to an auto insurance company, which listed Rodrigo's car by the vehicle identification number. It was a 1992 Chrysler. Pacella wrote down the VIN number of Rodrigo's car. There were also a lot of paid monthly American Express bills. Pacella went through them and saw that Rodrigo and Oscar ate out almost every night. It seemed that they usually partronized five restaurants in the Cambridge area.

Pacella remembered what Tavlin had said that morning. The victim in the East LA case was apparently lured into the kidnapping by a woman, probably Isabela Mendosa posing as a waitress. He copied down the names and addresses of the restaurants from the American Express receipts. Then he gave everything of interest that he found to Tennant.

Catalfumo's team had taken the second bedroom to search. McMahon found a box of thirty-eight-caliber shells under the bed, but no gun or holster. There was a picture on the dresser of a man standing with a woman and two children. Another picture on the nightstand showed the same man shaking hands with an older man. Sal showed that picture to Dunn, who was waiting in the living room.

"That's Oscar Barbero," Dunn said.

McMahon found a stack of letters under a pillow on the bed and gave them to Catalfumo. They were addressed to Oscar Barbero, from Nina Barbero in Peru. They were written in poor Spanish, but Catalfumo found from reading the letters that Oscar was Rodrigo's bodyguard and that he was supposed to return to Peru for a visit in August. Nina Barbero was Oscar's wife, their fifth wedding anniversary was June 27, they had two children, and everyone was always sending their love and looking forward to his visit. There was also an unfinished letter from Oscar to his wife. He wrote her that life with Rodrigo was still very difficult, but that he was trying hard and he would make her proud of him. Catalfumo gave the letters to Ervast, but he kept Oscar's pictures.

The search of the apartment turned up nothing else of value. It was apparent that Rodrigo hadn't been taken by force; everything was in order and there was no sign of a struggle. Besides, the alarm was a code type and had been set. Unless Oscar was in on the kidnapping, Rodrigo hadn't been kidnapped from the apartment. The investigators left, still with no idea of the location of Rodrigo's kidnapping.

Once outside, they broke up into teams to canvass the neighborhood. They rang every bell on Rodrigo's block. Nobody had seen anything unusual around July 4 and nobody even knew Rodrigo or Oscar.

But Catalfumo had seen something in Rodrigo's apartment. Before he had left, he went through the garbage in the kitchen and found a Slurpee cup and a sales receipt from a 7-Eleven, dated July 2. Catalfumo decided to try the 7-Eleven. He was working with Hoyt and he asked, "Where's the nearest 7-Eleven?"

"Two blocks, on Western Avenue. Why?"

"We know they've been in the store and we're getting nowhere here. Wanna give it a try?"

"Good idea. We'd work our way there sooner or later anyway, but sooner is better. It looks like nobody else in this neighborhood knows them. Let's try it."

They walked the two blocks to the 7-Eleven in a couple of minutes. Hoyt introduced himself to the manager and showed him the NYPD photo of Rodrigo.

"I don't know him," the manager said.

Catalfumo showed him the picture of Oscar.

"He's a customer. Comes in all the time. Carmen knows him."

The manager called over the girl who had been working the cash register. She was a small, pretty, dark-haired girl, about twenty years old. She said her name was Carmen Barron. Catalfumo showed her the photo of Oscar.

"That's Oscar Barbero. Did anything happen to him?"

"That's what we're trying to find out," Hoyt said. "He's missing."

Then Catalfumo showed her the photo of Rodrigo.

"That's Oscar's friend, Rodrigo."

"How do you know them?" Catalfumo asked.

"I used to see Oscar in the store every once in a while. He's from Peru and I'm an exchange student from Venezuela. A couple of weeks ago he asked me for a date and I went out with him. It was a double date. We went with Rodrigo, Oscar's friend. He had a date with another girl."

"Do you know the other girl?" Catalfumo asked.

"No. I met her that night. Her name is Miriam. She's from Chile. She's a waitress at a French restaurant, Chez Jacques. That's where Rodrigo met her. He's crazy about her. She's very tall, very pretty, and very smart. She goes to Radcliffe."

"Do you know where she lives?" Hoyt asked.

"No. She said she rented a house with some other students. It's way out in the country."

Catalfumo showed Carmen the two FBI sketches of Isabela Mendosa. It was the blond version this time.

"Tell us about the date, if you don't mind," Catalfumo said.

"It was a nice night. Rodrigo and Oscar picked me up at my apartment. Then Oscar drove to Chez Jacques to pick up Miriam. Miriam was waiting for us in front of the restaurant. Oscar drove us to La Andalusia. That's a nice Spanish restaurant where Oscar and Rodrigo go. On the trip Miriam told us some good stories about learning to be a waitress. Miriam ordered Mexican food for everybody. Rodrigo and Oscar never had Mexican food before. They only ate the Spanish food there. Everything was great. We stayed there till closing time, drinking pitchers of sangria."

"What did you talk about?" Catalfumo asked.

"Mostly we just listened to Miriam. She told how she happened to be living in Cambridge. She said she was from a rich family in Chile and that her father used to be a general in their army there. She had been everywhere and had everything. She went to school in Europe and spoke Spanish, English, French, and German. But a couple of years ago her life changed. Her father had to leave Chile after General Pinochet lost power. They came to Miami, but they had to leave everything and now she was poor. Miriam came to Cambridge to study at Radcliffe. She said she planned to start in September and was working in Cambridge for the summer to get enough money to live for the rest of the semester."

"Did you believe her?" Catalfumo asked.

"Sure. She was very nice."

Isabela's got some line, Catalfumo thought. "What did you do after La Andalusia?" he asked.

"After we left, Oscar offered to drive Miriam home, but she said she was gonna go home with one of her roommates who was also a waitress at Chez Jacques. So he drove back to Chez Jacques. Miriam got out of the car and Rodrigo followed her in."

Carmen smiled when she said, "He left me and Oscar sitting in the car for five minutes. Rodrigo was very happy when he came out. He got another date with Miriam for July fourth. She had given him directions to her house. Oscar was gonna drive him there."

"What did you do then?" asked Catalfumo.

"Then Oscar drove me home and told me he would call me again."

"Did he?" asked Catalfumo.

"No. I hope nothing happened to him. He's a very nice man. So polite, know what I mean?"

"No," Catalfumo and Hoyt answered together.

"He's different. He never tried anything," she said, blushing.

"Thank you. You've been very helpful, Miss Barron," Hoyt said. Catalfumo took down Carmen's address and telephone number.

"I hope you find him," Carmen said as they left.

Then they went back to Rodrigo's block and told the other two search teams what they had found.

"Chez Jacques is one of the restaurants listed on Rodrigo's American Express bills. He eats there all the time," Pacella said.

Everyone jumped in their cars and headed for the restaurant. When they got there, they had a conference in the parking lot and decided that just the Cambridge detectives would question the manager about Miriam. They didn't want to show too much interest in her in case she was still around. The two detectives went into Chez Jacques while everyone else waited in their cars on the street outside. They were back out in fifteen minutes.

"We talked to the manager," Hoyt said. "He told us he used to have a waitress named Miriam Salazar. She worked for one week, from the end of June till July third. Miriam told him that she was from Chile and that she was gonna attend Radcliffe in September. She was a good waitress and she spoke perfect English and French. She was supposed to work again on July fifth, but she never showed up. The manager called her home, but there was no answer."

"You got her phone number?" Pacella asked.

"Yeah. The manager insisted she give him a phone number he could verify before he hired her."

"Did she show him any ID?" asked Catalfumo.

"Yeah. He remembered that she showed him a Florida driver's license with her picture on it. Then we showed him the picture of Rodrigo and the family picture of Oscar. He knew them both. Frequent customers for the last six months. Miriam was their waitress the last time they were there. That was near the beginning of the month. Then we showed him the blond sketch. The manager said it was Miriam."

Hoyt called his office to run down the telephone number that the manager had given them. He found out that the telephone subscriber for the number was a Jacob Wilson. His address was an RFD number on a Wilson Road in Pinehurst.

"Anyone know where that is?" Tennant asked.

"I don't know where Wilson Road is," Hoyt answered, "but Pinehurst is ten or fifteen miles north of town. It's outside our jurisdiction so we won't be going. Just let us know if it turns out that the kidnapping happened in Cambridge."

"We'll let you know," Tennant said. "Thanks for your help."

Back to the cars and twenty minutes later the FBI agents and the New York City detectives were all at the Pinehurst post office. It was four o'clock. Pacella went into the post office with Ervast and Tennant. They identified themselves to the postmaster and he located the mailman who delivered to the Wilson residence.

The mailman was a short, thin man named Tom Herrington. He was just getting off work. Herrington said that he had known the Wilsons for twenty years. The Wilsons took in student boarders, but in June a woman had rented the whole house for the rest of the summer. The Wilsons were now staying at Mrs. Wilson's sister's house, which was about a mile from their own house. He was delivering their mail to them there. Herrington said that he never saw the woman who had rented the Wilsons' house because she never got any mail.

Herrington took the FBI agents and the New York detectives to Mrs. Wilson's sister's house. The Wilsons were there and said that they had rented their house to a woman named Miriam Salazar on June 20. At first, they only wanted to rent her a room, but Miriam had told them that she had family coming from Florida and she wanted to rent the house for the summer. She had offered the Wilsons $5,000 in cash and paid in advance, plus a $1,500 security deposit and a $500 security deposit for the use of the telephone. Mrs. Wilson said that she and Mr. Wilson decided to rent Miriam the house and spend the summer at her sister's house. Miriam had shown the Wilsons a Florida driver's license for identification.

"When was the last time you saw her?" Tennant asked.

"Not since we rented the house to her, but we just got the phone bill."

"Could we see the bill?" Tennant asked.

Mrs. Wilson retrieved the phone bill and showed it to Tennant. It was a small bill and there were no long-distance calls listed after June 20.

Pacella showed the Wilsons the blond FBI sketch of Isabela. Again, it was Miriam.

"Would you mind telling us what this is all about?" Mr. Wilson asked.

"We have reason to believe that Miriam Salazar is a federal fugitive," Tennant answered. "I'm afraid that we're going to have to search the house."

"Go ahead and search it," Mrs. Wilson told them.

"Not just yet," Tennant said. "We're going to get a search warrant first, just to keep everything legal."

They thanked the Wilsons for their cooperation and went down the driveway to their cars, along with the mailman.

"Why don't you go get the search warrant?" Pacella asked Tennant and Ervast. "Mr. Herrington can show us where the Wilson house is and we'll buy him dinner for his trouble."

"Fine," Tennant said. "Where should we meet you?"

Pacella asked Herrington for the name of a good restaurant and he gave them one in Pinehurst.

The FBI agents left and Herrington showed Pacella and Catalfumo where Wilson Road was. "There's three houses," Herrington said. "The Wilson house is the last one on the road."

Catalfumo drove them to the restaurant in town. The food was good and everyone ate with great appetite. Pacella and Catalfumo had eaten nothing all day except for some doughnuts at the office that morning, and they were starving.

When Pacella and Catalfumo could eat no more, they sat back and marveled at Herrington's gastronomical capacity. He was skinny, but he just kept on eating. Pacella excused himself and went to the phone booth outside the restaurant. He called Tavlin and told him everything that they had accomplished so far. It looked like they were going to be working late into the night. Then Pacella went back to their table and resumed watching the skinny mailman pack the food away.

Herrington had finally gotten to dessert when the FBI agents returned at six o'clock. Tennant came into the restaurant and said, "Let's go. We got the warrant."

"How'd you do that so fast?" Pacella asked. "Boston and back in two hours? You must be keeping a federal judge in your trunk."

"We brought some help too." Tennant said, pointing to the window.

Pacella looked out the restaurant window and saw that the FBI was loaded for bear. Tennant and Ervast had arrived at the head of a convoy. Outside the restaurant were parked two FBI heavy weapons teams, a Mobile Crime Lab truck pulling a generator, and a truck that appeared to be equipped with nothing but lots of lights. The FBI is gonna put on quite a show tonight, Pacella thought.

"Looks like we're gonna be unpaying spectators," Pacella said to Catalfumo.

Pacella paid the sizable supper bill and got the receipt for Tavlin. They thanked Herrington for his help and left him to walk the short distance from the restaurant to his car at the post office.

The two NYPD detectives got in their car and Catalfumo led the convoy to the beginning of Wilson Road. Once they arrived, an agent came over to their car and introduced himself as Warren McCoy, the special-agent-in-charge of the Boston office of the FBI. "I spoke to Chief Brunette," he said. "We're gonna give you complete information on anything we learn tonight, but would you mind just staying out of the way?"

"Fine by us," Pacella said. "We'll just tag along and watch."

Catalfumo waited at the side of the shoulder while the FBI convoy started down Wilson Road. Then he followed as the last car in the convoy.

The convoy paused at the first house while Tennant talked to the occupants. When he came out he talked with McCoy. Then McCoy pointed him to Pacella and Catalfumo's car. Tennant walked over and said, "They told me they haven't seen a strange car go down the road in a least a week. When the Wilsons first moved out, they occasionally saw an old tan van go down the road and they knew that it was parked at the Wilsons' house. They said they didn't get the plate number on the van because they always minded their own business."

The convoy continued to the second house on Wilson Road. Nobody was home.

Next came the Wilson house. It was a large, white colonial and the road ended in a circular driveway at the front door.

Then the show really started. Pacella and Catalfumo sat on a fallen tree trunk in the woods at the edge of the Wilson house and took the whole thing in.

The FBI heavy weapons teams surrounded the house. There were no cars in the driveway but it looked like two lights were on in the house, one upstairs and one down. They saw one of the agents use a mobile phone and they heard a phone ring inside the Wilson house.

After an hour the FBI finally stormed the house. They had everything. Dogs, gas, gas masks, automatic weapons, full flak jackets, and smoke grenades.

It was a great show, but the house was empty.

Then the FBI crime lab went to work. They were doing a complete job on the house when, unfortunately, the Wilsons came by. The FBI wouldn't let them in but the Wilsons saw from the front door that the entire interior of their house was being wrecked with fingerprint dust. The Wilsons went into a rage. They left and apparently called the Massachusetts State Police. When the state police arrived, the Wilsons demanded that the FBI agents be arrested for destroying their house.

The matter was finally resolved when the FBI promised the Wilsons that they would pay for all the damages. By this time Pacella and Catalfumo were gripped in uncontrollable laughter. "We better wait in the car with the windows rolled up and listen to Frank Sinatra or we're gonna be in trouble," Pacella suggested. They did.

It was just starting to get dark when the backhoe arrived on a flatbed truck. Most of the lab technicians inside the house were finished with whatever work they were doing and everyone started searching the grounds using the lights from the illumination equipment truck they had brought with them. At nine o'clock at night it still looked like high noon around the Wilson house. Anyplace the ground looked disturbed or unsettled the backhoe dug a hole.

They found Oscar Barbero in the third hole that they dug. At that time the laughing stopped and Pacella's and Catalfumo's respect for the FBI and their methods increased 1,000 percent.

Oscar had been buried in the woods in the rear of the house and two agents had to cut down a tree to get the backhoe to the spot where they wanted the hole dug. He was four feet down and the backhoe cut off his leg as it dug. Pacella and Catalfumo went over to take a look at the body. Pacella guessed that Oscar had been dead about a week and he could see that Oscar's shirt was bloodstained.

Everyone stood around for a while, waiting for the county coroner to arrive. Then it started to drizzle and Pacella and Catalfumo decided to wait in their car, listening to more Frank Sinatra and watching the agents get wet. Pacella enjoyed the music, but he noticed that Catalfumo seemed lost in thought. "Why so sad, kid?" Pacella asked. "We're doing good here."

"Oscar Barbero."

Pacella turned off the radio and said, "We don't know enough about this guy for you to lose any sleep over him. He still could've been one of the gang. Maybe they just had a falling out, or maybe he outlived his usefulness."

"He wasn't the type. He was a simple guy, the faithful family retainer, a real family man. He's a victim."

"What makes you so sure?"

"I read his mail."

Catalfumo told Pacella what he had learned about Barbero from the letters in his room and from Carmen Barron. When he finished, Pacella turned the radio back on and they each kept their own thoughts until the county coroner arrived. Then they rejoined the agents in the rain.

The coroner wanted the body removed from the hole, so two agents jumped into the grave. They tied the body up and had the backhoe operator use his machine to lift it out and place it on the ground. Then one of the agents jumped back into the hole. He found a thirty-eight-caliber Smith & Wesson revolver that had been under the body. Using a handkerchief, he opened up the cylinder of the gun. The revolver was fully loaded with five rounds.

The coroner examined Oscar's body. "There are two bullet wounds to the chest. I'd say that's the cause of death," he said.

Pacella saw that Oscar was wearing a small holster on his belt and he figured that the thirty-eight was Oscar's gun, which he had never gotten a chance to use. An agent then searched the body. There was no ID, no wallet, and no jewelry.

Pacella and Catalfumo got in their car and Sal drove back to town to call Inspector Tavlin. It was ten thirty and Tavlin was still in his office. Pacella told him about the FBI search and what they had found.

"Good work," Tavlin said. "McKenna's on his way back from Florida. Leave the FBI on good terms and get back. Got another big day tomorrow."

They drove back to the Wilson house and found Special-Agent-in-Charge McCoy. "You did a great job on the search of the house," Pacella told him. "We're impressed."

"Thanks for your help. Give my regards to Chief Brunette. Tell him I'll forward anything our lab comes up with on the forensic search of the house," McCoy answered.

Hands were shaken and backs slapped all around. Pacella and Catalfumo went back to their car. They were happy to leave McCoy.

They had begun to think that they all sounded like members of the Mutual Adoration Society.

"Wanna drive?" Catalfumo asked Pacella.

"No. You?"

"Not me. I'm beat."

"I guess you did enough for today," Pacella said as he reluctantly climbed behind the wheel. Catalfumo stretched out in the backseat to take a nap and was asleep in minutes. As he drove, Pacella couldn't stop thinking of Nina Barbero, her two kids, and the husband and father they wouldn't be seeing in August. He couldn't get the family picture out of his mind. The more he thought, the sorrier he felt, and the madder he got. Carmen Barron had said that Oscar was a nice guy, very polite. That didn't help his mood. There's not enough nice guys, he thought.

Tommy Pacella promised himself that, one way of another, *Sendero Luminoso* was going to pay for the sorrow they caused the Barbero family.

July 11   8:45 A.M.

"It looks like he's getting ready to leave, Captain."

Lieutenant Hardcass's irritatingly precise military monotone drummed into Sheeran's subconscious.

"Captain?" Hardcass repeated.

Sheeran made the effort. He opened his eyes and looked at the two television screens directly across the room from his chair. He saw Flavio Asturo putting on his pants from two different views. Hardcass was right. Flavio had spread his suit jacket, a white shirt, and a tie on the bed in front of him. "Did he pack?" Sheeran asked Hardcass.

"No, sir."

So Flavio's just going out and not checking out, Sheeran thought. Sheeran picked up the radio from the coffee table in front of him and said to his units outside, "Get ready. Looks like the subject is getting ready to move." Then he walked over to the window and looked at the scene on the street below him in front of the Intercontinental Hotel. Two Port Authority cops pulled their car to the front of the line of three yellow taxis waiting in the taxi stand at the entrance to the hotel. He watched as they moved the three waiting taxis out of the cab line and directed them out of the parking lot of the hotel. Sheeran wondered what the Port Authority cops had told the taxi drivers that made them move out of the lot so quickly. Then he saw the two police department taxis move into the now vacant

214

taxi stand. They were ready for Flavio. Sheeran looked across the parking lot to his two chase cars. They too were ready.

Richie White sat behind the wheel of the chase car with the two antennae. The car was fixed with location triangulation receivers that could follow the location beacon planted in each of the two police department yellow taxis. White saw Sheeran looking from the hotel window and waved at him. Sheeran said, "Good morning, Richie," over his radio.

White waved again.

Sheeran stood in front of the TV screens and watched Flavio as he finished dressing. Then Flavio started shining his shoes with the disposable kit that the hotel provided. "We got more shoe-shine kits?" Sheeran asked Detective Tonia Echevara, who wore the hotel maid's uniform and was assigned as Flavio's maid. She had more shoe-shine kits.

Sheeran took stock of his personnel in the crowded hotel room. In addition to Tonia Echevara, he had Detective Pedro Gaspar from TARU, to monitor and tape Flavio's phone calls. Detective Joe Mendez looked spiffy in the hotel room-service uniform. And there was Lieutenant Hardcass.

Besides the five people, the room was crowded with the maid's cleaning cart and the room-service serving cart, the desktop photocopying machine, along with the extra television monitors, the large tape recorder recorder, and the wires running along the floor. It was a mess, garbage cans overflowing with pizza boxes, used coffee containers, sandwich wrappers, and soda bottles. And we've got the maid up here, Sheeran thought.

Sheeran watched Flavio as he continued shining his shoes and compared the way Flavio kept the room directly under them with the mess in their own room. Clean and neat, not a thing out of place.

Flavio was adjusting his tie in front of the mirror in his room. He looks like what I'd expect a South American businessman to look like, Sheeran thought. About forty, thinning hair, solid looking. Then Flavio opened the door of his room and left.

"He's coming down," Hardcass said into his radio.

Sheeran watched from the window. Two minutes later he saw Flavio get into the front taxi. Everything was going according to plan. Taxi One pulled out of the hotel parking lot. A minute later Richie White's voice came over the radio, "They're northbound on the Van Wyck Expressway."

White's running commentary continued as the cab passed exits on the Van Wyck. When Taxi One had passed the Grand Central Parkway exit on the Van Wyck, Sheeran told Echevara and Mendez to get to work. They took the desktop photocopying machine and put it under some dirty sheets in the canvas bag of their maid's cart. They pushed the cart out of their room and a minute later Sheeran watched them enter Flavio's room on the television monitors. Together they set the photocopy machine on the floor, plugged it in, then started searching the room.

Taxi One got off the Van Wyck at Northern Boulevard, heading westbound on Northern Boulevard. That rang a bell with Sheeran. The taxi driver they had interviewed last night had told them that he had picked Flavio up at Junction Boulevard and Northern Boulevard and dropped him back at the Intercontinental Hotel. That was Corona, a Spanish neighborhood in Queens.

Sheeran returned to the monitors and continued watching the two detectives search Flavio's room. Mendez was going through the drawers while Echevara had pulled the sheets and blankets off the bed and pulled the mattress to the floor. Mendez found something. He brought it to one of the corners of the room and held it up. Gaspar zoomed in one of the pinhole lenses that had been placed in the small holes that they had drilled into the corners of the ceiling of Flavio's room from their room directly above. Mendez was holding up Flavio's Peruvian passport.

"What should I do with this?" Mendez asked.

The microphone in Flavio's room picked up his voice perfectly. Hardcass replied over his radio, "Photocopy all the stamped pages in the passport."

Then Richie White's radio transmissions started coming rapidly. "Flavio's out of Taxi One at Junction and Northern. Detectives following on foot."

"He's into a church at Junction and Thirty-fourth Avenue. Detectives still with him."

"He's in a pew all by himself. A mass is starting. The mass is in Spanish. Flavio seems to be praying."

"What's going on?" Hardcass said to Sheeran. "I thought this guy was suppposed to be a godless commie terrorist."

Sheeran had no answer. But he was getting a knot in his stomach. He said nothing and continued to watch the search in the room below. Mendez and Echevara were very thorough. They had the furniture upside down and were checking everything. What are we looking for? Sheeran thought. He didn't know. But he was sure of one thing. Flavio Asturo was the *Sendero Luminoso* messenger who was supposed to bring Rodrigo's finger back to Peru. Everything pointed to that.

Mendez had found Flavio's airline tickets in the nightstand drawer. Nothing else. No guns, no drugs, no messages, no maps, no directions,

216

no code books, no radio transmitters, no telephone numbers. He and Echevara began to make up the room. They had discovered nothing of value except Flavio's passport and his airline tickets.

The radio came on again and continued for the next five minutes. "Flavio's out of the church. He didn't talk to anybody and he didn't pick anything up. Taxi Two's got him."

"Southbound on Junction Boulevard."

"He's eastbound on Roosevelt Avenue."

"Now he's southbound on the Van Wyck. It looks like he's heading back."

As they listened to the radio transmission, Mendez and Echevara started to move faster. They were out three minutes before Flavio got out of Taxi Two in front of the Intercontinental Hotel.

The detective stationed in the lobby reported that Flavio was on his way up. Flavio still hadn't talked to anybody. Mendez and Echevara were back in room 739 with their cleaning cart in time to watch Flavio enter his room on the monitors.

Flavio settled into his familiar routine. He took off his suit and shirt, carefully hung up his clothes, turned on his TV, and sat on his bed in his underwear, watching television.

Sheeran looked over the photocopies of Flavio's passport and airline tickets. The businessman was well traveled: he had been to the United States, Mexico, Spain, Italy, Brazil, and Argentina. There were eleven entry stamps to the United States in the past year alone and this was Flavio's second visit to the United States this month. He had come here on July 4 and gone back to Peru on July 6, then returned to the United States on July 8.

Sheeran had already learned from the hotel management that Flavio had stayed at the Intercontinental on July 4 and 5 and that he had registered again on July 8, and that these were his first visits ever to the Intercontinental. Sheeran figured that Rodrigo's pinky had been delivered to Flavio at the Intercontinental on July 5, along with a list of *Sendero Luminoso*'s demands. Flavio had probably left immediately for Peru, arrived there on July 6, and somehow delivered the pinky and the demands to Rodrigo's family in Peru. Then he returned to the United States on July 8 for some more Rodrigo body parts.

But then McKenna had shot the *Sendero Luminoso* messenger on July 9, while he was on his way to deliver Rodrigo's ring finger to Flavio at the Intercontinental. So then Flavio didn't know what to do. He'd called his contact number, the pay phone at East 113th Street and Lexington Avenue, and somebody had given him instructions.

For some reason he had left the hotel on the night of the ninth, without checking out. The maid had told them that his bed hadn't been slept in that night. Where had Flavio gone that night after Rico was killed? And why was a member of a terrorist group involved in murder, kidnapping, and torture going to church every day?

Then Sheeran looked at the photocopy of Flavio's airline ticket. It was a Lan-Chile open ticket for the 6:05 P.M. flight from Kennedy Airport to Lima, Peru. All Flavio had to do was confirm his reservation with Lan-Chile on any day and he could take the flight out. He was just waiting for Rodrigo's next finger, Sheeran thought.

"He's using the phone," Hardcass said.

Sheeran watched and listened while Flavio dialed room service. He ordered a hamburger deluxe, cherry pie, coffee, and a bottle of wine. Joe Mendez took his serving cart and left for the kitchen to pick up Flavio's order.

Then five replacement troops arrived at the room from the Two-five. That's when the problem arose. None of his detectives wanted to be relieved. They all had been working for more than twenty-four hours, so everyone was making a lot of overtime. And nobody was killing themselves. It had become a very easy job. When Flavio slept, they slept. Last night this room looked like a teenage sleep-over party, Sheeran thought. They just needed one man awake for the monitors and one man in the lobby, in case Flavio got any visitors.

Sheeran had a total of eleven detectives assigned to the hotel, and most of them were his people. He realized that his detectives were all eventually going to be replaced by Brunette's and Tavlin's choices. Brunette expected good things out of this case, and he wanted to put his people in line for grade with a big case.

The thing that puzzled Sheeran was Richie White getting transferred from the Seven-one Squad to the Major Case Squad. It had happened so suddenly, and Richie had told him that he hadn't even put in for a transfer. His job on the case was still the same. Richie was still sitting downstairs waiting to follow Flavio wherever he went. But for some reason, someone had put Richie White on the fast track to Grade.

Sheeran knew, of course, that White had done the right thing with his "Police, Don't Move" story on McKenna's shooting investigation. But who had liked the story so much that he went out of his way to reward Richie? Even Richie didn't know. It had to be Brunette, Sheeran thought. But why? The only reason that Sheeran could figure was that, for some reason, Brunette had a soft spot in his heart for McKenna. That had to be it, Sheeran thought. Well, it's none of my business.

Which brought Sheeran to his own unique set of circumstances. By choice, he was in a dead-end job, with virtually no chance of promotion. A captain in the Detective Bureau is a great job, but it's a dead-end job. Under current department policies, captains must command a patrol precinct in order to get promoted to deputy inspector. Which was the last thing that Sheeran wanted to do. The promotion didn't mean that much to him and patrol was a big headache. He was happy being in the Bureau and had resigned himself to retiring from the job as a captain.

Then this case came up. The case had the potential to be something extraordinary. Sheeran knew that extraordinary promotions sometimes came out of extraordinary cases. Luck had placed him on the fast track. He knew that he had done a great job so far, and that he had placed himself in the limelight.

But he had stepped on some powerful toes to get his job accomplished, like Flynn from the Legal Bureau. Flynn was a power source, someone in a position in Headquarters to make his life miserable. Sheeran had come to the conclusion that if this case turned into a disaster, he had better retire. But if the case turned out well, he had a great chance of getting promoted while staying in the Bureau. That promotion would take him right out of harm's way and make the rest of his time in the job a wonderful thing. Once he was a deputy inspector, he could stay in the Bureau and just keep on getting promoted. Better make sure that I do this thing right, he thought.

Flavio's food was being delivered by the room-service detective. Flavio was still in his underwear. He signed for his bill and gave Mendez a five-dollar tip in cash.

"Five dollars!" Hardcass said as he watched the monitor. "Very generous! That's another pizza for the troops."

While Flavio ate, Hardcass indoctrinated the replacements. "Detective Echevara, you're off duty. Help clean up this pigpen before you go." He called the desk and told the hotel manager that he needed another maid's uniform. Joe Mendez had come back to the room. Hardcass said, "Give me the five dollars Flavio gave you. You're off duty, take off the uniform." He sized up one of the replacements and said to him, "You're now in room service. Get the uniform from Mendez." The other two replacements went to Taxi One and Taxi Two. He told them, "Send the other drivers up so I can sign their overtime slips." Then Hardcass called the Motor Transport Division and told them to deliver two replacement cabs to the Intercontinental Hotel, right away.

Having a genuine prick like Lieutenant Hardcass makes this job so easy, Sheeran thought. There's not too much for me to do. The whole job had become simple since they had secured the total cooperation of the Intercontinental. Sheeran knew that Brunette had called the director of security for the entire chain of Intercontinental Hotels. As so often happens, it turned out that the director was a retired chief from the NYPD, and after that eveything went smoothly.

Half an hour later they watched Phil Alarcon, the new room-service detective, clear away Flavio's food trays. Flavio was watching TV again. Everyone settled down into the routine for another hour.

At two o'clock Flavio picked up the telephone and dialed a long telephone number. The number showed up on the LCD screen on the TARU recorder as Flavio was dialing it. Pedro Gaspar looked at his book for telephone country codes and then said, "He's calling Peru." Sheeran recognized the number as one that appeared on Flavio's telephone charge bill. He had called the number two days ago, before the wiretap had been installed, and had talked for thirteen minutes. "Put it on the speaker," Sheeran told Gaspar.

A woman answered the phone. The tape was rolling. Sheeran and Hardcass were the only two people in the room who didn't speak Spanish and couldn't understand the conversation. They all stared at the speaker as they listened to Flavio's conversation.

The woman was crying as she spoke to Flavio. Sheeran heard her say something about *Sendero Luminoso*. Sheeran couldn't take it any more. "What are they talking about?" he asked Detective Maria Balazos, the new maid.

Balazos whispered to Sheeran, "The woman is Flavio's wife. *Sendero Luminoso* kidnapped their daughter a week ago. Flavio's wife keeps telling him to do whatever *Sendero Luminoso* wants him to do, and Flavio told her he was trying, but he didn't know what they wanted him to do next. He told her that he would know more at four thirty. Now Flavio's wife is telling him that their daughter is still alive and that she received another message from *Sendero Luminoso*. The message is that their daughter's life still depended on Flavio."

Gaspar had zoomed one camera in on Flavio's face, and they could see that Flavio was also crying. The conversation went on for another fifteen minutes and Sheeran asked no more questions.

When Flavio had hung up, Sheeran told Maria Balazos to give him a synopsis of the conversation. She told him that Flavio's daughter, Linda, had been taken by *Sendero Luminoso* at gunpoint last week while Flavio's wife was walking her to school. They had told Flavio's wife not to call the police, that they just had a job for Flavio to do. If the job worked out, their daughter would live. If not, she would die. Balazos told Sheeran that Flavio's wife blamed herself for the kidnapping, and she blamed Flavio for not getting the job done on time.

Sheeran said to Gaspar, "Make a copy of the telephone conversation tape." Then he sat down to think about this new information. Flavio was a legitimate businessman who was being forced to act as a messenger for *Sendero Luminoso* in order to save his daughter's life. That's why he keeps going to church, Sheeran thought. That explains a lot.

Hardcass surprised Sheeran by saying first the thought that was on everyone's mind. "So if we get *Sendero Luminoso* here, the little girl dies in Peru. That sucks!"

Pretty concise, Sheeran thought. Now, what happens at 4:30 that will give Flavio more information on his mission? He's either going to get a visitor, go to a meeting, get a phone call, or call the phone booth at East 113th Street and Lexington Avenue for further instructions. I'd better let Tavlin know what's going on, he thought.

Sheeran told everyone in the room not to mention a word of the conversation between Flavio and his wife to anyone. This could become a public relations disaster, he thought. Then he went down to the pay phones in the lobby of the hotel. He didn't want any of his detectives listening in on his conversation. He called Tavlin at the Two-five, told him what was happening, and promised him a copy of the tape. Steve Tavlin was known to have a conscience and Sheeran could hear from his tone of voice that the news hit Tavlin hard.

Tavlin said, "I'm going to have an Emergency Service truck with heavy weapons standing by near the hotel by four thirty in case you need them. I'll make sure the surveillance teams in the Two-five know that four thirty is the crucial time. Good job, Sheeran."

Tavlin hung up. Sheeran said to the detective he had stationed in the lobby, "Stay on your toes. Something's gonna happen at four thirty. Let me know if you see anybody suspicious." Then he went back to room 739 to wait.

At 4:15 Flavio turned off the TV and started pacing. At 4:25 he went to his pants that were hanging in his closet and pulled out his wallet. He took out a piece of paper, unfolded it, and placed it on the nightstand next to the phone. "Zoom in on the paper," Hardcass told Gaspar. No good. They couldn't make it out. It was too far, but they could see that it was a list of numbers. Hardcass picked up the radio and said, "Get ready, Two-five Surveillance Teams. He's getting ready to make the call." Sheeran heard Goldblatt's voice answer from the Two-five, "We're ready, but there's nobody near the phone."

"Open up a line to Telephone Security," Sheeran told Hardcass. Hardcass called New York Telephone Security, identified himself, and asked for the supervisor. Hardcass knew him. After thirty years in the Bureau, Hardcass knew everybody. He told the supervisor to stand by for a number and that he wanted a quick location on that number.

Sheern watched the monitor while Flavio picked up his phone.

Flavio read a number off the list on the nightstand as he dialed. Sheeran picked up the radio and said, "Two-five, he's dialing."

"There's nobody at the pay phone," Goldblatt answered from the 25th Precinct.

Hardcass gave the number to Telephone Security. It had a 212 area code. Manhattan. The phone rang once. Someone picked it up. Flavio said something in Spanish and a female voice answered him in Spanish. Then she hung up.

Hardcass got the location of the number. "Pay Phone. East 117th and Lexington," he said. Two blocks from the surveillance in the Two-five. Sheeran radioed the location to Goldblatt, and heard Goldblatt redirecting his people. "Just take a look," Goldblatt told them. "Don't make them suspicious. Don't hang around. Be careful."

One minute later, Sheeran heard a female detective assigned to the surveillance in the Two-five say, "There's nobody near the phone. What should I do?" He heard Goldblatt answer, "Stay away, but look at everyone close by. Don't blow it. Tomorrow's another day."

Sheeran knew that Goldblatt was right. It wouldn't do to blow it now. *Sendero Luminoso* might be looking at that pay phone right now. He hoped that Goldblatt was right about getting another chance tomorrow.

"What happened," Sheeran asked Balazos.

"Short and sweet, Captain," she answered. "Flavio just said, 'It's me,' and the female told him 'Everything's OK. Just stay there. Call me tomorrow at the next number on the list.' Then she hung up."

So we do get another chance, Sheeran thought. We've got to get that list from Flavio. Flavio folded up the list, put it back in his wallet, then put the wallet back in the pocket of his pants that were hanging in the closet. How are we going to get it? Sheeran asked himself. We need it so we'll know where to place our surveillance team tomorrow. We don't need another repeat of today's failure.

The obvious answer was to just go down and take it. But Sheeran felt that would insure the death of Flavio's daughter. To take the list, they would have to take Flavio. There was no guarantee that Flavio would cooperate. He was under a lot of pressure. No good, Sheeran thought. There had to be a better way.

Sheeran watched as Flavio poured himself a glass of wine. The wine? Sheeran thought. We could put something subtle in his wine to make him sleep a little better. Of course, that would be against all the rules, Sheeran knew. Slipping anyone a Mickey, even the bad guys, was strictly illegal. Besides, Flavio might not order another bottle of wine.

In any event, Sheeran figured that he would have to send two detectives to Flavio's room that night to get the list from his pocket.

Real dangerous, Sheeran thought. Better have my men look like burglars, just in case Flavio wakes up.

While Sheerean was trying to figure out a better way, a messenger arrived from headquarters. He had a bundle of mail. There were the paychecks for everyone assigned to the Intercontinental Hotel, a package from the Legal Bureau addressed to Sheeran, and a plain envelope, also addressed to Sheeran.

Sheeran gave Hardcass the paychecks to distribute. Then he opened the letter from the Legal Bureau. There was a little note from Captain Flynn apologizing for the delay in obtaining records. In the envelope were Flavio's AT&T statements and his American Express statements, along with his July charges, which were not yet billed to Flavio.

Sheeran looked through the American Express bills first. He saw that Flavio usually stayed at the Hilton Hotel in Manhattan when he came to New York. Then Sheeran compared the bills against Flavio's passport entries and found that Flavio always charged his flights to American Express. It was a business account in Flavio Asturo's name with bills paid by *Laxthaca Importadors y Exportadors, S.A.*

Sheeran looked at the July charges. Flavio's two round-trip charges for airline tickets to the United States were listed. The Intercontinental was also listed. But the most interesting thing was that there was a charge dated July 9 for the Holiday Inn on North Conduit Boulevard near Kennedy Airport. There was a room charge and a $36.20 telephone charge.

So that's where he went after McKenna shot Carlos Mendosa, Sheeran thought. He called his contact number in Spanish Harlem after Carlos Mendosa didn't show up and they told him to get out of the Intercontinental. Flavio left all of his things here and spent the night at the Holiday Inn, which was about a half a mile away. And *Sendero Luminoso* probably sent somebody here to check out the Intercontinental for police activity centered on Flavio's room. They would have wanted to make sure that Flavio hadn't informed on them to the police. They found no police activity because we didn't find out about Flavio until the tenth. Good thing, Sheeran thought. So then Flavio called the next number on his list of contacts on the tenth, and *Sendero Luminoso* told him to return to the Intercontinental, which he did.

Hardcass came back from distributing the paychecks to the troops downstairs. Sheeran told him to assign a team to go over to the Holiday Inn and try to get the list of Flavio's telephone calls for July 9 and 10. Then he opened the second letter. It was a short note from Chief Brunette instructing Sheeran to call him when he got a chance. There was a telephone number listed that Sheeran did not recognize as one of the regular department exchanges. Sheeran went down to the pay phones in the lobby again and called the number. Brunette picked up the phone right away. Sheeran was ready to report on the day's activities at the Intercontinental, but apparently Tavlin had already filled him in. It was something else.

Brunette said, "The Brooklyn DA worked out a deal with Murray Don't Worry. Murray said his clients had good information and he struck a hard bargain. The deal is that Chavez won't have his parole revoked because of his last arrest. He'll plead guilty to the present weapons and narcotics charges and get five years without possibility of parole. Torres had jumped bail on a murder conviction. He'll be sentenced on the murder and begin serving time. He'll plead guilty on the present weapons and narcotics charges and he'll get five years to run concurrently with his time served on the murder conviction."

"That's quite a deal for them," Sheeran said.

"That's why I need you. Your job is to see if the information they got is good enough to justify the deal. I want you to meet with the DA, Captain Flynn, McKenna, and Pacella tomorrow morning at ten thirty at the Manhattan House of Detention. Murray will give you an overview of the information that his clients can provide. If you think the information is vital to the case, tell the DA we need the deal. Then McKenna and Pacella will interview Torres and Chavez."

"What if they have something, but not enough?" Sheeran asked.

"If it's not enough to justify the deal, let them rot. It's up to you."

Sheeran hung up with a lot on his mind. If he authorized the deal, Chavez could be saving four years of jail time. Ordinarily, he would have his parole violated and he wouldn't begin serving time on his present charges until 1993, when his parole expired. Then he should get eight years on the weapons and gun charges. Torres would do even better. He would get no real additional jail time on the weapons and narcotics charges since the jail time on these charges would run concurrently with the time on his murder conviction. It bothered Sheeran that he would be the one to authorize it, since he personally felt that they both should be shot. Remember, it's just a game and we don't make the rules, he thought. In the back of his mind, he hoped that he could find an excuse to nix the deal.

Sheeran went back to room 739 and picked a slice of cold pizza out of the box on the coffee table. He sat down and joined everyone else watching the news. There was still nothing reported on the investigation.

The weather was on when Richie White came up to the room from his mission at the Holiday Inn. He had done a good job. On the night of July 9 and again on the morning of July 10 Flavio had called his wife in Peru from his room at the Holiday Inn. At 4:29 on the afternoon of the tenth Flavio had called 212-778-3214, a local New

York City number. Sheeran had given the number to Hardcass, who'd called it in to Telephone Security. It was a pay phone on East 117th Street and Third Avenue. Still in Spanish Harlem, Sheeran thought. He figured that Flavio had called the number on July 10 and they'd told him to go back to the Intercontinental.

Then Sheeran's mind back to the list of telephone numbers in Flavio's pocket. He couldn't find any answer that sounded right, so he decided to pass the ball. "I'm going to see Inspector Tavlin," he said to Hardcass as he got up and headed for the door. "I'll be back in a couple of hours."

19

July 11   11:00 P.M.

McKenna's plane was a half hour late getting into La Guardia. It was raining in New York and his plane had to circle the airport to wait for an available runway. As soon as he left the plane, McKenna found a pay phone and called home. No answer, so he called Brunette's mobile phone. Brunette answered at once. "Where are you, Ray?" McKenna asked.

"Still sitting in your living room. I didn't want to answer your phone."

"I guess Angelita's still not there?"

"Sorry, buddy. I'm here by myself. But your phone's been ringing every half hour or so."

McKenna wasn't surprised. Angelita wasn't the kind of girl to make idle threats. She said she was leaving and she's gone. McKenna was glad that Ray was there; he wasn't ready to go home to an empty apartment. "I'll see you in half an hour," he said, and hung up.

McKenna went to the baggage area and was surprised that his bag was one of the first on the carousel. He picked up his bag and went outside into the rain. There was a taxi waiting in the hack line. McKenna got in and gave the driver his address. The driver wasn't talkative and McKenna fell asleep in the back of the cab before they got to the Triboro Bridge. He woke up when they were a couple of blocks from his apartment. It was pouring and McKenna had the driver take him right to the front door.

McKenna smelled the steaks before he got his door open. "Welcome home," Brunette said. "You're just in time if you want your steak rare."

Ray was busy cooking up one of their five-minute meals—Minute rice, frozen vegetables, and rare steak. He had made himself at home and wore pajamas and a robe. The air-conditioner roared and the place was freezing. McKenna wasn't hungry after the big dinner with Raoul and Rosa in Florida, but he didn't want to spoil Brunette's fun. "I'll just have a little steak, Ray."

"Great! More for me. Get those wet clothes off and I'll get the food on the plates."

McKenna went into the bedroom and dressed in pajamas and a robe. When he opened his closet, he saw that all of Angelita's clothes were gone. He checked her dresser. Empty. A queasy feeling rose in the pit of his stomach. Trying to keep his focus on the case, McKenna joined Brunette at the table.

Brunette told him what Pacella and Catalfumo had learned in Massachusetts. "I just found out the worst part half an hour ago. The FBI found the body of Rodrigo's bodyguard buried in the woods behind the house Isabela was using. Two shots to the chest. Pacella and Catalfumo are on their way back to New York."

Brunette then gave him the news from the Intercontinental Hotel, leaving out the monitored telephone conversations between Flavio and his wife in Peru. He explained the problems of the surveillance in the Two-five, since Flavio called a different telephone number from the list of numbers in his wallet each time he contacted *Sendero Luminoso*.

While Brunette talked McKenna thought the problem over. He realized that the outcome of the investigation depended on being able to follow Flavio's contact to the place where Rodrigo was being held. Getting the list from Flavio's pants pocket while he was sleeping was the only way to keep the investigation on track. But that course of action was dangerous. If Flavio woke up during the search, the investigation would probably be blown and Rodrigo would certainly be killed. It seemed to be a necessary risk and McKenna said, "There's no other way. Flavio's room will have to be searched while he's sleeping."

"I haven't made up my mind about that yet," Brunette said.

McKenna was glad that he wasn't responsible for that decision. Maybe there's another way, he thought. "Why don't we put something in his food to make sure that he doesn't wake up while our men are in the room?"

"We might eventually have to, but he's already had dinner tonight. Let's keep that idea to ourselves."

McKenna's mind was racing. Maybe we should just grab Flavio and give him the facts of life. After all, he was involved in a capital crime in the United States. Maybe a deal should be made with him in return for his cooperation. But first it would be necessary to do some more research on Flavio to find out why he was with *Sendero Luminoso* and exactly how dedicated he could be expected to be to their cause. "We need to know more about Flavio and what makes him tick. Maybe we can make him talk to us. Has he made any more phone calls to Peru?" McKenna asked.

Brunette was waiting for that question. He folded his hands in front of him and looked McKenna straight in the eye. McKenna was surprised to see that his friend looked nervous. This isn't gonna be good, McKenna thought.

Brunette said, "Our job is to solve crimes committed in New York or capture persons who come to New York after committing crimes in the rest of the country. Right?"

That was simple, McKenna thought. "Right," he answered.

Brunette continued. "Unless we are specifically asked to, we don't try to solve crimes that are committed outside the United States, and we certainly can do nothing to prevent crimes from being committed outside the United States. Our job is to solve crimes committed in this country by arresting the persons responsible if they are in New York. We really can't be responsible for crimes committed outside the United States, or the consequences of our actions in other countries if we do the job that we are paid to do. Do you agree?"

"Sure," McKenna answered. What's the punch line, he thought.

"Flavio Asturo is not a member of *Sendero Luminoso*. He's working for them because they kidnapped his daughter and they're holding her in Peru to force him to work for them. He's a legitimate businessman, as far as we can tell."

"How do you know that?" McKenna asked.

"We listened to the phone calls between Flavio and his wife in Peru. They cry to each other twice a day. You don't want to hear the tapes," Brunette said. "We haven't been able to find out how old the girl is, but we know that she must be young. Her name is Linda and they took her from Flavio's wife on the street while she was taking her to school."

"Do the police in Peru know about this?"

"No. Flavio's wife apparently didn't notify them. These kidnappings must be pretty common in Peru and everyone there seems to know the procedure. Flavio's wife keeps telling him to do whatever they want and he keeps telling her that he will, but that he doesn't know what they want him to do now. Flavio and his wife are very upset about the delay."

"Do you think Flavio would work with us?"

"I asked myself the same question. I called in the department psychologist and gave him a rundown on Flavio and his situation. He listened to the tapes of Flavio talking to his wife. His conclusion is that Flavio's already involved himself in this kidnapping to save his daughter's life and that he won't make any deals with us on his own behalf. Flavio's primary concern is his daughter's safety, and he'll do nothing that would antagonize or work against the interests of *Sendero Luminoso* while they're holding his daughter. So forget that one."

McKenna was dumbstruck. All of a sudden, their investigation didn't seem so important. He thought about Flavio and the risks that he was taking to save his daughter's life. Linda's safety and the successful conclusion of this case were two totally incompatible situations. Rescue Rodrigo and get a little girl killed in Peru? Should we do that? Does First Grade mean so much to me that I have to get an innocent little girl killed to get it?

The McKenna remembered that Mark Bremmen from Brooks Brothers had told him that Rodrigo was a scumbag. Rodrigo has already lived a good part of his life, and from what I know now, he's had a pretty good life, McKenna thought.

The next thing that popped into McKenna's head came from nowhere and terrified him. It was, I need a drink. It wouldn't leave his mind.

"Feel like a drink, Ray?"

"You too? For the first time in a long time, I'm having a tough time with it. It might be the main reason I decided to come here tonight. I knew that you'd feel the same way and that we could help each other out. This whole Flavio thing makes it personal and helps me to focus. It's just another reason that I'm beginning to really hate *Sendero Luminoso*. They kidnapped Flavio's daughter and they make me want to drink."

"They haven't made it too easy for me, either. I just lost my girl over these dirtbags. I would've retired today and forgotten all about First Grade if it wasn't for them. I'd be happier than I am right now and I'd still have Angelita. Now I have to kill them before they kill me."

McKenna got a hold on is emotions. Drinking is always a bad idea for people like Ray and me, he thought. That would make *Sendero Luminoso* the all-around winners. It's time to concentrate.

Ray was watching him, waiting for him to collect his thoughts and get back on track.

"Obviously," McKenna said, "*Sendero Luminoso* didn't think that Flavio was involved in the shooting of Carlos Mendosa. If they did suspect Flavio of anything, they would have killed his daughter by now, or at least have sent his wife a couple of her fingers. I think they just attributed the death of Carlos to bad luck. But we have to do everything possible to make sure that it doesn't look like Flavio Asturo was any part of this investigation."

"I've already insisted on that. We don't even want him to know himself that he's helping us. But if worse come to worst, we're gonna grab him. We might have to try to get what he knows about these people. We have our jobs to do, and we both know what our job is with these people. This is America, not Peru, and they're operating in our country."

Brunette had obviously decided that the subject was closed. That's another decision I'm glad I don't have to make, McKenna thought.

Then the phone rang and McKenna picked it up. It was Angelita. "How you doing, hotshot?" she asked.

"OK. But I'd be doing a whole lot better if you were here. Where are you?"

"I'm still at my folks' house for the next week or so."

"And then?"

"I'm going to put in for a transfer to Florida. I hear that there are a few openings coming up and I've got enough seniority with the airline to get it, if I want it. I want to go and I figure that it'll be better for both of us if I get out of town."

"Florida's a long way to go, baby. Couldn't you go someplace a little closer? I just need a little more time. A week or two, at most. Then this case will be over and I'll get out. A couple of weeks isn't too much to ask after four years."

"That's just it, Brian. Four years was too long to wait. Let's not go over this again. It's not gonna change anything. I'll call you when I get settled and know what I'm doing."

Angelita hung up the phone. Thanks for calling, McKenna thought.

Brunette had cleared the table while McKenna was on the phone, and he had started washing the dishes. McKenna joined him in the kitchen with a dish towel. "Angelita?" Brunette asked.

"Forget it. What else is going on?"

Brunette could see that McKenna was not in the mood to talk so he explained the mission that Tavlin had given Cisco Sanchez and Wilfredo Gomez that morning. They had gone through the newspapers and made a list of 113 apartments that had been advertised as available between June 26 and July 4 in the target area. "It's twenty square blocks and everything we've learned so far tells us that they're holding Rodrigo somewhere in that area."

"Why make a list now? Why don't we just wait and follow whoever answers Flavio's call tomorrow?"

"Because of the way they operated in LA and Miami. If they rented two apartments here like they did there, then tomorrow we'll only learn about one of their apartments. But if we have a list ready of all the apartments that were rented during that time, then it'll be easy.

Once we find one location, we'll just have to do a little snooping to get the other one."

That sounded like a good idea to McKenna. If *Sendero Luminoso* had been that careful in Miami and East LA, they would certainly do the same thing here, he thought. They don't seem to be running out of money, and from everything that we've learned about them so far, they're certainly careful, if nothing else.

They finished the dishes and McKenna took two Kalibers out of the refrigerator. They sat down in the living room, drinking their beer.

"Let's talk about the FBI," McKenna said. "They still haven't come clean with us."

He told Brunette what had happened with Raoul Camarena in Florida, what he found out about Camarena's finances, and of his suspicions about the immediate FBI search of Raoul's home. "I think they already had a case going on Camarena before I shot Carlos and somehow the two cases are related. I just can't figure out why they're following Rosa."

"Maybe she's their informant," Brunette said.

"I can't see it. I think she's crazy about him."

"Let's not pull our hair out over this now," Brunette said. "Gene Shields told me he'll get me the answers and I believe him. We don't need them for our end of this case, anyway."

"Has the FBI contacted the Guiterrez family or the Peruvian government about the kidnapping?" McKenna asked.

"They sent couple of agents to Peru this afternoon to interview the family and find out why they haven't reported the kidnapping. Shields will let me know what they say."

"Anything else happening?"

"The Boston police found Rodrigo's car. It was parked near Boston Common. Somebody stole the tires. I spoke with the editors of the *Boston Globe* and with the chief of police in Boston. They're still gonna keep under wraps the fact that Rodrigo had been kidnapped and that the New York City police are close to finding him."

"We'd better find him soon," McKenna said. "We're not gonna be able to keep this case quiet for much longer. I'm surprised you've kept it out of the papers for this long. What are you doing with me next?"

"You and Pacella are going to meet Sheeran at ten thirty tomorrow morning at the Manhattan Men's House of Detention."

Brunette told him of the deal between Murray Don't Worry and the Brooklyn DA. "If Sheeran goes for it, you and Pacella are going to interview Chavez and Torres and wring everything they know from their devious minds."

McKenna turned on the TV and they watched CNN while they kept their own thoughts. Then the phone rang again. It was Pacella, calling from a rest area on the New England Thruway. He complained that he had tried to call earlier, but the phone was busy.

"When did you try, Tommy?"

"At ten thirty."

"You must've dialed a wrong number. Nobody was using the phone here," McKenna said. He told Pacella about the proposed interviews of Chavez and Torres at 10:30 in the morning.

Pacella was pleased. Ten thirty was one of the better times to travel from Long Island to Manhattan. Traffic wouldn't be too bad. "See you in the morning," Pacella said and hung up.

Then it hit McKenna. Pacella had dialed and gotten a busy signal. So he'd tried again later. Everybody does it. McKenna jumped up from the couch and asked Brunette, "Ray, were you using my phone at ten thirty?"

"No."

"Does TARU have the ability to interrupt Flavio's telephone calls as soon as they get the number he's calling?"

"I think so," Brunette answered.

"How long would it take to get the location of the telephone number that Flavio calls?"

"Under a minute."

"And how long would it take to move our surveillance teams to a new location?"

"If we had enough people working to cover the entire neighborhood, under two minutes."

Brunette got it right away. As soon as Flavio dialed the next number on his list at 4:30 tomorrow afternoon, TARU would cut off Flavio's call and feed him a busy signal. Then they would get the location that Flavio dialed from Telephone Security and set up the surveillance. They should have a couple of minutes before Flavio dialed again. If they weren't ready when he did, they would just feed him another busy signal. If Flavio's last phone call was any indication of the *Sendero Luminoso* procedure, Flavio wouldn't talk, he would just listen. He probably wouldn't question his contact on the busy signal.

"I think it'll work," Brunette said. "It'll take a lot of people to cover the neighborhood tomorrow, but I think it'll work. So we've got nothing to worry about. We don't have to worry about slipping Flavio a Mickey and searching his room for his telephone list. That's a load off my mind."

The TV news all looked good after that. The two men had another beer and then turned in for the night.

20

July 12   6:20 A.M.

The alarm went off for the third time. McKenna groped and found the snooze button again. He pressed it, then decided to get up. He shut off the alarm, went into the bathroom, brushed his teeth, and splashed some cold water into his eyes. He returned to his bedroom and heard the sound of Brunette's snores coming from the guest room.

McKenna put on his old running clothes and did his routine of stretching exercises. He felt good and was raring to go. He left his apartment and ran down the stairs to the street.

It looks like it's gonna be a nice day, McKenna thought. A hot day maybe, but at least it wasn't going to rain again.

McKenna ran to Hudson Street and started north. It was Sunday and the streets were deserted. Just the homeless and a few taxi drivers were around. On West 14th he made a right and started down the wide sidewalk toward the East River. He ran to the end of 14th Street, past Stuyvesant Town, and turned south, then across the pedestrian bridge over the East River Drive into Corlear's Hook Park. He picked up his pace as he ran south in the park along the East River.

Now there were people. He passed other runners and recognized many of these devotees. He had been running in the park on this same route for the past fifteen years with many of these same people. Then came the thing that McKenna hated most. He recognized the sound of the man behind him and he picked up his pace. The man was still behind him, gliding almost noiselessly. McKenna went flat out for a half mile and lengthened the distance between himself and his pursuer. He slowed down as he crossed under the Williamsburg Bridge, confident that he had won. But he didn't want to give his pursuer the satisfaction of turning around. That was a mistake.

McKenna was passing Marine 6, the Fire Department fireboat company, when Peter Bengard passed him at full speed with the flags fluttering on his racing wheelchair. "Not today, McKenna," he yelled as he passed, his massive arms pushing the wheels of his wheelchair along at what seemed like an impossible speed.

"God, I hate that guy," McKenna said under his breath as he smiled and waved at Bengard. He looked around to see if any of the other runners he knew had noticed it. Of course, there were two or three witnesses. McKenna felt like turning back, but his pride kept him going. He continued south to the Brooklyn Bridge, up the stairs to the wide pedestrian path, and began running across the bridge.

Halfway over, McKenna turned back. This was as close to Brooklyn as he ever wanted to get. He ran off the bridge and continued south to Battery Park, the end of Manhattan, crossed the park, and headed home, running north on the West Side Drive along the Hudson River. He went past the Battery Tunnel entrance, past the World Trade Center, and past the transvestite prostitutes waiting for customers from New Jersey. At West 14th Street he turned east again and sprinted at top speed past the meat market.

When he got back to Hudson Street, he slowed to a walk while he caught his breath. He looked at his watch. Five to eight. That didn't make him too happy. Ten miles in seventy-five minutes. Oh well, he thought. Still plenty of time to train. The New York City Marathon isn't until November.

McKenna walked south on Hudson Street to Mr. Sparacino's grocery store. Old Mr. Sparacino was there behind the cash register, as usual, in the same place he had been since 1941, seven days a week, twelve hours a day. McKenna had known him all his life.

"Morning, Brian. How'd you do today?"

"I beat everybody except for a guy in a wheelchair."

"Him again? Don't let him ruin your day, Brian. Go into the back and treat yourself to an avocado. They're soft and ripe, finally. Angelita will love them."

McKenna didn't feel like explaining his changed social status to Mr. Sparacino. It would be common knowledge in the neighborhood by the end of the week anyway. But an avocado sounded great. He went to the fruit section in the rear of the small store. Sure enough, the avocados were perfect. Next he stopped at the large refrigerated counter and picked out a quart of orange juice and a quart of milk. He turned toward the counter at the front of the store and froze.

234

The young Spanish kid stood in the doorway, next to the front counter. Mr. Sparacino was behind the counter with his hands up. The kid's hands gripped a TEC-9, pointed at McKenna. Over the kid's shoulder, McKenna saw an old tan van parked at the curb with the motor running. The passenger door of the van was open and the driver was staring at him and smiling. It was Alfonso Mendosa in a grandstand seat, waiting to watch him die.

The kid also smiled as he raised the TEC-9. McKenna backed up, but there was nowhere to go and nothing to do. His Glock was on his dresser in his bedroom.

The kid took a couple of steps toward him and fired a burst, breaking the glass doors of the refrigerator and splashing milk and orange juice all over McKenna. He dropped his groceries and prepared to meet his maker. The kid swung his TEC-9 to the right and fired another burst into the aisle on McKenna's left. McKenna was splattered with the contents of the row of soup cans that had been stacked on the shelves in the aisle.

The kid started laughing, enjoying himself. McKenna could see that Ali was also laughing in the van. Then the kid centered his weapon on McKenna's chest and walked forward. "This if for Carlos!" he said.

McKenna stared into the kid's eyes. He wanted to be able to recognize him if he saw him again in the next life. McKenna was ready to die.

Then McKenna saw Mr. Sparacino drop his hands and reach under his counter. McKenna kept staring at the kid and said in Spanish, "Just make it fast, *cabron*." The kid shifted his aim to McKenna's groin.

The kid was still having a great time when the first bullet hit him. McKenna dropped to the ground and Mr. Sparacino kept firing. The kid fell forward and McKenna reached up and ripped the TEC-9 from his hands as the kid hit the ground. McKenna turned the gun around and, from the floor, fired a burst through the front window at the van outside. He got up and caught a glimpse of Alfonso Mendosa as the van pulled from the curb, tires squealing.

McKenna ran to the front door, past Mr. Sparacino, who was still holding his revolver. He ran into the street and saw the van turn right on West 14th Street. There was nobody else outside.

McKenna went back into the store and walked over to the gunman lying on the floor. He had at least three holes in his back. McKenna rolled the kid over. He was dead, another hole in his chest. An exit wound, McKenna thought. I'm glad I dropped.

McKenna placed the TEC-9 on the kid's chest, walked back to the front counter, and took the revolver out of Mr. Sparacino's hand. It was a cheap gun, a five-shot .38-caliber Rohm. McKenna opened up the gun and emptied it. Five spent shells. Mr. Sparacino looked like he was going into shock. He was shaking and McKenna was surprised that he was shaking himself.

"Take it easy, Mr. Sparacino. It's all over."

"Are they going to arrest me, Brian?"

"You don't have a pistol license, do you?"

"No. They wouldn't give me one."

"Well, I think you've got one now. Thank you. I owe you my life. Now, give me the phone and sit down. And don't say anything to anybody."

McKenna heard the sirens as he dialed Brunette's mobile phone. Brunette picked up the phone on the fifth ring. "Wake up, buddy. And put on your chief of detectives hat. Get down to Mr. Sparacino's grocery store right away."

"What happened?"

"*Sendero Luminoso* tried to get me. Mr. Sparacino just killed one of them with an unlicensed pistol and saved my life. Alfonso Mendosa was driving the getaway van. He got away."

"I'll be down in a minute. Don't let Mr. Sparacino say anything to anybody." Then Brunette hung up.

McKenna put the TEC-9 and the Rohm revolver on the counter as the first patrol car pulled up in front of the store. The two cops got out of the car with their guns drawn and pointed at McKenna through the door.

McKenna raised both hands in the air and yelled, "I'm on the Job!"

The cops didn't move. They both kept their revolvers trained on McKenna. "Where's your shield?" one of them yelled.

"I'm Detective Brian McKenna from the Major Case Squad. I was out running and I don't have my shield with me."

They weren't convinced. "Keep your hands in the air."

A second patrol car pulled up. It was the patrol sergeant. "McKenna!" he yelled. "Are you OK?"

Thank God, McKenna thought. He didn't recognize the sergeant, but the important thing was that the sergeant recognized him. McKenna lowered his arms and walked over to the sergeant. "Put it over," he said. "An old tan van, New York plates, headed east on 14th Street, three minutes in the past. Male Hispanic driver, probably armed and extremely dangerous. And call an ambulance."

The sergeant lifted his radio and transmitted the messages. He told the cops to wait outside and followed McKenna into the store. He walked over to the gunman's body, bent over, and examined him. "You don't need an ambulance for this one, McKenna. Was he armed?"

"Extremely. This man was killed during a confidential operation that is being personally run by the chief of detectives. I'm sorry,

Sarge, but I can't tell you more than that right now, except that Mr. Sparacino is a hero and he's not to talk to anyone. The ambulance is for him. There's to be no notifications and no press. Just make sure that nobody else comes in here. That's the chief's orders, and he's on his way here."

The patrol sergeant stiffened, stunned. Then he did the obvious thing. He walked outside and yelled to his men, "Put your hats on and keep everyone away from the front of this store." Then he went to his car and put on his own hat. After all, the chief of detectives was coming.

Five minutes later Brunette arrived outside the store. By that time there were ten patrol cars and two ambulances at the curb. Every cop was in full uniform, complete with hats and nightsticks. McKenna saw the sergeant walk up to Brunette and salute. Brunette gave him some instructions during the next few minutes, then came into the store as most of the patrol cars began leaving.

"Your fly's open, Ray," McKenna said.

Brunette looked down. Sure enough, his pajamas were showing through his open fly. He zipped and said, "I got dressed in a hurry. Why won't anyone tell the emperor when he's wearing no clothes? But at least I didn't piss in my pants."

McKenna followed Brunette's discreet gaze to his own groin area. His old cut-off sweatpants were wet around the crotch. "That's sweat, Ray. Don't forget, I just ran ten miles."

Brunette smiled and said, "We might have to send those shorts to the police lab for analysis, Brian."

"Let's just agree it's sweat and forget it. Otherwise, they'll be breaking my balls for the next ten years."

"I'm kidding, Brian. Of course it's sweat." Brunette picked up the guns on the counter and looked at them. Then he walked over to the dead gunman. "He's about twenty years old, I'd say."

"Dead soldiers are always young."

"Did you figure out yet how they found you?"

"Either through DMV or they followed my taxi from the airport last night. Following me home is more likely. With a common name like mine and no date of birth, it would have taken them longer to find me if they got access to a DMV computer. Which means that Raoul Camarena must have let them know which flight I'd be on from Florida."

"I think you're right, buddy. This is going to really change your life-style. They know where you live."

"I've got the FBI to thank for that. Maybe if they would've told us what they're doing in Florida, none of this would've happened. Or at least I could've been ready. Weatherby's responsible for this. He's an incompetent little prick and I'm gonna straighten him out. What happens now? I can't go home until we get them?"

McKenna's voice was rising and starting to shake.

"Take it easy, Brian," Brunette said. "I'm gonna get right to Gene Shields. We'll get this straightened out today. I promise. If not, we'll go see Weatherby together. If that doesn't work, we'll go see the Director. Don't worry."

Just then the patrol sergeant came in again. He stood by the door until Brunette motioned for him to come over. He walked up to Brunette and said, "The 13th Precinct's got the van at 23rd Street and Broadway. It's empty, but there are four bullet holes in the right side. No blood, though. The van was reported stolen in the Bronx on June twenty-sixth."

"Have it towed into the 13th Precinct garage and safeguarded for fingerprints. Tell the 13th Squad to do a canvass at 23rd and Broadway to find out if anyone saw where the driver of the van went."

The sergeant saluted and left. You OK now?" Brunette asked McKenna.

"Sorry. I'm fine. Let's see if you can fix things for Mr. Sparacino."

They walked over to the old man. He was still shaking a little. Brunette had been in the store many times for groceries and Mr. Sparacino recognized him.

"How are you feeling now, Mr. Sparacino?"

"Fine, sir. Am I in a lot of trouble?"

"Of course not, Mr. Sparacino. You're a hero, as far as I'm concerned. You're one of the bravest men I ever met. You saved Detective McKenna's life and just did the right thing. Why would you be in trouble?"

"Because I don't have a license for the pistol."

"Did you ever apply for a pistol license?"

"Last year, after I was robbed for the third time. But they told me at Police Headquarters that I was too old or something like that."

"Nonsense, Mr. Sparacino. I think you're mistaken. I think that the police department issued you a pistol license for your pistol, but you lost it. I'll make sure a replacement is issued for you today. *Capisce?*"

Understanding slowly dawned on Mr. Sparacino. "I understand, sir."

"Good," Brunette said. "But there's more. You've killed a man from a very dangerous criminal gang and you're still in danger. Where do you live?"

"Upstairs."

"Do you have a family?"

"I live with my wife. My daughter is married and lives in New Jersey. My son is dead."

"You and your wife can't stay here for a while, Mr. Sparacino. It's too dangerous for you. The police department is going to send you and your wife on a vacation for a couple of weeks while we find you another place to live until this is over. All right?"

"Where will we go?"

"Wherever you want."

"What about my store?"

"I'll make sure that your store is guarded while you're gone. I'm sorry, Mr. Sparacino, but all this is necessary for your safety."

Mr. Sparacino obviously wasn't too happy, but he saw that Brunette was right. "What should I do now?"

"Go upstairs and start packing. You and your wife are going to be staying at a nice hotel tonight. There will be detectives guarding you. In the morning they'll take you to court with your pistol license. You'll meet a man named Captain Flynn and he'll help you. You'll have to tell the grand jury what happened. Then the detectives will take you to the airport. OK?"

"Yes sir. I'll start packing now." Mr. Sparacino walked around the counter and out the front door without even glancing at the man he had just killed. As he was leaving, Inspector Tavlin came in.

Brunette explained to Tavlin what had happened. He told Tavlin how he wanted the shooting handled and exactly what he wanted done. Tavlin had no questions.

21

July 12 9:00 A.M.

McKenna was expected, which didn't surprise him at all. Ray said he would arrange it, and he had.

McKenna arrived at the Manhattan office of the FBI at 26 Federal Plaza right on time for his meeting with Gene Shields and one hour after the shoot-out in Sparacino's. The receptionist brought him into Shields's office without subjecting him to the usual signing in and visitor's pass procedure.

Shields's office was impressive, on the fourteenth floor with a good view of the East River and the Brooklyn Bridge. The office was dominated by a large mahogany desk in the center of the room, which contrasted with the otherwise modern decor. Apparently it was Shields's own desk and he brought it with him whenever he changed assignments.

Gene Shields also contrasted with the modern decor. Shields and his desk were a matched pair. He looked like a prosperous professor at an Ivy League school.

McKenna knew the look because he was practicing it himself. They both wore tan Brooks Brothers suits, blue shirts, red striped ties, and brown penny loafers. Shields had forgotten the pipe and McKenna had forgotten the horn-rimmed glasses. Both men dressed for success and were ready to be believed, no matter how outrageous the lies they told.

Shields rose and offered McKenna his hand. "We meet at last," he said.

240

"Thanks to the chief," McKenna said as he sat down facing Shields's desk. McKenna took the opportunity to look around the office while Shields shuffled through two large files. McKenna hated to admit it, but Shields was probably a better liar than he was. Or, at least, he was believed by more prestigious people. The walls of his office were lined with pictures of Shields shaking hands with presidents, vice-presidents, governors, directors, police commissioners, corporate presidents, and other power sources. McKenna was impressed. He sat back in his chair, ready to watch, listen, and learn.

Shields got right to the point. "I heard about your problems this morning. I'm glad that everything worked out for you."

"This time it worked out. Next time I probably won't be so lucky. What happened to me this morning is one of the things I want to talk to you about."

"I understand. I'm told that you believe my agency has been less than candid in our dealings with your department in your investigation," Shields said.

"Less than candid? I think you've been lying to us, or you haven't told us the full truth, which I consider to be the same thing."

"Let's just say less than candid, OK? It sounds so much better."

"Whatever you say, Mr. Shields."

"Well, you're right. We have been less than candid with you. Not me, personally, but I take responsibility for the mistakes my agency made."

"I'm not blaming you personally. I blame Weatherby."

"So do I. He made a lot of mistakes. In his defense, he didn't think he was putting you or your investigation at risk. Then you surprised him with how much you learned in such a short time. You'll see that he had his reasons for being less than candid. I'm going to tell you everything you want to know, but first I'll need your promise that the things we discuss here today won't be revealed by you to anyone, won't appear in any of your reports, and that you won't testify on these matters without consulting with me first. Do you agree to this?"

"I don't think that I can without knowing more. Remember, we're still cops and we're trying to build a case here against kidnappers and terrorists. That involves reports and testimony."

"Let's put our cards on the table," Shields said. "There isn't gonna be a case against *Sendero Luminoso*. I was told by Ray Brunette, whom I know and trust, that you're prepared to do what's necessary. I'm relying on his judgment. More than that, I'm staking my career and my reputation on it. Are we in agreement on that?"

McKenna could see that he was wrong about Shields. McKenna believed him. This was the first time in his life that he had ever heard anyone else in a Brooks Brothers suit talk about doing the right thing, especially when the right thing might be considered murder by a righteous and zealous prosecutor. There was no double-talk with Shields. He was being straight, and McKenna trusted him. Enough about *Sendero Luminoso*, McKenna thought. They understood each other on that account. "What about Raoul Camarena?" he asked.

"I'll need your promise first."

"You got it. Nothing said to anyone except Brunette and my partner, who I trust, just like you're trusting me. But nothing in my reports and nothing in my testimony, if there's ever any testifying to be done. Let's have it."

McKenna's qualified assurance was good enough for Shields. "The person you know as Raoul Camarena is a Cuban spy. His real name is Colonel Esteban Cabrera of Cuban intelligence. We've had him under surveillance for most of the time he's been in this country and we've been able to do a lot of good things with him."

"Does he know that you're on to him?"

"We suspect he does now, since Weatherby had his house searched. Turns out that was a big mistake."

"What about Rosa Figueroa?"

"She's a deep-cover FBI agent."

"Not just an informant?"

"Nope. She's an agent. Has been since 1985."

Shields paused while McKenna digested his revelation. McKenna had liked Rosa Figueroa from the moment he'd first laid eyes on her. Now he respected and admired her. She was performing the most dangerous of assignments, living with the enemy as a deep-cover agent. "How'd you get Rosa into this operation?" he asked Shields.

"By accident. It's a long story. You'll have to hear the whole thing to understand why Weatherby acted the way he did. You got time?"

"That's what I'm here for."

"We got onto Cabrera by accident, the way it usually works. He arrived here in 1978 in a boat from Mariel, Cuba. He was led in handcuffs by the Cuban police to the boat. It was already full of refugees heading for the United States. The police beat him on the dock in front of the other refugees and then put him on the boat. The boat was then cleared for exit and left for Miami. Raoul told the other refugees on the boat that he had been a prisoner in the Isle of Pines prison since 1977. He said he was a fisherman from Pinar del Rio province who had been convicted of smuggling electric appliances into Cuba from Panama and he was surprised when the police took him from prison and placed him on the boat. The boat was towed to Miami two days later by the Coast Guard, out of fuel and out of food and water. All the refugees were placed in a camp outside Miami where they were interviewed and processed by the Immigration and Naturalization Service. The INS agents were immediately suspicious of Raoul Camarena."

"Why?"

"He had no documentation of any kind. The INS agents knew the Cuban government would try to plant intelligence agents among the legitimate refugees. The other twenty refugees who arrived on Raoul's boat were all connected to each other in one way or another, and INS was able to check them out fairly quick. They were processed and given political asylum."

"But not Raoul?"

"No. He was sent to a detention center in Arkansas for further investigation. He told INS he had a brother named Juan Camarena who came here a month before he did. They investigated and found that in July of 1978 a Juan Camarena had arrived here aboard another refugee boat. He had already been cleared and processed and was working as a deckhand on a fishing boat in Miami. Juan Camarena was interviewed by the INS and he identified Raoul Camarena as his brother."

"That's the same brother who Raoul was staying with in Miami?" McKenna asked.

"Right. He's a spy, too. So INS cleared Raoul Camarena for entry. Then they got a break. They were holding an identified Cuban intelligence agent at Raoul's camp in Arkansas. This agent had been infiltrated into the United States in a refugee boat that arrived in Miami in July. The INS got onto him and he confessed. They turned him over to us and we made a deal with him. In return for his complete cooperation, he could stay here under a new identity. So he identified Raoul Camarena as Major Esteban Cabrera of Cuban intelligence. He said he had served in Cabrera's unit in the Cuban army in Angola and that Cabrera was wounded in the chest and legs during a UNITA guerrilla ambush in Angola in 1976. We checked Camarena's medical file and found he had the scars on his chest and legs."

"So why didn't you just try to turn Cabrera?"

"It was too good an opportunity to pass up. The show the Cubans put on when they put him on the boat made us think he was a big shot. We had him before he had actually carried out any intelligence missions here. We looked at it as an opportunity to learn more about their operations in this country. We watched him for ten years with everything we had—electronic surveillance and wiretaps on him and Juan Camarena."

"What did you get?"

"Plenty. Cabrera went to work on a Miami sport-fishing boat, just like his supposed brother. They both joined anti-Castro organizations and began reporting to Havana on whatever these organizations were doing. We listened in and found out more about the anit-Castro movement than we ever knew. We also found out about lots of other Cuban agents. We got some of them to work for us as double agents, which gave the CIA a big advantage when the Cubans were causing mischief in Central and South America during the late seventies and the early eighties. Incidentally, the Cuban diplomat responsible for your latest run-in with the police administration was recruited by us after he had met with Cabrera."

"That's just another one I owe him," McKenna said.

"Listen. You're going to find out you owe him a lot more. We watched for years as Juan Camarena eventually got his own deep-sea sport-fishing boat. He did a good business, with Cabrera as his first mate. We placed surveillance and locating devices on his boat and watched as he picked up money, weapons, and other intelligence agents from rendezvous at sea and in the Bahamas. We found that the Camarenas and other members of their ring were involved in reporting the movements of the United States Navy Carrier Task Force that operated out of Mayport, Florida. We prepared a great case against them and lots of other Cuban agents. We were ready to prosecute them and expose the extent of Cuban intelligence operations in this country. Then, in 1987, the world political situation changed drastically and the role of the Camarenas also changed."

"What happened in '87?"

"The Cold War ended. We won."

"How'd that affect the situation with the Camarenas?"

"Castro gave them a new mission. The Russians were drying up as a source of revenue and he was running out of money. He was desperate and he needed a new source of income. He used the Camarenas to help him out."

"Drugs?"

"Right."

"Wasn't that kind of dangerous for Castro? If that got out, wouldn't the U.S. have an excuse to go down there and get rid of him, like we did with Noriega?"

"It would seem that way at first. As it turns out, he was in an almost no-risk position. Listen. When the Russian aid dried up, Castro was in a real bind. He needed cash to maintain his army, which he felt was the only thing that was keeping him in power."

"OK. So he's poor," McKenna said. "Why doesn't he just cut the size of his army? He doesn't need a big army if he's not sending them all over the world anymore."

"He can't. True, the Cuban army no longer has much of a purpose. The Cuban people know about the deal we made with the Russians

244

during the 1962 Cuban missile crisis, that we wouldn't invade Cuba. They believe it. After the Bay of Pigs fiasco, they knew there wasn't any danger of the anti-Castro groups coming back. Resentment toward the government was growing. So why maintain the army? they ask. Many party members asked the same question. Wouldn't it be more productive to use the money wasted on the Cuban army to import consumer goods and give the Cuban people a better standard of living? The Russian-aid cutoff caught Castro at the worst possible time. The reforms that Castro initiated weren't enough. But he knew that he had to keep his large army, which includes many combat veterans of overseas campaigns. He can't afford to release these soldiers into the population, which already isn't too crazy about him. He always maintained the loyalty of the army by promising them pensions. But the time for paying these pensions is close. Many of his higher ranking officers and senior NCOs had been in the army since the early sixties. He's got to pay these pensions if he cuts the army, and he had no cash. So . . ."

". . . he started smuggling drugs to the U.S."

"Right. It was the only way he could get the cash to stay in power. At first, he thought he was taking a big risk. But as time went on, because of a unique combination of circumstances, he found he was free to smuggle drugs into the United States with virtual impunity as long as he exercised a few precautions."

"How's that? I'd think if the American people found out, they'd demand an invasion, just like Panama."

"That's what we thought at first. But that's not the way it worked out. He started by using Noriega as an intermediary. He placed the government and island of Cuba at the disposal of the big Colombian drug dealers. The price was high, but the Colombians paid it. Besides supplying Castro with cash and gold, the Colombians also bought his surplus weapons at inflated prices. In return, Castro turned his intelligence operation in the United States into a drug-smuggling network. Cuba's only ninety miles away and it became an ideal base for the smuggling of large amounts of drugs into the United States."

"How'd he do it?"

"By sea. Cuban fishing vessels are immune to Coast Guard inspection as long as they remain more than twelve miles from the coast of the United States. Castro understood that the Coast Guard used the Fisheries Act as a subterfuge to search the vessels of foreign nations for drugs and contraband within two hundred miles of the United States coast. We do it by maintaining that we have the right to protect out fishing industry within these two hundred miles, and we recognize the right of other countries to enact laws to protect their own fishing industries within two hundred miles of their coastlines. But there's a problem. The entire country of Cuba falls within the two hundred miles. If the Coast Guard searched Cuban vessels who were more than twelve miles but less than two hundred miles from the United States coastline, then the Cuban government would enjoy the same rights and would be free to search all United States fishing vessels that were within two hundred miles of the Cuban coast and more than twelve miles from the United States. As a result, any vessel flying the Cuban flag and recognized to be a legitimate Cuban fishing vessel was immune from Coast Guard inspection as long as the twelve-mile limit was respected and as long as any smuggling activity was not blatantly overt and obvious."

"It worked?"

"Sure did. Starting in 1987 the Coast Guard and the CIA saw a big increase in the size of the Cuban fishing fleet fishing just outside the twelve-mile limit. This fishing fleet was equipped with the latest in LORAN and other navigational equipment. By watching the Camarenas and monitoring their conversations with other Cuban agents and diplomats, we immediately knew about Castro's decision to enter the drug-smuggling business. Cuban fishing vessels began dumping bundles of cocaine into the sea near the Florida coast. The Cubans rigged the bundles to float below the surface. We know that a lot of drugs got through, even though the DEA made some large seizures from boats that were picking up the drugs from the drop points. Juan Camarena ran the smuggling operation, and he was careful to use intermediaries. He only used boats owned by Americans to pick up the drugs. He kept the Cuban role insulated."

"You must've had enough on the Camarenas. Why didn't you do something?" McKenna asked.

"The thinking in the bureau at the time was that we should go public—arrest and charge the Camarenas and blow Castro's role wide open. We were overruled."

"By who?"

"The State Department. Through covert diplomatic contacts, they informed Castro twice that we were aware of his activities and warned him to stop. Both times he denied the accusation. Then he charged some high-ranking but out-of-favor Cuban government official with smuggling. The end result was the same in both instances. The accused Cuban was executed after a secret trial. This made the State Department happy. Then Castro just continued his smuggling operation. Only two things slowed him down."

"One had to be the invasion of Panama. What was the other?" McKenna asked.

"The Persian Gulf war. When we invaded Panama and put Noriega in jail, Castro stopped operations and awaited developments. In the

246

wecks after the invasion, members of the Cuban government were indentified by the United States press as having been involved with Noriega in smuggling drugs into the United States. Castro waited, but nothing happened. So he resumed smuggling. Then came the Persian Gulf war. That must've scared him. He saw the high-precision American bombing operations and he must've realized that the same degree of accuracy could be brought against him. The American people were feeling confident, so Castro stopped his drug-smuggling operation and waited for a reaction from the American government. Once again, not a peep. So in April of '91 he resumed."

"Why didn't we do anything?"

"That's the same question I asked. We had all the ammo we needed. But we don't make policy. I think that in April 1991 Castro and the FBI came to the same conclusion—the State Department had no interest in exposing the Cuban drug-smuggling operation."

McKenna leaned forward in his chair and Shields continued. "The State Department realized that if the Cuban drug-smuggling operations in the United States were publicized there'd be a lot of people who'd demand military action against Cuba. Castro had taken a number of precautions to insulate himself personally, and he was always ready to execute a few more Cuban officials if the noise in the United States became too loud. But the State Department and Castro realized that might not be enough to satisfy the American public if persons proven to be Cuban agents were tried and convicted. Military action against Cuba would be the only thing that would satisfy the American public. Of course we'd win. But it wouldn't be like Panama or Iraq. American casualties would be much higher. Castro had people who were prepared to return to the mountains, the place where their revolution got started in the first place. It'd be a guerrilla war against whatever government we put in Havana. And then where would we be?"

"The same place we were in 1958, before Castro."

"Right, and even if we got rid of Castro, would the drug-smuggling from Cuba be stopped?"

"Probably not," McKenna answered. "It didn't stop in Panama after we invaded. New operators sprang up to take the place of the old ones. The same would probably happen in Cuba. Instead of Castro making the money, it'd be run by some other gangsters. But the end result would be the same. Somebody is going to smuggle the drugs here from Cuba."

McKenna looked expectantly at Shields. He had received a lesson in history, geography, current affairs, and diplomacy. But nothing that related to the kidnapping of Rodrigo Oxcalo Guiterrez by *Sendero Luminoso* and nothing that the FBI would have needed to keep from the chief of detectives, except that Castro was involved in smuggling drugs into the United States and the State Department knew about it and wanted nothing done. McKenna didn't think that any of those revelations would have shocked Brunette. Then he remembered the National Security Agency report on *Sendero Luminoso* that Bobby Johnston had given him. It stated that *Sendero Luminoso* had received training and arms from Cuba, and that they were looking to use drugs to finance their revolution. That had to be Camarena's connection to them. McKenna looked at his watch. Nine forty-five. He had to meet Sheeran at ten thirty and he was getting impatient.

"What about Peru?" McKenna said. "That's our concern right now. How does this Cuban thing tie into *Sendero Luminoso?*"

Shields didn't seem to notice McKenna's impatience. He opened one of the files on his desk and studied it. After a few minutes he removed some reports, placed his hands together on his desk in front of him, and stared at McKenna without saying a word.

He's thinking over exactly how much he's gonna tell me, McKenna thought.

Shields began so suddenly that McKenna was startled: "In October of 1986 Raoul Camerena became an American citizen. In December of 1986 Camarena applied for and received a United States passport. In March of 1987 Major Esteban Cabrera, aka Raoul Camarena, disappeared from Miami and from our surveillance. We didn't locate him again until July of 1988, when he moved to Fort Myers Beach and bought his fishing boat, the *Pescador II*. We've learned since then that during the fifteen months we lost track of him, he had spent time in Mexico, Colombia, Peru, Cuba, Miami, and New York."

So that's it, McKenna thought. The FBI lets a Cuban intelligence agent stay in the United States so they can monitor his movements and snare other agents. Everything goes great for them for about ten years and they learn a lot. Then he slips their surveillance for over a year and starts traveling to some very interesting places—all of the places that figure in our kidnapping investigation. Peru and New York. That has to be more than just coincidence.

McKenna didn't say a word. He fixed his gaze on Shields's eyebrows, waiting for the rest. Shields still looked confident as he returned McKenna's gaze, but there was tension in the air and McKenna could sense Shields's discomfort.

"How'd you pick him up after you lost him for all that time?" McKenna asked.

"Luck. The agent you know as Rosa Figueroa was working undercover in a Fort Myers Beach real estate office in July of 1988. She was assigned on a Justice Department investigation into possible discrimination by Fort Myers Beach real estate agents against blacks looking to buy homes in the Fort Myers Beach area. Then Esteban Cabrera walked into the office and Rosa almost fell off her chair. She was based out of the Miami field office and they had been trying to locate Cabrera for more than a year. Cabrera took one look at Rosa, went over to her, and introduced himself as Raoul Camerena. Rosa got up and sold him a house. She's been with him ever since."

McKenna's respect for the FBI and the dedication of its agents increased tremendously. He smiled as he remembered all the disparaging remarks he had made about the FBI to Rosa. She must have had quite a few laughs on me, he thought. Now I understand the surveillance on her. Deep-cover undercover assignments are the most dangerous in law enforcement, and Rosa is quite a girl. "How'd she do it?"

"It's wasn't as hard as you might think. With Rosa, Cabrera's been very careful to remain the character of Raoul Camarena, the hard-working fisherman and law-abiding citizen of the United States. Rosa stayed in her job as a real estate agent while she reported on his activities. Cabrera's crazy about her, but she's managed to keep her distance so far. She wears the pants. . . ."

"She hasn't been sleeping with him during all this time?" McKenna asked incredulously.

"If she has, she didn't report it. Cabrera wanted her to move in with him, but she told him she was a traditional Cuban girl and that a traditional period of engagement was necessary. She maintains her own apartment in Fort Myers Beach. Naturally, Cabrera gave her the keys to his house and told her to make herself at home whenever she wanted to, and she has, whenever he was away. She found all of his hiding places."

McKenna remembered the rugs pulled away from the wall in Camarena's house. "Like under the rugs?" he asked.

"That was one of them. We wired his house for sound and heard him digging the hole for two days. She just went in and found it. There was nothing hidden in the hole at the time. He made a nice cover for the hole and it couldn't be seen once the rug was down. As time went on, Rosa became an expert at using a knee-slammer to stretch the living room rug every time she checked the hole. That's where she found Cabrera's passports."

"Passports?"

"He had two. His legitimate American passport in the name of Raoul Camarena and his Cuban passport in the name of Esteban Cabrera. She checked the entry stamps and found out some of the places he went when we lost him. In March of '87 he went to Mexico on his Camarena passport, and then to Cuba on his Cuban passport. He returned to Mexico in June of '87, then traveled to Peru on his

American passport. In October of '87 he returned to Mexico and then came to New York as Raoul Camarena."

"Where does the drug smuggling come in?"

"I'm getting to that. During the next couple of years Rosa watched and listened as he built up his fishing-boat business. He also got big in the anti-Castro groups on the Gulf Coast of Florida. He managed to recruit the owners of a number of American fishing boats for the Cuban drug-smuggling business, but once they were recruited he passed the control to other agents, mainly Juan Camarena. During this time Rosa was never able to identify the person who gave Cabrera his instructions, but we assumed it was one of the customers on his fishing boat. That was the only aspect of his life that wasn't absolutely monitored, although we had the boat wired and always knew its exact location. It began to look like Cabrera wasn't directly involved on an operational level with the drug-smuggling trade."

McKenna was surprised by the matter-of-fact way Shields made this revelation. Shields continued, "In November '91 Rosa went to the Fort Myers Beach town dock to meet the *Pescador II* when it came back from fishing. Cabrera had only two passengers that day, a man and an attractive blond girl. They were speaking in Spanish and she could tell by their accents that the couple was from South America. They had just one fish to show for the day, a four-foot mako shark. There was no first mate on the boat, and Cabrera told her he had given his mate that day off, since he knew that he would have only two customers and he wanted to save the mate's salary for the day."

"Was it Alfonso and Isabela Mendosa?"

"Yes, but at the time we had no idea who they were. Cabrera saw them off and then took Rosa out to dinner. At the restaurant, while he was paying the check, Cabrera noticed that his license and Social Security card were missing from his wallet. Rosa saw that he was very angry about that and she asked him how he could lose the documents and still have his wallet. He couldn't give any answers. She assumed that Cabrera's passengers that day had somehow taken his license and Social Security card without his knowledge. She reported this to her superiors and they checked their instruments for the locations of the *Pescador II* that day. They found that the boat had spent one hour at a spot eighteen miles off the Gulf Coast and they learned from the Coast Guard that a large Cuban fishing boat had also been operating in that area that day. A physical surveillance was set up on the *Pescador II* by the FBI. That night, after Rosa left Cabrera's house, he returned to his boat and removed two large wooden cases, which he brought home."

"What was in the cases? Drugs?"

"Worse. Rosa didn't get a chance to check Cabrera's house for a couple of days. When she did, she found the cases in the hole under his living room floor. They contained eight TEC-9 automatic pistols, lots of ammo, a box of blasting caps, and four bricks of plastic explosives. She reported her find and her superiors decided to wait. They knew that something was up with Cabrera's two new customers, but they weren't able to put it together then. Near the end of November '91 Rosa showed up at Cabrera's house and found him there with the South American couple. Cabrera said they were interested in investing in his fishing-boat business, but Rosa saw that he was nervous about her meeting them again. They made small talk for a couple of minutes. We got some photos of them when they left Cabrera's house. They got into a rented car, which we later found was rented by Cabrera with one of his credit cards. They drove evasively and the agents who followed them from Cabrera's house decided to discontinue the surveillance rather than risk being discovered. The photographs of the man and woman were circulated everywhere, but nobody could identify them at the time."

"Did she ever see them again?"

"No. But later she identified them as members of *Sendero Luminoso* from our Miami and LA sketches. But we still didn't know their names until you found out who they were."

"What happened to all the stuff under Esteban's rug?"

"The next time Rosa got a chance to check, everything was gone. In April of '92 Cabrera disappeared for four days. Naturally, she searched his house and found that only a few items of clothing were missing. When he returned, he apologized to her and told her that he needed to spend some time alone to think. Then he proposed marriage and told her that he wanted to get away. He said they could move anyplace in the world she liked. In line with her cover story, she accepted and a date was set for June 1993. Cabrera bought Rosa an enormous engagement ring and she noticed that he began to spend a lot of cash on their evenings together. Near the end of April 1992 she found a suitcase in the hole. It had La Guardia Airport airline tags on it and contained more than three hundred thousand dollars. She left the suitcase there and reported."

"So Cabrera's real dirty, making money, and wants out. He wants to take Rosa into the sunset and live happily ever after," McKenna said.

"That's the way we figured it. He wanted out, but he kept getting deeper. On June 27th of 1992 Rosa met the boat at the town dock. This time Cabrera had only one passenger. Once again he had given his first mate the day off. Cabrera told Rosa that he had to talk business with his passenger and Rosa said she understood. She went home, but she notified her superiors that Cabrera might be having some company that night. A surveillance van was sent to Cabrera's house to photograph his customer. He didn't get home for another two hours. His customer was still with him and we got some photos. They both went into the house, but they stayed for only three minutes. When they came out the customer was carrying a small suitcase that Rosa identified as one of Cabrera's. Cabrera drove his customer to the airport and returned home. The photos were sent to Washington and he was identified as Roberto Aguilar, a Colombian who's wanted by the government of Colombia as a drug financier. He's also wanted by the United States government and the State of New York for large-scale importation and distribution of cocaine. We checked the Fort Myers airport and found that Aguilar had boarded a plane for New York. The only information that we got from the taped conversation in the house between Cabrera and Aguilar was that Cabrera was loaning Aguilar some money. We assumed that his money was in the suitcase."

"Why don't you just take Esteban for espionage and drug smuggling?"

"We got him for espionage, but not good enough on the drug smuggling. It doesn't accomplish anything. Every time we arrest a Cuban spy here, Castro manages to arrest one of ours in Cuba. They're usually quietly exchanged after they spend a couple of years in prison, but out spies get the worst of the deal. We send the Cuban spies we capture to Leavenworth, but ours go to the Isle of Pines, which makes Leavenworth look like the Waldorf-Astoria."

"How come you didn't link *Sendero Luminoso* to Esteban sooner? You've been investigating the *Sendero Luminoso* killings since April."

"Weatherby."

"What's he got to do with it? He's not in charge in Florida."

McKenna could see from the change in Shields's demeanor that he had hit pay dirt. Shields rifled through the file in front of him for a few seconds. McKenna thought that he had caused Shields some consternation with his question. He was wrong. Shields had begun to smile, and after a second the smile filled his whole face.

"Weatherby's been involved with the Cabrera investigation in one way or another for years. He used to be a supervisor in the Miami office, which ran the investigation. Then in '86 he was assigned as my second-in-command here in New York. He still managed to stay involved with the case because he was in charge of counterespionage operations here. As one of his duties, he was charged with controlling the Cuban cultural attaché who we exposed as a Cuban spy after he met with Cabrera in 1982. This Cuban diplomat was Cabrera's supervisor in the United States and he told Weatherby everything he knew. Turns out that from 1982 to 1987 Major Esteban Cabrera of

Cuban Intelligence unknowingly reported directly to John Weatherby of FBI counterespionage. But Weatherby and the Cuban diplomat were both surprised when Cabrera disappeared and apparently returned to Cuba on his own. Esteban Cabrera was operating under a different set of orders when he returned from Cuba, and the emphasis of his mission changed from espionage to smuggling. The problem was that Cabrera had been promoted to colonel in the Cuban Army, outranked Weatherby's diplomat at the United Nations, and no longer reported to him."

"Weatherby still should have put it together."

"Right. We suspected that Cabrera had been placed in charge of the Cuban drug-smuggling operation into South Florida. Weatherby kept the operation under his control as a counterespionage operation. That was his mistake. He should have left it with the Miami office. But he sensed an intelligence coup. We had a deep-cover agent close to Cabrera and Weatherby wanted to make sure he was around to receive the credit. He kept the whole thing to himself. He knew that Cabrera had been in possession of the eight TEC-9 automatic pistols, but Weatherby was in New York. He didn't know that *Sendero Luminoso* had used TEC-9s to kill the people in Miami and LA until an internal memo was circulated to all field offices in April of this year. Then Weatherby knew he fucked up. If the Cabrera investigation had been left with the Miami field office, the connection between Cabrera and *Sendero Luminoso* would have been made much sooner."

McKenna was surprised when Shields began to laugh. "Lost my second-in-command over that one. The director sent him to Brooklyn after he found out about Weatherby's role in the affair. What a shame!"

McKenna was beginning to like this Gene Shields more and more. Anybody who was willing to do the right thing and hated John Weatherby besides had at least two redeeming qualities, as far as McKenna was concerned.

Shields was still laughing as he continued. "On July 9th as soon as Weatherby heard about your shoot-out in Brooklyn, the TEC-9, and the finger taped to Carlos Mendosa's back, he knew it was *Sendero Luminoso*. He thought that luck had sent him the way to get back in good graces. And then he stopped thinking altogether. He found out that Mendosa had the missing Raoul Camarena license and he figured that Cabrera might try to skip once he found out about the death of Carlos Mendosa. And he knew that Esteban Cabrera was in Miami with his supposed brother, Juan Camarena. So Weatherby had Cabrera's house in Fort Myers Beach searched. He figured that he would get something on Cabrera to implicate him in the kidnapping of Rodrigo, or at least find out something that would lead him to *Sendero Luminoso* in Brooklyn. He took a big chance and lost. They found nothing. It was all gone, except for the passports, which we could have gotten anytime. He probably ended Cabrera's usefulness to the FBI. Since the search, Cabrera feels that he's under surveillance. I don't think he's gonna be much use to us in finding Rodrigo."

"So why don't you lock him up?"

"We will. But first we'll wait to see how you do. You're the one who showed us who the players were when that Amnesty International doctor identified Carlos for you. We knew from Rosa they had been with Cabrera in November. But we had no names for them."

So they don't want to arrest Esteban right now, McKenna thought. I can see why. They can't afford to. The FBI will get quite a black eye if the newspapers get onto this story before the *Sendero Luminoso* affair is over. Too much would come out during any trial of Cabrera. The public would find out the FBI and the State Department knew of the Cuban government's involvement in smuggling drugs into the United States—and that nothing was done to stop it.

And now it was even worse for the FBI. *Sendero Luminoso,* a terrorist organization committing acts of terrorism in the United States, was dealing with Esteban Cabrera, a Cuban agent, a person under FBI surveillance, right under its nose. The FBI now knew that he supplied *Sendero Luminoso* with guns used in at least two terrorist homicides. They also knew that he probably supplied them with explosives, which they hadn't used yet. But the FBI didn't find out what Cabrera was up to until it was too late.

That's the trouble with being in on the ground floor, McKenna thought. The FBI was there when the foundation of this case was laid, but had no way of knowing how tall the building was gonna be. The problem for the FBI is that Esteban would be implicated if any case was made against any *Sendero Luminoso* members arrested as a result of our kidnapping investigation in New York. The agency would have to come clean on their involvement with Cabrera or risk accusations of a cover-up as big as the Iran-Contra affair. A major government scandal was brewing here, and the blame wouldn't be placed entirely with the FBI. No, McKenna thought, the major part of the blame for permitting Castro to smuggle drugs into the United States and, perhaps incidentally, permitting *Sendero Luminoso* to commit murder and who knows what else, belongs to the State Department, which, in theory, is an instrument of the president. The White House was going to hear about this one, if they didn't know already.

But why is Shields telling me so much? McKenna became aware that he was staring into Shields's eyes as he was pushing these questions through his mind, and that Shields was frankly returning his gaze. Answers came to McKenna and he suddenly became uncomfortable under Shields's stare.

He's telling me, McKenna thought, because he's got my promise that I won't reveal this information to anyone else, even in testimony. And he believes my promise is good. He can also feel safe telling me because he knows that I'm gonna get even deeper in this mess. I'm gonna clear up some of the FBI's loose ends by helping to kill everyone in *Sendero Luminoso* that comes into range. There'll be no trial for the kidnapping of Rodrigo Guiterrez. Nothing will be made public. Then Cabrera's involvement with *Sendero Luminoso* will never come up, and the FBI will be in the clear. They'll just deal with Weatherby on their own.

Of course, I'm not doing it for Shields, the FBI, or the United States government. I'm doing it for myself, because if I don't kill them, they'll eventually kill me. I'm the best partner Shields could have. I'm operating on my own behalf in his interests. He'll just give me information that he knows we'll need to finish the job, if we can. Then he can forget about me. So he might as well give me everything he knows. "What exactly is Cabrera using his boat for?"

"We have a theory that he's picking up people from Cuban fishing boats and smuggling them into the United States. According to this theory, *Sendero Luminoso* agents and people like Roberto Aguilar leave Cuba in Cuban fishing boats. Off the coast of Florida, they get into scuba gear and jump off the fishing boats at a specified location. An hour later Cabrera picks them up on the *Pescador II* and brings them into Fort Myers Beach. He always has lots of scuba gear on his boat. But it's still only a theory."

"What's the connection here between the drugs and *Sendero Luminoso?*"

"All the information we have at this point suggests that Cuba started to export Peruvian cocaine to the United States through a network set up by Cabrera. Our intelligence analysts speculate that the Cubans probably received some of this cocaine from *Sendero Luminoso* as payment for Cuban weapons and training. They think that Cuba is also smuggling the rest of the Peruvian cocaine supplied by *Sendero Luminoso* on a commission basis."

"Won't that make the Colombians mad?"

"Our analysts note that the old partners the Cubans had when they first became involved in smuggling drugs into this country are vanishing from the scene. Noriega is gone, the *Sandinistas* are out of power in Nicaragua, and the Colombian drug lords are being weakened by deals they're forced to make with the Colombian government to avoid extradition to the United States. The *Sendero Luminoso*

255

supply of cocaine came along at exactly the right time for Castro."

"How are they handling the distribution?"

"That was one thing about the whole operation that we didn't understand. We thought that *Sendero Luminoso* would have a problem distributing their cocaine once they got it into the United States. They had no contacts here and the DEA expected a major drug war as soon as they moved into established territories to set up their own distribution networks. None of this happened. We now assume that the lack of friction can be attributed to an agreement worked out by Cabrera and Roberto Aguilar."

"You got anything on the forged licenses?" McKenna asked.

"Yesterday when we found that Isabela Mendosa used the name of Miriam Salazar in Cambridge with a Florida driver's license for identification, we found and interviewed the real Miriam Salazar in Fort Myers. Her pocketbook, containing her driver's license, was taken at gunpoint in a Fort Myers parking lot in November of 1991. Our agents showed her a picture of Alfonso Mendosa and she said he might be the man who robbed her pocketbook. That makes three stolen licenses that *Sendero Luminoso* used to make forgeries for themselves—Tricia Flint, Miriam Salazar, and Raoul Camarena. All three were stolen in the Fort Myers area in November of 1991. We have no idea why they decided to steal the Raoul Camarena license, especially if Cabrera was the one who brought them into the United States. They must have been very nervous and anxious to obtain good identification papers in a hurry. We still don't know who used the stolen licenses to make the forgeries for them."

"You said you showed the real Miriam Salazar a picture of Alfonso Mendosa? Where'd you get a picture of him?"

"We've got lots more of them now. You'll understand in a few minutes."

"How about the Guiterrez family in Peru?"

"Hernan Guiterrez refused to speak to our agent, but the State Department is talking to members of the Peruvian government who are friends of the Guiterrez family. I'm optimistic that we'll eventually persuade Hernan Guiterrez to cooperate with us."

McKenna looked at his watch again. It was ten fifteen.

Shields could see that McKenna was in a hurry. He said, "Before you go, I have this for you." Shields reached into his top desk drawer and took out a large manila envelope. He handed the envelope to McKenna and said, "Everything in the file is very sensitive, so please be careful about who sees it. There are a number of copies of photographs, which you can keep and give to whomever you think should see them."

McKenna opened the manila envelope and took out a thick report and about fifty eight-by-ten photos. He opened the report to the first page. It was a Central Intelligence Agency report on Alfonso Mendosa, Carlos Mendosa, and Isabela Mendosa, dated July 11, 1992. He rifled through the batch of photos and instantly recognized the subject of one set of photos—Carlos Mendosa. The other two sets were of Alfonso Mendosa and Isabela Mendosa. McKenna wanted to go through the report, but he didn't have time. He put the report back in the envelope, shook Shields's hand and said, "I'm sure I can use this. Thanks."

Shields called to his secretary outside on his intercom and she came in to escort McKenna out of the FBI offices.

McKenna could see why Ray liked and trusted Gene Shields. Ray's a good judge of character, McKenna thought as he rode the elevator down.

July 12 10:30 a.m.

Once again, McKenna arrived right on time. The short walk across Federal Plaza to the Manhattan Men's House of Detention took under two minutes. The Men's House of Detention—commonly known as the Tombs—the Manhattan Criminal Court, and the New York County District Attorney's Office are all located at different entrances of the same building, 100 Centre Street.

The only one there was Pacella. McKenna wasn't surprised. He knew that 10:30 meant 10:30 for the troops, but that 10:30 meant 11:00 for the Bosses and politicians. As always, McKenna was happy to see Pacella. It seemed a long time since he had last worked with him, although it had only been the day before yesterday. They had both put on a lot of miles since then.

Pacella sat on the hood of his car, a new red Cadillac Sedan de Ville, drinking from a container of coffee. He had a container for McKenna too.

"Glad to see you, kid. I heard about your troubles this morning. How many times have I told you that running's no good for you?"

"I think that I'll listen to you from now on, Tommy. Where'd we get the car?"

"Joe Sophia gave it to me this morning. It's been assigned to the Major Case Squad for this investigation. It seems that Tavlin insisted that the best car should belong to the top gun."

Pacella gave McKenna the keys, and McKenna slid the CIA report on the Mendosas under the front seat. Then, while they drank their coffee and waited for the Bosses to arrive, McKenna talked about his meeting with Gene Shields.

Pacella was unimpressed. He lived in a simple, black-and-white world. Nothing was ever complex to Pacella: there were only good guys, bad guys, and victims. The motivations, politics, and backgrounds of the bad guys as they preyed upon their victims weren't important to Pacella. They were still just bad guys to him.

As a New York City detective, Pacella considered himself by definition to be one of the good guys. The job of the good guys was to find the bad guys and get them, any way they could.

At 10:45 Captain Sheeran arrived, driven by Richie White. Richie double-parked and waited in the car when Sheeran got out. The captain wore a fresh suit, but looked like he needed some sleep. He greeted McKenna and Pacella cordially. He told them that Flavio was at church again, but that they would be listening in when he got his instructions at 4:30 that afternoon. Sheeran said, "Inspector Tavlin will be ready in the Two-five. He's got enough people to follow whoever answers the phone when Flavio calls."

Captain Flynn came next, walking from the direction of police headquarters. Flynn looked well dressed and well rested. He acknowledged Pacella and McKenna's existence with a nod, but was effusive in his greeting to Sheeran.

"Dennis, you got all the court orders you need to keep everything legal?"

"Yeah, I got what I need," answered Sheeran, "but you better be ready. If things work out this afternoon, Tavlin's gonna need some eavesdropping warrants and search warrants in a hurry."

"I'll be ready for that. I'm gonna be at the Two-five myself at four thirty to draw up the applications. I've got a judge standing by to sign the warrants."

Bruce Mulvey, the Kings County district attorney, and Murray Don't Worry arrived together in Mulvey's official car. McKenna figured that they needed the ten minutes it took to travel from Brooklyn Court to Manhattan Court to iron out any little discrepancies in the deal they had between them. They didn't look like pals when they got out of the car.

Bruce Mulvey possessed a reputation for efficiency. He had prosecuted a number of big, newsworthy cases during his career, always winning a conviction and substantial jail time for the guilty. He was a big, good-looking, affable guy, obviously destined for bigger positions.

Nevertheless, cops hated him. As a politician, he would shake the hand of a bum in the street if he thought there was a 5 percent chance that the bum would vote on election day. But Bruce Mulvey displayed a basic lack of courtesy in his dealings with cops. He treated them like furniture. One well-known story among the cops in Brooklyn had happened a couple of years before Mulvey was elected as the district attorney. He'd been working as an ADA in Brooklyn, prosecuting a particularly violent group of drug dealers. There were some oblique threats tossed in Mulvey's direction and he had requested police protection for himself and his family for the duration of the trial.

Two uniformed cops from the Brooklyn precinct had been assigned to guard his house every night. One cop was stationed at the front of the house and that officer could sit in his police car while he watched the house. The other cop had to stand in Mulvey's backyard all night. It was winter and bitterly cold. The Brooklyn cops reported that not once during the month that the trial lasted did Mulvey or any member of his family ever so much as offer the cop standing in their backyard a cup of coffee or invite him in to warm up for a few minutes. It was a tough job and Bruce Mulvey hadn't tried to make it any easier.

Murray Plenhiem was another story. He was a large, extremely intelligent man who had won a reputation for himself by keeping his clients, most of whom were successful drug dealers, out of jail. Murray looked his part, the master of the deal. The fees he charged his clients reflected his track record, and criminals frequently boasted to cops about their lawyer when they were doing well enough in their life of crime to be able to afford him. Murray Don't Worry was expensive, and proud of it.

Mulvey already knew both Sheeran and Flynn, and Sheeran introduced Murray to everyone present. Murray greeted everyone warmly, especially McKenna. They had been adversaries once before when McKenna had arrested two of his clients for possession of loaded guns, and McKenna was rather proud of the fact that Murray was unable to convince the jury that McKenna had stretched the truth when he'd testified about the conditions under which he'd found the guns on his clients. Both had been convicted and both had gotten time. Murray was noble in defeat.

With Mulvey leading the way, everyone went into the Men's House of Detention. They were met in the lobby by the assistant warden from the Department of Correction, who brought them to a conference room on the third floor. It was a spacious, oak-paneled room with a large, polished oak table in the center and chairs for twelve people. The walls were lined with the official photographs of former New York City correction commissioners.

Mulvey took a seat at the head of the table. Sheeran and Flynn picked one side of the table and McKenna and Pacella sat on the other. Murray placed his briefcase on the far end, facing Mulvey. Murray had taken the position that McKenna expected; he knew that Murray wouldn't want anyone reading over his shoulder as he outlined the information that his clients were prepared to divulge as part of the deal.

Murray removed a large file from his briefcase, opened it, and began his presentation. "The district attorney and I have worked out the final details of the agreement on the sentences my clients will receive if Captain Sheeran determines that the information they possess and are willing to talk about is vital to the police department's present kidnapping investigation. We've agreed that my clients will tell everything they know in any prosecution under a grant of immunity. I'm prepared to give an overview, without specifics, of the information they possess. Then I'll await the decision of Captain Sheeran. He'll tell me whether or not it's enough. If he says it is, we've got a deal." Murray turned to Mulvey and said, "Am I right?"

"That's the deal. Go on."

Murray appeared satisfied and continued. "My clients are middle-level drug dealers. They buy drugs in multi-kilo weights from one major drug supplier and sell the drugs, uncut and in weights up to one kilo, to large-volume street-level dealers. They sell only to drug dealers that they know. Both Torres and Chavez felt that the threat of arrest was minimal in the type of operation they were running, and they attribute their present predicament to bad luck. They were set up in business in February by the brother of the man the police killed outside their door three days ago. He was known to them as Rico and they knew his brother as Ali. In February Ali gave them twenty kilos of cocaine on consignment. He told them they'd have one month to sell the cocaine and pay him three hundred thousand dollars, which was an extremely cheap bulk price for twenty kilos of uncut cocaine. It was the kind of high-profit, low-risk deal they couldn't resist. Since February they've been selling thirty kilos per month for Ali. During this time my clients witnessed two murders committed by Ali and Rico. They met with Ali on two occasions at a location in Spanish Harlem and they can identify three of his business associates, and they have a telephone number where they previously contacted Ali."

McKenna's mind raced. There was a lot about this deal with Torres and Chavez that no longer made sense to him.

The fact that Carlos and Ali Mendosa had committed two additional murders and that Chavez and Torres claimed to have witnessed these murders did not surprise McKenna. They were all in the high-volume, extremely competitive and territorial drug business, where people get killed all the time. If Chavez and Torres were present for two

261

murders, then the murders must have been drug-related. So who cares? Two more public service homicides.

McKenna couldn't see the importance of how many rival drug dealers *Sendero Luminoso* killed during the normal course of business. It wasn't vital to his present mission, which was to find them. McKenna knew that no members of the group were going to be arrested and charged with the kidnapping of Rodrigo Guitterez and the murder of Oscar Barbero. So why give Chavez and Torres, two low-life murdering drug dealers themselves, any kind of a break for information that wasn't going to be used?

The quantity of drugs that *Sendero Luminoso* supplied to the New York market also wasn't important. McKenna believed in the laws of supply and demand; if *Sendero Luminoso* didn't supply the drugs, someone else would, as long as the demand was there. It made no difference to McKenna how much coke they wholesaled in the last six months when his plans called for all members of the gang to be dead this month.

The fact that Torres and Chavez could identify three of Ali's business associates didn't matter either. It might be important to the Drug Enforcement Agency and the FBI, but not to him. McKenna wanted to get on with his life after this was over, not spend the next couple of years chasing down all the people that *Sendero Luminoso* made money with in the United States. Find them, kill them, and free Rodrigo was the optimal order of events that McKenna envisioned to end this case. Then take some time to sort out his problems and do whatever he had to do in order to spend the rest of his life with Angelita.

However, two pieces of information did interest McKenna, but he needed more specifics before he could evaluate their importance. One was the location in Spanish Harlem where Torres and Chavez said that they had met Ali, and the other was the telephone number that they said they used to contact Ali.

McKenna felt sure that Ali met Torres and Chavez in public places where he would not run into anybody he knew. The location of the meeting would probably be useless, he thought. The telephone number was something else. McKenna doubted if it was Ali's personal telephone number. *Sendero Luminoso* had already shown that they were too careful for anything like that. It would be another pay phone or a telephone number that couldn't possibly be traced to Ali's location. But, the telephone number might lead to at least one more person who knew Ali.

McKenna didn't know if he would accept Murray's deal, and he was glad that he wasn't the one responsible for making the decision.

Murray stared intently at Sheeran, waiting for him to make up his mind. Sheeran had been watching a spot on the wall directly above McKenna's head but he let his eyes drop to meet McKenna's. McKenna could see that Sheeran was having a hard time making up his mind about the deal.

Finally Mulvey said impatiently, "I haven't got all day, Captain. If there's any doubt in your mind whether the information that those two can give you is going to help you in your investigation, then let's forget the deal. They should both spend the rest of their lives in jail anyway."

That little jolt from the district attorney would have made up my mind, McKenna thought. But not Sheeran. He couldn't be pushed and he was still thinking. The silence in the room was becoming uncomfortable. Sheeran didn't seem to notice.

Finally Sheeran turned to Murray and said, "Is the place where your clients met with Ali a public place or an apartment?"

"It was a public place in Spanish Harlem."

"Is the telephone number your clients used to contact Ali a pay phone or a mobile phone?" Sheeran asked next.

"The information I get from them is that Ali carried a mobile phone with him, and they believe that the contact number was for the mobile phone."

Not good enough to cut these guys' sentences by years and years, McKenna thought.

It wasn't good enough for Sheeran, either. "Mr. Mulvey and Mr. Plenhiem, I'm sorry for wasting your time today. I know that you're both busy people with crowded schedules. But I need another day before I can make a decision about this deal. I'm not sure today that the information that Chavez and Torres can give us is worth the sentence arrangement that's been worked out in exchange. I need another day to think it over. I hope you'll be able to forgive my indecision."

Sheeran looked very humble. His stock kept rising in McKenna's estimation. He couldn't be pressured and he was always thinking. Why should Sheeran allow himself to be pressured into making a decision today? McKenna thought. It made more sense to see what happened at 4:30 when Flavio called his contact. There was a good chance, if everything went according to plan, that we wouldn't need the drug dealers' information to find *Sendero Luminoso*. The delay would also give Sheeran time to learn if anyone else in any other agency wanted the information that Murray's clients could provide. Sheeran merely had to make sure that he didn't burn any bridges with Mulvey and Murray.

Sheeran didn't. Mulvey was looking at Sheeran with undisguised contempt. He said, "I wish Brunette would have sent somebody here today who was capable of making a decision."

Sheeran took it on the chin. "I'm sorry, sir. It's a big decision and I need more time. Tomorrow I'll call you and we can probably do this whole thing over the phone, which will save you some of your valuable time."

Mulvey backed off at Sheeran's show of humility. McKenna knew then that Brunette hadn't bothered to inform the Brooklyn district attorney of the progress made in the investigation so far, since Mulvey didn't know that some substantial developments in the investigation were expected during the course of the day. Otherwise, Mulvey would have seen the wisdom of Sheeran's delay.

Murray took Sheeran's request in stride. He knew that he had negotiated a great deal for his clients, and the deal would keep another day. He said politely, "Do whatever you think is best, Captain. Just give me a call tomorrow with your decision, and I'll get it to my clients as soon as I can. I don't think one more day will make too much difference to them."

Pacella was the first to get up. He gave McKenna a look that said, *Let's get out of here.* McKenna nodded and they both headed for the door. It was the end of a very uncomfortable meeting, and everyone was glad it was over. Sheeran almost beat him to the door.

When they all got outside, Mulvey jumped right into his car. His driver took off immediately, leaving Murray Don't Worry to find his own way back to Brooklyn. Don't Worry didn't seem to mind; thirty seconds later he was in a taxi. Flynn congratulated Sheeran and told him that he thought the delay was a good idea. Then Flynn astounded everybody by offering to buy Sheeran lunch.

Flynn-skint is in danger of losing his reputation, McKenna thought. Sheeran thanked him but declined, saying that he wanted to get back to the Intercontinental Hotel as soon as possible. Flynn looked relieved as he turned to walk back to his office.

Richie White was in the car at the curb and Sheeran yelled over to him, "Where's Flavio now?"

"He's back from church," Richie yelled back. "He's in his room watching TV."

"Thank God," Sheeran said. "What are you guys gonna be doing tonight?" he asked Pacella and McKenna.

"Something in the Two-five, I guess," McKenna answered. "It depends on how you do, Captain."

McKenna wished him luck as Sheeran got into his car. Richie White took off, leaving McKenna and Pacella standing on the sidewalk.

McKenna turned. "Your humble servant wishes to buy you lunch at Mumbles. Would that be all right with you, Mr. Pacella?"

"Excellent idea! However, if memory serves me correctly, it's my turn to buy you lunch, Mr. McKenna. Mumbles will be fine. The New York City Police Department has even been gracious enough to provide us with this very fine car. Please allow me to drive you to our restaurant, Mr. McKenna."

How could I ever leave this job, McKenna thought.

23

The afternoon was heating up and the Sunday shopping traffic increased as Pacella drove uptown toward Mumbles at Second Avenue and East 33rd Street.

"Where do you think the police department got this car from?" McKenna asked.

"Some poor dope the Narcotics Division caught buying drugs."

"How do you know they didn't seize it from some drug dealer?"

"That's easy. Listen to the radio."

McKenna turned it on and pushed some of the station-selection buttons. Pacella was right. The previous owner of the car had set the radio to the country western, golden oldie, and light rock stations. Whoever he was, he certainly wasn't a New York drug dealer. He had probably bought some drugs, gone to jail, and lost his car besides. Too bad for him, but good for us, McKenna thought.

McKenna reached under the seat and pulled out the CIA report on the Mendosas. He began reading while Pacella negotiated the downtown traffic.

The report was addressed to the director of the Federal Bureau of Investigation from the assistant director of the Central Intelligence Agency. A cover letter stated that the report was in response to a request from the special-agent-in-charge of the New York office of the FBI for any information in the files of the Central Intelligence Agency on three individuals known as Carlos Mendosa, Alfonso Mendosa, and Isabela Mendosa. Because of the recent incorporation of the operational records of the now defunct East German State Security Service (STASI) into the CIA computer banks, the letter said, there was now a fair amount of information available on the three individuals, though much of this information had not been verified.

The intelligence services of Argentina, Chile, Peru, Germany, and Israel had also been consulted in the preparation of the report, but the specific contributions of each agency were not delineated.

McKenna turned the page and continued. He found that the report was candidly written and as he read he was unable to discern any particular political viewpoint. Almost everything he might want to know about Carlos, Alfonso, and Isabela Mendosa was there. The report covered their families, their educations, and their involvement in the *Montonero* movement in Argentina. As McKenna read, it became obvious that much of the information was from the files of the East German State Security Service, which had built up quite a dossier on the Mendosas while they lived in East Germany and Syria. The East Germans were very thorough, and McKenna was glad that the STASI records had been appropriated by the West German intelligence service after the reunification of Germany. Otherwise, he thought, he would be reading a very short and speculative report.

The last part came from the Peruvian military intelligence service and covered the suspected activities of the Mendosas in Peru and their involvement with *Sendero Luminoso*. The Mendosas had been very busy in Peru.

At the end there were a number of photographs of the Mendosas, apparently from the STASI files. Some of the photographs were surveillance-type, which led McKenna to conclude that the East Germans didn't entirely trust the Mendosas. McKenna looked at the first, apparently East German Immigration photos, all dated March 21, 1982.

McKenna saw that Carlos Mendosa hadn't changed much in the last ten years. He looked nearly the same standing somewhere in East Germany in 1982 as he did lying and dying in a project hallway in Brooklyn in 1992.

The next photo was of Alfonso Mendosa. He was definitely the man who had driven the getaway van that morning. McKenna saw nothing extraordinary in Alfonso's appearance, certainly nothing that suggested he was an international terrorist.

Isabela Mendosa glared arrogantly at the camera. With her blond hair and blue eyes, she looked like she belonged in Germany. She had the face of a teenager and McKenna tried to imagine how she would appear after ten years.

The rest of the photos were surveillance shots that showed the Mendosas walking into an apartment building, getting out of a car, and walking down a street.

By the time McKenna had the faces committed to memory, Pacella had reached Mumbles. McKenna got out of the car across the street from the restaurant and called the office from a pay phone.

Joe Sophia answered and told McKenna that the inspector wanted to talk to him. Tavlin came on the line and informed McKenna that the chief wanted to talk to him. He gave McKenna the number of Brunette's mobile phone and hung up.

McKenna then called Brunette. "How'd it go with the DA?" Brunette asked.

"Sheeran said no for today. They didn't have enough."

"That's all right. What are you doing for lunch?"

"We're in front of Mumbles right now."

"Why don't you wait for me?" Brunette asked. "I'll be there in half an hour."

"Good. I've got something to show you. Shields gave me the whole deal on the Mendosas. They're real badasses."

When McKenna got back into the car he found Pacella going through the photos. Pacella held up one of Isabela and said, "She's beautiful, but she looks like she's got some hard qualities."

"She's as tough as nails and hard as stone," McKenna answered. "She's put a lot of men in early graves in Peru, Argentina, and probably here too. You might as well read the whole thing. Ray's meeting us here for lunch in half an hour."

Pacella didn't mind the delay. He had been one of the select members of the McKenna-Brunette lunch club for ten years. He continued shuffling through the photos of the Mendosas and McKenna read the report again while they waited. This time McKenna took notes.

Brunette arrived right on time at 12:45 and came over to their car. He looked tired. McKenna noticed that everyone around him had been looking more and more that way since this case began.

"Sheeran called me about the meeting," Brunette said. "I agree with you. We've got nothing to lose by waiting another day to see how things go in the Two-five tonight. Let's go in and eat."

They went into Mumbles, took a table in the rear, and ordered burgers around. After the waitress arrived with their food, McKenna asked Brunette, "Want a rundown on the report Shields gave me while we eat? It's loaded with information and some pretty good pictures too."

"Let's have it. I'll read the whole thing later."

McKenna put his notes next to his plate and began. "First is Isabela. Born in 1957 in Osorno, Chile. Maiden name was Blier, daughter of German immigrants who settled in the German-speaking region of Chile after the First World War. Her father was a professor of linguistics. He taught at universities in Florida, California, and New York during the sixties and Isabela went to school in the United States. He published a number of books on languages, and money wasn't a problem for the family. In 1972, when Isabela was fourteen years old, her family returned to Chile. Her father took a post in the Allende government. He was a friend of Salvador Allende, and after his government was thrown out by the military in 1973, Isabela's father was sent to jail for a couple of years. While he was in prison, Isabela went to school in Switzerland. She was expelled when she was sixteen for 'inappropriate behavior,' whatever that means. When they let her father out of jail the family moved to Argentina and Isabela joined them there."

"So she's born with a silver spoon in her mouth and she's not crazy about the military? Learns some languages, develops an attitude, and gets thrown out of school. Go on," Brunette said.

"In 1976 she started at the University of Rosario in Argentina. There's lots of antigovernment agitation going on and the school's got a long tradition of opposition to government policies. Che Guevara got his start there. In her first year there Isabela went to some demonstrations against the military government of Argentina and they threatened to deport her to Chile. She cooled down, but then she met Alfonso Mendosa. He was a history professor, really antigovernment, one of the ringleaders of the student movement."

"So she knows him since '76. That's fifteen years," said Brunette.

"She's been with him since. Alfonso Mendosa was born in Rosario, Argentina, in 1946, first son of a rich doctor. Alfonso and his younger brother, Carlos, had it made. Alfonso was the athlete and Carlos was the student. Both went to college in Texas. Alfonso majored in history and economics. Carlos took pre-med. Alfonso returned to Argentina in 1969 and took a commission in the Argentine army. Carlos stayed in the United States and went to medical school in New York. Alfonso served in the army till 1975 and he did good. They even sent him to the Guerrilla Warfare School in Panama, which was run by the U.S. Army Special Forces."

"We gave *Sendero Luminoso* the best training we had?" Pacella interrupted.

"This crew got the best training anyone had. When the Argentine military overthrew the civilian government in 1975, Alfonso started to get cranky. By that time he was a captain and started a discussion group of officers who disagreed with the military take-over. Alfonso left the army in 1976 and he returned to Rosario, where he got his teaching job. In 1973 Doctor Carlos returned to Argentina and he opened a free clinic in a poor neighborhood in Rosario. He stayed out of politics; apparently he just wanted to cure the sick and treat the injured. But he got dragged into the shit anyway."

"By his brother, right?" Brunette asked.

"Right. In 1978 the military got Alfonso fired from the university. He joined the *Montoneros.* They were a guerrilla group fighting the government, and it got pretty bloody. Then Isabela Blier left school, married Alfonso, and joined the *Montoneros* too. Within a year Alfonso and Isabela were *Montonero* leaders and they were getting famous. Alfonso knew his stuff and he was beating the army bad. Then he started robbing banks to finance his operations. Isabela became a propaganda officer and a recruiting officer for the *Montoneros.* I don't have one, but she starred in one of their recruiting posters. Must have been pretty hot. It became a must-have item for any Argentine youth aspiring to manhood; it even got circulated internationally."

"Was she in on the military operations?" Brunette asked.

"Yeah, but later. A guy named Colonel Abate was made the *comandante* of the Rosario army barracks. The generals told him to clean out the *Montoneros,* no matter what. Abate knew Alfonso. He'd served with him when Alfonso was in the army. The first thing that Abate did when he got to Rosario was to have Carlos Mendosa arrested for providing medical care to injured guerrillas. The arrest caused a number of antigovernment demonstrations in the poorest sections of Rosario. The charges against Carlos couldn't be proven and were dropped. Carlos denied membership in the *Montoneros,* but he became somewhat of a local hero, since it was well known that the *Montonero* hero 'Ali' was his brother. Many people saw the release of Carlos as a defeat for the military government, so he was kidnapped one day by the secret police when he left his office."

"I remember this," Brunette said. "Alfonso rescues him and kills Abate and everybody else he thought had anything to do with the torturing of his brother, right?"

"Yeah, they got everybody, eventually. It took him a couple of years."

"What's Carlos doing all this time?" Brunette asked.

"Recovering. He was never seen in Argentina again. They got him to Uruguay, where he spent the next four months recovering from his wounds. We know they got him bad, and some parts of Carlos never healed. His two-day stay with the secret police changed him into a dedicated revolutionary. From Uruguay he went to Cuba, where he studied revolutionary ideology, theory, and tactics while he practiced medicine. In 1981 Alfonso and Isabela joined him there. Their war against the military government was a bust and they had decided to get out of Argentina while they could. The Mendosas came to the conclusion that any revolution that had to be financed by robbing banks and kidnapping businessmen wasn't worth starting. It was too

270

easy for the government to portray them as nothing more than common criminals."

"What'd they do in Cuba?" Brunette asked.

"Whatever they wanted. Alfonso and Isabela were welcomed as heroes. The Cubans did everything that they could for them and they tried to take advantage of Alfonso and Isabela's experience. Alfonso taught revolutionary tactics at the staff college of the Cuban army and Isabela wrote political dialogue for Radio Havana. But it didn't take long for the Mendosas to get bored. Everything was too easy. They were well-traveled people, and they discovered that Cuba was really just a small, rather boring island. Alfonso and Isabela needed some action, but there weren't too many places they could go. They were wanted for bank robbery and murder in Argentina. They could say that these were political crimes carried out by a rebel army in an insurrection against an illegal and repressive regime, but most likely they'd be yelling their arguments from a jail cell if they were captured in the Western world. Carlos wasn't wanted, but he stuck with Alfonso and Isabela. In 1982 they showed up in East Germany."

"All the crazies were in East Germany in the eighties," Pacella said.

"But the East Germans used them. They treated the Mendosas good, but the East Germans didn't believe in the idea of retired revolutionaries. They looked at the spread of communist brotherhood in the Third World as a lifelong work for any dedicated revolutionary. They liked what they saw in the Mendosas. They gave them psychological screening tests and found that all three had a sense of history and self-importance, which meant they didn't have any guilty feelings for anything they did to further their cause. The East Germans knew that a substantial lack of conscience could be a useful quality. What disturbed the East Germans was that the Mendosas knew all the communist ideology, but didn't necessarily agree with any of it. They just looked at communism as one of the ways to change the world. The East Germans also found that Alfonso and Isabela were experts in guerrilla operations. They had a few tricks that even the East Germans hadn't heard of. Carlos was willing to learn, and the East Germans thought that a doctor would be a big plus in any guerrilla operation. The Germans thought that it would be worthwhile to fine-tune the Mendosas' guerrilla-warfare skills with the latest tactics and technological innovations, and the Mendosas agreed. They were sent to Syria in 1983."

"If they didn't like Cuba, they had to hate Syria," Brunette said.

"But the Syrians had a lot to teach. Damascus in 1983 was the world center of terrorism. In 1982 Israel invaded Lebanon and gave the Syrian air force a real beating. The Syrians portrayed themselves as the champion of the Arab nation and they had thirty thousand troops in Lebanon. They couldn't beat the Israelis on the ground or in the air, so they used terrorism to get to Israel once they found out their very expensive air force couldn't do the job."

"Terrorism was a real bargain for the Syrians," Brunette said. "It was an instrument of their foreign policy. Their leader, al-Assad, found out that people were paying attention to what he had to say after a few of his terrorist operations. And it cost him almost nothing. He could keep a cell of terrorists in Europe for a year for less than the cost of one Mirage jet fighter. Recruits were no problem, either. They all wanted to be martyrs."

"That's what I get out of the report," McKenna continued. "In Syria the Mendosas learned everything there was to know about explosives, fuses, and booby traps. They became familiar with every military weapon manufactured in the world. They learned new assassination techniques, new communication techniques, new interrogation techniques, and the latest principles of command and control. But they couldn't wait to get out of Syria. Terrorism without revolution wasn't what they were looking for. They also couldn't get themselves excited about the Arab obsession with suicide missions and their emphasis on religion. Stopping everything five times a day to pray wasn't for them. Most important, Syria just wasn't very much fun. It made Cuba seem like Las Vegas. So in 1984 they returned to East Germany and settled in Leipzig."

"Did that make the Germans unhappy?" Brunette asked.

"No. The government gave them apartments and money to live on, but nothing to do. Every once in a while some government official would drop by to see them with a description of a crisis in some part of the world where the Mendosas might be able to help. But they all looked like losing propositions to Alfonso and Isabela, and they were sick of being on the losing side. On one visit an official suggested that the Cuban comrades in Angola could use a little help. The Mendosas looked at that one and decided it was just a case of tribal warfare between two impoverished tribes who had always been fighting each other. The only difference in the Angolan civil war was that each side managed to get some of their big friends involved. Another East German official came by and suggested that the *Sandinistas* could use a little help against the contras. The Mendosas didn't like that one either. The *Sandinistas* were the government in Nicaragua at the time, and the Mendosas weren't too impressed with the job they were doing in running the country. The *Sandinistas,* for whatever reason, had managed to alienate the United States, which was Nicaragua's major trading partner and the previous source of most of Nicaragua's foreign aid. Now, instead of foreign aid, the U.S.

was sending them contras. Carlos summed up the situation in Nicaragua when he said that there was room for only one Cuba in that part of the world. Then one day another East German official stopped by with another thought. How about Chile? he asked. The Mendosas agreed with him that Chile was a great proletarian cause. Everybody was getting fed up with Pinochet. The country was ripe for the introduction of well-organized, well-trained, and well-financed revolutionaries, except for one thing. It would have to be a suicide mission. Chile was totally under military control. There were checkpoints everywhere, thousands of government informers, and the Chilean army and the Chilean police were solidly behind Pinochet. They were highly trained, highly motivated, and highly paid. The Mendosas politely declined the East German's invitation to a death in Chile in another losing cause."

"They were waiting for Peru," Brunette said.

"That's what it looks like. The Mendosas had been in East Germany for a couple of years when they got an invitation to a reception at the Cuban embassy in Berlin. The reception was being held to honor the many revolutionary heroes from around the world to whom the generous East German comrades had given sanctuary. It was quite an affair and they met people who appeared on wanted posters throughout the Western world. There were Baader-Meinhof people, Red Army people, Abu Nidal people, and even a few old pals from the *Montonero* movement who had found their way to the Prussian People's Paradise. There also must have been a heavy representation of STASI people at the reception who reported on everything that happened there, which is why the CIA knows so much."

By this time Brunette, McKenna, and Pacella had all finished their dinner and McKenna took a breather while the bus boys cleared away the dishes from the main course. Brunette ordered coffee all around and, after the coffee came, McKenna continued.

"According to the CIA report, the Cuban reception was where the Mendosas first heard about the *Sendero Luminoso* operation in Peru. The Mendosas liked what they heard. They learned that *Sendero Luminoso* had been active for about eight years and had scored a number of successes against the government. They had a few popular heroes, a dedicated following, and they were reasonably well armed. They got the money from the cultivation of the coca leaf in the areas under their control. They had a vague ideology, which provided a little something for everyone. For Indians in the rural areas of the country, they promised that the land would be returned to them so that the farms could be worked in the communal way of ancient Indian society. For the government worker, they promised wages pegged to the sizable inflation rate. For the factory worker, they

273

promised nationalization of foreign factories and worker ownership. For the soldiers, they promised elimination of the traditional officer class. The only people in Peru they promised nothing good to was the two percent of the population that had always owned and run the country. Fortunately for *Sendero Luminoso,* the government got brutal when they fought *Sendero Luminoso* in the countryside and they alienated a lot of people. The Peruvian army was sent to provinces where *Sendero Luminoso* was active and they placed these provinces under direct military control, with suspension of all civil rights. Then the government, with the backing of the United States, started spraying the coca crop in the areas controlled by *Sendero Luminoso* to destroy their source of financing. That really got the people against the government because coca was the traditional cash crop in those provinces."

"Were the Cubans involved in Peru then?" Brunette asked.

"Not yet. *Sendero Luminoso* had asked Cuba to provide training and weapons. Cuba was undecided at first. They were in no hurry to antagonize the government of Peru, especially since, at the time, the secretary-general of the United Nations was from Peru. But they put out feelers. The Mendosas talked over the *Sendero Luminoso* request while they were still at the reception. They were interested. Alfonso sought out the Cuban military attaché and told him that, if Cuba decided to aid *Sendero Luminoso,* then he, his wife, and his brother would be interested in going to Peru to advance the *Sendero Luminoso* revolution and, incidentally, Cuban interests. One week later the Mendosas were invited again to the Cuban embassy. Two weeks later they were in Havana. Sometime after that they went to Peru. According to Peruvian military intelligence a guerrilla leader known as 'Ali' had been successfully operating with *Sendero Luminoso* in Ayacucho province since 1987."

"How successfully?" Brunette asked.

McKenna consulted his notes and said, "Very. They got a list of thirty-four incidents in which Ali was identified as a participant. There were fourteen bombings of government installations or power lines, nine ambushes of government troops resulting in the deaths of over three hundred soldiers, seven assassinations of government officials, and four kidnappings to obtain ransoms and concessions from the government. The last incident on their list was in September of '91, which makes sense since the Mendosas have been in the United States since November 1991."

"Don't the Peruvians know who Ali is?" asked Brunette.

"They have no idea. They suspected that he wasn't Peruvian. They describe him as an extremely capable military leader who's good at organizing ambushes in which explosives are used. He never takes prisoners unless they can be held for ransom and he doesn't hesitate to discipline his troops when they don't follow his orders to the letter. The Peruvian military says that since Ali arrived on the scene, they noticed that everything improved in the *Sendero Luminoso* troops—their discipline, their weapons, their morale, and even their military appearance."

"Sounds like he should be a chief on the Job," Brunette said. "What did they say about Isabela and Carlos?"

"Not too much, but they report that Ali sometimes traveled with a beautiful foreign woman who they thought was his wife. But here's something. The Peruvian government offered a reward of two hundred million intis for information leading to the arrest of Ali. How much do you think that is in dollars?"

"Probably couldn't pay for this dinner," Pacella said.

McKenna gave Brunette the photos of the Mendosas that came with the report. Brunette took a few minutes as he looked at all the photos. Then he took a pen and paper out of his pocket and did some calculations. When he finished, he said, "Isabela is a tall girl and should stand out. According to her picture she's one hundred and seventy-five centimeters tall, which translates to five feet nine inches. She should stick out in Spanish Harlem. Alfonso is the same height, which makes him a little taller than average."

Next McKenna told Brunette what he had learned that morning from Gene Shields about the activities of Raoul Camarena in Florida and about the Cuban government's role in smuggling cocaine into the United States.

Nobody seemed to be too surprised at the news. McKenna also told them about Rosa Figueroa's role and said, "I gave my word to Gene Shields that all this information would go no further than us."

Brunette and Pacella understood. "Your promise is good," Pacella said.

Then Brunette called for the check and said, "I'm gonna give you two a break and pay for lunch."

Neither Pacella nor McKenna complained. Brunette paid the check and Pacella left the tip. Brunette took a few copies of the photos of Alfonso and Isabela Mendosa and said that he would have them delivered to Sheeran at the Intercontinental Hotel. Before he left, Brunette told McKenna and Pacella that he planned to be at the Two-five by 4:00 and that he would see them there.

24

July 12   2:00 p.m.

There wasn't much conversation between McKenna and Pacella on the short ride to the 25th Precinct. McKenna didn't know the uniformed police officer assigned to the log book outside the Major Case Squad office, so he and Pacella just signed in and entered.

The office wasn't what McKenna had expected. It was almost deserted. Ernest Ford sat at his desk, answering the constantly ringing telephones. Joe Sophia made entries in a log at a desk in the corner of the room, and Cisco Sanchez did the same thing at another desk. Sergeant Goldblatt sat near the door of Tavlin's office, struggling with the complexities of the roll call for the evening. But there were no detectives pounding at typewriters. Then McKenna figured out the reason. Betty King was also there.

Betty sat at her word processor with a set of headphones on, typing away. She didn't see them come in and McKenna watched her work. She had obviously come up with an innovation. The detectives assigned to the unit just told her what they did on the case during the day, she recorded them while they talked, then typed their reports into her word processor at her leisure. She had computerized their reports. With just two days in the Bureau, Betty King had brought them into the twentieth century.

Betty King worked behind a solid wall of flowers. She was obviously appreciated, but she looked like she was typing in the middle of her own wake. McKenna went over and tapped her on the shoulder. She

276

took her headphones off, stood up, and McKenna kissed her on the cheek.

"I heard about your problem this morning," Betty said. "I'm glad you're OK. I'm beginning to really dislike those people."

"I'm beginning to dislike them too, Betty. How do you like working here?"

Betty King said that she felt like a queen, which made McKenna happy. He walked over to Cisco's desk and watched him make some entries in his real estate log. "They stuck me and my partner with the tough job, as usual," Cisco said.

"How you making out?"

"I'm almost done. We found two hundred and fourteen apartments they might be in. I hope somebody's gonna use this list after we get done."

"When you gonna finish?"

"My end? In five minutes. Then I'll give the list to Betty and she'll computerize it by block, date advertised, and whatever else she can think of. After that, I'm done till four o'clock."

McKenna saw that Joe Sophia was looking very busy, but it was only a show for the benefit of Sergeant Goldblatt. Joe was calculating the gas used during the past twenty-four hours by all the vehicles assigned to the unit, though the figures were already entered in the boxes in the vehicle log.

With Raggs off limits, there was absolutely nothing for McKenna and Pacella to do. Pacella made a fresh pot of coffee and they stood around drinking it and talking until 2:30. Then the office started filling up with the Hispanic detectives assigned to the case.

At 2:45 Tavlin called McKenna and Pacella into his office. He wanted to know what was going on, so McKenna described the meeting at the Tombs and summarized the information contained in the CIA report on the Mendosas.

"Leave the report with me," Tavlin said. "I'll give it back later. You can post some of the pictures of Alfonso and Isabela on the bulletin board outside so everyone else can see what they look like."

"What are you gonna have us doing tonight?" Pacella asked.

"You'll both be on the surveillance. Since you don't look Spanish, I'm putting you on the tracks over Park Avenue. From there you should be able to see most of the street activity on each block from Lexington to Park. Ford spoke to the railroad police and they're gonna deliver some track-worker uniforms here by 3:30. Get some tools and spotlights from Emergency Service."

Looks like we're headed for the sidelines, McKenna thought. They left Tavlin's office and saw that the squad office was now crowded with detectives. McKenna went over and posted the East German Immigration photos of Alfonso and Isabela Mendosa, writing their heights in feet and inches on the bottom of the photos.

At 3:15 Sergeant Goldblatt read the roll call. He had broken down the twenty-five detectives into eight three-man teams. Five of these teams had four-block areas of responsibility covering the twenty-block area where they thought the pay phone Flavio would call was located. He kept the other three teams in reserve, and assigned the extra man as his driver.

Goldblatt's instructions to the surveillance teams were simple. Look inconspicuous, blend in, stay alert, be careful, and don't get made once the *Sendero Luminoso* contact is located. Look for a back-up person for whoever answers Flavio's call. Check the pictures of Alfonso and Isabela Mendosa posed on the bulletin board.

Goldblatt kept it short. Everyone had heard Inspector Tavlin's pep talk the day before and there wasn't much more to say. By 3:30 the office was almost empty again. The detectives assigned to the surveillance teams had checked out their equipment and radios, studied the photos of the Mendosas, and left the office.

McKenna and Pacella had another cup of coffee while they waited for their track-worker uniforms and Brunette to arrive.

25

July 12   2:30 p.m.

Rodrigo heard the front door of the apartment open and close, followed by the sounds of muffled voices. They were back. Rodrigo didn't know whether to laugh or cry. He hadn't heard any sounds of movement in the apartment nor had he been visited by Miriam for a long time. He thought it must have been at least two days, but he couldn't be sure. Night and day were no longer relevant terms for him, since his world was dominated by the single light bulb in the ceiling fixture. But he knew it was daytime because of the street noise outside. They were daytime noises—radios playing salsa music, traffic, car horns, children yelling, and the occasional sound of a fast-moving train. The nighttime noises were different, mostly police sirens and occasional gunshots or fireworks.

Rodrigo was filthy, hungry, thirsty, and in great pain. He was sure that he had a fever and he worried that he was losing his mind. He lay on his back in a small room, tied to the bed by Velcro straps across his chest, knees, and ankles. He was naked, except for a straitjacket. A plastic shower curtain had been spread beneath him. His legs were wet with his own urine and excrement. The smell of feces made him gag if he thought about it.

His bed was against one wall of the small room. The walls were covered with lines of mattresses standing on end. Two meters from his feet a mirror had been mounted in the facing wall, and a hole drilled under the mirror, one meter from the floor. The entrance to the room was a locked door to the left of the mirror. Rodrigo had been told that it was a one-way mirror and that his guards could see what he was doing. The hole in the wall under the mirror would let them shoot him at their convenience.

But *Sendero Luminoso* had added something new, something that petrified Rodrigo and brought home to him exactly how expendable his kidnappers considered him. When Rodrigo had first woken up two days ago and surmised that he had been left alone, he saw a small block of plastic explosive taped to the front of his straitjacket. The top of the blasting cap was embedded in the explosive and the wires leading from the top of the blasting cap were connected to a small radio receiver, which was also taped to his straitjacket. For the past two days Rodrigo had been trying to ignore the small green light on the front of the radio receiver as it blinked on and off every second.

Rodrigo thought that somewhere close by a member of *Sendero Luminoso* had a radio transmitter tuned to the frequency of the radio receiver taped to his chest, and that this person would press a button on that radio transmitter if anything went wrong with their plans. He imagined a radio signal would then be sent from the transmitter to the receiver and the receiver would send nine volts of high-amperage electricity down the wires to the blasting cap embedded in the plastic explosive, which would cause the blasting cap to explode and detonate the plastic. Rodrigo pictured a reddish tint on the mattresses lining the walls.

A strip of tape closed Rodrigo's mouth and for the past two days he had experienced difficulty breathing. His right hand hurt and he thought that the wound resulting from the severance of his pinky was infected. His hand throbbed so badly that he could feel in his ears the pressure of each beat of his heart. Rodrigo suspected that his ring finger had also been removed by Miriam's accomplice two days ago while he was drugged, but he wasn't sure. He felt intense pain at the spot where his ring finger should have been connected to his hand, but sometimes he thought his ring finger responded to the orders of movement that he forced his brain to send. Even so, if that finger were gone, Rodrigo wouldn't have been the slightest bit surprised.

Even before he was kidnapped, Rodrigo had had some insight into how *Sendero Luminoso* operated. He knew that last November Miguel Sanchez, the only son of Colonel Rueben Sanchez, had been kidnapped while he was attending college in Miami. Colonel Sanchez was a close family friend and he had later told Rodrigo's father the details of the kidnapping. Colonel Sanchez had first learned of it when a messenger delivered one of his son's fingers, a photo of his son, and a list of demands. At the time, Colonel Sanchez had been the military governor of Ayacucho province, the province of Peru where *Sendero Luminoso* was strongest.

Sendero Luminoso had demanded that Sanchez arrange to have $500,000 in United States currency dropped in the jungle at a place they specified. They also demanded that he free twenty-five prisoners held by the government in Ayacucho, and that he not inform the Peruvian or the American governments of the kidnapping.

Sanchez had hurried to comply with as many of the demands as he could. But he hadn't been fast enough, and three days after he had learned of the kidnapping, another one of his son's fingers had been delivered to him.

Sanchez had immediately had the money dropped by helicopter at the place specified by *Sendero Luminoso* and he'd freed nineteen of the prisoners. He had been unable to free the other six because they had "disappeared" while they were in government custody. Two days later another one of his son's fingers had arrived. There was nothing more that Sanchez could do. He knew that his son had been killed by *Sendero Luminoso* when, one week later, the money that had been dropped in the jungle was returned to him by a messenger, along with another of Miguel's fingers.

When Rodrigo's father heard about the kidnapping of Miguel Sanchez, he insisted that Rodrigo bring a bodyguard with him to the United States, which is why Oscar had accompanied him here. Not that Oscar had made much of a difference, Rodrigo thought. He's dead and I'm still a prisoner of these maniacs. And I'm in for a lot more pain and suffering before this is over, one way or the other. After all, Miguel Sanchez lost four fingers before they finally killed him.

It wasn't his fingers, his pain, or his physical health, but his mental health that worried Rodrigo most. Rodrigo knew that he should have been relieved when Miriam and her accomplices left him alone two days ago, but he wasn't. He found that he longed for the human contact provided by his torturers. His eyes had been focused on the locked door and on the one-way glass at the foot of his bed for most of his waking hours. Now his kidnappers were back, and he felt a sense of relief. He wanted to see Miriam again, not just because he knew that she would clean him up and probably provide him with food and drink, but because he wanted to talk to her. There were so many questions that he needed answered.

Rodrigo's worrying was interrupted by the sound of the door to his room being unlocked. The door opened and Isabela Mendosa, the woman Rodrigo knew as Miriam, came in. She carried a bucket in one hand and a new plastic shower curtain in the other. Someone closed and locked the door behind her. Rodrigo saw that Isabela had done something different with her hair, but he couldn't tell exactly what it was. She was dressed the way a woman with a good figure likes to look for summer, wearing white shorts, a yellow halter top, and sandals. She also wore rubber gloves, which destroyed her fashion statement. Rodrigo thought that Isabela looked more Spanish and even more beautiful than she did the last time he saw her. She was getting darker and had obviously been sunbathing somewhere. Rodrigo was so happy to see Isabela that he felt tears form in his eyes, which surprised him. Rodrigo had never considered himself an emotional person. But a visit from Isabela meant more to him than just food, pain-killers, and freedom from his restraints for a while.

Rodrigo was sure that he loved her. Despite the fact that she was a dedicated terrorist, probably a murderer, and the person most responsible for his predicament, she was also beautiful, intelligent, witty, charming, and great in bed. He loved to think of their last moments together at her house in the country in Massachusetts. It was the last thing he remembered before he woke up in this room a day later, missing his pinky. They were naked, making love in her bedroom. He was on top of her and she had her arms and legs wrapped around his body, biting his shoulder in passion. He now knew that he was set up. He figured that there were men hidden in her bedroom closet who jumped out at that moment and injected him with whatever drug they constantly used to knock him out. But it was still so good. He spent a lot of time wondering how much pretending she did that day.

As always, Rodrigo initially felt embarrassed by the mess he had made on his bed. He knew that it didn't matter to Isabela. After all, he had no choice, since he was tied to the bed. But he was a wealthy young man and unused to his condition.

Isabela placed the bucket and the shower curtain on the floor, then touched a button on the radio receiver taped to Rodrigo's chest. The green light stopped blinking. Isabela wrinked her nose as she looked Rodrigo over disapprovingly. Then she smiled at him and said, "Sorry we had to leave you for so long, Rodrigo. But we were always thinking of you. Now everything's going to be fine. Do you remember your instructions?" For emphasis, Isabela nodded toward the one-way mirror.

Rodrigo remembered. He knew the type of behavior that was expected of him to keep from being shot through the hole in the wall by the man behind the one-way mirror. Rodrigo looked at Isabela and nodded his assent.

"Good," Isabela said. "I'm going to remove the tape from your mouth and answer any questions that you might have while I clean you up and give you something to drink."

This all sounded good to Rodrigo. Once again he nodded. Isabela reached down and quickly pulled the tape from Rodrigo's mouth. In the process she yanked out some of Rodrigo's whiskers, which were stuck to the tape. Rodrigo sucked in big gulps of air for the next minute as he stared into Isabela's eyes. She dispassionately returned his gaze for a moment, then began to unfasten the Velcro straps that secured Rodrigo to the bed. As she finished Rodrigo asked, "How many fingers do I have left, Miriam?"

"Eight," Isabela answered.

So they did cut off my ring finger, Rodrigo thought. I'm still in real trouble here, and the longer I stay with these people, the more weight I'm going to lose. What's wrong with my father? Why hasn't he given them what they want? Is it possible that they're asking more than he feels I'm worth?

Rodrigo became more worried as he reflected upon his worth to his family. He imagined his father thinking that he was fortunate enough to have had two sons, and that Hernando was still alive to carry on the family name. For the first time in his life, Rodrigo wondered if his father loved his older brother more than he loved him. He began to wish that he had been an only child. "Have you completed negotiations with my family?" Rodrigo asked Isabela.

"No," she answered. "Unfortunately, we had some problems from the American police and we were forced to discontinue the negotiations for a couple of days. But everything is all right now and we will resume negotiations with your family tonight."

"Does that mean that I lose another finger today?" Rodrigo asked.

Isabela smiled at him sympathetically. "No, Rodrigo," she answered. "Before our problems with the American police, our negotiations with your family were going fairly well. You know that we have already delivered your pinky to your family. We are sure now that they are convinced that we are serious. I don't think that we'll have to send them any more of your fingers. Now, stand up please, and I'll clean you up. Then I'm going to feed you and dress you so that we can take some more pictures of you to send to your family to show them that you're still alive."

Rodrigo ignored Isabela's order to stand up. The news that she was going to take more pictures made Rodrigo suspect that she was lying to him. These bastards are going to cut off another one of my fingers, he thought. That's the way they operated in the past.

Rodrigo remembered that the last time Isabela had dressed him for a photo session was the last time he was sure that he had a ring finger. Isabela had fed him and cleaned him up before the session. She had even combed his hair. Then she had brought his clothes, a chair, a newspaper, and a Polaroid camera into the room. Following her instructions, he had gotten dressed and then sat down on the chair while holding up the copy of the *Boston Globe* that she had given him. Isabela had taken six pictures. Rodrigo remembered that he hadn't been smart enough to be suspicious when she had taken the close-up pictures of his hand. I'll know better this time, he thought. If she takes a close-up of my hand, then I'll know what to expect. But a lot of things still weren't clear to Rodrigo.

"Stand up, Rodrigo," Isabela repeated loudly, with exasperation and menace in her voice.

"Please, Miriam," Rodrigo pleaded. "Just answer a few more of my questions and I'll do anything you want. You know I can't hurt you, but these questions I have are driving me crazy."

Isabela considered Rodrigo's plea for a moment. Then she seemed to soften. She looked toward the one-way mirror and Rodrigo followed her gaze. He saw, for the first time since he had been in the room, that the barrel of a gun was poking through the hole in the wall under the mirror. The gun barrel was pointed at him. Isabela waved her hand and the gun barrel was withdrawn from the hole in the wall. She turned to Rodrigo and said, "Ask whatever you like, Rodrigo."

For a moment, Rodrigo savored his first small victory over his kidnappers. Isabela had shown him that they weren't quite ready to kill him. Besides, he thought, she wants me alive and conscious for the photo session. Isabela was waiting impatiently. "Why did you leave me here alone for two days?" he asked her.

Isabela answered immediately. "We suspected that the American police might have learned our location here. So we left you here and watched this place from a distance."

"You said before that you've already delivered my pinky to my family. What about my ring finger?" Rodrigo asked.

"Unfortunately, your ring finger wasn't delivered. The person who was carrying it was killed by an American policeman. When that happened, we naturally thought that the American police had located us and were preparing to attack us here. So we left you here by yourself, along with some surprises for the police if they came here."

Isabela pointed to the bomb that was taped to his chest and Rodrigo understood. If the police came, *Sendero Luminoso* was going to detonate the bomb by remote control, killing him and any policemen who were unlucky enough to be close to him at the time. They would get some headlines out of that.

"Eventually, we're going to make the American police suffer for interfering with our plans," Isabela continued. "In the past few days we have learned a few things about the policeman who killed our comrade. His name is Brian McKenna and he was involved in the death of another comrade this morning."

"He killed two of your people?" Rodrigo asked.

"Yes. We'll deal with him later, I promise you."

Rodrigo believed her. *Sendero Luminoso* had a well-founded reputation for revenge. But maybe the American police are close, he thought. He had to know more. "Why did he kill the person who was carrying my finger?"

"This McKenna has a reputation in New York for being able to detect people carrying guns. Unfortunately, our messenger was carrying a rather large gun under his jacket and we think that's why this McKenna first noticed him. He started chasing our comrade and there was a gun battle between them that stretched over some distance. Our man managed to get rid of your finger before he was killed. We've concluded that the death of our messenger was an accident, which doesn't surprise me. He was a wonderful man and a good friend, but he had been unlucky all his life. The important thing, as far as you're concerned, is that we have nothing to fear from the American police, so far. Which means that you have a small chance of surviving all of this, Rodrigo."

After listening to Isabela, Rodrigo didn't think of much of his chances. Isabela's answers to his questions both angered and worried Rodrigo. He was angry at the American police for interrupting the delivery of his finger to his family and he was sure that this interruption would cause him additional pain and suffering. He had lost his ring finger for nothing and now, he thought, despite Isabela's denials, they would probably cut off another finger to send to his family in its place. Rodrigo was worried because Isabela had given him so much information in response to his questions. He had suspected that he was being held in New York. The streets outside were too busy to be anywhere else but New York. But Isabela had never given him that information before, even though he had asked. Now she had given him enough information so that he was able to infer that he was in New York, and he hadn't even asked her. And she told him that two of her people had been killed by the New York police. Why was Miriam so free with information today? Rodrigo wondered. Was it because they've already decided to kill me? If they do kill me, would she be the one? She's the only member of the group I've ever seen.

"I have a personal question, Miriam."

"I probably won't answer it, but you can ask."

"Where are you from? I know you're not from Peru."

"I'm from the human race."

"Then why Peru? What are you doing with *Sendero Luminoso*? I hope you'll forgive me, but from what I know of them, you don't seem to fit in. Which is a compliment. And don't tell me that you're just another dedicated communist. Not in this day and age."

She thought over the question for a while. "I'm not going to lecture you because you are what you are and you can't change. You were born to your life. I was born to the same life, but things were different for me. Something happened and I changed. I got to see life from the other side. Why Peru? Because Peru is the worst case. In your country, two percent of the population controls fifty percent of the wealth. That's your two percent, Rodrigo. The only work your class does is work directed at keeping and increasing your wealth. And your power. You allow a small middle class to service your needs. You allow them a degree of prosperity so that you may appear civilized to the international community. But seventy percent of the population lives in abject poverty. This must change and I hope that *Sendero Luminoso* can change it. Given, they are not the most delightful people in the world. Or the greatest conversationalists that I've ever met. But they are the only hope for now. They are poor because you keep them poor, and they are uneducated because they have no choice. So far, we're doing OK. In the end, the masses must prevail. Even if *Sendero Luminoso* fails, another peasant or Indian group will take our place. Things must change, and which group changes things doesn't matter."

"Then you're not a communist?"

"In Peru, I'm a communist. In another country with a different situation, who knows? Probably not. But Peru is the worst-case scenario. You've held power for too long. Centuries. You'll never willingly share. You don't know how. So communism seems the only answer in Peru. Total redistribution of land and wealth. Of course, I know that communism must fail in the end. There will still be corruption and a new power class, a new class of oppressors. But even then, things will still be better than they are now, once your two percent is gone."

"Then you think that you must kill me and my family?"

"I hope not. Of course, some of you will be killed. But not many. You aren't a notably courageous bunch. But many people will be killed during the struggle. Some poor unfortunates, like Oscar, along with many more of us. In the end, you'll see the hopelessness of your position. You'll just leave. Like Batista in Cuba. Like Marcos in the Philippines. You'll simply pack up and go to places like Miami and Spain. Most of you have houses in those places and you spend a lot of your time there anyway. It won't be too painful for you. You'll take what you can. Of course, you won't be permitted to take the fifty percent of the country that you think you own. In the end, some of you might even have to work. Then you'll sit on the sidelines to tell the world what a mess we've made of your democratic country. I just hope that all this is accomplished in my lifetime. I'm looking forward to reading some of your émigré newspapers. I know I said I wouldn't lecture you, but I did. Now, enough questions and enough lectures. If Harvard can't teach you, then I sure can't. No more questions, Rodrigo. I want to finish cleaning this mess up and get rid of the stink in this room."

"One more, please. Why did you kill Oscar? Why didn't you just take him like you did me?"

"I would've liked it to be that way, but we couldn't. I liked Oscar. But he had a gun and we had to shoot him with a rifle while he was guarding you outside my house. We couldn't take a chance. You might be interested to know that one of our demands is that your father give his wife one hundred thousand dollars to compensate for her loss."

Isabela had given Rodrigo a lot to think about and, in his condition, thinking made him dizzy. But, now Isabela seemed to be in a hurry once again.

"Now stand up, Rodrigo," she ordered. Following her instructions, Rodrigo swung his legs over the edge of the bed and sat up. He felt light-headed and his vision started to blur. Rodrigo closed his eyes. He decided to sit still for a few moments until he felt a little steadier. Isabela seemed to understand and stood watching him. Then she turned toward the mirror and made a drinking motion with her hand. A second later there was a knock and Rodrigo heard the door unlock again. Isabela went over and opened it. A pitcher of ice water and a glass were on the floor outside. Rodrigo opened his eyes and strained to see into the next room. He glimpsed a green wall and the shadows of two people against it before Isabela picked up the pitcher and the glass, and the door closed behind her.

Isabela poured a glass of water and held it to Rodrigo's lips while he drank. It was the first water that Rodrigo had had in two days and it tasted wonderful to him. After a few moments Rodrigo began to feel better. He finished the glass and Isabela poured him another. Then she reached into her pocket and took out a handful of pills. "Open your mouth, Rodrigo."

"What are they?"

"There's six pills. You need them all. Two are antibiotics for the infection in your hand, two are pain-killers, and two are sleeping pills."

To Rodrigo, they all sounded like things that he needed. He opened his mouth and Isabela placed the pills on his tongue. Next she put the glass of water to his lips and Rodrigo kept drinking until the glass was empty.

"Ready?" Isabela asked him. Rodrigo nodded and she grabbed the back of his straitjacket and helped him to stand up. Rodrigo felt wobbly for a moment and thought that he was going to fall, but then his strength started to return to his legs. The throbbing in his hand intensified. He walked to the wall and Isabela hooked the dog leash that was attached to the back of his straitjacket to a hook embedded in the wall between two of the mattresses. Then Isabela removed the soiled plastic shower curtain from the bed and replaced it with the new one that she had brought with her into the room.

It only took her a couple of minutes to finish cleaning the bed. Then she turned to Rodrigo and said, "You know what to do. Face the wall, place your head on it, and move your legs away from the wall."

The routine had become familiar to Rodrigo during his captivity. He did as he was told until he was in a position where Isabela could easily knock him to the floor if he tried anything. Once he was in position, Isabela approached him from behind and washed his genital area and his legs. When she was finished, Rodrigo felt her back away from him and heard the sound of the door being unlocked. "Stay there for a moment more, Rodrigo," she ordered.

Rodrigo heard the door open and close, then he heard the sound of it being locked again. He smelled food and saw Isabela place a chair next to where he was standing. On the seat of the chair in a large, neat pile were his clothes, a newspaper, some rope, a Polaroid camera, a plate of food, and another pitcher of water. Isabela took everything off the seat of the chair and placed these items on the floor out of his reach. Then she said, "Turn around and sit down on the chair."

Rodrigo did as he was told. Isabela had a tin plate of food and a spoon in her hands. Rodrigo surmised that the food was a take-out order from a local restaurant. Steak, mashed potatoes, and string beans. "The menu doesn't change very much around here, does it?" he asked. Except for the last two days, Isabela had fed him steak, mashed potatoes, and string beans almost every day since he first had woken up in this room. As usual, the steak had already been cut into small pieces.

"Sorry, Rodrigo. What do you want to eat tomorrow?"

"Hamburgers and french fries. I've been dreaming about them. But steak will do for now. I'm starving!"

"OK, tomorrow I'll bring you hamburgers and french fries."

Isabela leaned over Rodrigo and began to feed him, a spoonful at a time. Rodrigo ate everything. When the plate was empty, Isabela gave Rodrigo more water until he was satisfied. Then she asked, "Ready to get your bandage changed and take some pictures?"

"I'm always ready to take this jacket off."

The thought of taking off the jacket made Rodrigo as close to being happy as he could be under the circumstances. He relished the thought of being able to move his arms again. He also wanted to see what his hand looked like since they cut off his ring finger.

Isabela started the dressing procedure and Rodrigo remembered the steps from the last time. She picked up Rodrigo's pants from the floor and he raised his legs from his chair so that she could slip his pants on over his feet. She helped him to stand up again, pulled up his pants and fastened his belt. Then Rodrigo sat back down. Isabela took two lengths of rope and tied Rodrigo's legs to the legs of the chair. When she was finished, Isabela stood up and loosened the two buckles on the front of the straitjacket that held his arms to his body. Rodrigo stretched his arms. The pain in his hand increased as he stretched, but he didn't care. Then Isabela told Rodrigo to lean forward in his chair. When he did, she unhooked his leash and also the buckles on the back of the jacket. Isabela stepped back from the chair as Rodrigo finished taking off the straitjacket. As soon as he did, his nostrils were assailed by his own pungent body odor. It was unpleasant, but the most important thing to Rodrigo at that moment was his injured right hand.

The bandage on Rodrigo's right hand was stained with blood where his ring finger should have been. Rodrigo pulled off the adhesive tape around the bandage and started unraveling the gauze. His dried blood stuck to the gauze and it hurt to unroll the bandage, but his curiosity was greater than his aversion to pain. He was relieved to see that his hand felt worse than it looked. The ring finger was gone, but the wound was nicely closed with stitches. There was some swelling and redness that he suspected was the beginning of an infection, but nothing life-threatening. The pinky wound was also healing and it looked like the stitches were ready to be removed. Rodrigo looked up and saw that Isabela was staring at his hand. "You people are getting pretty good at cutting off fingers, Miriam."

"We got the idea from your people, Rodrigo, and we're still not as good as them. We haven't had enough practice, yet."

Rodrigo didn't question Isabela on her meaning. The forces of his government had been accused of being overzealous when they interrogated suspected members of *Sendero Luminoso,* and he knew he was in no position to argue with Isabela about which side was more brutal in the war. He would have to lose any argument that he had with her.

Rodrigo was getting tired; the sleeping pills that Isabela had given him were beginning to work. With his belly full and his curiosity about his hand satisfied, Rodrigo had an overwhelming desire to close his eyes and go to sleep.

But there was still the matter of his body odor. Rodrigo could see that Isabela also smelled him from where she was standing. "It must be real hot in that jacket," she said.

"It is," Rodrigo answered.

Isabela went to the door and knocked on it. When the door was unlocked and opened, Isabela told one of the people to bring some more soap and water and a towel. She waited by the open door and once again Rodrigo strained to see what was on the other side. He saw the green wall and the shadows the two people cast against it. Then a third shadow appeared and Rodrigo saw a pair of hands give Isabela the bucket and a towel. She brought them over to Rodrigo and placed them next to his chair. The door closed and locked behind her. Rodrigo noticed that whenever Isabela moved around the room, she was always careful not to place herself between him and the hole in the wall. The person on the other side of the mirror had a clear shot at him at all times.

The bucket had been filled with fresh soapy water, and a sponge floated on the surface. Rodrigo picked it up and began to wash himself. The water was pleasantly warm and he took his time. When he had finished his upper body, he carefully washed his injured hand, then dried himself with the towel.

Isabela picked up his shirt from the floor and handed it to him. Rodrigo started dressing, but he was getting more tired with every minute that passed. He had trouble buttoning the front because of his injured hand, and Isabela impatiently told him to forget about the buttons. She gave him the newspaper and told him to hold it up in front of his chest. Once again, it was the *Boston Globe.* Rodrigo looked at the front page, searching for news of himself, but found that he had trouble focusing. Isabela was holding up the camera. "Hold the newspaper up, Rodrigo," she said. "I'll let you read it later."

Rodrigo turned the newspaper around and held it in front of his chest. Isabela took three pictures of him, then came closer and snapped a photo of his hand.

Oh no! Rodrigo thought. Another finger. Rodrigo dropped the newspaper and stood up. He tried to move toward Isabela, but couldn't; his legs were tied to the legs of the chair. Tired as he was, Rodrigo began to feel foolish. Isabela looked at him with an air of contemptuous amusement. He glanced at the hole in the wall. The gun barrel poked through the opening, pointing directly at his chest. He felt he was very close to death as he struggled to regain his composure.

"Sit down and pick up the newspaper, Rodrigo!" Isabela ordered coldly.

Rodrigo sat and reached to the floor for the newspaper. A wave of fatigue swept over him as he placed the paper across his chest.

"Open your eyes, Rodrigo!" Isabela ordered.

Rodrigo struggled to keep his eyes open. Isabela stepped forward and focused the camera on his right hand as he held the newspaper.

"You lying bitch!" was the only thing Rodrigo could manage to say. He closed his eyes again and fell asleep. A few minutes later the newspaper dropped from his hands and he began to snore.

26

July 12   4:15 p.m.

Flavio Asturo spoke to his wife in Peru from his telephone in the Intercontinental Hotel. One floor above Flavio's room, their conversation in Spanish was being attentively followed by everyone except for Captain Sheeran and Lieutenant Hardcass. Sheeran watched Flavio on the monitors, pacing within the short limits that his telephone cord allowed. Without understanding a word of Spanish, Sheeran could guess the gist of the conversation from Flavio's and his wife's tones of voice. Flavio's voice seemed firm and consoling while his wife was crying and pleading with him.

The conversation lasted less than five minutes. The translation came to Sheeran without his asking for it. Detective Tonia Echevara, who was assigned as the hotel maid in Flavio's room, told Sheeran that Flavio's wife had received a telephone call from *Sendero Luminoso* that morning and they had let her talk to their daughter. The girl had sounded scared, but she told her mother that she was being treated well and was fine. Flavio's wife again begged him to do whatever *Sendero Luminoso* wanted in order to get their daughter back. Flavio told her not to worry, he would do nothing to jeopardize their daughter's safety. He hoped to be home soon.

That was good news to Sheeran. He too wanted to get home soon. It had been a boring day since Sheeran had returned to the hotel room from his meeting at the Manhattan House of Detention that morning. Flavio had gone through his normal routine of church, lunch, nap, and television. But Sheeran knew that Flavio wasn't bored

292

at all. He tried to put himself into Flavio's head, but found that he couldn't. Flavio's predicament was beyond his understanding and experience.

Sheeran watched the businessman pour himself a glass of wine. It's all up to you now, Sheeran thought. Good luck, Flavio!

It was 4:25. The radio had been busy for the last few minutes as one by one the surveillance teams in the 25th Precinct reported that they were in position and ready.

Hardcass dialed Telephone Security. They expected his call and the supervisor came on the line. Everything that could be done has been done, Sheeran told himself.

Flavio drank his glass of wine and poured the remnants from the bottle into his glass. Then he took his wallet out and removed the folded list of telephone numbers, spreading it out next to the phone on the nightstand.

Sheeran was ready. While Flavio had been at church that morning, TARU had installed another camera in his room and a third monitor in their room. The pinhole lens was mounted in the ceiling above the nightstand. Sheeran watched this monitor as Detective Gaspar zoomed in on Flavio's list.

"Got it!" Gaspar said.

The images were being recorded on one of the VCRs in the room and Sheeran could read Flavio's entire list of twelve telephone numbers. But which one is he going to call? Sheeran wondered.

Hardcass was also watching the monitor. "It should be 212–465–7707," he said to the supervisor from Telephone Security.

Hardcass was probably right, Sheeran thought. That number was next on the list below the number that Flavio had called yesterday.

Flavio lifted the phone and the sound of the dial tone filled the room. As Flavio dialed Gaspar called the numbers out from his LCD monitor and Hardcass repeated them to the New York Telephone Security supervisor. 2...1...2...4...6...5...7..7...0...7. Two seconds after the last number Gaspar pushed a button on his audio recorder and the sound of a busy signal came on. All eyes watched the monitors as Flavio took the telephone from his ear and squinted at it, puzzled. After a few seconds he replaced the telephone on the receiver and took another sip of wine. Then he put his glass on the nightstand and stared at the phone.

Sheeran looked at Hardcass. The seconds seemed like hours. Thirty seconds later Hardcass put his radio to his mouth and said, "Two-five surveillance teams. Target location is a pay phone at the northwest corner of Third Avenue and 118th Street."

"Two-five Base to Hotel Base. Read your transmission. Northwest corner of Third and 118th."

293

Telephone Security got the location faster than we expected, Sheeran thought. Now we just have to hope that one of the surveillance teams gets there before Flavio tries again.

Thirty seconds later Flavio picked up his telephone again and began to dial. Sheeran watched the LCD display. 2 . . . 1 . . . 2 . . . .

The radio crackled. "Two-five Team Three has location under surveillance."

. . . 4 . . . 6 . . . 5 . . . 7 . . . 7 . . . 0 . . . 7. Gaspar was looking at Sheeran with his finger on the button that would feed Flavio another busy signal. Sheeran shook his head.

"Two-five Team Three to Hotel Base. There are two pay phones on the corner and both are being used."

The phone rang once and was answered. The conversation between Flavio and a female was short and in Spanish. Sheeran understood what she had done. The *Sendero Luminoso* contact had stood at the pay phone at Third Avenue and 118th Street and pretended to be talking on the telephone so that nobody else would use her phone. But she had kept the receiver hook depressed so that she could receive Flavio's call.

"Two-five teams, subject is a female Hispanic," Hardcass transmitted.

"Two-five Team Three. We got her. Female Hispanic, black hair, age thirty, tall, wearing white shorts, yellow top, tan sandals. Looks like Isabela Mendosa. She appears to be alone. She's now walking West on 118th towards Lex. She's got a large tan pocketbook."

"Two-five Team Four is at 118th and Lex. We'll pick her up."

Sheeran recognized Goldblatt's voice as he came on the air to direct the surveillance operation. "Surveillance Supervisor. Team Two, go to 117th and Lex. Team One, go to 119th and Lex. Team Five, go to 118th and Park. Track Team, what's your location?"

Sheeran heard Pacella's voice answer, "On the tracks, 118th and Park."

"Stay there."

Sheeran saw that Flavio had taken his suitcases from his closet and started packing. "What happened?" he asked no one in particular, and three voices at once began to tell him. Sheeran held up his hand and pointed to Tonia Echevara. "The woman who answered the phone asked Flavio if he was booked on the six-o-five flight. Flavio told her he was. Then she told him to pack up and be standing in the lobby of the hotel at five twenty, and that he should be ready to check out of the hotel at five thirty."

"Nothing about the busy signal?" Sheeran asked.

"No, sir."

Perfect! Sheeran thought. But now what do I do? He was interrupted by the radio.

"Two-five Team Four has got her at 118th and Lex. She's southbound on Lex, east side of the street. This is too easy. She's gorgeous and everybody looks at this girl. She's not going to make us."

"Two-five Team Three to all Two-five units, be advised subject has a possible backup. He's westbound on 118th, hawking all around. Male, Hispanic, possible Indian, thirty years of age, five-foot-five, mustache and beard, blue shorts, red shirt, white sneakers, carrying a blue gym bag."

"Two-five Surveillance Supervisor to Team Six. Can you pick up the backup?"

"We'll be there in two minutes, Sarge."

"Team Two to Surveillance Leader. She's crossing 117th on Lex. Still heading south."

"Team Seven is at Lex and 115th. We'll pick her up."

"Team Six to Surveillance Supervisor. That possible backup man is now standing on the corner of 117th and Lex, looking down the street toward the subject. He looks like the Real Deal."

"Surveillance Supervisor to all teams. Be alert for additional backups."

At East 116th Street and Lexington Avenue, Isabela Mendosa approached Detective Cisco Sanchez and Detective Sylvia Maldonado. Detective Sanchez put his arm around Detective Maldonado and gave her a kiss on the cheek. It was something that he had wanted to do for the past two years, and he prided himself on never missing an opportunity. As soon as Isabela had passed them, Detective Maldonado took her beer in her brown paper bag and poured it on Detective Sanchez's crotch, giving him the "I had to pee and I couldn't hold it" look. This was something that she had wanted to do for the past five years. The third member of their team, Detective Wilfredo Gomez, transmitted from the roof of a building on Lexington Avenue, "Team Seven to Surveillance Supervisor. Subject crossing 116th, still southbound on Lex."

"Team Six to Surveillance Supervisor. The backup man's still standing on the corner of 118th and Lex and he's still staring down the block at the female subject."

Sheeran didn't have time to listen to this anymore. He had to think. He looked at his watch. Four forty. If Flavio had to meet someone from *Sendero Luminoso* outside the hotel at five twenty, then that person must already be on his way from the Two-five, if that's where he's coming from. Or the contact could be here already, he thought. He looked out the window. He saw Taxi One, Taxi Two, and his two chase units in the hotel parking lot. Everyone was in their cars and Sheeran knew that they were all listening to the progress of the surveillance teams in the Two-five. They didn't know yet about Flavio's imminent departure and probable meeting with someone from *Sendero Luminoso* at the hotel. And Sheeran didn't want to interrupt the surveillance transmissions on the radio to tell them what was going on.

Sheeran called Hardcass over and said, "Tell the teams downstairs what's going on here at five twenty." Hardcass was at the door in an instant. "Tell them to be on their toes." Hardcass nodded and left.

Better let the chiefs know what's going on, Sheeran thought. Maybe I can pass the ball and someone will give me some ideas on what to do next. Sheeran dialed the Major Case Office in the 25th Precinct, and was shocked when Chief Brunette picked up the telephone. Sheeran told Brunette about Isabela Mendosa's instructions to Flavio. The line was silent as Brunette thought over that information. Then Brunette asked, "You got enough manpower there, Dennis?"

Ball three, full count. The catcher smiled and returned the ball to the pitcher. Enough manpower for what? Sheeran thought. "Yes sir," he answered.

"Good. I knew I could count on you. Call me back in fifteen minutes." Brunette hung up.

Sheeran felt like a two-hundred-pound meteor entering the earth's atmosphere. He wondered how much of him would be left when he hit the ground.

It took Sheeran ten minutes to come up with a plan and put it into operation. Flavio was not going to appear to be involved in their operation in any way. Sheeran had convinced himself that Flavio Asturo's daughter was as important as Rodrigo Guiterrez and more important than any promotion he might get out of this. He hoped that the chief had not compromised her safety in any way by informing the Peruvian government of the police department operation here. If the Peruvian police knew of Flavio's involvement as an unwilling *Sendero Luminoso* agent, Sheeran suspected that they would either follow him from the airport in Lima or arrest him in the airport and take him somewhere for questioning. Either course of action would put Flavio's daughter in even graver danger than she was in already.

Hardcass was back. Sheeran said to him, "Send Richie White and his partner to the Lan Chile departure gate. Tell them to just make sure that Flavio gets on his flight at six-oh-five. Then take the team from the other chase car and put them in the lobby where they can see but not be seen, and stay with them. Tell them to be careful. *Sendero Luminoso* might already be in the hotel somewhere."

As Hardcass was leaving, Sheeran told him to report back by radio if there was anything suspicious in the lobby. Sheeran searched his mind for anything that he might have missed, but couldn't think of another thing to do.

On the monitor, Flavio had finished packing his two suitcases and was sitting on his bed and staring into space, apparently lost in thought.

The radio transmissions from the surveillance teams in the Two-five hadn't stopped. Sheeran listened with half an ear. Isabela had been wandering up and down Lexington Avenue for twenty minutes. From what Sheeran gathered, she wasn't more than normally suspicious. She was just being careful, Sheeran hoped. Her backup man stood on the corner of East 117th and Lexington Avenue when, at five o'clock, Isabela went into a tanning salon on Lexington between East 117th and East 118th Street. The Two-five surveillance operation shifted into neutral.

At five after five Hardcass's voice over the radio broke the silence in the hotel room. "Hotel Supervisor to Hotel Leader. It looks like our guests have arrived. Two male Hispanics just got out of a gypsy cab in front of the hotel. One is in the lobby and one is outside. In the lobby we have a male Hispanic, forty years old, about five foot ten inches tall, with a beard and mustache, wearing a gray suit, white shirt, blue tie, and sunglasses. He's just looking around. I can't see the other one now. The gypsy cab is leaving."

Why two guys? Sheeran thought. And what's the other one doing? He got his answer in a second. "Taxi One to Hotel Leader. Subject number two is walking around the parking lot. He might be looking for us. He's a male Hispanic, about twenty-five years old, clean-shaven, five-foot-four, wearing black pants, white shirt, white nylon Windbreaker, carrying a newspaper. I'm right behind him. Do you want me to pick them up when they leave?"

Sheeran picked up his radio and said, "That would be wonderful, Taxi One. Taxi Two, what's your location?"

"Taxi Two to Hotel Leader. I'm two cabs behind Taxi One."

Sheeran's mind started racing. Wouldn't it be nice to find out where these two go after they leave the hotel? We have to make sure that they get into one of our cabs. And we have to make sure that no one else causes a scene by trying to hire them. Sheeran said into his radio, "Hotel Leader to Taxi One. Get out of your taxi and raise the hood, so no one else tries to hire you."

A minute later Sheeran heard, "Hotel Supervisor to Hotel Leader. The number one guy is pretending that he's talking on the phone in the lobby, but he didn't put any money in. He's watching the elevators.

He has his sunglasses off. Number One is Alfonso Mendosa. He looks just like his picture."

"Taxi Two to Hotel Leader. Number Two is finished checking out the parking lot. It looks like he's on his way into the hotel."

A minute later Hardcass's voice again came on the radio. "Hotel Supervisor to Hotel Leader. Number Two is sitting in a chair and reading a newspaper like he doesn't know Alfonso."

Sheeran took in all of this information as he stared at the monitor. He was also doing some arithmetic. The New York City Police Department now has four members of *Sendero Luminoso* under surveillance, including two of the ringleaders, he thought. How many people could they have in their gang? We could probably take all four in the next two minutes without losing a man. If a lot of things go wrong later on in the operation, Sheeran thought, then we'll probably look at this moment as a great missed opportunity.

At 5:15 Flavio checked his watch and got up off his bed. He put on his tie and jacket, left his suitcases on the bed, and walked out the door. Sheeran picked up his radio. "Flavio is on his way down."

A minute later Hardcass transmitted, "Flavio's out of the elevator and standing in the lobby by himself. Alfonso and his partner both see him, but they're not making a move. Looks like Flavio doesn't recognize either of them."

Nothing happened for another couple of minutes. They're just being careful, Sheeran thought. They want to make sure that Flavio's alone and they probably like to keep him nervous. Then Hardcass radioed, "Alfonso's approaching him. They're talking. Now they're walking back to the elevators. Number Two is still just sitting in the lobby. They're in the elevator." He paused, then said, "Now the elevator is stopped at Flavio's door."

Sheeran watched the monitors as Flavio and Alfonso entered the room. Alfonso left Flavio standing in the middle of the room as he checked out the bathroom, the closet, and under the bed. Then Alfonso said something in Spanish, and Sheeran watched as both men took off their ties, jackets, and shirts. Alfonso had a large automatic in a holster on his belt and an envelope and a plastic case taped to his back. He turned around and Flavio ripped the stuff off his back and put them on the bed. There was another short conversation in Spanish, and then Flavio turned around. Alfonso took a roll of surgical tape out of his pocket and taped the envelope and the plastic case to Flavio's back. Both men dressed again, with Alfonso giving Flavio orders.

Sheeran turned to Detective Echevara and asked, "Does Flavio know he's got a finger taped to his back?"

"It didn't come up in the conversation. Alfonso just told Flavio to deliver the envelope and the case to Hernan Guiterrez by twelve o'clock tomorrow, Lima time. That's the last thing he has to do. Then his daughter would be returned to him by tomorrow night."

As soon as Alfonso finished dressing, he left Flavio's room. Sheeran picked up his radio and said, "Hotel Leader to all Hotel Units. Alfonso is on his way downstairs. He has a pistol in a holster on his belt."

"Taxi One to Hotel Leader. I'm ready to take them. I'm going off the air."

"Hotel Supervisor to Hotel Leader. Alfonso's out of the elevator. He's being joined by Number Two in the lobby. They're both leaving the hotel. They're getting into Taxi One. I'm sending the chase team after them."

"Taxi Two to Hotel Leader. Taxi One is pulling away. Should I follow him?"

"Negative, Taxi Two," Sheeran transmitted into his radio. "Flavio will be leaving in a minute. Take him to the Lan Chile terminal."

Sheeran didn't want to take a chance of following Taxi One too closely, since he thought that would put the detective driving the taxi in too much danger. Alfonso was very careful and he would probably be looking for a tail. Sheeran thought that it would be better to let the chase team follow Taxi One. Taxi One had a locating transmitter installed on it and the chase team had the tracking equipment in their car so they could follow from a distance. The chase team started reporting a minute later. Taxi One was northbound on the Van Wyck Expressway.

Sheeran watched as Flavio picked up his suitcases and left the room. Two minutes later Hardcass reported over the radio that Flavio was at the hotel desk checking out. He then walked out of the Intercontinental Hotel and got into Taxi Two.

Then it started in the 25th Precinct again. "Two-five Team Three to Surveillance Supervisor. Isabela is out of the tanning salon. She's southbound on Lexington Avenue. She just passed her backup man standing on the corner. Now she's westbound on 117th Street."

McKenna saw her as soon as she turned onto East 117th Street. He was on the elevated tracks above Park Avenue and East 117th, one block west of Lexington Avenue. Pacella waited on the tracks at East 118th Street. McKenna lay on his stomach, watching Isabela through a pair of binoculars. She walked toward him through the crowded sidewalks like she didn't have a care in the world. She looks beautiful with that tan, McKenna thought.

McKenna saw her backup man following her down 117th Street, half a block behind. A minute later Isabela crossed Park Avenue directly under the spot on the tracks where McKenna lay. She kept heading west on East 117th Street, which puzzled McKenna. Park

Avenue was the unofficial border of Spanish Harlem, and going west from Park Avenue, as Isabela was doing, the neighborhood got increasingly blacker. She's going to come back, McKenna thought. One more block, and Isabela and the rest of her pals won't blend in at all.

Isabela stopped on the corner of East 117th Street and Madison Avenue, one block west of McKenna's position. She was joined on the corner by her backup man, and they stood on the corner talking together.

Sergeant Goldblatt had arrived at the same conclusion. He told his surveillance units to give Isabela and her backup some room and not get too close. There was no need to. McKenna could see them perfectly from the tracks. For a few minutes, Isabela and her friend seemed to be taking note of the passing traffic on Madison Avenue. Then they both turned and started walking back toward Park Avenue, passing below McKenna and continuing on East 117th Street until they reached a tenement building halfway between Park Avenue and Lexington Avenue. They stopped in front of the building, took a final look around the neighborhood, then went in. From his position McKenna couldn't see the address of the building, but Team Four could. Team Four reported that Isabela and her backup had gone into 132 East 117th Street, a five-story tenement building.

These people don't have too much respect for us, McKenna thought. The building was just two blocks from the Two-five station house on East 119th Street. McKenna had been listening to the radio and it sounded like Isabela would be joined by her husband in less than half an hour. Alfonso Mendosa and the other member of *Sendero Luminoso* were in Taxi One on the Grand Central Parkway, heading toward Manhattan. Every couple of minutes the chase unit gave their location, and they were getting closer to Spanish Harlem. The chase unit said that they had Taxi One in sight and were about 100 yards behind them.

Sergeant Goldblatt wanted all of his units to be ready for the arrival of Alfonso Mendosa. He told McKenna's team to stay where they were so that 132 East 117th Street remained under surveillance. Then he started assigning the rest of his teams to specific locations between Park and Third avenues so that no team was closer than one block to the tenement.

At 6:00 McKenna recognized Richie White's voice on the radio. Flavio was on his plane and he was alone when he boarded. At 6:10 White reported that Flavio's plane had taken off. At 6:15 Taxi One dropped Alfonso Mendosa and his backup man at East 117th Street and Second Avenue. Like Isabela, the two men took a leisurely stroll through the neighborhood. They looked all around them as they walked, apparently trying to make sure that they weren't being followed. At 6:25 McKenna saw Alfonso Mendosa and his backup man walk into 132 East 117th Street. Everybody's home, McKenna thought.

Nothing else happened for a while. By 8:00 McKenna was convinced that it was going to be a long night. One by one, five of the eight surveillance teams had been ordered back to the station house. But not McKenna and Pacella, who had walked along the tracks to McKenna's position. They speculated that the Bosses had forgotten they were there. They had been dodging the fast-moving commuter trains of Metro North for four hours and thought they deserved a break. It was starting to get dark, and the tracks were becoming increasingly dangerous.

McKenna saw that one of the TARU surveillance vans that had been parked in the parking lot of the 25th Precinct was now double-parked on the street below him. He figured the driver was waiting for a spot to open up near the door of 132 East 117th Street. Four remote-controlled television cameras were mounted in the van, two on each side. Red reflectors attached to the sides of the van hid the small lenses of the cameras. Each camera could be remotely operated from a quarter mile away.

At 8:10 a car left a parking spot directly opposite 132 East 117th Street and the surveillance van pulled in. The driver locked it and left. Pacella knew him, Pedro Gaspar from TARU. A minute later they heard Gaspar radio Goldblatt that the van was in place. Goldblatt then radioed McKenna's team and told them to report to the station house, which made them both happy.

McKenna and Pacella were all set to walk down the tracks to the little-used Metro North station at 125th Street when they saw Isabela's backup man come out of the building. He walked east on 117th Street to Lexington Avenue, made a right, and disappeared from McKenna's view. Pacella radioed the information to Goldblatt, and was relieved to hear that another surveillance team had the man under observation. He had gone into Hector's Spanish Luncheonette on Lexington Avenue between East 115th Street and East 116th Street.

Team Five reported that Detective Muriel Navara had followed the suspect into Hector's. Fifteen minutes later the suspect left, carrying a large bag. A minute passed and McKenna saw him turn the corner onto East 117th Street from Lexington Avenue. He brought his bundle of food back into the tenement.

Two minutes later, he was back on the street again. He had the same bag that he had just carried from Hector's, but it was no longer full. He walked past the parked surveillance van, crossed the street, and went into another building.

"Team Five to Surveillance Supervisor. The subject just came out of 132 and went into 129 East 117th Street carrying some of the dinners." McKenna looked around for Team Five, but couldn't see where they were hidden.

McKenna and Pacella talked over this latest movement by Isabela's backup man, and they both had reached the same conclusion. *Sendero Luminoso* did have two apartments right on the same block.

Which building is Rodrigo being held in? McKenna asked himself. 132 or 129? Probably 129, he thought. Most of the food stayed in 132. I'll bet there's just one person assigned to guard Rodrigo, and Isabela's backup man was probably just delivering supper to Rodrigo and the guard. If Rodrigo is still alive, that is.

"Let's get back to the station house before we get smeared by one of these trains," McKenna said to his partner.

"Good idea," Pacella said. The two men walked down the tracks to the 125th Street station.

27

July 12   9:00 p.m.

Joe Flaherty was again manning the sacred log book outside the Major Case Squad office.

"Where you guys been?" he asked McKenna and Pacella.

"Dodging trains," Pacella answered. "What's everybody else doing?"

"Nothing. Tavlin told most of them to wait in the CCAU office. There's only a couple of teams left out there."

McKenna and Pacella signed in, and McKenna noticed that Sheeran had checked in ten minutes earlier. They went into the squad office. Four television monitors had been set up on a table near the wall, with a joy-stick control in front of each monitor. Only two were on, each showing images of the front of a building. One monitor was labeled 129 ENTRANCE and the other 132 ENTRANCE. Gaspar watched the monitors while VCRs recorded the images. McKenna assumed that the pictures were transmitted from two of the cameras in the surveillance van.

The only other people in the office, Joe Sophia and Cisco Sanchez, were busy talking on the phone. Sophia interrupted his conversation to yell, "The chief wants to see you guys. He's in Tavlin's office."

McKenna knocked and they both went in. Tavlin, Sheeran, Flynn, and Brunette were sitting at the conference table, with Brunette at the head. As McKenna and Pacella entered, he rose from his seat and said, "Congratulations, Brian. I just got off the phone with the police commissioner. I told him how we're doing and how we happened to get so far. He asked me to tell you that he thinks that you're doing a first-grade job. And you haven't been doing too bad either, Tommy. But of course, we expect first-grade work from First-Grade detectives."

Ray then walked over to McKenna and Pacella and shook the hand of each man. He told them to sit down and explained what had happened in Flavio's room at the Intercontinental Hotel that afternoon, which was all news to McKenna and Pacella. Then he said, "I think we're running out of time if we're serious about rescuing Rodrigo. He's being held two blocks from where we're sitting, he's apparently lost another finger today, and *Sendero Luminoso* doesn't have a doctor anymore. He's got to be in a lot of pain, if he's still alive. Alfonso told Flavio that today's mission was his last, so we can assume that *Sendero Luminoso*'s run out of patience with the Guiterrez family, which means that time's running out for Rodrigo. It isn't our job to find Rodrigo's body. I want him rescued, if possible, and every member of *Sendero Luminoso* in New York City dealt with. I've talked with the mayor, the police commissioner, and the Feds. It's been decided that both apartments being used by *Sendero Luminoso* are gonna be assaulted by our department. We're not gonna negotiate with them for the release of Rodrigo Guiterrez because that would set a bad precedent in the way we deal with terrorists here."

There was a lot that Brunette hadn't specifically said that was understood by each man in the room. He hadn't said that he wanted every member of *Sendero Luminoso* arrested. He wanted them dealt with. The implications were clear.

Brunette continued. "Next we come to the other people living on East 117th Street. They're all in danger and I want as many of them as possible evacuated from both 132 and 129 before we hit. But it's got to be done without the knowledge of *Sendero Luminoso.* Any overt evacuation would tip them off. At the very least, I want all of the apartments evacuated that are adjacent to, over, and beneath whatever apartments *Sendero Luminoso* are using in the buildings. Then we'll convert them to police use. Crosby's on his way here from the Intercontinental Hotel. He's just supervised the removal of all his equipment and it's all gonna be set up in 129 and 132 as soon as we find out exactly which apartments *Sendero Luminoso*'s using. I want to know exactly what each member of *Sendero Luminoso*'s doing when the time comes to take them. Flynn . . ."

"Yes sir."

"Get busy drawing up the search warrants and eavesdropping warrants. Just leave the apartment numbers blank. We'll fill that in later."

"It's already being done," Flynn said. "I'll have the warrants signed an hour after we find out which apartments they're in."

Just then Captain Delaney, the commanding officer of the 25th Precinct, walked into the room. "There's seven of them," he told

Brunette. "One of my cops knows Hector Santos, the owner of Hector's Luncheonette. Turns out that *Sendero Luminoso*'s been his best customers for the past week. Hector couldn't help but notice them. They phone in an order twice a day and the guy who picked up tonight is the one who usually picks it up. This morning it was seven orders of sausage and eggs. Tonight it was eight orders of hamburgers and fries. I figure the extra order's for Rodrigo."

Delaney's message wasn't good news. "Seven," Brunette said. "That's a lot of bad guys to deal with at one time."

There was a knock at the door and Captain Keller from Emergency Service and Lieutenant Crosby from the Technical Assistance Response Unit came in and stood along the wall. There wasn't enough room at the conference table for them to sit down. McKenna and Pacella began to feel uncomfortable sitting there.

Brunette noticed and said, "Go out and help Cisco. He's trying to find out which apartments they're using. We're making our plans here on the assumption that you're gonna find out where they are, so get to it."

Cisco showed them what he had been doing. He had already come up with two newspaper advertisements that had listed apartments available in 129 and 132 East 117th Street. An apartment in 132 East 117th Street had been advertised as available in *El Diario,* one of New York's Spanish language newspapers, on June 26 and June 27. The ad described the apartment as a two-bedroom and gave a telephone number to call for further information. Cisco found that the June 27, 28, and 29 issues of *El Diario* also listed an available apartment at 129 East 117th Street, described as a one-bedroom ready for immediate occupancy, with a telephone number to call.

"I just called the number for 132," Cisco said. "Turned out to be the super's number. He told me he rented the apartment on June 27. I told him who I was and then I said that the people who'd rented the apartment are wanted for murder. I asked him to come here, but he sounded scared. Then I told him there might be a reward and he said he'd be here in ten minutes."

"Make that five minutes," Gaspar yelled over to them, pointing to one of his monitors. A short Hispanic man who looked to be about fifty years old was leaving 132 East 117th Street. He disappeared from the screen when he made a right and started walking toward Lexington Avenue.

Cisco left to go to the front of the station house to wait for the super and bring him up to the squad office. A couple of minutes later they came in. McKenna didn't know what Cisco had told him, but they seemed to be the best of friends. Cisco introduced the super, Julio Ramirez, to McKenna and Pacella. Cisco did everything that he could to make Ramirez feel at home. He poured him a cup of coffee and sat him down at his own desk, but the super still looked uneasy.

"I'm worried about all this," Ramirez said. "What if they find out I'm talking to the police?"

"Nothing to worry about," Cisco said. "We'll protect you and they'll never find out anyway. We're watching your building twenty-four hours a day."

Cisco showed Ramirez the monitor that covered the front of his building. Ramirez seemed to be impressed and said, "I'll help as much as I can. What about the reward? How much is it?"

"Depends on exactly how much help you give us," Cisco said. "What apartment are they in?"

"Second floor, front."

"Tel us how you rented it," McKenna said.

"The building owner ran an ad in *El Diario* on June 26 and 27. The first day a woman came to see the apartment. She liked it and she rented it."

"What's her name?" McKenna asked.

"Miriam Salazar."

"How much was it?" Pacella asked.

"Four hundred dollars. She gave me one month's rent and two months' security in cash."

"How about a tip?" McKenna asked.

"Two hundred dollars," Ramirez answered sheepishly.

McKenna showed Ramirez a photo of Isabela Mendosa.

"That's her," Ramirez said.

"Did she show you any ID?" McKenna asked.

"Yes sir. A Florida driver's license."

"When did she move in?" Pacella asked.

"The next day. Some of her friends helped her. She didn't have a lot of furniture. She told me the rest of her furniture would be arriving from Florida in a couple of weeks."

"How many people live there?" McKenna asked.

"I don't know. A lot, but they're quiet and nobody else in the building's complaining, so why should I?"

At McKenna's request, Ramirez drew a floor plan of the apartment. There were two apartments on each floor, and Isabela had rented the front unit. There was a living room, two bedrooms, a kitchen, and a bathroom. The living room and the kitchen faced the street.

"How about the apartments around them. Any of them empty?" McKenna asked.

"No, Every apartment in the building is occupied."

"You know everybody in the building?" Pacella asked.

"Of course. I been the super for sixteen years."

"You got all their phone numbers?" Cisco asked.

"Everybody except for Salazar. She's got a phone, but I didn't get the number yet."

"How do you know she's got a phone?" Pacella said.

"I had to let the telephone man into the basement when she had the phone put in right after she moved in."

"You been in the apartment since she moved in?" McKenna asked.

"No, sir."

"Where's your apartment?"

"First floor. Right under theirs."

"Do you know the super of 129 East 117th Street?"

"Yes, sir. That's Roberto Flores. He's a good friend of mine. He's a good man."

At Cisco's request, Ramirez called Roberto Flores and asked him to come to the station house immediately, without telling a soul. Flores wanted to know more, but when Ramirez told him that it was a matter of life and death, Flores said that he would be right there. Ten minutes later, Roberto Flores was in the task force office.

McKenna sat Flores down and started to question him about the apartment that was listed in *El Diario.* "Where is the apartment?" he asked.

"Third floor, front."

"Who'd you rent it to?"

"Raoul Camarena."

McKenna showed Flores a picture of Carlos Mendosa.

"That's Raoul," Flores said.

"When did you rent it?"

"June twenty-seventh, I think. It was the first day it was advertised."

"When did he move in?"

"Last week. Him and a friend wanted to fix the place up before they moved in. They brought in some Sheetrock and lumber and worked on the place for a couple of days."

"What happened when they moved in?"

"They showed up with a truck and three friends and moved their furniture in."

"Any large pieces of furniture?"

"Yeah. A big, heavy, wood closet. They had a lot of trouble carrying it up to the third floor. It took all four of them."

"They have a phone?"

"I don't think so."

"Anything suspicious about them?" McKenna asked.

"Just one thing. A couple of days before they moved in Raoul and some friends came in a truck and brought about twenty new mattresses up to his apartment. But I didn't ask him about it."

"How much did they give you for the apartment?"

"One month's rent and two months' security."

"In cash?"

"Yes, sir."

"How about a tip?"

"Two hundred."

"Did Raoul show you any ID?"

"He showed me a Florida driver's license."

McKenna showed Flores a picture of Alfonso Mendosa. "Do you know him?"

"I see him around the building sometimes. He's a friend of Raoul."

McKenna asked Flores to draw a diagram of the layout of the apartment. The apartment had one bedroom, a bathroom, and a living room and kitchen which faced the street. The surrounding apartments were occupied.

Both supers told McKenna that they would give him the keys to the front doors of their buildings. McKenna asked them about keys to the apartments being used by *Sendero Luminoso*. They did have keys for the apartments, but Flores said that Raoul had installed new locks. Ramirez wasn't sure if Miriam had put new locks on her apartment.

McKenna decided that it was time to inform Brunette. He told the super, "The chief of detectives is probably gonna want to talk to you. Wait here for a couple of minutes."

McKenna and Pacella were ready to go into Tavlin's office when Gaspar called them over to his monitors. He had been listening attentively to the interview of the two supers.

All four monitors were now on. Gaspar pointed to number three and said, "I got one of the cameras in the van focused on the second-floor windows of 132."

McKenna looked at the monitor. The windows of the apartment were open and he could see a man looking from a window to the street below. Gaspar used one of the joy sticks to zoom in. It was Alfonso Mendosa. Gaspar had focused the other camera in the surveillance van on the third-floor windows of 129 East 117th Street. The windows were open, but nobody was visible.

These guys are still on their toes, McKenna thought. They had lost two men and they didn't want to lose anymore. McKenna was happy to see Alfonso Mendosa as the lookout at the moment. The Bosses in their organization have to pull guard duty, McKenna thought. They must be stretched pretty thin on personnel. It was a good sign.

McKenna and Pacella went into Tavlin's office to report, leaving Cisco to entertain both supers. They both had the feeling that they were interrupting something. Brunette was pacing and all of the other Bosses had pads in front of them on the conference table, taking notes on whatever Brunette was telling them. "You find out which apartments they're in?" Brunette asked.

"Yes, sir," McKenna answered.

"Good," Brunette said, indicating with his hand that McKenna should stand at the head of the conference table. "Tell us what you've got so we can put our heads together and try to come up with the best plan."

Consulting his notes, McKenna told the bosses everything he had learned. Then he passed around the layout of the *Sendero Luminoso* apartments that the super had drawn. Nobody looked happy, including Brunette.

"We can assume that Rodrigo is being held in 129," Brunette said. "He probably arrived last week in that closet that took four men to drag up the stairs. Also, 129 is the building where all those mattresses were delivered, and in the photo of Rodrigo that McKenna took from Carlos's body there were mattresses in the background. Rodrigo's probably being guarded by one or two of these guys at a time, since that was a small bag of dinners that went to 129 tonight after the crew in 132 took their share. Anybody disagree with that?"

Does anybody want to be in uniform? Then just disagree with the chief of detectives was the universal thought passing through the room. Nobody disagreed.

Then Brunette focused on Crosby, who was still studying the apartment layouts. "Can you do the same wonderful things in these two apartments that your men did at the Intercontinental Hotel?" Brunette asked Crosby.

"If I can get my people into the building, they can have the equipment installed by morning. But I'll need the apartment above them and, ideally, the apartment next to them vacant. And we'll have to have access to the basement of 132 to do the phones right."

Crosby knew how to make Brunette happy. "That's what I was hoping you'd say," Brunette said. "We'll get those apartments empty for you." He turned to McKenna and asked, "What kind of people are these two supers, Brian?"

"I think they're both reliable, good, hardworking people. We can probably trust them. We've sort of promised them some kind of reward for their help."

Brunette thought this over. "Rewards are no problem. We don't have a budget on this case, and I'm not worried. We'll give them something. We need these two. A lot is going to depend on how much help they give us. Bring them in and let's talk to them."

Pacella went to the door and called Ramirez and Flores. Brunette went right over to them and introduced himself. The supers both appeared nervous and in a state of shock. Brunette introduced them to each person at the table, explaining the title and job of each of the bosses. Then Brunette sat Ramirez in his chair and brought Tavlin's chair from behind the desk and sat Flores down. Ramirez and Flores both looked very uncomfortable sitting at the head of the table. McKenna got ready for the show. He had seen the master in action before. All of a sudden, he had an insatiable urge for some popcorn.

Brunette started pacing as he spoke. "Mr. Ramirez and Mr. Flores, we need your help. Through no fault of your own, you both rented apartments to the most dangerous group of killers in the country. They've probably killed hundreds of people, and if we don't get them, they're going to kill hundreds more. We're gonna get them, but it's gonna be very dangerous. We need you two gentlemen to help us so that none of your friends and neighbors gets killed by them. Are you ready to help us?"

Flores and Ramirez sat glued in their chairs, stupefied. Finally Ramirez asked, "They've killed hundreds?"

"Hundreds," Brunette replied instantly. "They could kill you and your family today and not remember it next week. We've got to get them. Without your help, it's possible that many more innocent people will be killed. Will you help us?"

"I'll help," Flores answered.

"Me too," Ramirez said a second later.

"Good," Brunette said. "You look like the kind of men we can count on. I give you my promise that any help you give us will be kept strictly confidential. Now, Detective Sanchez mentioned something about a reward, didn't he?"

"He said something," Ramirez answered.

"It's five thousand dollars if you're able to help us do whatever needs to be done," Brunette said.

Flynn dropped his pen on the floor. Every other Boss in the room knew that if Flynn were the chief of detectives, Flores and Ramirez would be working for minimum wage on this one. Flynn knew that when the New York City Police Department talked about rewards, they were usually talking about hundreds of dollars, not thousands. But Brunette didn't miss a beat. "That's five thousand each," he said. McKenna thought that Flynn was about to have a seizure of some kind. But Brunette had just created two highly dedicated counter-revolutionaries. Special Agent Julio Ramirez and Special Agent Roberto Flores were completely at his disposal.

"I want the apartments all around the apartments that you gentlemen rented to these killers to be empty in a few hours. And I want you to show us how to get my men into those apartments tonight without the killers finding out. You know your tenants and you know your buildings, so give me some ideas."

Flores and Ramirez were at a loss for words, but then greed took over, and in ten minutes they had given Brunette all the ideas he needed.

310

July 12   11:00 p.m.

McKenna knew that he was about to attend the most important meeting in his twenty-three years in the Job, and possibly the strangest in the recent history of the New York City Police Department. They were in Tavlin's office again, and Brunette had just asked Tavlin, Crosby, and Flynn to leave the room and send in Sal Catalfumo and Cisco Sanchez. The plans had been made and the soldiers were about to receive their instructions. Tavlin, Crosby, and Flynn had already guessed the subject of the meeting, and they weren't at all unhappy to leave.

Captain Sheeran sat next to McKenna and Captain Keller was across the conference table, next to Pacella. Brunette leaned on Tavlin's desk, looking out the window in the direction of East 117th Street. Catalfumo and Cisco came in and closed the door behind them. They didn't look at all surprised by the summons from the chief. They sat down at the table and everyone waited while Brunette collected his thoughts. It was time to put the cards on the table, so all the players would know the score.

McKenna liked the company he found himself in. He knew each man at the table; each was someone he had grown to respect and trust. There were no jokers in this game. Brunette had chosen his people well.

Brunette turned and took silent measure of each person seated at the table. He appeared satisfied and made his decision. The dealer was ready and the cards were coming.

"Not one person in this room is here by accident," he began. "I know and trust you all. And you all have one thing in common. You've all been tested and passed the test. You've all fired your guns in the line of duty and won. You've all taken a human life while acting in the interests of the citizens of this city. Tomorrow you're going to do it again. For sure."

While Brunette paused to collect his thoughts, McKenna saw that not one man in the room looked surprised at the news. But then Brunette astonished even McKenna. He sat down, leaned back in his chair, and closed his eyes. Brunette seemed to be collapsing under the weight of the decision that both of them had already made two days ago. But McKenna's astonishment lasted for only an instant. Then he remembered that this was Brunette, the master showman, waiting for some audience participation while he appeared to be struggling with his conscience. The uncomfortable silence stretched on for a minute before Keller stood up and took the bait.

"Chief, we all know what has to be done," he said.

Keller was perfect, McKenna thought. Brunette passed him the deck.

"It's as plain as the nose on my face, Chief. They're a disease and a blight that's worked its way into this country and they must be eliminated so no more people who are lawfully in the United States are tortured and killed by them."

Keller thought he had made his point clearly enough and he sat down. But Brunette wasn't through with him. "Eliminated?" he asked.

Keller answered so easily that Brunette might have just asked him what time it was. "Each and every one of them on East 117th Street has to be killed. If we simply capture them instead of killing them, other members of their group are going to take some Americans somewhere in the world as hostages to obtain the release of their friends resting in our jails in New York. Then they're going to start killing these innocent Americans while our politicians and newspaper columnists wonder what to do. This would all happen if I didn't have the courage to pull the trigger when the opportunity presented itself. I know I'm right, and I don't wanna have to live the rest of my life with those dead Americans on my conscience. So, speaking only for myself, I would kill them all on a Sunday morning after confession and before Holy Communion, and not worry at all about my immortal soul. You don't have to report to God every time you step on a cockroach. I figure that's why He gave me size fourteen feet. He knows I'm bound to step on a few cockroaches in my lifetime. And these people are cockroaches. So if you don't want them killed, don't send me in after them."

Keller sat back in his chair. He had said all he was going to say. Nobody in the room raised any objections.

McKenna found himself admiring Keller's style. Clear, concise, and to the point, he thought. To the uninformed mind, it might appear that Keller should be institutionalized and locked in his room at night. But for tomorrow, Keller was the perfect captain of police for the job. I want this guy in my foxhole, McKenna thought.

"Anybody disagree?" Brunette asked. Nobody said a word. It was time to toss another chestnut into the fire. "Sal, suppose they want to surrender?" he asked Catalfumo.

"Same scenario, Chief. I think that we still have to kill them."

"Cisco, suppose that they're sleeping when we get to them?"

"Chief, it's got to be easier to kill them when they're sleeping. I hope they're all sleeping when we get to them."

"Pacella, suppose you have to shoot an unarmed woman who is a member of the group?"

"Bang!"

"Captain Sheeran, say that you're in charge of the assault on their apartments. *Sendero Luminoso* discovers what we're up to and they offer to exchange their hostage for their freedom."

"They've killed before and they'll kill again, if we let them get away. We still go in."

McKenna was starting to enjoy the meeting as Brunette forced each one to expose his soul and dunked him in the barrel. He was having so much fun that he was actually surprised when his turn came.

"Brian, suppose one of them is holding a gun to Rodrigo's head when you get to them? Do you shoot and take a chance on the hostage being killed, after all the trouble that we've been through to save him? Remember, the press will chew us up if you do."

Why do I always get the hard questions? McKenna thought. He thought about it until he could arrive at only one conclusion. "I guess I'd just have to let the press have some fun with us. That's what we have all those personalities in Public Information for. I shoot."

The air in the room couldn't have been clearer. Then Brunette made it pristine with the good news. He said, "We're not alone in our outlook on the situation we're in. This decision of ours, which I anticipated, has aleady been unofficially reviewed at the highest levels of government, and I've extracted some promises and assurances from the politicians that we're going to have to deal with after this is over."

McKenna wondered who Brunette meant by the "highest" levels of government. Did he mean the president? The governor? The

313

mayor? Who aleady knew what the seven people in this room had just decided to do tomorrow, and who had agreed to bend the rules in their favor? Brunette didn't spell that out as he continued.

"I'm assured that there will be no federal grand jury investigation into our actions tomorrow. Naturally, there has to be a county grand jury investigation into any deaths caused by the police, but that investigation will be perfunctory. The DA won't be seeking any indictments, and we all now that the DA runs the grand jury. I've also talked to the police commissioner about an idea that's been on my mind, and I've gotten him to agree with me. Before this is over, we're going to take some pages from some other good books. We're going to do things the way the British, the Germans, and the Italians do whenever their police deal with terrorists. No member of this department involved in the action tomorrow is going to be identified by name or rank. Not to the grand jury and not to the press. You're all just going to be numbers in the reports, and only the highest-ranking members of the department will know who belongs to what number. *Sendero Luminoso*'s last adventure with Detective McKenna pointed out that we've been doing something wrong. I don't want any man in this room having to worry for the rest of his life about his own safety and the safety of his family because he did his job and, as a result, caused the deaths of some terrorists. They're not gonna find out who you are, and you're not gonna tell them. The only person who's going to be giving any interviews to the press tomorrow is me, and that's the way it's going to be."

That's the way it should be, McKenna thought. But I don't see how that's the way it's gonna be. Not in this department, where leaks to the press are made as a matter of course and where every detective numbers at least one reporter among his good friends. And not with the cops on this job, who all have scrapbooks containing every press photo of them ever printed, along with every line of copy in every story in which their name is ever mentioned. That's one traditional police practice that'll be almost impossible to break. And besides, how are cops gonna get medals and promotions if nobody knows who they are? Good idea, Ray. But impossible.

Brunette had been reading McKenna's mind and the thoughts of every other man in the room. "We're real serious about this," he said. "The police commissioner is working on some revisions to the *Patrol Guide* and *Detective Guide,* which will be issued sometime this week. These revisions will make unauthorized disclosure of the identity of any member of this department involved in a counterterrorist operation a dismissible offense. It'll be right up there with bank robbery and raping your mother. Anybody gets caught whispering a name to his friends in the Fourth Estate, he's fired."

314

I guess I was wrong, McKenna thought. I forgot and violated the First Rule—never underestimate Brunette.

"Now it might have crossed your minds somewhere that, if nobody knows who you are, then nobody can get any promotions and pretty medals out of this. But, don't worry, I know who you are, and I won't forget. So I want everyone making their novenas and prayers for my continued good health, and I'll try to make everybody as happy as I can. Everybody except for you, Pacella."

Everyone followed Brunette's gaze. "You and I have gone about as far as we can go in this department. And we're both already exactly where we want to be and doing exactly what we want to do. We both already have our reward."

No doubt about it, McKenna thought. Tommy's a First-Grade detective. He's gone as far as he can go in his chosen profession. He's right up there with the Pope and the president. And Ray's the chief of detectives of the New York City Police Department. Who would want to be more than that? Not Ray, I know.

Brunette continued. "I've done my homework and got promises from everyone I could think of to protect us if we can do what has to be done tomorrow. But let's remember, it's just politicians that I've been talking to, and just politicians' promises that I've gotten. They're not people like yourselves. But I've done everything that I can. Now it's time to make a decision. Are we together in this?"

Each man nodded his assent. "I thought so," Brunette said. "Now, I don't think that I even have to say this, but I'm going to anyway. Strictly interpreting federal and state statutes, we've all just conspired to commit murder. If we're successful tomorrow, each or all of you may do it. We're all agreed that these'll be justifiable homicides, but there'll be a lot of people in the press second-guessing us. For reasons that must be obvious to all of you, I can't go with you on the actual assault. But you all should know that I'm here to back you up. Anybody have anything else to say while we're on this subject?"

"Let's all agree that this meeting never happened and that we'll never mention this again to anyone or even talk about it among ourselves," Sheeran said.

"Agreed?" Brunette asked. The motion was carried unanimously.

"Good," Brunette said. "I want to take this opportunity to invite each of you to a party that I intend to throw in your honor tomorrow. This is an official invitation from the chief of detectives and, I'm sure you all realize, it'll be in your best interests to make sure that you attend. I'll accept no excuses. So if any of you get killed or injured tomorrow so that you can't come to my party, I'll be as mad as hell at you. Keep that in mind as you go about your work tonight and tomorrow. Be careful. I want every one of you to be at the party, partly because I like the sound of it. The Magnificent Seven. It has a ring to it. Much better than the Stupendous Six or the Fabulous Five. So don't disappoint me. I want us all there. Now, to the next order of business. Pacella, ask Inspector Tavlin, Captain Flynn, and Lieutenant Crosby to rejoin us."

Pacella got up and left the office. A minute later he came back in, followed by Tavlin, Flynn, and Crosby. The only chair available at the conference table was the one that Pacella had just vacated. There was a moment of discomfort while everyone stared at the empty chair. Tavlin unexpectedly resolved the issue when he said, "Please sit down, Tommy. I have a feeling that you're going to be working much harder than any of us tonight."

Pacella self-consciously took the seat while the three Bosses aligned themselves along the wall. McKenna was sure that New York City Police Department history had just been made in the room. Three Bosses were standing while four detectives were sitting. Brunette didn't seem to notice and got right to business. "Steve, how are we making out with the telephone company?" he asked Tavlin.

"They're giving us everything we want," Tavlin answered. "They're ready to cut off service to each phone in both buildings, as soon as we give them the word. And they'll turn them back on whenever we want. The phone company just wants a personal assurance from you that they'll be covered on any legal problems that they might get out of this. As far as Isabela's phone is concerned, I have a man putting a wire on the telephone that she had installed in 132 and the telephone company is going to keep their phone on. We got lucky on that one. The junction box for the whole block is in a basement on East 118th Street. There's been no telephone service installed in the apartment they're using in 129, so we only have one wire to put in."

Brunette turned to Flynn and asked, "What are the legal ramifications of shutting off the phone service to the tenants in both buildings?"

"I don't think it's ever been done before, but I think it's probably illegal," Flynn answered. "They're all paying customers and, technically, we're interfering with their First Amendment rights when we cut off their phone service. I've talked to the city corporation counsel and he assures me that the city will defend the telephone company and provide reimbursement for any damages that they may incur as a result of any future legal action on the part of the tenants. But, honestly speaking, I can't see it coming to that."

"OK," Brunette said. "The phones go off. We have to let the tenants know we're coming and I don't want them talking to each other or calling the press. Give me a phone number of somebody in the phone company who I can talk to later and I'll make it easy for them. Next order of business. Lieutenant Crosby, what've we got on their communications?"

Crosby was ready. "We've been scanning the block for radio transmissions and we just got their frequency. They're communicating between the two apartments at 135.117 megahertz. Their signal is strong, about six watts, and it probably has an effective range of about ten miles in the city. Fifteen minutes ago we monitored a transmission in Spanish that definitely came from the block. One party said, in effect, that everything was fine and that the dog was still sleeping. The other party acknowledged and told the first party to stay awake. Now that we've got the frequency, I've had both sides of the block triangulated with locating receivers. The next time they exchange messages, I'll be able to tell you which side of the block is saying what. Also, we can jam their transmissions any time you want."

Brunette seemed satisfied with Crosby's answers. "Lieutenant, when I submit the Detective Bureau budget next year, remind me to put you in for some new toys. You can get a little crazier than usual with your requisitions. You got enough equipment to wire up both apartments?"

"Get my men in there, and by tomorrow I'll be able to tell you which one of them is farting."

"How many men do you need for each building?"

"Two will do."

"Are they ready for some excitement?"

"They were good detectives long before I picked them up for my unit, Chief. They remember how to play."

"I'm sure they do. Now, let's get to tactics. I think we all agree that the ideal situation would be for us to empty every apartment around them and get our people in those apartments without *Sendero Luminoso* knowing that they're there. Then Crosby's men would set up their equipment in the empty apartments so we can monitor them, know where each and every one of them is, know the weapons they have, and know what they're saying to each other. Of course, we would also expect to find out exactly where they're keeping Rodrigo. Then, once we have all this information, we pick up the optimal moment to hit them with a heavily armed force, keeping our casualties to a minimum and completely avoiding the possibility of any civilian casualties. Have I missed anything?"

Just one thing, McKenna thought. When did this job get phasers, transporters, and tri-corders? This sounds like a mission for the *Enterprise*. But nobody said that the chief of detectives had missed anything.

"With the help of Mr. Ramirez and Mr. Flores, I think we can pull it off," Brunette continued. "They've been on the block for a long time and they know everybody. They're going to be our heroes."

Brunette outlined his plan. The *Sendero Luminoso* lookout in the window of 132 East 117th Street had the block covered, and the police couldn't move on the block without making them suspicious. But the lookout couldn't see what was happening on Lexington Avenue. One thirty-two was six buildings from the corner of Lexington Avenue and 129 was seven. All of the tenement buildings on Lexington Avenue and East 117th Street were the same height—five stories. And they were all conneced. Ramirez and Flores knew the supers of some buildings on Lexington Avenue on both sides of East 117th Street. They could get the keys to the front doors of these buildings. Then it would be possible to get police into the buildings on Lexington Avenue without the lookout seeing them. The police teams could go to the roofs of the buildings on Lexington Avenue and walk across until they were standing on top of 129 and 132. Ramirez and Flores would unlock the roof doors to their buildings. According to the plan, the police teams could get into 129 and 132 without *Sendero Luminoso*'s knowing.

Then Brunette explained how he would evacuate the tenants from the building and put his men in their apartments. The supers would call each of their tenants in both buildings. They would follow a script that he would prepare, telling the tennats that terrorists were in the building and that these terrorists were planning to take over the building tomorrow and hold all the tenants as hostages. Then the supers were to tell their tenants that their lives were in danger, that the police were coming to rescue them, and that they shouldn't talk to anyone or leave their apartments until they received further instructions. The supers would say that telephone service was going to be cut off until later on that evening, but that the tenants should be ready to leave when their telephones rang again. When the tenants were evacuated from their apartments, they would all be taken to some nice hotel, courtesy of the city, until their apartments were ready for occupancy again.

Brunette said, "I don't feel too bad about having the supers stretch the truth to their tenants, since it might be exactly what *Sendero Luminoso* plans to do in the event of a police attack. I don't want the tenants evacuated by walking past *Sendero Luminoso*'s apartment. Everyone moving out at once would certainly make them suspicious. It's better that the tenants wait in their apartments for us to take them out over the roof. The tenants in the apartments on the same floor as the *Sendero Luminoso* apartments will be taken out by the back fire escapes. We'll cut each tenant's telephone service as soon as their super completes his call to them and we'll restore it to tell them when it's time to move out. That way they'll be ready to go without causing a fuss."

Then Brunette covered his plan for the actual assault.

"It's imperative that both apartments be hit at exactly the same time to keep them from killing Rodrigo. There'll be two separate assault teams. Captain Keller will command one and Captain Sheeran will command the other. Problem number one is the lookout. He has to be eliminated right before the assault to give our units on the ground some time to clear civilians from the street. Problem number two—we can only hit them when every member of the group is in the apartments. I don't want any of them getting away. Problem number three is the press. The press and every other member of the department not involved in the operation will be kept in the dark until it's all over."

Then Brunette asked Keller, "What kind of manpower can Emergency Service supply for the assault team?"

Keller had already given it some thought. "Let's see," he said. "That's two men from TARU in each team, and two of your detectives in each team. I figure that you'll need five of my men. Two for 132 and three for 129. The third man assigned to 129 will be assigned to take out the lookout in the window of 132 with a sniper rifle. Counting myself and Captain Sheeran, that'll make seven men in one team and eight men in the other. I see no point in involving the whole job in this."

McKenna translated Keller's manpower assessment into "Let's keep the witnesses to a minimum." McKenna could see that Brunette agreed with Keller's arithmetic. "Do you know which of your men you're gonna use?" Brunette asked.

"Sure, Chief. I know exactly which five I'll use. They're just my ordinary, run-of-the-mill, highly experienced, highly trained, highly motivated Marine combat veterans who worship the ground I walk on and who owe their very existence to me. I can personally vouch for their high character and low moral fiber because, in every incident that I've been involved in with them over the years, they've always had to ask me what they saw before they could remember a thing. Will they be OK?"

Even Brunette had to laugh. If Keller's serious, he's certifiable, McKenna thought.

"I'm impressed. But are you sure you haven't let any former paratroopers slip into your group?" Brunette asked Keller. "They're insidious, you know."

"I wouldn't allow it, Chief. We have to maintain our high standards, you know. I know that these paratroopers are always trying to hang around with the real men, so I have to stay on top of these things."

McKenna realized that Keller had hit upon the common denominator for the men whom Brunette had chosen for his Magnificent Seven. They must all have been in the Marine Corps. He knew that Brunette was a former Marine, Keller must've been, and Pacella, Catalfumo, and Cisco had all done their time. The only one he wasn't sure of was Sheeran, but he had to be. After all, he was a relatively young captain and he was assigned to the Detective Bureau. And the Marine Corps is and always had been the most basic hook in this job.

"Anything I missed?" Brunette asked.

"Just the manpower details on the street on who does what when the time comes," Tavlin said.

"You, me, and Delaney will go over the details, so you can get Delaney back up here. I'll let Keller and Sheeran plan with their men exactly what they're going to do when the time comes to hit these places. I'm sure they're going to have a lot to talk about and I don't want to interfere with good men doing a hard job. They'll come up with the right plan. Now I'm going to set it up with the telephone company and then Cisco and McKenna can make sure the supers follow my script when they talk to their tenants. Anything else?"

There was nothing else.

July 13   3:15 a.m.

Finally it looked like the couple had had enough romance for one night. McKenna watched them through his night-vision binoculars as they packed up their blanket, cooler, and radio for the second time. For the past two hours he had felt a little guilty as he had watched them drinking wine on the roof during their infrequent intermissions from lovemaking. The binoculars were so good that it was like he was hiding in the closet of their bedroom, although the two lovers were seven roofs down the row of tenements from where the police were hiding. Through the binoculars, McKenna had enjoyed an X-rated movie in which all the characters were green, performing in an all-green world for the illicit gratification of the degenerate members of the New York City Police Department.

Now I understand why the Hispanic population of this city is growing geometrically, McKenna thought. These two are good.

McKenna lowered the binoculars and noticed that he was the only one to take a break from the high-quality voyeur session that the taxpayers were giving them. The other six men in the team still had their binoculars glued to their eyes as they lay on the tar roof. "It looks like they're leaving, Captain," McKenna said in a whisper.

Keller didn't budge. "That's what we thought the last time," he whispered back as he watched the couple through his binoculars. "These two should be in movies. But I'll tell you one thing. I swear, if they jump onto that blanket again, I'm going to run over and find out about their diets. They must eat things that the Irish haven't even heard of to make them fuck like that. Whatever it is they're eating, we'll sell it in jars and all get rich."

Sometimes Keller made a lot of sense, McKenna thought as they all watched the couple finish packing again. The last time, they had packed up and made it all the way to the roof door when the romantic urge had hit the girl again. She had whispered something in her boyfriend's ear and pulled him away from the door. The cops hiding on the roof were amazed when the show resumed. It was no problem for the boyfriend. He just spread the blanket on the roof again, turned the radio back on, took another swig of wine, and was ready for action for the fourth time since the cops had sneaked onto the roof at a little after one o'clock.

Until the couple had come on to the roof, everything had been going according to plan. The two supers, Ramirez and Flores, had gotten the keys to the front doors of the two buildings located on Lexington Avenue on opposite sides of East 117th Street, just like they had said they would. Shortly before one o'clock, McKenna's team had parked their old van near the corner of Lexington Avenue and East 117th Street. The seven members of the team, all in dirty civilian clothes, simply entered the corner building and carried their three trunks of equipment to the roof. Nobody on the street had given them a second look, since midnight was the preferred moving time in Spanish Harlem, usually practiced by a family when they were three months overdue on the rent.

By one fifteen Pacella's team had reached the roof of the corner building on the opposite side of East 117th Street. Captain Sheeran, the team supervisor across the street, had reported to Keller that there were no problems. Hardcass, watching the monitors in the task force office, told Keller over the radio that everything looked good. He said that the *Sendero Luminoso* lookout in the window of 132 East 117th Street couldn't see what was happening on Lexington Avenue and hadn't moved from his position. Everything had been "Go" until the lovers came onto the roof and spread their blanket, catching McKenna's team by surprise. They had all been forced to drop to the roof and wait behind one of the parapets that separated the roof of each building in the row.

While McKenna's team waited, Cisco had been thoroughly amusing everybody with his assumed air of Hispanic sexual superiority. Everybody but McKenna. He was starting to drive McKenna crazy. It's not him, McKenna kept telling himself. It's me. He knew that he resented Cisco's presence on his team only because he was Cisco, not Pacella. Ray had come up with the crazy idea that two partners as close as he and Pacella should not work together on a job as dangerous as this one. "It might impair your judgment and ability to act if one of you gets wounded or killed during the mission," Ray had said.

Cisco didn't seem to notice McKenna's attitude. He just kept chattering on and on as they watched the acrobatics and contortions of the young Spanish couple. It was his duty to explain to the cold-blooded gringos the mechanics and complexities of the couple's romantic feats. He had originally predicted that the couple would be on the roof until two thirty. "We're not like you folks," he told them. "We always go at least three times, or we don't bother." But number four had caught even Cisco by surprise, and placed him squarely in the boyfriend's secret fan club. McKenna had already been in the club for about an hour.

The lovers reached the roof door for the second time. Cisco rolled over and whispered into McKenna's ear, "This must be it. I think they're out of wine, *Gracias a Dios.* Otherwise, we'd all be lying here with stiff cocks till morning."

Cisco was right. Everyone heard the roof door slam as the lovers disappeared for the night. McKenna's team lay on the roof for another five minutes, waiting for Keller's order.

Finally, Keller was satisfied that lover boy was out of ammo for the evening. "Let's get the vests and helmets on," he said.

Everybody in McKenna's team got up and stretched. Then one of the two Emergency Service police officers assigned to the team opened one of the trunks they had carried to the roof and began handing out the heavy flak vests and steel helmets. McKenna looked at the roof across East 117th Street and saw Pacella standing in the middle of his team like a giant among a tribe of pygmies. They were also putting on vests and helmets.

The flak vests were heavy, bulky, and hot. The Kevlar helmets weren't much better, but they fit nicely over the radio headset that each man wore. The headset only covered one ear, which left the other ear free to listen. McKenna thought that the headsets were a good idea because they let the team members monitor their radios without anybody else hearing the noise. To transmit, they only had to push the talk button on the mike clipped to the tops of their shirts.

Once everyone had their vests and helmets on, Keller gave the order to hand out the weaons. An Emergency Service police officer, George Landon, distributed the guns from one of the trunks. Landon and the other ES officer, Bobby Garbus, got full-automatic, .556-cal-iber Mini-14s. Pedro Gaspar and Angel Morales, the two detectives from TARU, took Remington 12-gauge pump-action shotguns. Keller, McKenna, and Cisco pulled their Glocks out of their holsters. McKenna felt very comfortable with his weapon and was glad that he didn't have to carry a shoulder weapon over the roofs and through the tenement.

"Lock and load," Keller ordered. Landon and Garbus loaded their automatic weapons with thirty-round magazines and silently slid their bolts home on a live round. Gaspar and Morales each pumped a round into the chambers of their shotguns. Across the street McKenna saw that Sheeran's team was armed and ready. Sheeran gave them a wave.

Keller said into his radio, "Assault Leader to Two-five Base. We're ready to go. Tell the supers to call their people and have them ready in two minutes."

McKenna knew that telephone service had just been restored to the tenants in 129 and 132. Ramirez and Flores were calling their tenants and telling them that the police were almost there and to get ready to let them in.

A few minutes later McKenna heard the message for Keller on his radio. "Two-five Base to Assault Leader. Everybody notified. Go get them out."

McKenna watched the roof across East 117th Street where, according to plan, Sheeran's team took up positions first. Sheeran's eight-man team started heading up East 117th Street along the rooftops, staying to the rear of the building so that they could not be seen by the *Sendero Luminoso* lookout in the second-floor window of 132 East 117th Street. Their target building, 129, was the seventh building from the corner of Lexington Avenue. The members of Sheeran's team took their time and were careful to stay to the rear of the air shafts between each building. McKenna knew from recent experience that the three trunks full of sensitive equipment they carried were very heavy, and he watched how Sheeran's team operated as they lifted the trunks over the low parapet separating the roof of each building. In ninety seconds Sheeran's team stood on the rear of the roof of 129 East 117th Street.

One of the men in Sheeran's team detached himself from the rest of the group and started crawling across the roof along the parapet to the front of the building. McKenna knew that it was Emergency Service Police Officer Johnny Pao, one of the best marksmen in the department, and that Pao was carrying a Winchester Model 70 with a scope attached. A minute later McKenna heard Pao report over his radio, "Post One to Assault Leader. I got their lookout whenever you want him. It looks like he's got no idea we're here."

The lookout also has no idea that this is his last day on earth, McKenna thought. Now it's our turn to get into position.

Keller gave the order to move. McKenna and Cisco each grabbed an end handle of one of the trunks and followed Keller, the Emergency Service officers, and the TARU detectives across the row of roofs. The only one of them not attached to a handle of one of the heavy trunks was Keller. *Sometimes it's great being the boss* was the thought that crossed the mind of every man in the team, including Keller. A minute later they reached the roof of 132, the sixth building from the corner of Lexington Avenue.

"Assault Leader to Two-five Base. We're going in now." McKenna and Cisco went to the rear of the roof and started down the fire escape while the rest of the team opened the roof door and started down the stairs. They left the trunks on the roof.

The fire escape of the old building was in reasonably good shape. McKenna and Cisco reached the rear window of the first-floor rear apartment noiselessly and without a problem. The apartment windows were open and the detectives were expected. As soon as McKenna tapped on the windowsill, he heard the whispered question from inside the apartment. *"Policia?"*

"Sí, Señora."

McKenna and Cisco quickly brought Señora Lopez and her three children to the roof. The kids were good and didn't make a sound. The roof was getting crowded. The rest of the team had already cleared all the tenants from the apartments on the third, fourth, and fifth floors and Keller was doing his best to keep everyone calm and quiet. The only apartment left to be evacuated was the second-floor rear apartment, and that was McKenna's and Cisco's job. Pao reported over the radio that the lookout was still standing in the window. So far, so good. McKenna followed Cisco back down the fire escape.

They had reached only the fifth floor when Cisco stopped short. "There's somebody below us."

McKenna strained his eyes to see. Cisco was right. There was movement. Somebody was on the fire escape two floors below them. The movement stopped. McKenna figured that whoever was on the fire escape had seen them.

"Only one way to go," McKenna said to Cisco.

They both resumed their descent. The person below them didn't move. When the detectives got closer, they saw two people standing on the third-floor landing of the fire escape. Two old people, a man and a woman. It was Mr. and Mrs. Llantos from the second-floor rear apartment. They were resting on the landing and had been waiting for McKenna and Cisco. They explained that they had seen them bring the Lopez family up the fire escape, and were afraid that they might have been forgotten by the police. Mrs. Llantos was very unhappy that they had taken the Lopez family first. Doesn't being a senior citizen count for anything anymore? she asked more than once as they started their trip up.

325

Getting the elderly couple to the roof proved to be quite a job. Mr. Llantos used a cane to climb the steep fire-escape steps. He tired easily, and they had to rest on each floor. Cisco suggested that they carry the old man, but he was proud and refused. Still, he didn't complain; Mrs. Llantos did the complaining for him. During the climb she managed to enlighten the two detectives on everything that was wrong with everybody in town. City workers were her specialty. It took fifteen long minutes to finally reach the roof.

Keller was waiting for them on top. He took one look at Mr. Llantos and understood the delay. It didn't matter. There was plenty of time, he said. He had already started the process of bringing the tenants in small groups across the rooftops to the building on Lexington Avenue. McKenna could see that Sheeran's team was doing the same thing across the street.

Cisco and McKenna started the trip with Mr. and Mrs. Llantos. By the time they reached the corner building, Mr. Llantos was out of steam and had to be carried by the two detectives down the stairs to the small lobby of the building on Lexington Avenue. On their way down they passed Gaspar and Morales returning to 132. When they finally reached the lobby, they found that it was empty. There was nothing to do but wait.

Unfortunately, waiting meant answering questions, and Mrs. Llantos had lots of them. McKenna had run out of answers by the time the bus pulled in front of the building. None of his answers had satisfied her. She said that a little gunfire was no reason to move. There was shooting every night in Spanish Harlem, and nobody else in the other buildings on the block had to move. Why did she have to go? she asked as McKenna opened the front door of the building and guided her and her husband toward the waiting bus.

The bus was an express, driven by Richie White. It was on a special run to the Hilton Hotel via the Two-five station house. McKenna hoped that Mrs. Llantos would enjoy her stay there, but he doubted it. He didn't think that she'd be happy in heaven, if heaven was more than three blocks from East 117th Street. McKenna was sure heaven wasn't that close and he wasn't sorry to see her leave.

McKenna and Cisco went back up the stairs and across the rooftops to 132. The only one still on the roof was Keller, holding his shoes in his hands. He said, "You're lucky you missed the job of carrying the trunks downstairs."

McKenna and Cisco didn't feel so lucky. Following Keller's lead, the two detectives took off their shoes and the three men tiptoed down three flights of stairs to the Garcia apartment, third floor, front. There were three children's bicycles chained to the banister of the third-floor landing. They looked old, but they were all freshly painted a bright shade of red. Mr. Ramirez had told them that Mrs. Garcia lived with her four children in the apartment. If there was ever a Mr. Garcia, he didn't live there.

George Landon was waiting for them at the apartment door. They all went in and Landon locked the door behind them. He remained on guard, with one eye glued to the small peephole mounted in the door.

McKenna and Cisco gave themselves a tour of the apartment. They had already seen Ramirez's layout drawing, and this place was no different than hundreds of other front tenement apartments that McKenna had been in over the past twenty-three years. Most tenement buildings in New York City were built more than a century ago and there were no awards given for innovative design. If you've seen one, you've seen them all. McKenna knew that the rear apartment would have the same basic layout, with one less bedroom.

The Garcia apartment was a railroad flat. There was no center hall, and all the rooms, with the exceptions of the kitchen and the bathroom, connected directly in a line, just like the cars on a train. The living room and a small kitchen faced East 117th Street. The bathroom was off the kitchen and right next to the entrance into the apartment. Behind the living room was the children's bedroom with two beds. Next in line came Mrs. Garcia's bedroom, holding a double bed and a crib.

Since the rear two bedrooms of every tenement do not face the street, the designers had come up with an innovation to give tenants the legal luxury of a window in every room to provide a measure of air and light—the air shaft. Although all the tenements on the block were connected in a row and presented a unified face, front and rear, the air shaft separated each building from the one next to it.

The tenement air shaft never served the purpose for which it was designed. It didn't provide very much light, except to the apartment on the top floor, and the air coming through the windows facing the air shaft was stale, at best. It usually stank. Most tenement dwellers usually nailed their air-shaft windows shut, since they were just one more way for burglars to get in.

As he looked around, McKenna was again struck by how neat Mrs. Garcia managed to keep the place. The whole apartment was freshly painted red and immaculately maintained. The furniture looked new and was covered with clear plastic. But it wasn't new, just well cared for; the plastic covers had started to yellow with age. The rug was a red shag and had been rolled up by Gaspar and Morales, who had already emptied their trunks and spread their equipment on the floor. McKenna saw that they had four television cameras, four monitors, two VCRs, many microphones of various sizes, rolls of cable, lots of tools, and a number of electronic devices that he couldn't figure out. Gaspar was busy drilling holes in Mrs. Garcia's living room floor, using a large variable-speed electric drill that made absolutely no noise. The drill bit looked about two feet long. Morales also drilled a hole in the wall next to the front door.

McKenna and Cisco had seen enough. They knew that *Sendero Luminoso* occupied an identical apartment downstairs and, as they surveyed the Garcia apartment, it became easier for them to visualize the tentative assault plan that had been drawn up by Keller and Sheeran.

They started looking for things to do and came up with nothing. The TARU men wanted no help. Magicians never show the uninitiated exactly how their tricks are accomplished. The Emergency Service men didn't seem to need them, either. Landon was peeking through the closed blinds of the living room window and Garbus now looked out the peephole of the front door. Keller sat on one of the kids' beds, drinking from a bottle of soda that he had found in the refrigerator. He seemed as comfortable as if he had lived in the apartment all his life. He had only one suggestion for them.

"You two should take a break," he said. "My men just started work at four yesterday afternoon and they're still fresh. You guys have probably been going straight for days. I'll call you when we need you. Besides, I don't want too much walking around in this apartment. I want to make sure that our pals downstairs get their sleep tonight."

Keller's idea sounded good to McKenna and Cisco. McKenna lay down on the other bed and Cisco went into Mrs. Garcia's bedroom. McKenna hadn't realized how tired he really was until he hit the bed. Then he had a hard time keeping his eyes open. He listened for a while to the radio traffic over his headset. Sheeran reported that his men had started to install their television monitors in 129, and that everything was going great. Johnny Pao said that he was moving his location from the roof of 129 to the fourth-floor front apartment of 129, and that the lookouts had just changed shifts. The new lookout was a male Hispanic, clean-shaven, about twenty-five years old. Pao said that it looked like he was wearing a bulletproof vest under his shirt.

McKenna was just about to doze off when Keller said to him, "You'd better make yourself a smaller target. Remember, right now we're only eight feet from the enemy. If they think we're up here, they're going to start shooting through their ceiling at us."

Keller had gotten McKenna thinking. He stood up, took his flak vest off, and spread it on the bed. Then he climbed on top of it and pulled himself into the fetal position. He used his Kevlar helmet for a pillow. McKenna closed his eyes and began to relax.

30

July 13   6:00 a.m.

McKenna felt the weight of a five-pound hand shaking his shoulder. "McKenna! The chief wants to talk to you!"

It was Keller. McKenna opened his eyes and sat up. Keller held a mobile phone in front of his face. He took the phone and spent a moment taking note of the changes in the apartment.

There were one-inch holes drilled everywhere in the wooden floor of the apartment. A web of cables stretched along the floor and connected different devices to a control panel set up on a table in the living room. It was Mrs. Garcia's kitchen table, and they were using a bomb blanket for a tablecloth. Four video monitors were mounted on the table, along with a host of complicated-looking electronic devices with flashing red and green lights. Gaspar sat in front of the table, watching the screens.

McKenna felt like he was in the NASA Mission Control. I'll ask him what all that stuff is later, he told himself. And when he tells me, I'll make believe that I understand.

McKenna raised the mobile phone to his face. "McKenna here, Chief."

"Listen to the tape. The number they called is a pay phone at the town dock in Fort Myers Beach. Call me back and tell me what you think. Talk to you soon, buddy." Brunette hung up.

McKenna handed the phone back to Keller and said, "The chief said that I'm to listen to the tape." I hope after I listen to it I'll have some idea what Ray's talking about, he thought.

Except for Cisco, who was still snoring in the bedroom, everyone in the apartment was looking at McKenna as Gaspar handed him a headset. Gaspar said, "Alfonso called a 415 area code telephone number at 5:29. The call lasted fifty-two seconds."

McKenna took off his radio headset and replaced it with the headset that Gaspar gave him. Gaspar pushed a button on the tape recorder and McKenna heard the sound of a touch-tone phone being dialed. The phone only rang once before someone answered. McKenna recognized Esteban Cabrera's voice. Cabrera did most of the talking. The conversation was entirely in Spanish.

Cabrera said that he would be at the Delta baggage carousel at La Guardia Airport at 1:15. He would be with another man, and this man would be picking up a yellow golf bag from the carousel. They would have two suitcases full of clothes and they expected that they would be exchanged for clothes that fit correctly. Cabrera asked Alfonso if he agreed on the sizes that they had discussed yesterday and Alfonso said he did. Alfonso told Cabrera that the man who would meet them with the clothes to be returned was named Octavio. He would be wearing a plaid sports jacket and carrying a red suitcase and a green suitcase. The smaller size clothes would be in the red suitcase. Then one of them hung up.

Gaspar shut the tape off and McKenna gave him back the headset. That's why the FBI wiretap of Cabrera's phone didn't turn up too much, he thought. He's been doing his business at the pay phone next to his dock.

Keller was waiting impatiently. "What do you make of it?" he asked.

"Our pals downstairs think that at least one of them is going to be at La Guardia airport to give a lot of money to a man I know from Florida, probably in exchange for a lot of drugs. But are any of them gonna be alive at one fifteen?"

"That's up to the chief. I know that Sheeran is pressuring him to wait till this afternoon to hit them. He's concerned about Flavio's daughter. He thinks that they're going to release her this afternoon, and he doesn't want to spoil it by hitting these guys sooner." Then Keller looked closely at McKenna and said, "But something tells me that, for some reason, the chief's waiting to hear what you have to say before he makes his decision."

Keller didn't push it. McKenna needed some time to think. Of course, he agreed with Sheeran. The later the assault, the better. Flavio's daughter had been on McKenna's mind ever since he'd found out about her kidnapping. Alfonso's promise to Flavio that his people in Peru were going to release her sometime after noon today had pushed McKenna into backing Sheeran's position. It was better to wait. Noon in Lima was 11:00 A.M. New York time. Two hours and fifteen minutes before Esteban Cabrera, aka Raoul Camarena, was scheduled to arrive in town. McKenna knew that Flavio was going to deliver Rodrigo's finger and the latest photos to the Guiterrez family before noon today, according to Alfonso's instructions. So why not wait and hit them after they released Flavio's daughter? he thought. But McKenna knew that the timing of the assault depended a lot on Rodrigo's condition and any plans for his health that *Sendero Luminoso* might have.

"Think about it for a while before you call the chief back, McKenna," Keller said. "Meanwhile, why don't you let Gaspar answer any questions you might have and show you how busy he's been. Him and Morales have been impressing me for the last couple of hours."

McKenna did have a lot of questions for Gaspar. "How'd you get the wire on their phone from here?" McKenna asked.

"I didn't do anything. Some people from my unit went to the telephone junction box somewhere on 118th Street. They disconnected Mrs. Garcia's wires and just ran a set of wires from Isabela's phone posts to Mrs. Garcia's phone posts. Then I hooked up our recorder to Mrs. Garcia's phone. So every time they pick up their phone downstairs, our recorder goes on."

Gaspar pointed at one of the video monitors and said, "They've been really busy packing up the correct sizes of 'clothes.' "

The monitor was labeled KITCHEN. There was some glare on the left side of the screen, and McKenna guessed that it came from a light bulb mounted in their ceiling downstairs, but he could still see everything in the room. The camera lens was mounted in the corner of the ceiling. There were two people in the room. Their backs were to the camera and McKenna could only see the tops of their heads.

"Alfonso and Isabela?" McKenna asked.

"In the flesh, *amigo*."

Suitcases were on the kitchen table and a duffle bag lay on the floor. One of the suitcases was open and the other one was closed. Alfonso took wrapped bundles of money from the duffle bag and placed them on the table. Isabela kept count on a piece of paper as she stacked the bundles in the open suitcase.

"They finished filling the other one about five minutes ago," Gaspar said. "Wanna hear what they're saying?" he asked, handing McKenna the headset again. "It's all being recorded, anyway."

McKenna put the headset on and Gaspar flipped a switch on his control panel. He heard the sound of the woman counting, but she was counting in French. Then she asked the man something in French and he answered in kind. Why French? McKenna thought. Maybe they didn't want the other members of the group to understand what they were saying to each other, especially how much money they're counting out. McKenna took the headset off and gave it back to Gaspar. "We got anybody up here that speaks French?" McKenna asked.

"None of us, unless Cisco does. The chief had a translator standing by at the base in case we needed him, but Keller said to forget it. Anybody that speaks French can't be trusted and doesn't belong with us up here. He said those bigmouth sissies haven't won a battle since Napoleon, and get this—he absolutely insists that Napoleon was a Guinea anyway. I don't think he plans on losing today and he's not taking any chances."

"What if Cisco speaks French?"

"Keller said he'd have to go."

How come I haven't run into this Captain Keller before this case? McKenna wondered. They must have just released him from somewhere by mistake, and they're probably looking for him right now. He thought about telling Keller that Cisco spoke French, but then decided against it. Maybe later.

Gaspar went back to his control panel and McKenna asked him to explain the rest of his toys. Gaspar assumed an air of authority, and McKenna could see that he was proud of his work. "Each of the rooms in the apartment downstairs is covered by a video monitor. Me and Morales drilled holes in our floor through to the ceiling of their apartment for the camera lenses and mikes."

"How big are the holes?" McKenna asked.

"For the mikes, we only had to drill a one-eighth-inch hole through our floor and their ceiling. The mikes are very small, but very sensitive. For the motor housings for the camera lenses, we drilled a three-quarter-inch hole in our floor. Then we drilled a three-sixteenths-inch hole in their ceiling for the lenses. The camera lenses are only one-eighth-inch wide with an eighteen-millimeter fish-eye lens. The lens housing is painted white, so that they'd never see it in the corner of their ceiling unless they knew what they were looking for and got really close to it. The problem with the group downstairs is that they do know what to look for. They're using equipment that's almost as good as ours. I'm gonna pan the camera in the kitchen toward their front door so you can see what I mean."

Gaspar moved his joy stick in front of the KITCHEN monitor and McKenna watched as the lens slowly swept across the room downstairs. When the camera stopped, McKenna could see a small camera with a video display standing on a small table next to their front door, with a cable leading from the camera into a hole in the wall. "Now go look at our front door," Gaspar said. McKenna walked over and saw that TARU had installed the same setup that *Sendero Luminoso* had on their front door. Bill Garbus was watching the monitor that showed the hallway outside. The cable leading to the camera had another pinhole lens attached to it and was mounted in a small hole in the wall.

McKenna walked back to Gaspar and said, "So *Sendero Luminoso* can see every time somebody enters the hallway outside their door?"

"If they're watching. As you can see, nobody's looking at their monitor right now. I just hope their equipment isn't as good as ours. Our monitor also beeps whenever there's any movement in the hallway, and theirs might, too. Now I'll show you how serious they are. See that small rectangular box bolted to their front door?"

It only took him a moment to recognize it. He hadn't seen one in twenty-four years, since Vietnam.

"I see it. It's a Claymore."

"That's what I think. When they see some people they don't like on their video monitor, they blow them up. It's my guess that they don't care much for visitors."

McKenna kept staring at the KITCHEN monitor. The door was an old wooden panel door, and the Claymore mine was fixed with two metal straps bolted to the door. Two wires ran from the top of the mine into the darkened living room, where McKenna knew the detonator must be. Gaspar's right, he thought. If they detonate that Claymore, nobody standing in the hallway outside has much chance of survival.

McKenna remembered the Claymore as one of the most effective killing devices that American ingenuity had ever produced. It was an electronically detonated directional mine loaded with hundreds of fragments of .32-caliber steel pellets, backed by a sizable amount of plastic explosive, all attractively packaged in the rectangular green box. Claymores were placed around the perimeters of marine defensive positions, and the wires connecting the mine to the detonator switch were run back to the position. If the enemy was in our concertina wire in front of the Claymores, one twist of the detonator turned them to mush. The .32-caliber steel exploded from the front of the Claymore in an expanding arc, slicing up anyone standing in front of it.

McKenna recalled a favorite trick of the Vietcong. Every once in a while one of them would manage to sneak through the barbed wire and turn the marines' Claymores around, so the side marked THIS SIDE TOWARD ENEMY would be facing the Marines. Then he would slip back to his lines. When the VC attacked, the marines would twist their Claymore detonators. But instead of killing the VC, they would be ripped apart by their own mines. McKenna imagined that the VC must have gotten quite a laugh every time they managed to pull that one off.

Gaspar panned the KITCHEN camera until it pointed to the refrigerator. McKenna saw two TEC-9 automatic pistols on top of the refrigerator and eight magazines of ammo. Then Gaspar panned the camera back so that it focused again on Isabela and Alfonso, who were still packing the second suitcase.

Gaspar continued his equipment demonstration. He pointed to the monitor labeled LIVING ROOM. The room was fairly dark, with some light spilling in from the kitchen. McKenna looked closer and saw the motionless lookout leaning against the window frame. He couldn't tell if the man was armed or not. But he still hadn't moved.

"Is he sleeping?" McKenna asked.

Gaspar picked up his radio and said, "Johnny, is the lookout sleeping?"

Pao answered from across the street, "Nope. He's wide awake. He just doesn't move much."

Then Gaspar gave McKenna the headset again. "Here's what's keeping him awake."

McKenna put the headsets back on and Gaspar turned up the volume in the living room. The lookout was listening to the police radio calls in the Two-five. While McKenna eavesdropped, he heard Two-five Sector David accepting an assignment of a 10-20, past robbery, at East 115th Street and Park Avenue. McKenna looked at the monitor, searching for the radio that was the source of the police transmissions. He couldn't see it. He guessed that it must be on the floor next to the lookout.

Brunette was right, McKenna thought. He had figured that they might be monitoring our transmissions. It's a good thing the frequency we're using is secret and beyond normal scanner range. Otherwise, they would've heard us while we were still on the roof.

Next Gaspar pointed to the monitor marked FRONT BEDROOM. It was almost totally dark. Gaspar flipped the switch on his control panel labeled FRONT BEDROOM MIKE. McKenna could hear the sound of heavy breathing. He guessed that there were two or three people sleeping in the room and said so.

"That's what I figured," Gaspar said. "We'll know for sure when we get some light."

Then Gaspar pointed to the screen labeled REAR BEDROOM. It was totally dark. "It's empty," Gaspar said. "It's Isabela and Alfonso's room. They put a light on in the bedroom when their alarm went off at five twenty-five. They'd been sleeping fully clothed on a mattress laid on the floor. They're living out of suitcases. They had a TEC-9 on each side of the mattress. They turned out the light and took the pistols with them when they went to the living room at five thirty to make their phone call to Florida."

So there's five or six of them downstairs and they keep their weapons close to them all the time, McKenna thought. And they've probably set up some booby traps. That's exactly what we expected, in the downstairs apartment at least. And exactly what Keller and Sheeran planned on. We can do the job on our side of the street. But our side isn't the most important side.

The plan had been made based on the theory that the life of the hostage was the primary consideration. If Rodrigo was killed during this operation, the press was going to have a great time chewing up the department and Brunette for the next week or two. But Brunette had been very candid in explaining his thoughts and feelings to the members of both assault teams before they'd left the Two-five last night. He told them that the important thing to him was that each member of the assault teams be alive at the end of their dealings with *Sendero Luminoso*. He said that he wouldn't trade ten Rodrigos for any member of the teams.

But, whatever Brunette said, Rodrigo was still the primary consideration for each man in the assault teams. Nobody wanted to see Brunette barbecued by the press.

"How's Sheeran's team making out across the street?" McKenna asked. "I haven't heard too much on the radio from them."

"That's because Sheeran doesn't do too much talking on the radio. Keller and Sheeran have been talking to each other on their mobile phones. I was just spinning some dials on my equipment while they were talking to each other, and their conversation miraculously sounded in my headset. But keep that to yourself. You know that the Bosses never want the troops to be too smart. It makes them too difficult to bullshit."

"What'd they say?" McKenna asked.

"Rodrigo's there. Sheeran's got the same setup over there that we have here. He reported that the bad guys only have one man guarding him. He's awake and heavily armed. They got a video camera at the front door, along with a Claymore strapped to the door. Same setup as here, except the detonator is mounted right on the refrigerator door. Sheeran's got a camera on Rodrigo and from what I gather, they've got him in some kind of bad shape. He's tied to a bed and wearing a straitjacket, but here's the bad news. The straitjacket is wired with a small block of plastic explosive with a radio remote detonator attached. As soon as we hit them, the first thing one of them is gonna do is hit the button on the transmitter for that detonator and make Rodrigo part of the landscape. Keller and Sheeran aren't sure what to do about that, yet. Besides, there's another hitch."

"What's that?"

"Sheeran thinks that Rodrigo knows we're here. When they drilled the mike hole in the ceiling in the room he was in, it turned out that the hole was right over his bed. They didn't know that. Then they drilled the lens hole and put the lens in. When they turned the camera on, they saw that Rodrigo was staring right at them. Apparently they keep the light on in Rodrigo's room all the time and they've got him tied down so that he's got nothing to do but stare at the ceiling. That's the only reason he saw the lens."

"Does the chief know all this?"

"Sure."

Is it good or bad that Rodrigo knows something's up? McKenna wondered. He had no answer. Just then, he saw the lookout in the living room raise a radio to his face. One of the recorders in front of Gaspar clicked on. Gaspar held up his hand while he listened through his headphones. The conversation lasted for a couple of seconds. Shortly after McKenna saw the lookout lower his radio, the tape recorder clicked off. Gaspar said, "The guy guarding Rodrigo across the street checks in with the lookout every fifteen minutes. He just reported that everything was fine and that the dog was still awake."

"What are you gonna do about their radios when we hit them?" McKenna asked.

"I'm looking forward to it," Gaspar answered. "They're using six-watt radios. We've got ten watts set to their frequency. Whatever we transmit will drown out any transmissions they might try to make. Did you see *Apocalypse Now*?"

"Sure."

"Remember the attack music the air cav played over the loud-speakers in their helicopters when they hit the VC camp?"

" 'Flight of the Valkyries'?"

"Right. I brought the tape with me. That's what they'll hear over their radios when we hit them. Remember Robert Duvall's line?"

" 'I love the smell of napalm in the morning. Smells like victory.' "

"That's the one. I only hope those characters downstairs saw the movie. That way they'll know in their final seconds that they're being blasted with some feeling by some very artistic dudes. Whatta ya think?"

"Good idea," McKenna said. We've got one more Keller prototype model here, he thought. Gaspar is another authentic bedbug. I think one Keller would've been enough.

McKenna kept watching the monitors while he thought over what he would tell Brunette. Nobody else in the apartment was doing too much of anything. Keller was stretched on the child's bed reading *Trinity* in paperback. Morales was asleep on the bed that McKenna had just left. Landon stood at the window and Garbus was in the kitchen, making some noise with some pots. McKenna thought he smelled coffee.

On the KITCHEN monitor Alfonso and Isabela had finished filling the suitcases with cash. Alfonso started making a pot of coffee and Isabela left the room carrying the two suitcases. McKenna watched her progress on the other three monitors. She walked through the living room, through the darkened front bedroom, and entered her bedroom. She left the door open and turned on the light. In the reflected light from Isabela's room, McKenna could see that there were three men sleeping on cots in the front bedroom. Two of them were sleeping on their backs holding TEC-9s across their chests. The third man seemed to be awake.

"Captain, there's three of them in the front bedroom," Gaspar said over his shoulder to Keller.

Keller put his book down and joined them at the monitors. He stared at the FRONT BEDROOM monitor for a moment and said, "All TEC-9s, thank God. Not too much penetrating power. Dumb assholes!" Then he went back to the bed and his book.

McKenna continued watching Isabela. She had placed the suitcases containing the money in a closet and opened one of the suitcases on the floor next to her mattress. She was picking out clothes, and also took some shampoo and deodorant from the suitcase. She stacked the clothes, underwear, and toiletries and left the room. Once again, McKenna watched her progress through the apartment. She had a short conversation with Alfonso and went into the bathroom, closing the door behind her.

"I knew that we should have brought an extra camera for the bathroom," Gaspar said. "That's a fine-looking woman about to take a nice hot shower."

"What'd Alfonso tell her?"

"He told her not to take too long. The coffee would be ready in five minutes."

McKenna decided that it was time to call Brunette back. He asked Keller for the mobile phone and Keller took it from his pocket without looking up from his book. McKenna dialed the office, Joe Sophia answered and then connected him to Brunette.

"How are things going up there, Brian?"

"Fine, except for the complications you already know about. But if we hit them hard enough very fast, we might be able to get Rodrigo out of this in one piece."

"What do you think of the other men on the team?"

"Top shelf."

"Was that Cabrera that they called in Florida?" Brunette asked.

"I'm certain of it. I recognized his voice right away."

"When do you think we should hit them?"

"Later on this afternoon. After they pick up the drugs and, hopefully, after they release Flavio's daughter."

"I was hoping you'd say that," Brunette said. "I've been receiving some pressure from Gene Shields. Rosa thinks that Cabrera's out fishing today. He left in his boat this morning, so his mate must've put him ashore at another dock. Which makes me wonder how often he makes these trips to New York. The Feds are very interested to see who's coming to New York with him."

"It's got to be somebody big. Isabela and Alfonso just finished loading up two suitcases with a lot of cash."

"Good," Brunette said. "The Feds also think that it'll look better for us when this is all over if there are a lot of drugs in their apartment, and I agree with them. I'm going to arrange to have them watched while they're at La Guardia. Then we'll find out what flight Cabrera's taking back. The Feds think that it'd be best to hit them while Cabrera's plane is in the air on the way back. That way they can meet the plane in Florida and arrest Cabrera and whoever he's with. What do you think?"

"Sounds like a good idea. We'll be ready."

"Be careful. I'll talk to you later. Now you can put Keller on and I'll give him the news."

McKenna gave the phone back to Keller and returned to the monitors with Gaspar. Alfonso had made four cups of coffee. He went into the front bedroom and talked to the man lying on the cot who had been awake before. The man got up and followed Alfonso into the kitchen.

Gaspar said, "Alfonso called him Octavio and told him it was his turn at the window. Octavio called Alfonso 'Ali.'"

Octavio was about twenty years old. With his almost angelic face, he looked like anything but a vicious killer. Gaspar read McKenna's mind. "He looks like an altar boy, doesn't he?"

"He sure does. But he has to be a killer to be in this group. The guy who tried to kill me yesterday morning looked just like this one, and he was a hard dude," McKenna answered.

Octavio dragged the duffle bag into the living room. It looked like it was still about half full. Then he picked up two cups of coffee and took them to the window in the living room. Octavio and the lookout both started chatting as they drank their coffee. Octavio opened the blinds and flooded the living room with light. There was no furniture in the room except for a small table near the window. Suitcases were everywhere. McKenna could now follow the wires leading from the Claymore. The detonator was taped to the living room wall, about six feet from the front door. He figured that whoever detonated the Claymore wouldn't be harmed by the blast. The two men continued talking and seemed to be having a good time. "What are they talking about?" he asked Gaspar, who was listening intently through his headphones.

"Isabela. They're talking about how nice it would be to be in the shower with her right now. The lookout just said that he's tired and wants to go to bed, but he can't leave yet. He said he was thinking about her and his dick is so hard that he's afraid that Ali will notice. Then Octavio said that he would wear a straitjacket for a week if Isabela would wash his balls just once."

"They seem healthy enough," McKenna said.

The two men kept talking for another five minutes, then the lookout reached down and picked up an M-16 off the floor where he had been standing and placed it on the table. They shook hands and the lookout who had just been relieved started walking toward the front bedroom. Octavio called to him and he returned. He took a small electronic device from his shirt pocket and placed it on the table next to the M-16. It was a little square box about the size of an electronic garage door opener, with a small light flashing on the front of it.

"Rodrigo's detonator," Gaspar said. "Perfect. The lookout's gonna be the first one to go."

"The lookout is the only one that can really hurt us," McKenna said. "That M-16 uses the same rounds as our Mini-Fourteens. They'd go right through this floor and right through us. Better tell Pao."

Gaspar lifted his radio and told Pao that the lookout was armed with an M-16 and had Rodrigo's detonator.

"Not to worry," Pao answered. "I think this new guy's got a bigger head than the other one. I can't miss and I'm still waiting. But I get relieved in an hour."

"It won't be for a while, Johnny."

"Just as well. I hope my partner takes him. This one looks kinda young. I don't think he's a keeper."

Nothing much happened for the next couple of hours. Isabela went back to her room after her shower and fell asleep. Alfonso woke up one of the other men and told him to go get breakfast. He was the same man who had been Isabela's backup on the street yesterday. His name was Antonio. He called Hector's Spanish Luncheonette and ordered seven plates of bacon and eggs. He left in ten minutes and returned in twenty. Then Alfonso woke up everybody to eat.

The thing that struck McKenna was that they were all so young. Except for Alfonso and Isabela, none of them was over twenty-five, and none of them would reach twenty-six. McKenna kept telling himself that they were old enough to kill, and therefore they were old enough to be killed. We didn't start this particular war, and we're not in their country kidnapping, torturing, and killing people, he thought. Still, it didn't make him feel much better.

Antonio left with two of the plates and took them to the other apartment across the street. Five minutes later Sheeran reported that they were both eating over there. Rodrigo was still awake, but got no breakfast.

Downstairs, Alfonso and Isabela ate in their room. Then they went to sleep. Octavio remained at the window while he ate. The other two men sat at the kitchen table. When they finished eating, they played dominoes while they watched the front-door monitor.

Upstairs, Keller finished his book, which was bad news for everybody. He woke up Cisco and Morales and said, "Time for a practice run. We'll practice on the people downstairs in the locations they're in now."

Everybody knew the plan and followed the drill. Gaspar and Morales moved each monitor into the room that the monitor covered downstairs. Keller went to one of the trunks and took out four more Mini-14s. He gave one to Cisco, one to Gaspar, one to Morales, and he kept one for himself. Each man got three thirty-round magazines. Then he took four Kevlar bomb blankets from the trunk. McKenna got two twelve-gauge shotguns, each loaded with eight rounds of ammo.

"Remember, this is practice," Keller told them. "So make sure that you don't poke your gun barrels through their ceiling."

McKenna watched while Garbus went to the rear bedroom and Landon took the front one. Keller took the living room and Cisco had the kitchen. Each man placed his monitor on the floor close to the place where anyone from *Sendero Luminoso* was located downstairs. Then each spread a bomb blanket on the floor, lifted the monitor on to the blanket, put their two spare magazines on the floor next to their monitor, and knelt down on the bomb blanket. They placed the muzzles of their rifles through the closest hole that had been drilled in the floor, and aimed their guns at the people downstairs by watching them on their monitor. Everyone felt confident they would've hit their targets if this were the real thing.

While they were still in position, Keller did an inspection tour. He determined that a few more holes needed to be drilled in the floor of each room. He marked those spots on the floor with a piece of chalk. Then he held his instructional critique. He called everyone into the living room and said, "When you get the signal from me or hear the first shot, start shooting at your targets downstairs. After the first couple of shots your bullets should open up a big hole in their ceiling downstairs. Then just push the barrels of your rifles through their ceiling for better aiming leverage. We brought up plenty of ammo, so don't stop shooting until you hear from me or until you run out of ammo. Stay on the bomb blanket as much as you can, and keep your monitor protected."

Keller was speaking as matter-of-factly as if he were explaining how to stroke a cue ball. "Remember," he said, "if they hit your monitor, they've hit your eyes. And be ready to move to a new hole if they run to a spot in your room where you can't hit them. If no hole is handy, just start firing through the floor. The rounds we're using will go through eight inches of wood, and the floor is only one inch thick. You'll get them. And you won't have too much to worry about. The TEC-9s they've got won't go through the bomb blanket."

Keller concluded by making sure that Gaspar and Morales understood that they were to replace any man who was hit.

McKenna didn't have to worry about the critique. He wouldn't even be in the apartment when the shooting started. His job was to wait on the stairwell outside with his two shotguns. At the sound of the first shot, which should signify the death of the lookout, he was to start firing into the front door of the apartment downstairs, first with one shotgun, and then the other, until both were empty. He knew that he should try to miss the Claymore, but that shouldn't be a problem. Keller wasn't going to give the order to open fire if any of the bad guys were standing next to the detonator switch. One thing is sure, McKenna thought. Nobody was going to make it alive out the front door.

And nobody was going to make it using the front fire escape. Pao would see to that.

McKenna knew that Pacella had the same job in the building across the street as he did. It was probably the best job. They wouldn't see who they were killing. They both had agreed when the plan was formed last night that the people downstairs had about as much chance of surviving as Bonnie and Clyde. And Bonnie and Clyde had none.

July 13   5:45 p.m.

All systems had been go until Alfonso's call from Peru. Now everything was on hold until the chiefs and politicians decided what to do. The call threw the whole operation into confusion. Morale on McKenna's team had started to fall and the troops were grumbling at the delay.

The call had come in at 5:35. Apparently Alfonso expected it, since he was sitting in the living room next to their phone. It had lasted only twenty-seven seconds and couldn't be traced, but from the contents of the conversation, it probably originated in Peru. When Alfonso picked up the phone, a male voice had informed him in Spanish that the family had agreed to the demands, that the money had already been delivered, and they expected the release of prisoners to be completed by midnight. Alfonso only said one thing during the conversation. He asked about Linda, Flavio's daughter, and was told that she had been returned. Alfonso hung up and announced the news to his men, who had surrounded him. He told them they had won. Everyone was going to get a rest for a while, and some of them were going home.

Alfonso's men instantly broke into celebration. There was a round of hugging, handshaking, backslapping, and kissing all around. Then came five minutes of singing and dancing, which McKenna feared would go on for hours. Alfonso ended it with a word. He told them that they were good soldiers who had just won an important battle, but the war was still going on and their brothers were still dying.

342

They were still in danger and much remained to be done. Alfonso's speech had a sobering effect on the group.

The assault team upstairs didn't need any calming down. If anything, they needed a boost. The news that had made *Sendero Luminoso* so happy had thoroughly depressed them. Keller called Brunette immediately. Brunette already had the news. Isabela's phone was also being monitored from the junction box on East 118th Street. Brunette told Keller to do nothing until he received further instructions. Then Keller phoned Sheeran, who thought it was good news. Keller obviously didn't.

Until the phone call downstairs, everything had been perfect. As far as both sides were concerned, Octavio's mission to La Guardia Airport had gone off without a hitch. The results were better than Brunette had anticipated. The whole transaction was monitored and photographed. Cabrera and his companion got the two suitcases full of cash and Octavio took three suitcases from them. When Octavio returned to 132, the assault team saw that the suitcases were filled with drugs.

Then Brunette called them with the bonus. The man with Cabrera at the airport had been identified as Roberto Aguilar, one of the most wanted men in the Western Hemisphere. He had disappeared from Colombia a year ago and was thought to have sought refuge in Cuba.

But here he was, in the United States, currently thirty-four thousand feet over Georgia. Cabrera and Aguilar had boarded the same plane at La Guardia Airport at 2:45 for their flight back to Florida. Cabrera changed planes at Atlanta. He was returning to Fort Myers Beach. Aguilar stayed on the plane, bound for Miami. Both of them were scheduled to be arrested by the FBI when their planes landed. It was originally planned that the assault on *Sendero Luminoso* would have been over by the time Aguilar and Cabrera were arrested. But that was before the phone call.

The plan made by Keller and Sheeran, along with a fair degree of participation from every other member of the assault teams, was to hit them while they were eating supper. That way everybody except the lookout would be sitting with their hands full. Sitting people make bigger targets than standing people when they are being shot at from above. They would have to drop their food to get to their weapons. They would have to get up to reach the detonators. Best of all, their forces would be more evenly split between the two apartments, if their past practices were any indication. Somebody would take food over to the sentry guarding Rodrigo. That would leave only five of them to be handled in 132, and two to be dealt with by Sheeran's team. The time was getting close and everyone was anxious to get it over with.

After the call, everyone in the assault teams assumed that *Sendero Luminoso* would release Rodrigo shortly, which meant they could no longer tell themselves that they were engaged in a rescue operation and that killing everybody downstairs was the only way to rescue Rodrigo. Of course, they could still carry out the plan. But if Rodrigo were killed or injured during the assault, Brunette would have to retire. The press would kill him. Why didn't Brunette wait until *Sendero Luminoso* released the hostage, and then arrest them? they would ask. The press would publicly reason that, after all, the job of the police is to arrest criminals, not kill them. There would be commentaries by columnists who would publicly wonder if the New York City Police Department was filled with homicidal maniacs just waiting for the chance to spray ghetto apartments with automatic weapons.

McKenna knew that even before the phone call, and even if they successfully rescued Rodrigo without a scratch, there would still be a measure of bad press.

Of course, no one would even try to explain the true reason for the assault. The assault teams were to kill every member of *Sendero Luminoso* downstairs to save American lives, lives that would be taken by *Sendero Luminoso* in the future if they were arrested instead of killed.

Then came the mechanics of arresting the people downstairs. Arresting them would be infinitely harder than killing them. How would that be done? they were asking themselves. Nobody has an easy answer. Everyone agreed that before they could be arrested, Rodrigo would have to be free and safe. Suppose they left one man to guard Rodrigo and the rest of them left town? Gaspar asked. While the teams were waiting for Rodrigo to be released, what would they do? Follow the terrorists and try to arrest them in the street? Impossible and stupid to try. Cops would get killed and some of the terrorists would still get away. Nobody wanted the job of telling them that they were under arrest. This group downstairs didn't look like the surrendering type. Everyone agreed on that.

Of course, they could destroy the tape of the call from Peru and go on with the assault as planned. McKenna didn't worry about anyone in the apartment with him. They had already made their decision. If Brunette told them to go ahead, then the tape never existed as far as they were concerned. But Brunette had made a mistake. Just like Nixon, he had overtaped. There was another copy of the tape and McKenna didn't know the man from TARU who was sitting on the wiretap on East 118th Street.

They all agreed that Brunette would have to be crazy to authorize the assault now. If he did, it was very possible that it would be his last major decision as the chief of detectives. There was too much of a chance that the story of Rodrigo's possible release would come out later. At least one too many people already knew.

The phone in Keller's pocket rang and brought everybody to their feet. Keller stood up and answered the phone. Again, the customary chorus of "Yes, sirs." Then Keller gave the phone to Gaspar. Gaspar just listened. He started rewinding the tapes on all the recorders in front of him. He knew that everybody was watchng him and he raised his thumb in the air. It was still on. Gaspar handed the phone to McKenna as he began erasing his tapes.

"McKenna here, Chief."

"Everybody up there ready to go, Brian?"

"We're ready to do the job. But I think you're taking too much of a chance. They might kill you on this one."

"Heavy's the head that wears the crown, buddy. That's why they pay me the big bucks. It's got to be done. But don't worry too much about me. I've covered myself pretty well."

"I don't see how you could have," McKenna said.

"Never underestimate the power of the chief. I'll see you at the party. I just wanted to set your mind at ease. Now put Keller back on. Then stand back and enjoy the show. I'm going to wind him up some more."

McKenna handed the phone back to Keller and stood back. The conversation had a few more "Yes, sirs," a "You can count on me, Chief," an "I appreciate your confidence, Chief," and ended with, "I'll be sure to tell the men that."

Keller's eyes were starting to get a little glassy by the time he put the phone back in his pocket. He lived for this stuff. While Keller composed his speech, everybody stood in place, waiting for the pep talk.

They were saved by Gaspar. He took his headphones off and told them, "The little ugly one just ordered eight steaks from Hector's. And Alfonso told him to pick up four bottles of champagne. Looks like they're planning a little celebration."

Keller thought that was funny. "Celebrating the end of the line," he said. "Let's get ready."

32

July 13   5:55 p.m.

Rodrigo knew the danger had intensified. He realized that the police were upstairs and figured that they were going to stage an assault on *Sendero Luminoso* to free him. As he stared at the blinking green light of the detonator attached to the block of explosives on his chest, he didn't see how he could possibly survive the assault. He was terrified.

Hours ago, he had lain awake when the small drill bit penetrated the ceiling over his head. The bit had been instantly withdrawn and the hole filled with a small white plug. There was no sound, and if he hadn't been watching he never would have noticed the small white dot on the ceiling. At the time, he couldn't imagine what was going on. Then he saw another drill bit penetrate the ceiling. This one was larger than the first. The hole was directly over his head, and some plaster dust drifted into his eyes. Once again, the hole in the ceiling was plugged, but this plug was different than the first. It was white, but there was glass in the middle. He knew it was glass because it caught the glint of the overhead light in the ceiling. He had watched the reflection on the small piece of glass in the ceiling as it moved slightly in the hole. Then the glass had stopped moving and blended once again into the ceiling. But Rodrigo knew that it was there and it was all he could look at.

The realization that the glass over his head was a miniature camera lens had come to him in a moment of inspiration. That was the only thing that it could be, he thought. The American police had found

346

him! His euphoria had lasted for only seconds, replaced by terror. He was waiting for the sound of the first gunshot, which he was sure would be the last sound he heard before his chest exploded to all corners of the room.

The pain from his hand was driving him crazy and making it difficult for him to concentrate. He found himself drifting in and out of consciousness as he watched the ceiling and struggled to order his thoughts. He knew that he had a fever and that his hand was badly infected. The pain was constant. Not the throbbing pain that he had grown accustomed to. It was searing pain that started at the place in his hand where his fingers used to be and continued up his arm to his elbow. Even breathing hurt. He was wrapped so tightly in the straitjacket that, every time he inhaled, the rough canvas fabric of the jacket glided for an inch across his hand and sent a rocket of pain shooting up his arm.

Even sleep did not suspend the suffering. Sleep brought the dreams and hallucinations, nightmares just as bad as the nightmare he was living. His recently recurring dream was just like his life. He could never move as the man in the mask started on him with the bolt-cutter. First his fingers, then his toes, one by one. Each time the bolt-cutters closed on one of his appendages, he heard Miriam say, "Sorry Rodrigo." What were they going to do after he ran out of fingers and toes?

He could not stand to lose another finger the way they had cut off the last one. He had woken up when they jabbed the hypo into his hand. His straitjacket was off and his arms were tied to the metal sides of the bed. All that he could see was the ceiling, the light, and the man in the ski mask. And for a brief, terrifying instant, the bolt-cutters. Then came Miriam's voice. She had said just one thing as he felt the blades of the bolt-cutter cut through the flesh and bone of his index finger. "Sorry, Rodrigo." Her voice and the pain had exploded in his brain at the same time. He'd lost consciousness and, when he woke up again, he was back in the jacket. It could have been minutes or days later. He had lost track of time.

Before he had seen the camera lens, Rodrigo had already given up hope and just wanted the ordeal to end. He had lost the will to live, but was afraid of the pain of dying. He didn't want to die. He just wished that he never existed. But he would prefer to die before they came in and cut off another finger. He would rather die than go through that pain again. But now death was closer than ever and he couldn't think. He could only feel. He stopped trying to concentrate through the pain and confusion and gave his emotions free rein.

Besides fear, the only other emotion he felt was hate. But his hate wasn't focused on his captors, which astonished him. His fear of them was so boundless that his brain didn't have room for another feeling about them. He shared a common purpose with them—the fulfillment of the ransom demands. His hate was reserved for his father. For days, he couldn't figure out why his father had not met their demands. Hernan Guiterrez was wealthy and influential. Rodrigo was sure that his captors were informed enough to know the extent of his wealth and power when they had presented their demands. They wouldn't have included anything that he couldn't give. But Rodrigo now believed that they had demanded more than his father was willing to give in exchange for the life of his son. Rodrigo was convinced that his father had elected to keep the family wealth and power intact, had chosen to disregard the pain and suffering of his second son in order to preserve for future generations the traditional position of the Guiterrez family in Peru. After all, Rodrigo thought, Hernan Oxcalo Guiterrez had another son. The thought hurt him.

Just then, Rodrigo heard the sound of the door to his room being unlocked. A wave of terror took hold of him. Rodrigo felt every muscle in his body tighten. By the time the door had opened, his legs were shaking uncontrollably within the limits allowed by his Velcro restraints. His terror abated slightly when the door opened and he saw Miriam, wearing her rubber gloves and carrying her bucket and a new shower curtain under her arm. She put the bucket and shower curtain down next to the bed and stood staring down at Rodrigo's shaking legs. Rodrigo felt his customary embarrassment as Miriam stared at him, shaking in fear and lying in his own filth.

Miriam seemed to understand his embarrassment. She smiled at him and said, "I have some good news for you, Rodrigo. Try to calm down. I know that all this has been very hard for you." Miriam then reached down and pushed a switch on the remote-controlled detonator taped to his chest. The green light stopped blinking.

Rodrigo's legs stopped shaking. For a moment, he forgot his worries over the camera lens in the ceiling, his embarrassment, his fear, and his pain. It had been so long since he had heard any good news. For the first time in at least a week, Rodrigo felt something besides hate and fear. It was hope. He longed to speak, but all that he could manage were some muffled sounds through the tape across his mouth.

"Calm down, Rodrigo. I'm going to leave the tape on your mouth for only a few minutes more while I give you the news. I don't want you yelling or screaming or doing anything else that might get you shot when you're so close. So just listen. I'll answer your questions later." Miriam began washing Rodrigo's legs as she spoke. "You will be in a hospital by morning. It's over, Rodrigo. Your family has met our demands."

Rodrigo felt tears forming in his eyes. Released? he thought. I'm going to live? He had given up all hope. He knew that Miriam wasn't lying to him. When he saw that the man who had cut off his finger had worn a ski mask, he knew that they would release him if their demands were met. Still, he had given up hope. Even if his father did meet their demands, he thought he would be dead by then. His eyes cleared as he felt the tears streaming down both cheeks. Involuntarily, his eyes focused on the tiny camera lens in the ceiling over his head, and the terror returned. He felt like a man suffering a fatal heart attack with the winning lottery ticket in his pocket. He couldn't breathe. I'm about to be killed just as they're about to release me, he thought. He struggled to think, to compose his thoughts, to plan.

Miriam didn't notice his panic. She continued chatting while washing his genitals. Her tone was conversational, like she was discussing whether to have red wine or white with dinner tonight. Then she did start talking about dinner. "We have something special for dinner tonight, Rodrigo. I brought you a great steak. I even brought a bottle of champagne. There's no reason we have to leave each other with hard feelings, you know. In the end, I hope you'll think of your stay here with us as just an unfortunate matter of politics. You'll have something to tell your grandchildren about, and you'll have some scars of honor to show off to the other members of your class. You'll be quite a hero to them."

Rodrigo thought he heard a movement upstairs. Somebody had dropped something on the floor. Miriam didn't seem to notice as she gloated on her victory. Then she started humming as she rinsed her sponge in her bucket. Rodrigo recognized the tune. It was the *"Internationale,"* the communist anthem. She was laying it on heavy for his benefit, he thought. He had to know more.

Miriam stood up straight and dropped the sponge in the bucket. "Remember the rules, Rodrigo." She nodded her head toward the mirror. "He'll still shoot you if you don't follow the procedure." She leaned over his face and stroked his cheek with the back of her hand. "Poor Rodrigo," she said. "You've been very brave, you know. My comrades can't even imagine why I'm doing this dirty job for you tonight. They think I should leave you here a filthy mess for the Americans to clean up." Then she grabbed a corner of the tape covering his mouth and slowly ripped it off.

Rodrigo didn't feel the pain this time. Miriam began loosening the Velcro straps holding his legs to the bed as she continued humming. Rodrigo started to speak, but felt his lips crack. He moistened his lips with his tongue and said in French in a tone as relaxed as he could manage, "How do you plan to release me?"

Miriam followed his switch from Spanish to French and answered, "We'll just go. Once we're a safe distance away, we'll call the American police and tell them who you are and where you are. Then they'll come and take you to a hospital."

"When will you leave?"

"Sometime tonight. You'll be free by morning."

"What time is it now?" Rodrigo asked, keeping the conversation in French. If they were able to listen, he hoped that the police above him didn't understand what they were saying.

"A little after six." She seemed amused by his question. "Why, Rodrigo? Do you have a date with another woman tonight?"

I'm trying to avoid the date with death that the American police have set up for all of us, he thought. I might even save your life in the process.

Rodrigo's mind was racing, searching for a plan, something to keep him alive as he considered all the possibilities. It would be hours before he was released. Too long. What were the American police planning? When would they attack? Would they try first to negotiate with them for his release? The only conclusion that he could draw was that, if the police were here, they knew the people that they were dealing with. They would never let them escape just to save the life of a foreigner. He was grasping at straws as he committed himself to his plan.

"Miriam," he said in French. "I'm going to tell you something that can save your life. Keep calm."

Rodrigo realized that something in his voice and in what he said changed Miriam's whole demeanor. She seemed to stiffen for a second. Then she continued loosening the straps that held his chest to the bed.

"You must leave now. I think that we are about to be attacked by the American police." He placed special emphasis on *we*.

Miriam's hand brushed over the detonator device as she was loosening the straps. Rodrigo saw the green light blinking again. But it was too late. He had committed himself.

"You don't have to kill me," he continued. "Just leave now. You can get away."

Miriam had finished loosening the straps. She stood up and said with a smile, "What makes you think all this, Rodrigo?"

"Don't look, Miriam, but I think there is a small camera lens over my head. The police are upstairs and they are watching us."

Rodrigo realized his mistake as Miriam raised her eyes to the ceiling. He shouldn't have said *I think*. He should have sounded more emphatic, more assertive.

She didn't see it at first as she searched the ceiling. Then she caught the reflected glint from the ceiling bulb on the lens. She recognized it at once. They had been using these same lenses since they had

350

arrived in the United States. Just as quickly, she realized her mistake. She turned and waved to the mirror. Then she started walking calmly toward the door. Isabela reached the door and waited impatiently for a couple of seconds. Then she heard the sound of the lock opening.

Upstairs, directly over Rodrigo, Captain Sheeran had been standing beside Emergency Service Police Officer Dionisio Molina, watching Isabela Mendosa stare into the camera lens. Molina was kneeling on the floor next to Sheeran with the barrel of his Mini-14 thrust through one of the holes in the floor. When Isabela turned, Sheeran said into his radio, "Get ready. Isabela saw the camera." Sheeran's message put the plan into motion.

In the apartments on both sides of East 117th Street, fingers tightened on triggers as seven police officers crouched over Mini-14s. The gun barrels poked through holes in the floor as the officers tracked their targets on their video monitors.

On Park Avenue near the corner of East 117th Street, Police Officer William Watson and Police Officer Arnold Freely turned on the roof lights of their marked patrol car and got out of the car in full uniform with their summons books in their hands. At the corner of East 117th Street and Park Avenue, Detective John Monroe of TARU pressed a button at the end of the electric cord leading from his hand to the traffic-control box, and the traffic lights at the corner shined a steady red in all directions, bringing traffic on Park Avenue to a stop and preventing any cars from proceeding into East 117th Street, a one-way street.

As the lights turned red, a caravan of six ambulances turned from East 118th Street and parked behind Freely and Watson's patrol car, their motors running.

In the middle of the intersection of East 117th Street and Lexington Avenue, Police Officer Felipe Santos and Police Officer Juan Bosco, both of the 25th Precinct Anti-Crime Unit and both in civilian clothes, began to argue loudly. A second later, Bosco punched Santos in the stomach and Santos punched Bosco in the face, which caused Detective Maria Balazos to fill her ample lungs and shout in Spanish, "Fight! Fight!" the guaranteed gathering call of the ghetto. Everyone who had been standing on East 117th Street began running toward the corner, lest they miss the greatest attraction of the day.

Police Officer John Pao, standing in the middle of a darkened room on 129 East 117th Street, pointed his rifle at the window and placed the cross hairs of the scope on the left ear of Victor Reyes, age twenty-two, lately of Ayacucho, Peru. Victor leaned out the window of 132 in order to see the commotion on the corner of East 117th Street and Lexington Avenue.

McKenna left the third-floor apartment in 132 and Pacella left the

351

fourth-floor apartment in 129. Both detectives started down the steps with their shotguns ready.

Eleven seconds after she had first stared into the camera lens, the door opened in front of Isabela. As she crossed into the living room, the rain of death began.

Manuel Lorca, age twenty, of Huancayo, Peru, had a tin plate of steak and french fries in his left hand and his right hand rested on the doorknob of the open door. He was standing in the living room of the apartment. The first burst of bullets caught him in the top of his head and stitched down his back as he fell forward into Isabela's arms. Just behind Isabela, the floor of Rodrigo's room was being torn up by the bullets coming through the ceiling. The bullets traced a path along the floor toward Isabela, who stood with the bloody body of Manuel in her arms. The floor stopped exploding a foot from her. They couldn't reach her.

Octavio DeJusus, age nineteen, of Ayacucho, Peru, sat at a table pushed against the living room wall, eating his steak and french fries. The table was between Rodrigo's door and the one-way mirror that looked into Rodrigo's room. On the table were the portable radio, Manuel's TEC-9, and four loaded magazines for the TEC-9. He had come to the apartment with Isabela and the food. It was his turn to assume the boring job of guarding Rodrigo. Octavio reacted instantly to the deafening roar of gunfire in the apartment. By the time the eighth bullet had entered the body of Manuel, Octavio had pushed himself away from the table and taken his 9-mm Smith & Wesson Model 59 pistol from his belt. He located the source of death in the ceiling and fired five rounds at the protruding gun barrel. The barrel swung toward him. Octavio ran into the kitchen and was caught immediately by a burst of gunfire from the kitchen ceiling. He was hit in the left leg by two bullets and his left foot was shattered by another bullet. The front door of the apartment was being blasted by gunfire, with large holes appearing in the door at two-second intervals. He fired three rounds at the gun barrel poking through the kitchen ceiling. One of the rounds struck it. The barrel of the Mini-14 rifle exploded as the next round of full-automatic fire raced down its length. Octavio turned back toward the living room as another large hole appeared in the front door.

The gun barrel in the living room ceiling had returned to Isabela. She pushed Manuel's body forward and jumped to the right, picked up the TEC-9 from the table with her right hand and the radio with her left. She raised the radio to her mouth. "Blow him up!" she screamed. Then she heard the music coming from the radio and threw it to the floor. She grabbed one of the loaded magazines from the table and ran toward the kitchen. A trail of bullets pursued her.

Octavio stood in the doorway that separated the kitchen from the living room, firing at the living room ceiling. He was badly injured and leaning against the wall with his left arm braced against the doorway for support. Two bullets from another spot in the kitchen ceiling caught his left arm and hand, but he kept firing until his pistol was empty. Isabela ran past Octavio and across the kitchen, yelling "Get out!" She had just passed the front door seconds after another shotgun round broke through it. She reached the refrigerator and twisted the detonator for the Claymore strapped to the front door.

The front door of the apartment exploded forward, with fragments of wood accompanied by hundreds of fragments of steel rod racing down the hallway at twelve hundred feet per second. The steel fragments tore into the banister of the stairway, into the walls of the hallway, into the apartment door of the rear apartment, and into the back of the stairs leading up. The destruction was enormous, but the stairs remained standing. Tommy Pacella did not.

When Isabela detonated the Claymore, Pacella had been standing on the third step of the stairs between the third and fourth floors. He was twenty feet away from the door and he had just fired the last round from his first shotgun. His back faced the door. He had his second shotgun in his hand and was preparing to turn and lean over the banister to resume his work. He was pushed forward by the force of the blast and deafened by the noise. Six fragments of shrapnel made it through the wooden stairs and pierced his legs. One metal fragment pierced his neck at the unprotected point between the Kevlar helmet and the flak vest. Many other fragments hit his vest and helmet. Pacella's legs gave out under his weight and he fell face forward down the stairs into the hallway. He lay on the floor of the hallway, on top of his loaded shotgun. He never saw Isabela.

Isabela was out the front door so quickly that she might have been part of the explosion. She ran down the hall and, as she leaped over Pacella's prone body, she fired a downward burst of six rounds from her TEC-9. Then she started running up the stairs. Two of the 9-mm rounds hit Pacella's vest, but did not penetrate. Two of the rounds hit the back of his right leg. One of these rounds severed his femoral artery.

In the fourth-floor apartment, Detective Catalfumo was kneeling on the kitchen floor. He had just emptied his Mini-14 through the floor at Octavio in the kitchen below and was putting a fresh magazine into the receiver. Emergency Police Officer Tomas Romero lay on the floor behind him. Romero's hands had been mangled when his Mini-14 had exploded and he moaned in pain. The apartment door was open. Catalfumo heard the video monitor next to the door beep, indicating movement in the hallway. He quickly pulled the slide back, putting a round in the chamber of his Mini-14. He started to pull the rifle from the hole in the floor. The front sight-blade caught on the edge of the hole and Catalfumo was trying to free it when Isabela passed the open apartment door on her way up the stairs. She fired a burst of seven rounds at Catalfumo and Romero. One round hit Catalfumo in the left forearm and traveled up his arm, following the ulna bone. It exited his arm at the elbow and continued forward, hitting Romero in the right ankle. Four other rounds hit Catalfumo in his flak vest, knocking him backward.

Isabela continued climbing the stairs. Sheeran ran out of the living room and saw Catalfumo lying on his back. He leaned over and yelled, "What happened?" The force of the 9-mm bullets hitting Catalfumo's flak jacket had broken one of his ribs and knocked the wind out of him. For a few moments, he didn't know what happened to him. He hadn't seen Isabela. Then he said, "I think she went up."

Sheeran yelled to the other officers that he was going up, but nobody heard him. As ordered, Police Officer Nick Somoza was still pumping rounds into the body of Manuel Lorca. Sheeran yelled into his radio, "Cease fire in 129! Officers injured in 129. Suspect headed toward the roof." There was no sound coming from 132. Then Sheeran ran out the front door and up the stairs. Police Officer Pao followed him.

In the third floor hallway, Pacella struggled to stay conscious as he stared through the shattered door of the apartment at Octavio De-Jesus. Pacella was bleeding heavily from the wounds in his neck and legs.

Octavio leaned against the kitchen wall. All firing had stopped. Octavio still had his pistol in his hand. Pacella could see that the slide of the pistol was back. It was empty. Pacella tried to pull his shotgun from under his body, but didn't have the strength.

Octavio pushed himself from the wall and stumbled to the floor. The two men locked eyes and Octavio began crawling toward Pacella. Pacella opened his mouth to yell, but no sound came out. Octavio reached Pacella and pulled the shotgun from under his body. Pacella grabbed him and tried to stop him, but couldn't. Octavio rose to his feet, using the shotgun as a crutch and holding on to the shattered railing with his free hand. He turned toward the stairs and began descending. Pacella reached under his flak vest and pulled his Glock pistol from his shoulder holster. Octavio stumbled again and fell forward. He caught himself on the banister as Pacella extended his pistol over the shattered stairway railing. He pointed the pistol down the stairs and fired until the pistol was empty.

Pacella's first round hit Octavio in the top of the head. Five more rounds hit Octavio as he tumbled down the stairs. He was dead before he hit the second floor.

Pacella heard him fall. He smiled and closed his eyes while his lifeblood flowed from his wounds. First-Grade Detective Tommy Pacella died alone, thirty-five years to the day after he joined the New York City Police Department. At sixty-two years of age, he was the oldest New York City Police Officer ever killed in the line of duty. He didn't die mowing lawns in Massapequa.

Sheeran and Pao had just reached the open roof door when they heard the sound of Pacella's shots. Sheeran took a quick look up and down the row of tenement roofs. Isabela was nowhere to be seen. They turned and started warily down the stairs toward the sound of the gunfire.

In 132, on McKenna's side of the street, everything had gone off without a hitch. When Sheeran's order to open fire sounded in his earphone, Alfonso and two of his men were sitting on the living room floor, laughing, eating, and drinking champagne. The lookout still leaned from the living room window, watching a fight in the street. Johnny Pao's first shot hit the lookout in the head, killing him instantly. His second shot exploded the radio remote-control detonator on the table next to the window.

McKenna heard the unbroken bursts of automatic fire from the apartment upstairs and he started pumping rounds into the apartment door with his shotgun. He aimed at the bottom half of the door, just below the place he knew the Claymore was taped on the other side. After his third shot he had made a big enough hole in the apartment door to see inside. Suddenly, he had something to shoot at. As he fired his fourth round he saw a leg on the other side of the door. The force of the shotgun pellets knocked the target's legs out from under him and he fell forward against the door. By the time McKenna fired his fifth round, he was shooting into the man's chest. A head fell through the hole in the door and McKenna stared into the dead eyes of Alfonso Mendosa. He chambered another round in his shotgun and aimed at the dead man's head, but decided not to waste it. Someone upstairs was doing enough, still filling Alfonso's body with lead.

There was a four-second lull in the firing while the men upstairs changed magazines. McKenna kept his shotgun trained on the front door, waiting for another sign of movement from the apartment. There was none. Then the firing continued from upstairs as they expended another magazine into the bodies below.

It was over in twenty seconds. McKenna heard Keller's voice in his earphones, "132, Cease Fire! Cease Fire!" and realized that Alfonso and his men had not managed to return a shot.

McKenna lowered his weapon. The firing was still going on across the street in separated bursts. Then he heard the explosion across the street, instantly followed by Keller's order in his earphones, "132, hold your positions!" The gunfire continued across the street. Then came Sheeran's transmission that an officer was down.

McKenna disregarded Keller's order. He picked up his second shotgun and bounded down the steps and out of the building. He was crossing the street when he heard the sounds of Pacella's Glock firing. An ambulance raced down the street and stopped short in front of McKenna. The ambulance attendants were getting out of their ambulance as McKenna ran into 129. The inside lobby door was locked. McKenna looked through the glass window and saw nobody. He fired two rounds from his shotgun into the lock of the door and kicked it open. He entered the building with his shotgun ready. Two ambulance attendants followed him in.

McKenna ran up the stairs and saw Octavio's bullet-riddled body on the second-floor landing. The ambulance attendants were seconds behind McKenna and they started the obviously useless procedure of checking the body for vital signs. "Forget him!" McKenna ordered.

McKenna slowly climbed the stairs to the third-floor landing, where he found the smiling body of his friend. He yelled for the attendants and in seconds they started working on Pacella. One attendant rolled Pacella over and started giving him mouth-to-mouth. Nothing. They started CPR and were still over Pacella when, seconds later, Sheeran and Pao reached them on the third-floor landing.

Sheeran and Pao took one look at Pacella and saw that he was dead. Then they looked at McKenna and quickly turned their eyes away, in order to avoid embarrassing him. McKenna's eyes were filled with tears. He started sobbing uncontrollably.

33

"Close that door!" Vinnie yelled over the bar to Joe Flaherty, the unofficial doorkeeper for the evening's festivities. Joe ignored him. He held the door open while he tried to explain to two lovely ladies why he couldn't admit them to the party. The girls looked great, attractively bundled in their best rabbit-fur coats, out for an evening of fun. The icy wind whipped down the bar through the open door and everyone was holding on to their money to keep it from blowing onto Vinnie's side of the bar, where it would be lost forever. Vinnie would charge it off as "God's will."

Finally, Lieutenant Roberti had had enough. "Flaherty, if you don't close that door right now, you're going to find yourself working with the white people in the morning!"

The ultimate threat, as far as Flaherty was concerned. Expulsion to the "spit and polish" police department of White-World, where he would be forced to work with some rookie who read the *Patrol Guide* during lunch. In White-World he would have to listen all day to white people whining about the traffic ticket they got two years ago for going through the light that was still yellow, whining over the thirty-dollar fine they had to pay, and whining about the increase in their auto insurance. "The cops around here have nothing better to do," they would say. Joe would think they were right. Then they would whine about the kids hanging on the corner who were always playing their radio too loud, keeping everyone in the neighborhood awake. "Why don't you do something about those punks?" they would say.

White-World was not for Flaherty. It terrified him. He much preferred working in Spanish Harlem, where the necessary number of tickets were given, received, and subsequently discarded with a common air of joviality, and where the only thing that kept the citizens awake was the occasional stray bullet whizzing through their windows.

Flaherty closed the door in the faces of the protesting young lovelies, breaking his own heart in the process. Then he locked it again.

The occasion was the invitation-only "secret" retirement party for Detective Betty King, Detective Sal Catalfumo, and Detective Tomas Romero. All had won the "Civil Service Lottery." They were retiring on "three-quarters," which meant that they had been so "disabled" in the line of duty that they were forced to retire. They would have to exist every year for the rest of their lives on three-quarters of their annual salary, tax free.

Betty King got her three-quarters because of a minor heart attack. It was rumored that her heart attack had been supervised by Chief Brunette. Sal Catalfumo and Tomas Romero were deemed to be disabled as a result of the injuries they had received in the famous gunfight on East 117th Street four months ago.

Once they had been promoted, all three had accepted their "misfortune" gracefully. They were expected to miraculously recover just after they cashed their first pension checks.

Raggs was jam-packed, standing room only. Betty, Sal, and Tomas were the centers of activity at three different spots along the bar. Their devotees gathered around them to receive their blessings. People who managed to get three-quarters without going to the trouble of becoming a chief are generally venerated in the New York City Police Department as Masters of the System.

It was four A.M. and Vinnie decided that, since it was supposed to be closing time anyway, he would start charging for drinks. The money that had been collected to finance the party had run out by midnight, and Vinnie estimated that he was losing about five hundred dollars an hour. But it wasn't the money. Vinnie was tired and he wanted the party to end, so he figured that charging for drinks was the quickest way to end it.

Everyone had the customary unbroken twenty-dollar bill on the bar in front of them. Then Vinnie made a mistake. The first twenty that he took belonged to Joe Sophia. As Vinnie walked to the cash register with his money, Joe's mind was working overtime, searching for a way to avert this tragedy. Then he found it. He stood on his

358

barstool, raised his glass in the air, and shouted, "Detective Tommy Pacella."

Immediately one hundred glasses were raised into the air and one hundred voices shouted, "Tommy Pacella!"

Vinnie was beat. He returned Sophia's twenty to its permanent place on the bar, then he and Laura rushed to fill the latest round. He knew the party would be on till dawn, at least. But he was happy with the knowledge that he was no longer losing money. He kept track of the number of drinks he provided, did some calculations, and presented the bill to Joe Flaherty. The drinks would be charged to the Pacella account that was secretly donated by Hernan Guiterrez to the 25th Precinct Club, with the instructions that the money be used for these emergencies. He had said that he wanted to be sure that the brave man who had died while rescuing his son would never be forgotten.

Hernan Guiterrez had gone further than that. He had flown to New York from Peru after his son was rescued, attended Pacella's funeral, and made a speech that was televised nationally. He was effusive in his praise for the New York City Police Department and the FBI for their heroic efforts in their fight to combat international terrorism. He visited the site where his son had been held and publicly apologized to the American people for the acts perpetrated by criminal elements from his country. Then Hernan announced that he was buying 129 East 117th Street, the building where his son had been held and where Pacella had died. When renovations were completed, the building would be opened as the Thomas Pacella Memorial Home for Troubled Boys. Hernan Guiterrez understood the proper application of money and power.

Rodrigo was still learning. When he had been rescued from the carnage, he had deliriously stated to Captain Keller that *Sendero Luminoso* had been ready to release him just before the police attacked. Rodrigo was put in a private room at New York Hospital and placed under heavy guard. The press was denied access to him until he was sufficiently recovered. Chief Brunette picked up Hernan Guiterrez at the airport when he flew up to see his son. They had a long talk on the way to the hospital, and they understood each other perfectly by the time they reached it.

After Rodrigo saw his father, Brunette thought that he was recovered sufficiently to be interviewed. The press conference that took place in Rodrigo's room was attended by representatives of all the major national and international papers. Rodrigo told them that *Sendero Luminoso* was just about to kill him when the police attacked. He said that his captors had told him that they were going to kill him no matter what—even if the ransom were paid and all of their demands were met. Rodrigo closed the interview by expressing his undying gratitude to the New York City Police Department for saving his life.

McKenna had finished his drink with the rest of them. When Laura got to his empty glass, she raised a questioning eyebrow. McKenna nodded and she mixed him another rusty nail. When she returned with his drink, he held up two fingers. She reached under the bar and put a pack of cigarettes next to his drink. McKenna opened the pack and lit up a smoke. Then he took a sip of his drink, his third of the evening. I've got to pace myself, he thought. Tonight might be the night.

Detective First Grade Brian McKenna was universally acknowledged to be the most miserable man in the department. In a room full of friends, he was drinking alone.

He'd made it through the hectic week after the shoot-out on East 117th Street, and later the grueling week of the grand jury investigation into the death of Pacella and the six members of *Sendero Luminoso*. There had been a few minor inconsistencies, but everything had gone according to Brunette's plan. They were all heroes although, officially at least, nobody knew who they were.

He had held up during Pacella's funeral, which turned out to be a spectacular media event attended by over six thousand police officers from departments all over the world. The governor, the mayor, the police commissioner, and even the director of the FBI had all been there and they all made speeches that got them some mileage. Against his wishes, Angelita had joined him for the funeral, saying she would stay with him for a while to make sure that he was OK. But he put her off. He told her that he needed to be alone. It had broken his heart to do it, but he knew it had to be that way.

It was at Brunette's party for all the men and women involved in the operation that McKenna fell apart. He had taken his first drink in seventeen years and he hadn't stopped. Brunette joined him, and they'd both gotten rip-roaring drunk. The difference was that Brunette hadn't touched another drink since then. It was his one fall from the wagon in seventeen years. McKenna didn't climb back on, and he drank every day. He never got drunk again. He just drank, two or three a day. He told himself that he was under control, that he was ready for Isabela Mendosa. He knew that, eventually, she would come for him.

McKenna was looking forward to the day—win, lose, or draw. He knew that it had to be soon. Isabela Mendosa was destroying his life and he was slowly caving in under the pressure.

They now knew how she'd gotten away. After she had shot Catalfumo, Romero, and Pacella she had run over the rooftops to a building on Lexington Avenue. Isabela had climbed down the fire escape, found an open window, and gone into the apartment. She had closed and locked the window behind her. The apartment had been empty. Everyone had left to watch the show on East 117th Street, where the police were going crazy. There were helicopters overhead, lots of ambulances, reporters eager to interview anyone in the neighborhood, and police everywhere. The mayor and the police commissioner had been there, too.

The police had stopped all traffic for blocks. They were on the rooftops, on the fire escapes, in the lobby of every building. They were searching every apartment on the block for Isabela Mendosa. After a while, the mayor had made an appeal on one of the police loudspeakers. He wanted everyone to get off the streets and go home. He had told them to wait in their apartments for the police. He had been generally ignored and the streets were full of people for hours.

When the Medina family returned home, Isabela was waiting for them. Once the family was inside she had jumped out of the bathroom with her TEC-9 in hand. She told them that she was the one that the police were looking for, and that she would kill them all if they didn't do everything she said. Her clothes were bloody and they had no trouble believing her.

Although they had been terrified at first, they'd quickly settled into the routine that Isabela mandated. Mrs. Medina had cooked supper for Isabela while the family watched the news on television. Isabela's picture and the story of Rodrigo's kidnapping were the lead feature on all channels. The stories told how the police were able to locate Rodrigo after Detective Brian McKenna shot Carlos Mendosa in a gun battle in Brooklyn. Isabela paid close attention and she had had the Medinas tape the show on their VCR.

By the time the news was over the two young Medina boys had been very impressed with the pretty celebrity who was visiting with them. They saw that she was sad because her husband and her friends had just been killed by the police. She had been crying while she watched the news. Isabela told them that her husband had been a very brave man and that she had loved him very much. The boys, at five and seven, had been very impressionable.

Mr. and Mrs. Medina acquired a different point of view from the news. They had become further convinced that Isabela Mendosa was a dangerous person who would kill them without hesitation.

The police had knocked on the door at ten o'clock. Nobody answered and they went away. A news special about the gunfight on East 117th Street was announced for eleven o'clock and Isabela politely asked Mrs. Medina to let the boys stay up to watch it. She consented and the boys had glued themselves to the screen to hear more about their visitor.

There were more details on the gunfight. The police had found more than seven million dollars' worth of drugs and over a half million dollars in cash in the apartment. The FBI had also arrested two men at Florida airports in connection with the case. One of them, Roberto Aguilar, was wanted everywhere by everyone. The two men had had more than three million dollars in cash in their luggage when they'd been arrested.

After the news, the Medinas sent the boys to bed. Once they were asleep, Isabela had tied up Mr. and Mrs. Medina in their beds. She'd left the lights on in their room and told them that if one of them opened their eyes, she would suffocate the other one with a pillow. Once again, they believed her.

Isabela had woken them up at seven o'clock the next morning. She'd had Mr. Medina call in sick to his job. Then Mrs. Medina called the super and told him that they were going away for the day. At nine o'clock there had been another special on the news, about *Sendero Luminoso* and the civil war in Peru. Isabela seemed to enjoy it immensely, and she'd taped this show also. At 10:30 A.M. the police had knocked on the door again. Again, nobody answered and the police left.

At eleven o'clock, Isabela sent Mr. Medina to the bank to withdraw one thousand dollars from his savings account. He had more than three thousand dollars in the account, but she said that she only needed a thousand and that she would pay him back. She'd given him a shopping list of clothes to buy for her, along with her sizes. She'd also told him to pick up some blond hair dye and added that, if he wasn't back by noon, she would kill his family. He was back in time with everything she wanted. He told her that he had run into the super, and had explained that the family had decided to stay home after all. The Medinas and Isabela spent the whole day watching television and playing games with the kids. She had tied them up again that night.

When the Medinas woke up the next morning, Isabela was a blonde. At 10 o'clock she called a gypsy cab company and ordered a cab for Fort Lee, New Jersey. The dispatcher had told her that the cab would be downstairs at 10:30. Isabela was all packed, and at 10:30 she'd taken the Medinas' youngest son downstairs with her. She'd told Mr. and Mrs. Medina that he would be back with them in a couple of hours as long as they didn't call the police. Once she was outside the apartment, she had put her gun in a shopping bag. The taxi had been waiting downstairs and they jumped in. She told the driver that she had to pick up a friend at Grand Central Station on Forty-second Street, and that she would give him an extra ten dollars. That was fine with him and he didn't call in the extra stop on his radio.

When they got to Grand Central, Isabela had told the driver that she had changed her mind. They wouldn't be going to Fort Lee after all. She had given him thirty dollars and left the cab along with the Medina boy. Then she'd put the boy in another taxi, given the driver twenty dollars and the Medinas' address, and told him to take the boy home. As the taxi pulled away she had waved at the boy, who was waving at her through the back window of the taxi. Then she had disappeared.

Two days later, the Medinas had received two thousand dollars cash in the mail. The envelope was postmarked Grand Central Station. The police took the money and dusted all the bills for fingerprints. A couple of days later, they'd given the Medinas two thousand dollars in new bills.

Tavlin had sent men to all the banks in the Grand Central Station area and found that Isabela had a large safe-deposit box in the name of Miriam Salazar at the Dry Dock Savings Bank at Grand Central Station. She had visited the bank on July 15 at 11 A.M. Tavlin had gotten a court order for the box. She had cleaned it out.

McKenna took another sip of his drink and lit up another cigarette. He was at the stage where he started feeling sorry for himself, once again. Except for me and Pacella, everybody made out very nicely on the case, he thought. Ray could be the next police commissioner, the next director of the FBI, or even the next senator from New York. Tavlin was a full inspector and Sheeran and Keller were both deputy inspectors.

Even Esteban Cabrera hadn't done that badly. Once the FBI had given him the facts of life, he'd decided to cooperate fully. It turned out that he, like nearly everyone else in the world, had already decided that communism wasn't the way to go. He had told the FBI everything he knew about Castro's operations in the United States, Mexico, and Peru. It turned out that he knew quite a bit. More than 100 arrests followed. The FBI also did a thorough investigation on Cabrera's finances and concluded that, while he'd dealt in sizable quantities of drugs and large amounts of cash, he hadn't profited personally from those transactions he had arranged and conducted. He was just a loyal Cuban agent, a military officer with a nice salary, doing the difficult job that he had been assigned to do. He probably would have refused to cooperate, except for three things. He had grown disillusioned with the rationale behind his difficult mission, he had grown to love living in the United States, and he was in love with FBI undercover agent Rosa Figueroa. So he had cooperated and made a deal.

Now the Justice Department had the goods on many high-ranking members of the Cuban government. Cabrera wasn't able to implicate Castro personally, but the Justice Department lawyers felt that they had enough on everyone around him to make a *prima facie* case against the Cuban government. They pushed for indictments. They had been overruled by the State Department, which had a few ideas of its own.

Working through intermediaries, the State Department had arranged a meeting with Castro. They had showed him the evidence provided by Cabrera of Cuban complicity in drug smuggling and Cuban support of terrorist groups operating in the United States. They had been undiplomatically blunt. If these activities didn't stop immediately, then the evidence they had would be made public. The State Department officials openly speculated that the American people would be incensed and drummed into a war fever, and shortly thereafter, military operations against the Caribbean People's Paradise would be inevitable. The American public and many of the politicians representing them would demand it. They had reminded Castro that the Russians were no longer in the game, and pointed out that it was an election year, when a nice short war against a despised enemy would help the incumbents. They'd also mentioned out that there were small cells available on both sides of General Manuel Noriega.

Castro had gotten the point. He had denied all of the allegations made by the Justice Department, but said that if he were smuggling drugs into the United States, and if he were supporting terrorists, then he would stop. According to all indications, he had. Cocaine was getting scarce on the streets and was up to $100 a gram.

Esteban Cabrera, under the name of Raoul Camarena, had pleaded guilty to one count of possession of a controlled substance and had been sentenced to three years at Allenwood. No mention was made of any espionage activities. Brunette had told McKenna that Felice Espinosa, aka Rosa Figueroa, had resigned from the FBI and was practicing law as an immigrants'-rights advocate in Allentown, Pennsylvania, while waiting for Camarena to be released.

Cabrera's short sentence was one of the things about which McKenna felt bitter. Cabrera admitted that he had gotten a message to Alfonso Mendosa when McKenna had left Florida so that Alfonso could arrange to have McKenna followed from La Guardia Airport to his home. He had never been charged with conspiracy to commit murder.

Because of Cabrera, *Sendero Luminoso* had been able to ambush him at Sparacino's Grocery Store. And because of Cabrera, Isabela Mendosa knew where he lived. McKenna placed the blame for a large part of his unhappiness on Esteban Cabrera.

Another loser in the whole affair was Special-Agent-in-Charge John Weatherby. His contribution to the case had been recognized and he had been assigned a position commensurate with his abilities. Weatherby was now the assistant to the assistant special-agent-in-charge of the FBI's three-man field office in Helena, Montana, where his duties consisted primarily of ensuring that the local Indian tribes had been issued a federal tax stamp before they held bingo games on their reservations.

Betty King came over and said good-night to McKenna. She told him it was way past the time when all good little old ladies were in bed. She tried to cheer him up, and he made a pretense of smiling. He felt good for her, glad for her promotion, and happy that she had gotten three-quarters. Once Betty left, McKenna finished his drink and ordered another. Four drinks in eight hours wasn't bad at all, he told himself. The rusty nails go down nice. He decided that the next drink, if he had one, would be to celebrate his own promotion.

Of course, McKenna had been promoted to First Grade, but that no longer meant much to him. Like all long-term goals, it didn't seem to be so important once he had achieved it. He had lost interest in the Job. There was nothing left to be done that he hadn't done already. He had been transferred back to CCAU so that he could remain in Spanish Harlem after the Major Case Squad returned to their permanent home in headquarters, but he hadn't made an arrest since Pacella was killed. If he had been anyone else, Roberti would have transferred him to the Missing Persons Squad by now, where his main duty would be to fingerprint all unidentified bodies at the morgue. But Roberti understood. He knew that McKenna was just along for the ride, collecting a paycheck every two weeks. And waiting for Isabela.

Isabela was the only thing holding him on the Job, holding him in the city. He knew that she would come for him. She was just biding her time, waiting until she was absolutely ready, waiting to catch him by surprise. Over the months, he had come to realize that nobody else was going to catch her, if they hadn't caught her yet. She had probably had plenty of money stashed in that safe-deposit box, which meant that she had places where she could hide out, waiting.

McKenna often asked himself where Isabela was and what she was doing, or if she was thinking about him at that precise instant. He wondered if she spent as much time thinking about him as he did about her. He hoped so. He hoped that his existence on the planet disturbed her enough to put her in motion soon, while he was still able to deal with her, while he still cared about living.

She had changed his life and destroyed his happiness. He wanted Angelita, and he couldn't have her as long as Isabela was alive. He didn't even dare to see her. He had nightmares about Isabela killing both him and Angelita at the same time. Isabela would enjoy that, he thought.

Angelita had transferred to an airline job in Orlando, Florida. She called him from time to time, and he always loved hearing from her. He wanted to retire and join her immediately. He was ready to live wherever she wanted, to meet all her conditions. But he couldn't tell her that. He didn't know how long Isabela was going to take. Angelita was a young, good-looking girl, and he couldn't ask her to wait forever. Nor could he tell her why he hadn't retired. Angelita would say that they could go somewhere where Isabela wouldn't find them. McKenna didn't believe it for a minute.

McKenna decided against another drink. No reason to make it easy for her, he thought. He lit up another smoke, left his twenty on the bar, and made for the door. Catalfumo asked him if he wanted a ride home, but he declined. He wished Catalfumo and Romero good luck in their retirement and told them that he would stay in touch. He didn't think that he would.

There was a gypsy cab waiting outside Raggs, but McKenna waved the driver off. It was freezing. His bulletproof vest helped to protect him against the cold, but he had to adjust his scarf to shield his face from the wind. He carried his pistol in his coat pocket with two extra magazines in his other pocket. He kept his hand wrapped around the pistol grip. He looked around for a few minutes, then started walking south on Park Avenue.

At East 116th Street, he flagged down a fast-moving gypsy cab and told the driver to take him to Park and Fifty-ninth Street. He kept checking the back window on the way down. At Fifty-ninth, he paid the driver and caught a yellow cab. He gave the driver his address and sat back to relax for a couple of minutes. What a way to live, he thought.

McKenna had the driver stop a block before his apartment building. He took a look around, paid the driver, and got out. This was the most dangerous time for him. He figured that she would try him when he was coming in or out of his building. He liked to get home late so that nobody else would get hurt and so that he would have a better chance to spot her. It was one of the things that kept him drinking. There wasn't much else to do while waiting for midnight.

McKenna took a slow walk around his neighborhood. He tried to glance in every parked car that he passed without being too obvious.

366

Not only was he looking for Isabela, he was also making sure that Ray hadn't assigned anyone to watch his house tonight, and maybe scare Isabela off or make her more cautious. Sometimes Ray used to be there himself, watching his apartment door and waiting for him. But not for months. He didn't see too much of Ray anymore. They had lost a lot of the things that they'd had in common, and McKenna knew that Ray disapproved of the changes in his life-style. But Ray was still a great friend, and occasionally McKenna still found a couple of detectives watching his house. McKenna knew that it would just postpone the inevitable.

McKenna walked past his apartment to the corner, then back. He went into his building and took the stairs up, his pistol in his hand. When he got to his floor, he peered both ways down the hallway before he left the stairwell. Then he checked his locks and his door before he unlocked and went in. He locked the door behind him and, as usual, checked the whole apartment before he relaxed. He was alone.

The lack of a woman's touch was becoming more and more apparent. McKenna hadn't figured out a way to make the sandbags he had piled against the kitchen wall look homey. He slept on the floor, behind the sandbags. The kitchen wall was the most distant point in the apartment from any window. After he had read Argentine police files on Isabela, he had concluded that he didn't have to worry about a grenade through his window or a bomb under his floor. Isabela liked to look into her enemies' eyes when she pulled the trigger. That's the way she had done it in Argentina. She wanted her enemies to know why they were dying and who was killing them. Blowing him up while he slept wasn't her style. She could afford help, but she would be the one to pull the trigger. But no use taking chances, he reasoned.

McKenna had removed all traces of Angelita from the apartment, just in case Isabela got in. Her pictures had been replaced with pictures of Isabela. Isabela with black hair, Isabela with blond hair, Isabela with gray hair, Isabela with red hair, Isabela with a mustache, Isabela with a beard, Isabela as an old lady. Isabela everywhere, in every possible guise that the Photo Unit could produce. McKenna knew them all. He talked to them all. "I'll know you when I see you," he said to the redheaded version.

McKenna undressed. He placed his coat, jacket, and shirt in the hamper that was full of dirty clothes. He had to use his foot to stuff them in. Then he sucked in his breath and loosened his pants, feeling the extra ten pounds he had put on since Isabela had forced him to stop running. He couldn't very well jog around the neighborhood without a gun. That would make it too easy for her. So he was putting

367

on the pounds. If Isabela didn't come this month, he was going to have to buy new suits in a larger size.

When McKenna was done, he put on some jeans, a flannel shirt, and an old pair of running shoes. He didn't want to be caught on the street in his underwear in case he had to leave in a hurry. He took his police radio out of the radio charger on the shelf in his closet. It was tuned to the 6th Precinct frequency, his direct link with the local precinct. Then he lay down on his mattress behind the sandbags, police radio in his left hand and his Glock in his right. He stayed awake past dawn, listening to the sounds, real and imagined, on the fire escape and in the hallway.

34

McKenna knew that he was going to be late for work again. The same old story: awake all night, listening and waiting, finally falling asleep sometime after dawn. Then he had slept all day. It was three thirty by the time he left his building. He had to report by four, and he needed to find a cab to make the trip uptown to the Two-five in rush-hour traffic. There was no way he could make it on time.

He took a look up and down the block, saw nothing suspicious. It was still cold and people were walking with their heads tucked into their collars to avoid the harsh wind sweeping down the street from the Hudson River. He walked to the corner of Hudson Street and tried to hail a cab. For five minutes he stood with his hand in the air, without success. All the cabs were occupied by people from the Wall Street area heading home.

McKenna decided to call the office and let them know he would be late. As he walked back to the pay phone on the corner, he searched his mind for an excuse that he hadn't used in a while. Roberti's number was ringing when the gray, late model Buick station wagon pulled to the corner. There were two nuns sitting in the front seat, dressed in the old-style black habit, gown and cape.

There's something you don't see too much anymore, McKenna thought. He was a traditionalist, and he missed the days when the nuns looked like nuns, the way they had when they'd taught and tortured him through eight years of grammar school. They're probably assigned to Our Lady of Pompeii on Carmine Street, he thought.

That's the only place left in the neighborhood with the occasional traditional nun. The nun on the passenger's side got out. The line kept ringing. Maybe this is my lucky day, McKenna thought. Maybe Roberti's late.

The nun came toward the pay phone, fumbling in her pocketbook for change for the phone. She was tall, McKenna thought, and pretty.

McKenna got ready. He hung up the phone and said, "You can have the phone, Sister. I'm done."

He looked her in the eyes as he fired the first round into her chest. As she fell backward, her finger jerked on the gun in her pocketbook and it went off. He managed to hit her three more times before she fell. He yelled "Tommy Pacella!" as he pulled the trigger again and again.

The station wagon, driven by the other nun, pulled away, tires squealing and out of control. The first cab hit the station wagon broadside. The second cab hit it in the left rear quarter panel. The wagon plunged nose first into a delivery truck double-parked on the other side of the street. McKenna looked at Isabela lying on the ground. She was dead.

McKenna ran halfway across Hudson Street toward the station wagon and stopped. Traffic had come to a halt. He crouched and trained his Glock on the nun who had been driving, waiting for some movement, for a reason to fire, for an excuse. Hoping. The driver slumped over the wheel, motionless. The worst scenario was unfolding in front of him, visible over the front sight of his Glock trained on the driver's head—a *Sendero Luminoso* prisoner. It was the reason for the death of Tommy Pacella—an all-out assault with no prisoners.

McKenna felt rather than saw the people behind him. Lots of people. He continued across Hudson Street, running in a crouch with his gun in front of him, always trained on the driver. The crowd followed him. They started to scream. McKenna reached the station wagon and put his Glock in the driver's ear.

Then he found out something that he didn't know about New York. You can shoot your mother in Times Square at high noon, and everybody will run. But you can't shoot a nun. The first blow, a rock, came from the back of the crowd that had followed him across the street. His head hit the roof of the car. They were all over him.

"Police officer!" he screamed, but nobody seemed to care. He was taking punches from truck drivers, kids, and old ladies. He fired two shots in the air and screamed again, "Police officer!" They were beginning to understand. The crowd backed away a foot.

Mary Lucas ran out of the real estate office on the corner. McKenna and Mary had gone to school together. She was yelling, "He's a cop! He's a cop! Leave him alone!"

The crowd backed away further. Then McKenna reached into the car and dragged the semiconscious driver out and threw him on the ground. He pulled off the nun's habit, which was bloody from the impact of his head hitting the windshield. It was a young Hispanic male, about eighteen years old. He was wearing street clothes under the gown. McKenna reached into the car and took a Colt .45 automatic from the floor on the driver's side. Then he dragged the driver back across the street to Isabela's body.

She was lying on her back on the cold ground with her eyes open. McKenna was glad to see that she wasn't smiling. Isabela looked surprised that death had found her. Her hand was still in her pocketbook. McKenna saw the bullet hole in the pocketbook and knew that Isabela's hand was still on her gun. He didn't move anything.

McKenna heard the sirens coming from all directions. They were close. Then Mary Lucas told him that he was bleeding.

"I know," he said, rubbing his head. His hand came away bloody.

"Not your head, Brian. Your leg."

McKenna looked down. His right pants leg was soaked in blood, just below the knee, but he didn't feel a thing yet. By the time the first patrol car arrived, he had rolled his pants above a deep cut on his calf. Isabela's bullet must have bounced off the sidewalk and hit me, he thought. I'm gonna play this one up. He was leaning on Mary by the time the first two uniformed officers got out of their car.

He held up his shield and said, "I'm Detective McKenna." Then he pointed to the body and said, "And that's Isabela Mendosa." McKenna gave one of the cops the .45 automatic and pointed to the driver lying next to Isabela. "That belongs to him."

He didn't have to say more than that. The cop walked over to the driver and cuffed him. The patrol sergeant arrived a minute later. He talked to one of the cops and then took charge. He had the street closed off and started looking for witnesses. The ambulances began arriving and the sergeant had the driver of the station wagon loaded into the first ambulance. He assigned three cops to guard him and told them that the prisoner was to talk to no one. Then he told the ambulance attendant not to move the ambulance until he said to.

The sergeant looked around for something else to do, something he might have forgotten. There was nothing. He had nothing to do but wait for the first captain to arrive. He walked over to McKenna and asked him if he wanted to go to the hospital.

"Not just yet, Sarge. I've got some things I want to do. I'll be in the real estate office across the street, when you want me."

"Whatever you say, sir."

Sir? McKenna thought. I guess I've just been knighted. He held on to Mary and hobbled across the street to her office, refusing all offers of help from the other cops. The cold was starting to hurt his leg. Mary took him into her office in the rear and sat him down at her desk. He started to unwind while she made him a cup of coffee. She placed the coffee in front of him on her desk and asked, "You want something stronger, Brian?"

"That's all right, Mary. I don't drink anymore." He enjoyed the coffee while he thought for a couple of minutes. Then he asked Mary if he could make a long-distance phone call.

"Make yourself at home, Brian."

McKenna called information in Florida and got the number for the United reservation desk at the airport. He dialed the number and asked for Angelita Morena. A minute later she came on the line. "Hello! This is Angelita. May I help you."

"Yes you may, young lady. I'd like to make a reservation from New York to wherever in the world you want to spend the rest of your life with me. Are you still available?"

Angelita recognized his voice and laughed into the phone. "Will that be round trip or one way, Brian?"

"One way, Gorgeous."

"Then you've got it, Brian. I'm available. What do you think I've been waiting for? Are you sure you've finally had enough of the Big Time?"

"I've had enough. I'll call you at home later with the details. I've got a lot to do."

McKenna hung up the phone and turned to Mary. "You still want to sell my apartment, Mary?"

"No problem, Brian. I can sell it tomorrow if the asking price is right."

"I'll leave it to you. The price is right."

McKenna watched the scene of controlled bedlam through the window of the real estate office. Inspector Keller arrived and took charge. A few minutes later Keller climbed into the ambulance. The three cops whom the sergeant had assigned to guard the prisoner left in a hurry by the back door. McKenna decided not to watch. He returned to concentrating on his coffee.

Twenty minutes later Ray found him. Ray had made the trip from headquarters in record time. He started to make a big deal over McKenna's leg. McKenna told him it was fine, but Ray insisted that he was probably permanently disabled. It wasn't what McKenna wanted to talk about. The prisoner was on his mind. He had created a monster. All he could say to Brunette was, "Sorry about the prisoner, Ray. There was nothing I could do. I couldn't shoot him and he couldn't run away. I figured that if I couldn't kill him, it would be best if he escaped."

372

"So that's all that's on your mind," Brunette laughed. "Don't worry about him. He's not one of them. He's local talent. He's Dominican. He just met Isabela today."

"How do you know?"

"Keller told me. He was here by the time I got here. He cleared the ambulance and then went in and gave your prisoner his Miranda rights. Then I guess that he gave him his Miranda lefts. Anyway, your prisoner wants to be our friend. He swears that he didn't know that Isabela was going to kill anybody. She just gave him five hundred bucks this morning and told him there was somebody carrying a lot of money who she was gonna rob in the street. It sounded good to him, so he took the money and agreed to drive the getaway car. His story checks out. He just got off Rikers Island three days ago. He's not a terrorist. He's just another mugger."

The news turned it all around. There were no loose ends, nothing left to worry about. "What were you saying about my permanently injured leg, Ray?"

"I was saying that you shouldn't waste this one, Brian. You can limp your way to three-quarters. Just play it up. And try not to laugh. Remember, you're a police hero. Nobody will fight you on this one. Just put your papers in."

"Can I do the paperwork by air mail, Ray? Right now I'm spending my last day on this job."

Brunette wasn't shocked. He thought for a minute. Then he smiled and said, "Me, too, buddy. Let's go fishing!"

Epilogue

It was a nice night for a flight, cool air and clear skies. It was beginning to feel a lot like Christmas. Today's the day they lit up the big tree at Rockefeller Center, McKenna thought. First time I missed that in a long time. Wonder if I'll ever see it again?

McKenna took the window seat in first class on the port side of the plane. It was the first time he had ever allowed himself such an extravagance and, after he settled himself in, he wondered what the big deal was, anyway. An extra $700 for a bigger seat on a three-hour flight? It didn't make a lot of sense to him, but then again, he wasn't sure if a lot of the things he'd done in the last month made any sense. Besides, he reasoned, he could afford it and he was sure money wasn't going to be one of his problems.

Everything hadn't gone exactly according to plan. When Mary had looked at the fortress his apartment had become, she figured that it would take at least a week to get it in shape before she could show it to any prospective customers. It took two weeks for painting, a new kitchen, and a new bathroom. Then McKenna sat back and waited for the promised flood of buyers. A week later the first one walked through the door and McKenna sold him the apartment at $30,000 under the listed price. But McKenna didn't care. He felt like he had robbed a bank with a 400 percent profit on the place.

Retiring wasn't as easy as McKenna had imagined. He had spent two days in the hospital after the shoot-out, and then he was home for three weeks, officially sick, while living among the mess and the workmen.

When he'd finally gotten to the Pension Section, he had had another shock. He retired that day, but he had ninety-five days on the books, so he wouldn't be "officially" retired until sometime in May. And it wouldn't be three-quarters until he was approved by the Medical Board. But the arithmetic was still great for a First-Grade detective with twenty-three years on the Job. He certainly wouldn't starve.

He had to return to headquarters the same day to turn in his guns and shield. He was told he couldn't get a pistol permit because he wasn't going to be living in New York City. McKenna had mixed feelings as he turned in the tools of the trade that had been part of his dress code for so long. He left the building for the last time, some pounds lighter but with a heavy weight on his mind.

Then there was Ray. McKenna had hoped that Ray would be filling the seat next to him for the one-way flight to West Palm Beach, but it didn't work out. McKenna believed that Ray wanted to leave and was sure that Ray's wife wanted it, but the problem was the kids. They were getting older, had minds of their own, and wanted to stay. His oldest boy was starting the Academy next month, and Ray felt obliged to stay on until the kid was off probation in case he needed a hook. McKenna knew the kid well and was sure he would.

The plane took off and McKenna forced himself to look at the good points. There was Angelita, of course. She had quit her job and moved into his condo in West Palm Beach. She was meeting him at the airport and he longed to see her again. He smiled when he thought of her. She called him every day with honeymoon plans and ideas about a new home where they would raise many children. She talked incessantly of names for girls and names for boys and told him about the schools in this country or that. He figured that he had cut his phone bill by just listening and agreeing to everything she said. It all sounded good. Duller than life on the Job, but good.

The plane banked left and headed south. The pilot directed McKenna's attention to the window and the sights to see. Below him the city was lit up for his inspection. He figured the plane was somewhere north of the Bronx, but he could still see Manhattan—the skyscrapers, the blocks of Harlem tenements, and all the glittering bridges connecting the Bright Lights to the less interesting parts of the world. As he surveyed his former kingdom he felt a knot growing in his stomach. So he turned from the window, pushed back his seat, switched off his overhead lamp, and closed his eyes.

About the Author

Dan Mahoney was born and raised in New York City. After serving with the Marine Corps in Vietnam, he followed in the footsteps of his father and grandfather and joined the New York City Police Department. He served in patrol and detective commands and retired as a Captain in 1989. Along the way he attended John Jay College of Criminal Justice and graduated as class valedictorian in 1977. He now works as a private investigator in New York. He is the father of three children and lives in Manhattan with his wife, Yvette, who is also a New York City Police Officer.

Detective First Grade is Dan Mahoney's first novel.